The Rules of the Game

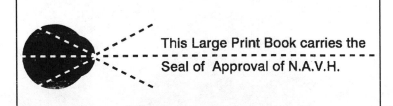

THE RULES OF THE GAME

LEONARD DOWNIE, JR.

THORNDIKE PRESS
A part of Gale, Cengage Learning

GALE
CENGAGE Learning™

Detroit • New York • San Francisco • New Haven, Conn • Waterville, Maine • London

LIBRARY OF CONGRESS CATALOGING-IN-PUBLICATION DATA

Downie, Leonard.
   The rules of the game / by Leonard Downie, Jr.
     p. cm. — (Thorndike Press large print thriller)
   ISBN-13: 978-1-4104-1516-5 (alk. paper)
   ISBN-10: 1-4104-1516-3 (alk. paper)
   1. Women journalists—Fiction. 2. Political corruption—United
States—Fiction. 3. War on Terrorism, 2001——Economic
aspects—Fiction. 4. Profiteering—Fiction. 5. Women
presidents—United States—Fiction. 6. Political fiction. 7. Large
type books. I. Title.
PS3604.O944R86 2009b
813'.6—dc22   2009001056

Published in 2009 by arrangement with Alfred A. Knopf, Inc.

Printed in the United States of America
1 2 3 4 5 6 7 13 12 11 10 09

For Janice, who has made this and everything else possible

1

It was a moment Sarah Page had been working toward ever since she first walked into the *Washington Capital* newsroom six summers earlier. Yet it felt as though she was being punished.

"I have rules," Ron Jones, the political editor, was warning her. "And I expect you to follow them."

Jones, a big, burly man, overwhelmed the little desk that separated them in his cramped, glass-walled office on the edge of the newsroom.

"Do I have to explain it all over again?" Sarah asked. She knew she had to keep her composure or miss this opportunity to move onto the national politics staff. She sat as tall as she could in a chair facing Jones.

"Of course not," he told her, softening his tone. "And I'm not blaming you. Evans should've known better. He was an editor."

"He wasn't really my editor," Sarah said.

It was important that she not be seen as a victim, a naïve young woman seduced by her boss. She didn't want special treatment.

"Investigative projects get pretty intense. At least this one did," she said, figuring he knew all about it. "Is that why I'm being moved?"

"Hell, no," said Jones. "I wouldn't let the local staff dump anyone on me. I asked for you. You did good work on those lobbyists in Maryland.

"And you were tough but fair with the governor," he added, "even though she's a woman."

Sarah hated being constantly reminded that politics was still mostly a man's game. In Annapolis, the suggestive comments of leering legislators and dismissive slights by some of the veteran reporters had made it clear she would never be one of the boys. In the newsroom, she had faced the widespread assumption that male colleagues had the inside track to the national politics staff.

Before she could respond, Jones smiled knowingly, as though sharing an inside joke.

"C'mon, look at me," he told her, spreading wide his huge arms. "Don't you think people have always seen a big bad black man before thinking anything else? It's only made me more aggressive. Sometimes, in this business, it helps to have a chip on your shoulder."

Sarah thought about that for a moment. "You think I do?"

"I know it's a cliché," Jones said, looking at her intently. "But I see a determined young woman fighting for respect. I also see something of an idealist, but we'll cure you of that."

Sarah saw herself as a fighter, too, but not necessarily an idealist. Her parents, who had grown up in the sixties and worked as reporters in Washington, had always talked about a sense of mission in journalism after Watergate. But that was before they switched to public relations and lobbying, where the money was.

"So why aren't there more women on your staff?" she asked Jones.

"Fair question. I inherited these guys, and nobody ever leaves. So I asked for you the minute I heard they wanted to separate you and your editor friend."

"Former friend," Sarah shot back. "He dumped me."

"Sounds like you're still pissed."

"I am. It's all over the newsroom, for heaven's sake. But I'm dealing with it. I just have no social life."

"You don't have to be a nun," Jones told

her. "But there're no secrets in political reporting. So it's not a good idea to fraternize on the beat.

"Some of my guys aren't happy about you," Jones added. "They don't think you've had enough experience. And a couple of them are close to Evans. They resent your coming over here after what happened to him."

"So you're really not doing me any favors."

"Listen. I know how badly you wanted this. And you're getting it a few years early." Jones leaned back in his chair. "You know, when you think about it, you should be kissing my ass."

They both laughed, and Sarah relaxed enough to make her pitch.

"I'd like to cover money."

"That's just what I figured." Jones smiled at her directness. "And I don't have anyone on it full-time yet. The Democrats are raising and spending more than ever to take back the White House, and the Republicans are matching them dollar for dollar. I'm particularly interested in what Trent Tucker will be doing."

Sarah nodded.

"You know who Tucker is, don't you?" Jones asked. "He's running Monroe Capehart's campaign for the Democrats. I think he did some work for Elizabeth Tawney in Maryland."

Sarah froze for a moment. Was he testing her?

"I met him when I was covering Governor Tawney," she said carefully. "He was a consultant for her campaign."

"Well, he might be a good place for you to start," Jones said. "He's a walking conflict of interest. A consultant *and* a lobbyist. He helps put them into office and then he lobbies them on behalf of his business clients. If Capehart wins, Tucker will have the run of the White House."

Sarah had known she wouldn't be able to avoid Tucker if she covered money and politics. But she felt she had prepared herself for it.

"I'll send you to the conventions so you can meet everyone," Jones said. "You'll have a few weeks to do some homework before the Democrats go to Chicago. I'll make sure your new colleagues help you."

"I'm okay on my own," Sarah said. "I've always been pretty independent — you know, the only child of two workaholics."

Jones could already tell she was a loner, the kind of instinctive outsider who, in the news business, often gravitated to investigative reporting. But he wondered who she was trying to convince, him or herself?

Less than five minutes after Sarah left Jones's office, Mark Daniels strolled in. Jones made a show of looking at his watch.

"What took you so long?"

"You're not really bringing Sarah Page over here, are you?"

Mark knew the decision had been made, but he didn't like it.

"Why not?"

"She doesn't understand politics," Mark said, casually perching himself on the edge of Jones's desk. "She's really an investigative reporter."

"She was investigating politicians."

"That was in Maryland. This is the big leagues."

"C'mon, Mark," Jones said. "Your real problem is your friend Evans. He gets busted. She gets promoted. And that doesn't seem fair to you. Do married guys who fool around have some kind of club?"

"Low blow." Mark slid off the desk and flopped onto the worn black leather couch on the other side of the office. "I've never messed around with anyone in the newsroom. Anyway, whatever became of consenting adults?"

"They had to be separated." Jones went through the motions of explaining what

Mark already knew. "Evans was one of her supervisors on Metro. He broke the rules, so he gets exiled to a suburban bureau. I asked for Page because she has potential, and I needed more bodies for the campaign. I wanted someone who could do money, which she did in Maryland."

"I heard she thought everybody in the legislature was on the take."

"Some of them were, including a couple of the governor's allies. Page did Tawney a favor."

"Tom told me he had to rein her in."

Jones leaned forward over his desk.

"So," he said, slowly and emphatically, "Evans wasn't just screwing around behind his wife's back. He was also bad-mouthing his girlfriend behind *her* back."

"I shouldn't have said that." Mark straightened up on the couch.

"Damn right," Jones told him. "Sarah's part of the team now. I'm sending her to the conventions, and I want you to show her around."

A few days later, on the Fourth of July, Sarah allowed herself to sleep late in the small house she shared in the old Palisades neighborhood, just beyond Georgetown on a bluff above the Potomac River. Her housemate, a lawyer, who was intent on becoming a partner in her firm, had already left to spend the holiday working downtown. Sarah's task for the day was nearer at hand.

The late morning sunlight was filling her upstairs bedroom. She threw on a T-shirt, shorts, running shoes, and a baseball cap that covered her short black hair. Rather than going for a run or to the gym, as she did most mornings, she walked over to MacArthur Boulevard, where she knew the Fourth of July Palisades parade would be starting.

It was a distinctly neighborhood affair, with fire trucks from the local engine house and police cars from the Second District sounding their sirens, a big refrigerated truck from Safeway honking its air horn, and open convertibles carrying parents and children from local churches and schools. It was traditionally political, with the mayor and members of the city council marching amid supporters who handed out campaign buttons and bumper stickers. It was also eclectic, with representatives of the Oldest Inhabitants association in antique cars, a Bolivian dancing troupe in brightly colored costumes, Scottish bagpipers in plaid kilts, and a gay marching band called D.C.'s Different Drummers.

Sarah walked the length of the parade route down to the edge of the Georgetown Reservoir and back toward Palisades Park, studying faces in the crowd through a reporter's curious eyes. She encountered neighbors, newsroom colleagues who lived nearby, and a lawyer who had once been a source of hers.

When she saw the energetic young mayor coming toward her, shaking as many hands as he could, Sarah decided to introduce herself. He was only a few years older than Sarah, and she noticed how fit he looked from his well-publicized running and exercise regimen. His shaved head glistened like polished mahogany in the sunlight.

"Good to see you again, Miss Page," the mayor said, taking her by surprise. "We met last year, when I was visiting the governor in Annapolis. I hope you haven't been demoted to covering me. You're too tough."

Sarah was impressed that he remembered her and flattered by what he said. She was about to tell him about her new assignment when the mayor recognized an older woman pushing toward him.

"Mrs. Landry, so good to see you," he said, reaching out his hand. "Thanks again for that reception in your beautiful home."

I guess I'm not *that* important to him,

15

Sarah thought, remembering that it wasn't the first time she had taken a politician's fleeting attention too seriously. She slipped away and continued down the street.

Just as she neared Chain Bridge Road, a winding lane that tumbled downhill into MacArthur Boulevard, she spotted Trent Tucker. Wearing a loud Hawaiian shirt, with shorts as white as his legs, open-toed sandals, and a floppy hat and sunglasses, he was off by himself, sprawled in a lawn chair on the grassy hillside.

"Sarah Page, my darlin'," Tucker called out before she could reach him. He took off his sunglasses to better assess her tanned, athletic body. "Aren't you still a fine-lookin' woman."

How could I have forgotten that down-home accent he uses when he turns on the charm? Sarah thought. She knew that Robert Trent Tucker III, who hated the traditions of old Southern families like his own and never used his full name, liked to manipulate people.

"I didn't know you lived around here," Sarah said, acting surprised. Actually, she had already looked up his address — just up the hill on Chain Bridge Road — and had spied on the castle-like stone house from outside its gates. She had also checked on what he paid for the house and the amount of the mortgage, which, according to city land records, was held by a company called Malin Associates.

"No 'Hello, how've you been?' darlin'?" Tucker drawled, easing into the lopsided grin that women found inexplicably captivating. "I know it's been a long time, but there's no need to be cold about it."

"Just businesslike, Trent. They've moved me to the national political staff."

"We're reunited? Hallelujah!" Tucker waved his sunglasses in mock celebration but made no move to get up. Sitting in his lawn chair, his chalky legs splayed in front of him, he was at eye level with Sarah, who was standing just below him on the hillside.

"So," she asked, as though she hadn't heard him, "do you live around here now?"

"Sure do, darlin', back a ways up the hill and round the bend." He motioned toward Chain Bridge Road. "What about you? Are you a neighbor? Or are you here workin' the parade? I saw the mayor come by a while ago." He paused, still grinning. "But then, you just said you were coverin' *national* politics now, didn't you?"

"I live on the other side of MacArthur, toward the river," she said, ignoring the teasing she had once found so amusing.

"Sounds nice. Maybe we can take a walk round the 'hood some time."

"You don't walk, Trent," Sarah said. "I wonder how you're going to get back home when the parade's over."

Tucker laughed.

"That's my car, parked right over there, the big Beemer. I drove down, darlin'. That hill's real steep."

"They've assigned me to campaign finance," Sarah told Tucker, turning serious to put him on notice. "I'll be in touch after I get up to speed. And I'm going to the convention in Chicago. Maybe I'll see you there."

"Happy to see you anytime, darlin'."

Tucker put his sunglasses on, and Sarah walked back down into the crowd watching the parade. He's got a bit more paunch, she thought, but otherwise he didn't seem to have changed much. But everything else had. Once, she had been his quarry. Now he would be hers.

2

Waiting for Jeanne to call, Mark Daniels stared impatiently into the night from the window of his room on the twenty-third floor of the Fairmont hotel. Why, he wondered, did everything feel so different with her?

Mark could see the Sheraton just a few blocks to the left, across the Chicago River. The streets and bridges leading to the hotel were empty, sealed off by police cars and barricades. He knew Jeanne was somewhere on a floor secured by the Secret Service at the top of the Sheraton, taking care of last-minute details in Monroe Capehart's suite and meeting with the rest of the advance team.

In the darkness that shrouded Lake Michigan, Mark saw the beckoning lights of the Navy Pier, where he knew thousands of other journalists would be enjoying free food and drink at the preconvention media party. There was a time, many years earlier, when he would have been there with them, tagging along after older journalists and exchanging hopeful glances with young women liberated by the exhilarating atmosphere of a national convention.

Now Mark might have gone instead to the crowded bar at the Democrats' headquarters hotel to gossip with other insiders and perhaps to arrange a more discreet assignation. But he had stayed in his room at the Fairmont to wait for Jeanne. As the hours passed, he phoned his wife back home, took a shower, and checked his e-mail on his BlackBerry, before standing vigil at the window. Finally, Jeanne called.

"I can't talk long. I'm stuck in a countdown meeting with the Secret Service. It's going on forever," she whispered. "It's crowded and hot in here. And I'm starving. Can you order room service for us before it's too late?"

"What should I get?" They had been together fewer than a dozen times and seldom for more than a few hours, but Mark was already devoted to her in a way he had not been with anyone else for a long time.

"You decide," she told him. "Bye."

Like Mark, Jeanne Gale lived according to her own rules. She worked when she wanted to in a small Washington travel agency she owned with her sister. A lifelong Democrat who had once worked on the Hill, she served her party periodically as a volunteer advance person on major trips for its presidential candidates. She was the mother hen of the "RON" team, the mostly young and female staffers and volunteers who looked after the candidate when he "remained overnight" on a trip.

Jeanne was in charge of Monroe Capehart's hotel suite and personal arrangements, making certain in her meticulous way that everything was exactly the way he wanted it. She adjusted the air-conditioning, unpacked his clothes, turned down his bed-covers. She stocked extra towels, unwrapped the soaps in his bathroom, and set out his robe, slippers, and an extra pair of reading glasses. She made certain the suite con-tained fresh flowers, newspapers, a platter of his favorite fruit, and plenty of Diet Cokes and fat-free cookies. When the candi-date's wife traveled with him, Jeanne did much the same for her. Jeanne was often the last person to see the couple before they went to bed at night and the first to greet them in the morning.

Mark waited another half hour before call-ing room service. He ordered two filets mi-gnons medium rare, salads with dressing on the side, a bottle of Pinot Noir, and a small vase of flowers. He knew what Jeanne liked.

Mark and Jeanne had met several months earlier, in the spring, on the sidewalk outside the Mark Hopkins hotel in San Francisco, where Monroe Capehart had stayed while raising money in the Bay Area. As the likely nominee, the senior senator from Pennsylvania was traveling with full Secret Service protection and a large entou-rage in chartered planes and long motor-cades with police escorts. Mark and Jeanne were each catching a ride in Capehart's motorcade back to the San Francisco airport. The coordinator had put them in the same overflow van a dozen vehicles behind Capehart's limousine, just ahead of the press bus.

"Why haven't I seen you before?" Mark asked, chatting up the tall, slender woman with expressive eyes and an easy smile who was sitting next to him.

"This is my first trip with Capehart," Jeanne had told him. "I do hotel advance for long stays. I started with the Gores when he was vice president. After what happened in 2000, I skipped the Kerry campaign. Capehart's people talked me into coming on the road again."

Jeanne had missed the drama and camaraderie of the campaign, the familiar rhythms of deadlines to meet and goals to accomplish, the privileged insider access with special credentials, Secret Service badges, and code names, and the motorcades with sirens, flashing lights, and streets cleared of traffic. It was fun, a game with its own unique rules, which sometimes included intimate relationships confined to the campaign, away from what insiders referred to as "real life."

"How does it feel?" Mark asked Jeanne as

the motorcade started to roll.

"Like I never stopped." She looked out the window. "But I have to admit the other girls keep getting younger. And the Secret Service guys, too, not that I mind that."

She glanced over at Mark. He appeared to be about her age and was still boyishly handsome, with a nearly unlined face and tousled hair the same dark brown as hers. He was a possibility.

"Capehart's relatively easy to take care of," Jeanne told him. "His people know what they're doing."

"Well, he's been around for a long time," Mark said. "If he gets elected, he'll turn seventy during his first year in the White House. How did he look to you, up close, on this trip?"

"Oh no, you don't," she said. "I don't know you well enough for that."

As they continued talking in the van on the way to the airport, Mark found himself increasingly captivated. Jeanne was beguilingly warm and womanly, an attractive grown-up who was clearly comfortable with herself, unlike the hard, striving young women he often found himself with on the road. When he eventually asked, Jeanne gave him her phone number at the travel agency.

A few days later, in Washington, Mark

called and invited her to lunch at the Oval Room. Located just across Lafayette Square from the White House, the restaurant was a favored place for lobbyists and journalists to dine with politicians and administration officials. Mark had chosen it to impress Jeanne. Everyone knew him there.

When Jeanne arrived a few minutes after him, strikingly dressed in a gray pin-striped pantsuit, Mark watched from his usual table as the maître d' warmly embraced her. They whispered into each other's ear, laughing, before he took her to Mark's table. Jeanne, too, was known at the Oval Room.

As she sat down, Jeanne reached out and squeezed Mark's hand. "You look good all dressed up," she told him. "But then you looked good on the road, too. It's easier for men."

"I've been doing it for a while," he said, sensing an opportunity. "I'll be going back out with Capehart soon. How about you?"

"Not until the convention in Chicago. I'll get there a week before Capehart arrives so I can have everything ready at the hotel. I won't get much sleep. That's why I only do big trips. I leave the others to the younger girls."

"You don't look any the worse for wear," Mark said lamely.

"Thanks." Her smile told him he didn't have to try so hard. "I'm not complaining. It could be my last chance to end up advancing a president."

"No matter who wins, I want the White House beat," Mark told her. "I'd be in Washington more."

Jeanne had noticed his wedding ring and wondered what that might mean for her. Relationships with married men usually meant fewer demands.

They met again for dinner that Friday at Chef Geoff's, a neighborhood restaurant near American University. In its cozy, anonymous confines, their conversation became more personal. Mark talked for the first time about his wife, a congressman's press secretary when they met and now a public relations executive.

"It's been hard for her," he said. "Anne's got her job and our two boys, and I'm gone so much. When I'm home, I try to make up for lost time with the kids. That doesn't leave much for her."

"Have the two of you talked about it?"

"Not really. But I can sense her resentment. We seem to get along best when I'm traveling and we're e-mailing or talking on the phone about the trivia of our days."

"And you fool around when you're away?"

Jeanne asked. "I know what campaigns are like."

"You expect me to answer that?"

Mark looked at Jeanne for a moment, calculating how much he should tell her, just as countless news sources had done with him over the years.

"Well, yes," he said. "The younger women these days seem to like commitment-free sex."

"That's your rule? No commitments?"

"I don't have much choice."

"I've got rules," Jeanne said. "I need to be in control."

"What does that mean?"

"I was married once to a lobbyist I met on the Hill. He was a lot older, and he took good care of me at first. But I got tired of being a Washington 'wife of,' without any life of my own. Then I caught him fooling around. Everyone knew about it. In the divorce settlement, I got enough money to buy my independence. So I bought the travel agency with my sister. Now I do things my way."

When they had finished dinner, Jeanne invited Mark back to her apartment in a stately old building on Connecticut Avenue. The living room was filled with comfortable-looking furniture and a baby grand piano.

"Do you play?" Mark asked Jeanne as they sat near each other on a small couch, sipping white wine.

"I took piano lessons for years as a girl and got tired of it," she said. "I bought this one at one of those sales at the Kennedy Center. I thought it would look good in this room. And then I started to play. Without the pressure, it became fun again."

"I've started feeling that way about covering politics — about my whole life, actually," Mark said. "The pressure's been getting to me. Maybe I'm too old for it all."

"You still look pretty good to me," Jeanne told him, running her free hand through his hair and leaning over to kiss him. Then she took him by the hand to her bedroom.

Their uninhibited lovemaking had surprised them both with its easy intimacy. They couldn't stop talking afterward, lying comfortably in each other's arms. They told as much as they dared of their life stories.

"You know," Mark said to Jeanne at one point, "you sound as detached from other people as I am most of the time. Your relationships with customers at your travel agency and with the pols you advance are just like mine with my sources. You cultivate them without becoming too involved. Your personal life seems the same way. I thought only journalists were like that."

"I thought only divorced women were like that," Jeanne said. "We're wary of becoming too attached to anybody else again."

"You don't have to be afraid of me," Mark said. "My only real attachment is to my work. And I'm not so sure about that anymore."

After a few hours, Jeanne had insisted that Mark leave. He reminded her that his wife had already left with their sons for a weekend at the beach, where he would join them the next day. But Jeanne was adamant. It was one of her rules.

It had continued that way right up to the Democratic convention: businesslike lunches downtown, furtive romantic dinners in out-of-the-way restaurants, and passionate trysts at Jeanne's apartment. They had stayed overnight together only once, in a New York hotel, where they had scheduled coinciding business trips. Although she was beginning to feel affection for Mark, Jeanne had long ago grown comfortable with this kind of relationship. Mark, unusual for him, had become a bit befuddled. He found himself increasingly anxious to see her and wistful when they parted. Yet he had done nothing that would disrupt the dependable routine of his work or home. He kept each part of his life in its separate box. Only in Jeanne's presence did he feel any threat to his emotional detachment from almost everything in life — work, family, and most of the many women he had known.

Finally, just before midnight in Chicago, the phone rang again in Mark's hotel room. It was Jeanne telling him that she was on her way over from the Sheraton. When he opened the door for her, she rushed in and kissed him quickly. She shook her long dark hair out of a no-nonsense ponytail and unceremoniously took off her blouse and skirt.

"I'm so hot," she said. "I felt like I couldn't breathe anymore."

It was a strange striptease, as Jeanne matter-of-factly removed her clothes with her back to Mark. Seemingly oblivious to his presence, she took a glass of water from the room-service table and pressed it against her brow before drinking it down. Then she turned toward him, reached back and unhooked her bra, freeing her breasts. Mark stood there awkwardly, staring at this effortlessly sexy woman.

"Come on, I don't have much time," she said, grabbing his hand and turning toward the bed. "We can eat later."

Afterward, as they lay naked on the bed,

picking at the cold food on the room-service table Mark had pulled over next to them, Jeanne talked about what she would soon be doing as the new day began over at the Sheraton. To Mark, she seemed to be talking around something she didn't want to tell him.

"You've done advance for the nominee at a convention before," he told her. "Is this one any different?"

"Well, usually the candidate would have picked the vice president by now," she said. Capehart's advisers had persuaded him to postpone the announcement of his choice for a running mate until the first day of the convention to inject more excitement into his candidacy. "It's a major pain that we have to deal with the announcement tomorrow."

Jeanne knew that one of the cardinal rules of advance was never to tell the press anything, to leave all substantive contact with the news media to the candidate and his press staff. But she had a strong urge to share inside information Mark would want to know. She ran her hand down his body and smiled enticingly. He tossed the remains of a dinner roll back onto the table and gave her his full attention.

"Who do you think Monroe will pick?"

she asked in a way that hinted she knew.

Mark handicapped the half dozen governors and senators on everyone's short list. "Bennett's too Southern and nearly everyone in Louisiana politics has a big old skeleton in his closet," he said. "Hamilton had to put through that tax increase in Michigan. Coleman has moved up quickly in the Senate, but I don't think the party's ready to put him on the ticket at his age. Robinson looks great on television, but he's only been in the Senate for five minutes and he's a car dealer. Wilkinson's numbers are great as governor, but they don't need him to carry New York."

Jeanne moved her hand to where she would distract Mark the most.

"Are men all you think about?"

3

"This is Trent Tucker. Who's calling me at this hour, for Chrissakes?"

It was just after six o'clock in the morning, and Tucker was sitting in his undershorts in the middle of the bed in his room in the Sheraton, surrounded by speech drafts, polling numbers, and campaign advertising budgets. A half-eaten bar of Lindt dark chocolate lay in its foil wrapper

31

on the bedcover next to him.

"It's Mark Daniels. I knew you'd be up by now. It's convention week."

After Jeanne had left his hotel room a few hours earlier, Mark realized what was going on. He had called Tucker while still in bed himself.

"I underestimated you guys," he told Tucker. "I didn't think you'd have the guts. She's such a big risk. And you don't really need her for California. The country loves her, but that's *People* magazine stuff. Will voters be comfortable with her a heartbeat away?"

Tucker leaned over his belly to reach the chocolate. Reporters fished like this all the time. When it worked to his advantage, he allowed himself to be hooked. He always got a rush making high-risk, split-second decisions about what would be best for a client or himself. This one was especially risky, the kind of perverse calculation of conflicting interests that he knew could produce a big bang.

"How can you possibly know that?" he asked. "It's been airtight. They even interviewed her in secret while Monroe was out raising money in Beverly Hills."

"What do you mean 'they'?" Mark asked

back. "I thought you were running this campaign."

"Yeah, I am." Tucker cradled the phone against his bare shoulder so he could break off a piece of chocolate. "But this is Monroe's idea. I've been the one asking hard questions. Is she ready for a national campaign? What kind of baggage does she carry from all that stuff with her ex? Will her Princess Di image overwhelm Monroe's message?"

This was a sanitized version of Tucker's fears. Putting Senator Susan Cameron on the ticket was one of the worst ideas he had heard in a lifetime of watching and working on campaigns. Wronged young political wife divorces cheating multimillionaire senator, takes his seat in the Senate after he resigns in disgrace, becomes a red-hot media celebrity, and is picked by a much older presidential candidate to be only the second woman vice-presidential candidate on a national Democratic ticket. You couldn't sell that scenario to the movies.

Tucker, though, was a realist. He came from a Georgia family that had always had plenty of land and not enough money. His grandfather, the first Robert Trent Tucker, was a popular governor who got caught taking cash in envelopes from highway builders. After being acquitted by a jury of loyal supporters, he started an insurance agency with the money he had left. He did well enough to send his only son to prep school, college, and law school. Bob Tucker, as straight as his father was bent, won election to the State Legislature, then three terms in the U.S. House and one in the Senate before being sent back home to his small-town law firm by a conservative opponent who distorted his do-gooder record as being too liberal for Georgia.

His son, Trent, who was raised mostly in Washington while his father was in Congress, took to politics as his birthright. But he had decided to avoid the pitfalls and relative penury of elected office. He found it much more rewarding to work behind the scenes, advising politicians and their campaigns. Win or lose, he took for himself a sizable share of the ever-larger amounts of money they raised and spent trying to win elections. In addition to his fees and expenses up front, he collected, as many consultants did, a percentage of what each campaign spent on the advertising, polling, and fund-raising he directed. He then collected still more from the business clients he had acquired over the years, buying influence with the same politicians he had helped elect to office.

All this made politics a very lucrative business for Trent Tucker. In addition to his expensive house in Washington, he owned a co-op apartment in New York and a condo in Palm Beach. He drove a BMW 740, was a regular at A-list Washington parties, watched Redskins games from his own suite at the stadium, and had his own table at several of the city's best restaurants. He played high-stakes poker in the most exclusive game in town — with a couple of U.S. Supreme Court justices, a rotating group of senators and congressmen, and several of the country's best-known newspaper and television journalists.

Tucker was convinced that a Capehart-Cameron ticket was bound to be a train wreck. Cameron's inexperience would make Dan Quayle look like a statesman and, given Capehart's advanced age, could become a big issue in the campaign. She was more rock star than politician, someone who hadn't yet learned how to play by his rules. She could be difficult to control.

But this was Capehart's infatuation, to which he was stubbornly clinging in the face of opposition from most of his advisers. When Mark Daniels called that morning, Tucker decided at that moment his last chance to derail the old man's decision would be to leak it just in time to publicly expose its folly before the scheduled announcement.

For his part, Mark was landing a great story. He was already out of bed and pulling on clothes as he dialed the cell-phone number Jeanne had given him. She must already have been up and at work in Capehart's suite, because he got her voice mail.

"Sorry to bother you, but call me as soon as you can," Mark said into the phone. "I found out about Susan Cameron."

He ordered coffee, juice, and pastry from room service, sat down at the desk and turned on his laptop. He downloaded news stories and biographical information about Cameron from various Web sites, along with his own stories in the *Washington Capital* about Capehart's search for a running mate. He had just started writing when Jeanne called back.

"You're lucky I check my messages all the time," she said, skipping pleasantries. "Do I have to remind you this is a Democratic Party phone?" She didn't wait for a response. "I'm not a source. But you're safe. Good-bye."

Mark made one more call, to Susan Cameron's young press secretary, Alison Winters.

They had first met when he tried flirting with her in the bar of the Wayfarer Inn outside Manchester during the New Hampshire primary one winter. She had been working for a long-shot presidential candidate who later dropped out after finishing badly in the primary. For a romantic relationship, she had told Mark bluntly, she would prefer someone nearer her own age. Mark was more impressed than angry, and they became friends. He was the first reporter she called when she unexpectedly landed the job with Cameron.

"Oh my God, Mark, this is a horrible way to wake me up." He had reached her on the cell phone she reserved for personal calls, so he had no idea where she was. "I just can't talk about this, and the senator won't either."

"Look, I'm sorry," Mark said. "But I've got the story and I'm putting it on our Web site. I just wanted to give you a heads-up so the senator has a chance to comment."

"Yeah, thanks for nothing," Alison said. "I won't wave you off, but that's it. On the record, we have no comment and no plans. I've got work to do."

Mark finished writing the story on his laptop, e-mailed it to his editors, and started telephoning them. An editor for the newspaper's Web site was already at the *Capital*'s work space in the sprawling press tents outside the United Center arena, where the convention would soon open. Mark asked her to get the story ready to go onto the site as soon as he cleared it.

Then he called Ron Jones, waking him up in his room at the Fairmont. Mark told him the identities of two of his sources, who would not be named, and left Jeanne out of it. Jones quickly read the story on his computer and woke his bosses before calling Daniels back to tell him to go ahead. Minutes later, just after 8 a.m. in Chicago, the story appeared on washingtoncapital .com.

By Mark Daniels

CHICAGO — Freshman California Sen. Susan Cameron, the country's most popular politician in opinion polls, has been selected by Pennsylvania Sen. Monroe Capehart to be his running mate when he is nominated this week as the Democratic Party's candidate for president, informed sources said today.

Capehart, the 69-year-old Democratic front-runner, who has already amassed enough delegates to win the presidential nomination at the party's national convention here, plans to announce Cameron as his surprise choice for vice president at a press conference later today.

Cameron, 42, won her first election only two years ago after being appointed by California Gov. Davidson Black to fill the Senate seat vacated by her former husband, high-tech multimillionaire Michael Cameron, when he resigned in the wake of financial and sex scandals.

The story was immediately picked up by all the networks, which credited Mark and the *Capital.* Ignoring the steadily ringing phone in his hotel room, Mark showered quickly, put on a suit, and took a taxi to the United Center. He spent the rest of the morning in the press tents outside the arena, accepting congratulations from colleagues and giving television and radio interviews about his story and what it might mean for the presidential campaign.

Trent Tucker's gamble failed spectacularly. By early afternoon, instant polls taken by cable networks and Internet news sites indicated overwhelming initial support for

Susan Cameron's selection. Democratic politicians and women's group leaders rushed onto news and talk shows to sing her praises as a senator focused on what mattered most to voters: education, health care, and security in old age. Republicans and the White House were silent as uncertain party leaders waited for their campaign war room to draft a strategy for doing battle with an unconventional opponent whose record was as scant as her popularity was great.

Monroe Capehart's makeshift headquarters in the ballroom of the Sheraton was flooded with media interview requests, congratulatory telephone messages and e-mails, and offers from women all over the country to volunteer in the campaign. Hours before the convention's opening gavel, the press tents outside the United Center were filled with journalists frantically chasing the runaway story. Swarms of credentialed talking heads — party activists, consultants, and political scientists — roamed from tent to tent, analyzing it all for eager reporters. The usually quiet first day of convention week had become a circus.

Tucker, wearing one of his trademark three-piece suits, was among those moving through the press tents. Having recovered

40

his equilibrium, he was coolly extolling Capehart's "inspired choice" of Cameron in one media interview after another when his cell phone rang and he was summoned back to the Sheraton for a meeting with Capehart and Cameron. The scheduled formal announcement of her selection at an outdoor press conference on a terrace of the hotel overlooking the Chicago River was less than an hour away.

Monroe Capehart, standing tall and trim in a well-tailored dark blue suit, was alone with Susan Cameron in the parlor of the presidential suite at the Sheraton when Tucker was ushered in. Looking even younger and more glamorous than when Tucker had last seen her, Cameron was wearing a soft beige suit and cream-colored blouse that set off her blond hair and California tan, with a skirt that revealed just enough of her long legs. An unseen aide closed the door from outside the room.

"Ah, Trent, you've met Senator Cameron before, haven't you?" asked Capehart. "Why don't we chat for a minute before we go downstairs to face the press."

Cameron leaned back comfortably in her chair, and the two senators exchanged knowing glances. Watching them, Tucker realized that Capehart must have told Cameron that Tucker had fought against putting her on the ticket and may even have leaked the story. He wondered what other secrets Capehart had shared with her.

"Susan's rather new to all this," Capehart began, leaning toward Tucker, "and I figured, Who could be a better teacher than Trent Tucker? Don't you think?"

How could Capehart do this to me? Tucker thought. Tucker was at the top of his game, more than ever *the* man to see if you wanted to get something done in Washington. It would be the crowning achievement of his career in politics if Capeheart won. Tucker had worked meticulously to put together the campaign that had made the veteran senator the inevitable nominee. Now, if he could work from inside the White House for an agenda of his own, in addition to those of his clients, he could accomplish things more lasting than just making more money. Deep down, Tucker was a Southern populist, like his father and grandfather before him. He believed government had a responsibility for the basic welfare of all Americans, not just those who could afford to buy what they wanted through lobbyists like him. He didn't see any conflict in that, or in behaving more like his grandfather while believing in ideals more like those of his father. For all he had done that he knew could not withstand public scrutiny, Tucker saw himself as a patriot.

"Trent," Capehart said. "I just want you to get Senator Cameron's campaign going."

Tucker didn't need this. Capehart's selection of Cameron and his expectation that Tucker would take the time to mentor her was putting everything at risk. But he wouldn't let himself lose control. He couldn't throw away the golden opportunity he had with Capehart.

"Senator Cameron, ma'am," he said, summoning his Georgia drawl. "We're goin' to have a damn fine time together."

They were all standing now, moving toward the door. Tucker clasped Capehart's shoulder.

"Monroe, my friend," he said, man to man, as though they were leaving the locker room of a country club for a big money golf game, "Susan and I are going to kick some ass."

Then he slipped behind the two senators as they opened the door to a gaggle of aides waiting to take them downstairs and outside for the announcement. He watched, with satisfaction, as Susan Cameron glanced anxiously toward Capehart while the two walked on together.

She knows I'll be in charge, Tucker thought.

In fact, she had simply taken an instant dislike to Tucker. She had no reason to know yet how much trouble he would cause her.

4

"Is this what you do on the national staff?" Elizabeth Tawney asked. "Stake out boring parties?"

Recognizing the voice, Sarah turned to find the governor of Maryland and her husband arriving at the entrance to the InterContinental hotel near Lake Michigan. Her timing could not have been better.

"I'm covering money and politics, Governor," Sarah told her. "And this is where the money is tonight. Can I sneak in with you?"

"Stay close," Tawney said. "We'll see what happens."

Even when Sarah's reporting had caused the governor grief in Annapolis, Tawney had respected her aggressiveness. Sarah, in turn, had been impressed by the governor's determination to make her mark in Maryland's macho political culture.

When the three of them reached the ballroom, a young party worker focused his attention on the governor's husband and asked to see his delegate's badge. The young man's face flushed when Tawney showed him hers instead. Seeing who she was, he quickly waved them all through.

"Thank you, Governor," Sarah said when they were inside the crowded ballroom. "If you don't mind, I'll go mingle now."

This was one of the most exclusive of the many parties that filled Chicago's hotels, restaurants, and clubs each night of the convention. These events gave big campaign contributors face time with prominent officeholders and candidates, along with Hollywood personalities and other celebrity supporters. The politicians were there to keep the money flowing, while the contributors' presence reminded them of what was expected in return for their money. No matter how much campaign-finance laws changed, this kind of influence peddling flourished at fund-raising receptions, dinners, golf outings, and resort weekends all year long, all over the country. But it was most visible every four years at both parties' national conventions.

Several of the guests in the InterContinental ballroom reacted with surprise and discomfort when Sarah introduced herself as a reporter and began asking questions.

When one congressman suggested she leave, Sarah disappeared into the crowd and wandered around as inconspicuously as she could, making mental notes on who was there and what she could overhear.

Sarah fit comfortably into the role of an almost unseen observer. As a child, she had lived on the edges of a mostly adult world with her parents in the gentrified Adams Morgan neighborhood of Washington. She watched and listened at the late dinners that featured an ensemble cast of her parents' friends, most of them journalists, who seldom noticed she was there.

Sarah was popular at Georgetown Day high school because she was cute, smart, and noticeably mature. She got along with almost everyone but had few real friends. At Columbia University, she moved out of the dormitory as soon as she could and melted into Manhattan. Most of her contact with other students came at the *Spectator,* where she became the editor. After winning a summer internship at the *Washington Capital,* she did well enough to earn a full-time position.

All good journalists recognize and cultivate their otherness. For Sarah, it was instinctive. She never felt the need to be on the inside of what she witnessed; observing and writing about it were satisfaction enough. She seldom identified with those she covered, and became almost clinical about the targets of her investigations. She had tried to keep her private life separate from her work; whenever she had made an exception, she had come to regret it.

At the fund-raiser in the InterContinental ballroom, Sarah blended in with the well-dressed guests in a sleeveless black sheath that showed off the body she worked so hard for in the gym. She succeeded in chatting up several eager young men, eliciting what information she could without disclosing her purpose. As she moved around, she noticed a woman who appeared to be almost twice her age doing much the same thing. The other woman was wearing a low-cut, silver lamé dress with a silver cross on a delicate chain dangling between her breasts. Inevitably she came face-to-face with Sarah.

"Hi, I'm Kathleen Morgan," she said, extending her hand, "but everyone calls me Kit. Are you a reporter?"

"How'd you know?"

"The way you were looking around, taking everything in, asking questions," Morgan said. "You had to be either a reporter or a spy."

"You mean a Republican spy?"

"Actually, somebody told me you were a reporter," Morgan said. She smiled knowingly. "You made the mistake of identifying yourself to him earlier. He's looking for you now so he can have you thrown out. Want to hide out with me?"

"I'm Sarah Page of the *Washington Capital*," Sarah said. "Are *you* welcome here?"

"Most of them know me," Morgan answered with a wave of her hand. "I get around."

"What do you do?"

"Ah, the classic Washington question."

"And you're evading it."

It was Sarah's turn to smile knowingly. She was enjoying this game.

"I'm in business in Washington," Morgan said. "You know, helping people out with the government."

"What kinds of people?"

"Too many questions for this time and place," Morgan said, staring intently at someone behind Sarah. "Why don't I look you up at home? We'll do lunch."

Morgan was looking over Sarah's shoulder at Trent Tucker, who was engaged in conversation with a trim, erect, balding man wearing an expensive doubled-breasted suit.

"Who's that?" Sarah asked, after turning to look herself.

"Trent Tucker. He's —"

"I know *him*," Sarah interrupted. "I meant the old guy with him. A politician or a big contributor?"

"Much more powerful than either." Morgan seemed nervous. "I don't want him to see me here. If you don't mind, I'll try to find you later."

As she hurried away, Sarah started toward Tucker.

"My dear Miss Page," he drawled. "You look more beautiful tonight than ever."

"Why, thank you, Mr. Tucker." When Sarah looked expectantly at the man with him, she noticed it was Tucker's turn to look anxious.

"Miss Page," he said somewhat stiffly. "I'd like you to meet General Carter Phillips. He runs Palisar International, an investment firm back in Washington."

As Phillips took her hand, Tucker said, "Miss Page is a reporter for the *Washington Capital*."

Phillips's handshake was almost too firm and his gaze actually felt threatening. He made an indelible impression.

"I believe Miss Page may have come upon our little gathering by mistake," Tucker assured him. "If you'll excuse me, General, I'll help her find her way."

Tucker purposefully guided Sarah across the ballroom and out the door. "Sorry, darlin'," he whispered as he gave Sarah a parting kiss on the cheek. "You ran into the wrong gentleman."

On the sidewalk, she stopped to scribble some notes, including the names of Carter Phillips and Kathleen "Kit" Morgan. I need to find out more about both of them, she said to herself as she headed south on busy Michigan Avenue toward the Chicago River and the Fairmont, where she and the other *Capital* reporters were staying. A man who looked like Mark Daniels was walking ahead of her among the late evening strollers. As she passed the Tribune Tower, the man, accompanied by a tall, dark-haired woman, disappeared down some steps to a promenade along the river.

Continuing onto the bridge above them, Sarah looked up at the chalk-white, historic Wrigley Building, bathed by spotlights, and then down at the ink-black river and the dimly lit promenade. She leaned against the wall at the end of the bridge to take in the moment. She was thrilled to be covering her first national political convention for her hometown newspaper, but as she watched couples strolling hand in hand on the promenade below on the beautiful summer night, she felt lonely.

When she noticed the man with the tall, dark-haired woman again, Sarah saw that it *was* Mark Daniels. She was not surprised because she knew his reputation. Mark and the dark-haired woman kissed one long, last time before the woman hurried off toward the Sheraton Hotel, where Sarah knew Monroe Capehart and Susan Cameron were staying. Sarah saw Mark climb up the steps and start across the bridge toward her. She turned away before he could see her, and hurried ahead of him to the Fairmont.

5

On the huge video screen above the podium, Susan Cameron walked through an empty San Jose courtroom, talking about how she had helped protect working people from crime during her days as a prosecutor there. She reappeared in an elementary school classroom, surrounded by children as she sat on the edge of a student's desk, discussing what she had learned about the importance of education while serving, as a senator's wife, on a task force on the future of America's children.

"This is impressive," Mark Daniels told Sarah, as they watched from their perch in the press seats in the upper deck of the United Center. "How did they do it so quickly? It must be her ex-husband's Hollywood connections."

"Why would she have anything to do with him or them?" Sarah asked.

Her story on fund-raising at the convention had already been published — the first front-page story on her new beat. Ron Jones had rewarded Sarah by assigning her to help Mark cover the climactic act of the Democrats' carefully scripted show in Chicago. Mark wasn't too pleased about it, and, because Sarah knew about Tom Evans's friendship with Mark, she wasn't surprised by his obvious discomfort. She had prepared herself for worse.

"This is politics," Mark answered with condescension in his voice. "I don't care what he did to her."

Up on the screen, Susan Cameron was climbing the white marble steps of the Capitol in brilliant sunshine, talking into the camera about how she fought as a senator to improve the lives of ordinary people all across the country. At the top of the steps, she joined a group of veteran Senate Democrats, the majority of them women, who testified one by one about her caring and leadership.

"Look at them." Mark nudged Sarah and pointed down to dozens of perfectly groomed, look-alike men and women lining the arena's mezzanine level — reporters from television stations across the country. They were all speaking into cameras, their backs to the crowded convention floor.

"They're like a bunch of Barbie and Ken dolls," Mark said. "They don't care what's really going on here. They're just using the convention as a backdrop for their stand-ups. Most of them are probably talking about Susan Cameron. She's become a rock star."

It was the convention's closing night, which usually would be dominated by the acceptance speech of the presidential nominee, still two hours away. Instead, the United Center, brightly decorated in red, white, and blue, was already filled for Cameron's debut as his running mate. The traditional warm-up had become this convention's main event.

The rows of seats reserved for the press on either side of the speakers' platform were packed with reporters already hard at work. Even as he provided Sarah grudging commentary on what they were watching, Mark kept typing away on the laptop in front of him. He added a description of what was happening in the convention hall to background material he had written earlier. He wouldn't start writing the main part of the story until first Cameron and then Capehart had started speaking and their written texts had been distributed to reporters. He would wait as long as possible to write his lead — the first few paragraphs of the story, which would sum up everything.

As always when writing on deadline, Mark had loosened his tie and unbuttoned his shirt at the neck. He nervously ran his hands through his thick, dark brown hair. The adrenaline rush he felt facing a computer screen, knowing from long experience that somehow a satisfactory story would materialize there, was one of the things Mark enjoyed most about being a newspaper reporter. Deadline writing gave him a thrill that never required emotional investment.

"I can't remember a presidential nominee being upstaged like this at his own convention," he told Sarah. "But I hear Capehart doesn't mind. He's even got Trent Tucker working on Cameron's message and delivery."

"How well do you know him?" Sarah asked.

"Capehart?" Mark's tone made clear he

didn't think much of the question. "I've been covering him since before he declared. I can't remember how many times I've interviewed him."

"Sorry," Sarah said. "I meant Tucker."

"Oh." Mark wasn't expecting that. "We've been running into each other on campaigns for years. He's been a source on occasion."

And then he switched the subject. "It'll be interesting to see what Tucker does with Cameron. She's got a good story to tell."

Sarah and everyone else already knew most of Cameron's story from the extraordinary media coverage of her rapid rise from disgraced senator's wife to vice presidential nominee. The only child of two Stanford University political science professors, she had grown up in a comfortable, book-filled house a few blocks from the campus in Palo Alto. There was never any doubt that Susan would attend Stanford herself. She met Michael Cameron when she was a junior there and soon moved into his apartment off-campus. They married within a year.

Michael, the son of a Hollywood producer and one of a succession of actress wives, took for granted his good looks and privileged life. He enjoyed the attention of would-be starlets at Beverly Hills High, but was ready for something more challenging than life in the entertainment industry. At Stanford, he fell in with students working on new ways to make money with computer technology, eventually helping them to finance and market early Internet ventures. He became a Silicon Valley venture capitalist and proselytizer for the entrepreneurial high-tech economy.

Susan went on to earn her law degree at Stanford and work as a local prosecutor in San Jose. She and Michael bought a spacious home in the hills above Palo Alto. Influenced by her parents, they also became interested in politics. Michael discovered that the intricacies of campaigns and elections fascinated him as much as the burgeoning technology business. While Susan eventually joined a private law practice and did some work for Democratic candidates, he became a popular speaker and fundraiser for the party.

Eventually, he chose the historic Julia Morgan Ballroom at the top of the Merchants Exchange Building in San Francisco's financial district, where many successful Silicon Valley start-ups had staged their announcement parties, to launch the first technology-industry political action committee. The unprecedented gathering of celebrities from Silicon Valley, Hollywood, and Washington attracted attention across the country. After that, no prominent Democrat came to California to campaign or raise money without paying court to young Michael Cameron. He became intrigued with the possibility of pursuing politics to Washington.

When California's senior senator decided to retire, Michael quickly amassed enough money and support to preempt the Democratic field, while the ideologically split Republicans selected a right-wing conservative. The novice candidate's moderate "New Democrat for a New Economy" message, broadcast incessantly throughout the state with millions of dollars' worth of television and radio advertising, catapulted Michael Cameron into the United States Senate at the age of thirty-four.

Susan Cameron felt uncomfortable at first with all the attention that she and Michael drew as the attractive new political couple in Washington. But she came to realize that she could take advantage of it to work on things that mattered to her, including the welfare of women and children. It helped to make up for Michael's reluctance to have children of their own and the limits of her supporting role in his political career. She found herself speaking out on issues, taking on leadership roles, and giving media interviews.

Susan's increasingly busy life also filled a growing gap in her marriage. Michael spent long weekday hours on Capitol Hill and traveled most weekends, campaigning in California or raising money for the party around the country. So it came as no surprise to anyone who knew her that she appeared to be completely in the dark when news broke about Michael's other life.

In a nationally televised interview, a woman who worked in Cameron's venture-capital firm in California said she had carried on a long relationship with Michael before discovering that he had had affairs with other women during his travels. She also revealed questionable stock transactions he had made in high-tech firms before being elected to the Senate and putting his holdings in trust. Michael escaped prison only by agreeing to resign from the Senate, admit to insider trading and stock fraud, pay a hefty fine, and provide federal investigators with information that implicated a courtroom full of high-tech entrepreneurs, stockbrokers, and accountants. He insisted that Susan knew nothing about his cheating in business or in their marriage.

The scandal focused intense media attention on Susan, of course, as the wronged wife who had worked for good causes and blindly supported her husband. At the urging of many political women who had become her friends, she played out her role articulately in public. Interviewers expanded their questioning from how Susan felt personally about Michael, and what he had done, to what she thought about the issues his sensational case had pushed to the top of the national agenda. She gave thoughtful, confident answers, and soon she was deluged with supportive mail and job offers.

The governor of California, responding to public opinion polls, decided to appoint Susan to replace her estranged husband in the U.S. Senate. Backed by Michael's old technology-industry coalition and supporters in Hollywood, as well as leaders of women's groups, she kept the seat in the next election.

Now, just a few years after her husband's downfall and their divorce, Senator Susan Cameron was the literally larger-than-life star of the Democratic convention. After the video ended, she appeared live on the giant screen, walking down a United Center corridor to the speaker's platform, wearing a fitted royal blue jacket and skirt that subtly highlighted her figure. When she finally reached the podium, the thunderous roar of the crowd in the packed arena rivaled what Michael Jordan must have heard each time he stepped onto the court there. A choreographed demonstration took over the convention floor, with delegates waving CAPEHART-CAMERON and WE LOVE SUSAN signs for the television cameras.

"I love you, too," Susan responded as she gestured for the crowd to subside. Her delicate features, framed by her blond hair, filled the video screen behind her like the visage of a glamorous movie star. She began her speech by thanking Monroe Capehart for boldly picking a woman as a running mate. She then disarmingly acknowledged her relative inexperience in public office.

"In California, I benefited from what has become a habit of electing women to the United States Senate," she began. "But I still have the perspective of someone who has not spent that much time in Washington. I still know what matters to real people living real lives all across this great country. I know they want good schools, good jobs, good health, and good years ahead of them after they retire.

"And I know the special responsibilities shouldered by the many women who both work and care for their families. I hear their voices. I know their hopes and fears."

"She's touching all the bases," Mark said to Sarah. "And she sounds good."

Then came the surprise.

"Warner Wylie doesn't know what life is like for ordinary Americans," Susan declared, her voice rising. "He had an address in Missouri when he was governor. But Warner Wylie grew up in Washington, D.C. He went to private schools and an Ivy League college. He got his first job in his father's old law firm. What could Warner Wylie know about real life? And what has he learned about it since he became vice president?"

"Now, this is interesting," Mark mused aloud, as he rapidly punched the keys on his laptop. "They're using her acceptance speech to attack the opposing presidential candidate. That's usually the job of a warm-up speaker. It was Ted Kennedy's specialty."

Warner Wylie, the son of a former long-serving senator who had been a rich Kansas City lawyer, was the governor of Missouri when he was asked to be the second-term running mate of the incumbent president. The Republicans chose him to replace an aging warhorse with a heart condition who had helped the ticket the first time out but would have had no chance of winning the White House on his own. As vice president, Wylie was kept out of controversy while being groomed as a presidential nominee.

"Too many Americans are still waiting for loved ones to return home alive and well from Iraq. Where was the leadership to help the president find a better way out of his mismanaged war?

"Where was Wylie?

"Incompetence and bureaucratic chaos continue to undermine our emergency preparedness and homeland security. Where was the leadership to better protect our citizens from terrorism and natural disasters?"

As her electrified audience started to pick up the refrain, Susan paused for an instant, her arms outstretched to conduct the chorus.

"Where was Wylie?"

"The Social Security and Medicare time bombs are still ticking. Where was the leadership to ensure good health and a secure retirement for all Americans?"

Everyone, from delegates on the floor to guests in the V.I.P. suites high above them, chanted along with her.

"Where was Wylie?"

"Where was Wylie?"

Mark Daniels typed away methodically. He found the performance impressive, although he had seen variations of it over the years. But Sarah tingled with an excitement that surprised her.

Pledging to help "retake the White House and bring strong leadership back to the country," Cameron finished her speech with a flourish. She basked in a long, loud ovation that subsided only when she disappeared from the podium. Politicians rushed from their seats in the state delegations to praise her on camera to television reporters working the convention floor. Commentators for the national networks, which had expanded their meager coverage of the convention to broadcast her speech live, said it confirmed Cameron as a major player on the national political stage.

During the scheduled interval for television commercials and the arrival in the convention hall of the presidential nominee, Mark's cell phone rang. He turned away from Sarah when he heard Jeanne's voice, but his change in demeanor was obvious.

"I'm way up here in the friends and family box, waiting for MAC's speech," Jeanne told him, using the Secret Service acronym for Monroe Arthur Capehart. "Didn't you think Susan Cameron was impressive?"

"You know I'm not going to answer that. But it's a great story. And it's great to hear your voice. I wish I could see you."

"I can see you right now through my binoculars. And you look good. I've missed you," Jeanne added softly. "Who's the babe?"

"A colleague," Mark answered quietly as he turned further away from Sarah. "It's her first convention. She's doing campaign-finance stuff."

"Well, she's too young for you."

"Stop it. I'm on deadline. I'm writing about how they're exploiting the Cameron phenomenon. Have you heard Capehart talk about her?"

"Nothing in particular, but he seems happy with how the week's been going," Jeanne said. "Let's get together later to-night."

"I'll be real late."

"That's okay. After I tuck in MAC, I have to go to a RON meeting for the bus trip he and Cameron are starting in the morning."

"Tell me about it," Mark said. "I have to be up at the crack of dawn for the baggage call."

"I'll let you know when I'm ready to go to the Fairmont," Jeanne said before hanging up.

"Who was that?" Sarah asked after Mark turned back to his computer.

"A source," Mark said impatiently. "I've got to get this story done. At this rate, it's going to be all Susan Cameron. Go find the press people and tell them to give us the Capehart text now, or he won't be in the first edition."

After Sarah returned with copies of Capehart's speech, Mark picked up his open laptop, with the story still on its screen, to go back to the *Capital*'s work space in the press tent. Grabbing Capehart's speech, he told Sarah, "I'll put some of this in the story and file it for the Web site. You stay here and listen. I'll watch on TV."

Sarah took off her suit jacket, draped it over the back of her chair, and opened her own laptop. It felt good to be back on her own. While waiting for Capehart's entrance, she stared across the tumultuous convention hall. She could see why political reporters lived for events like this.

Mark removed his jacket and tie when he reached the *Capital*'s work space and sat at one of the long tables filled with rented computers, printers, and telephones. At a temporary television setup nearby, another reporter was doing a video interview with a congressman for the Web site. Mark juggled two phones and his computer as he worked hurriedly on his story while talking to sources returning calls he had made from the convention hall.

One of the first to call back was Rush Ripley, a Trent Tucker lieutenant. Like some of the others who worked for Tucker, Ripley was an obnoxiously ambitious young political operative. Mark told him there was no need for the usual spin on Susan Cameron's speech. But why, he asked Ripley, did she attack Wylie like that?

"Wylie has some real liabilities," Ripley told him. "We've done the research."

Mark couldn't let such a fat pitch go by without a swing.

"What research?"

6

"Marge, I think I've got a live one."

"Good," the researcher told Sarah. "What can I do for you?"

A tall, graying woman with grandchildren, Marge Lawson was a news librarian who took pride in having returned to the newsroom in her fifties after a break to raise her family and mastering the techniques of exploring the rich information resources in cyberspace. Her cluttered cubicle, with its high-powered computer, was a popular destination for reporters. And Sarah was one of her favorite pupils.

"I'm looking at Trent Tucker's lobbying clients," Sarah said. "So far, I've found an oil company, a pharmaceutical maker, a mining company, and a bunch of government contractors. They've given a lot of money to members of Congress he's worked for as a political consultant. And some of their votes have helped his lobbying clients. Patent protection for pharmaceuticals. Oil drilling rights in environmentally sensitive areas. Preferential access to Pentagon contracts."

Sarah had never known about this part of Tucker's business. Had he built it since she first met him in Maryland? They had talked only about politics back then.

"Money has always bought votes in Washington," said Lawson.

"But Tucker's playing both sides of the street," Sarah said, sounding as though she had just discovered gravity. "Politicians pay him to get elected. And business clients pay him to lobby those same politicians."

"It looks like I've taught you well," Lawson said. "Lobbyist registration forms. Campaign contribution lists. Congressional voting records. You must've hit them all.

What do you need from me?"

"I want to see how much further I can follow the money, Marge."

"I'll get right to it as soon as I finish with Warner Wylie."

"Who asked for that?"

"Daniels," Lawson said. "He sent me a list of things to look for in his campaign contributions, and it's all checking out."

"He's poaching," Sarah said. "Political money is my beat now."

"Don't get too big for your britches," Lawson replied. "Mark Daniels has been covering politics since you were a schoolgirl."

Her words sobered Sarah. She still had to prove herself. What should she do while waiting for Lawson? She remembered how Carter Phillips had reacted when Tucker had introduced her to him in Chicago. Sarah decided it was time to find out why.

She was surprised to discover that Phillips was a retired commanding general of the Army's Special Forces who had briefly been director of the Central Intelligence Agency before starting Palisar International. The privately held firm had grown rapidly, from winning government contracts for intelligence and security work to investing in companies in defense contracting, construction, energy production, and mining all over the globe. Palisar maintained only a small headquarters in Washington and didn't have to file reports required of publicly traded companies.

Its Web site showed that Phillips was only one of many Palisar partners and executives who had held high positions in the U.S. and foreign governments. Past news coverage had raised questions about whether those connections gave firms it controlled the inside track on government contracts and concessions. Sarah noticed that some of the companies Palisar owned — Dorsey Energy, Mammoth Mining, and the military contractor Smith and Hawley — were among the clients listed on Trent Tucker's lobbyist registration forms.

This is interesting, Sarah thought. Tucker and Phillips must be doing business together. There could be a story in any influence peddling involved.

She couldn't yet imagine that such a story would open the door to much more than the political corruption that had become commonplace in Washington.

A few days later, working half a dozen desks away from Sarah, Mark Daniels finished his story about Warner Wylie.

"Since when did you become an investigative reporter?" Ron Jones asked Mark while editing the story. "You're not usually interested in this kind of stuff."

"I got a good tip," Mark told him. "Marge did the heavy lifting."

"Well, it's a great get. Just like the Susan Cameron story. Everyone's going to have to chase you again."

Jones knew the story would be good for him, too, as one of the few black senior editors in the newsroom. He had put in years and years as a political reporter for other newspapers before being hired at the *Capital,* where he waited for what seemed like too many more years before being promoted to political editor. He knew his reporters respected his deep reservoir of political knowledge and sure-footed judgment, but he wasn't sure he had the complete confidence of his own bosses.

By evening, the story was ready for the *Capital*'s Web site and the next morning's newspaper.

By Mark Daniels

Republican presidential nominee Warner Wylie, while he was governor of Missouri, received tens of thousands of dollars' worth of free plane trips and golf vacations from pharmaceutical companies, while they fought state and federal efforts to hold down the cost of drugs for Medicare and Medicaid recipients.

One multinational drug company, Templeton Mannheim, loaned its company planes to Wylie for dozens of political fund-raising trips around the country. It and other pharmaceutical firms also paid for Wylie to attend industry outings for lobbyists and politicians at exclusive golf resorts in Florida, California, and Hawaii, according to campaign-finance records.

"Yes, he has been one of our frequent fliers," said a Templeton Mannheim official who did not want to be named. "But we extend our hospitality to many friends."

Executives of pharmaceutical firms, including Templeton Mannheim, have contributed hundreds of thousands of dollars over the years to Wylie's political action committee, Missourians for Progress. The PAC has helped fund both Wylie's national political campaign activities and the campaigns of other Republican politicians who have supported his presidential ambitions.

Templeton Mannheim also was one of Wylie's top-paying clients when he worked, before being elected governor, in the Kansas City and Washington offices of his father's law firm, Wylie, Drew and Roberts, according to sources with knowledge of the relationship. A spokesman for the firm said he would not discuss its clients.

The story dominated television news shows and media Web sites the next morning. Monroe Capehart, interrupting a brief vacation on Cape Cod to speak at fundraising gatherings in Boston, ignored reporters' shouted questions about it. But in California, Susan Cameron, who was campaigning and visiting her family there, was quite ready to discuss the story. She held an impromptu sidewalk press conference on Nob Hill in San Francisco, where she had just delivered a speech at the Pacific-Union Club.

"This report, which appears to be fully documented by public records, is a shocking revelation," she told reporters, who were eager for a newsy confrontation early in the race. "Now we know why health-care and prescription-drug reform has gone nowhere in the current administration. Warner Wylie has been in the pocket of the big drug companies."

Susan made her reaction seem spontaneous, looking out over the microphones into the faces of the reporters surrounding her. "The drug companies flew Warner Wylie all around the country while he was governor," she continued, as a breeze ruffled her hair. "They paid his way to luxurious resorts to play golf. They're helping to underwrite his campaign for president. Warner Wylie cannot be trusted to protect hard-working and retired Americans from high health-care and drug costs. The American people cannot afford to have Warner Wylie in the White House."

Keeping the story at the top of the network shows and newspaper front pages, Susan Cameron wounded Wylie while Monroe Capehart stayed above the fray.

Sarah spent a fretful morning in the newsroom the next day before working up the nerve to walk over to Mark's desk and confront him.

"You're a terrific reporter," she began

nervously. "But do you know that Templeton Mannheim is one of Trent Tucker's lobbying clients? Wouldn't that explain how he knew the company had provided Wylie with planes and golf trips and contributed so much money to his PAC?"

Once she had gotten started, the adrenaline flowed. Her muscles tightened as she stood over Mark, who was leaning back in his chair. Her intense, dark eyes focused on him as though he were on a witness stand.

"Wasn't it awfully easy to get that quote from the spokesman for Templeton Mannheim? And a statement that the company was a client of Wylie's law firm? Who might those 'sources with knowledge of the relationship' be, anyway?"

"Whoa," Mark said, still relaxed in his chair. "Can't you just say, 'Great story, Mark,' and leave it at that? You sound jealous."

"I don't work that way," Sarah snapped.

She paused to take a breath. She had thought carefully about this.

"Look," she said. "I happen to have been going through Tucker's lobbying disclosures when I found the Templeton Mannheim stuff. You probably didn't know about that. And I didn't know your story was going to be about Wylie's relationships with drug companies."

She paused again.

"But it looks like Trent Tucker took you for a ride. He had Susan Cameron ready to run with your story."

"That's enough," Mark said, now sitting upright, eye-to-eye with Sarah. It felt to him as though Sarah was baiting him to confirm Tucker as his source.

"Everything in that story was right," he told her. "And this newspaper should be holding Warner Wylie accountable for what he does, just like we do with the rest of them. It doesn't really matter who opened the door for me. I got the story. If Tucker's clever enough to take advantage of it and Cameron delivers the goods, so be it. When they cross the line, we'll call them out, too. Meanwhile, we'll cover what the Republicans say when they fight back."

Sarah couldn't really argue with any of that. And she didn't know what to say next.

"Isn't this exactly the kind of reporting you do?" Mark asked her. "I'm sure your sources had their reasons when they helped you in Maryland. Everything's just rougher and tougher at this level. Presidential politics is a full-contact sport."

"Well, I've told you what I thought," Sarah

said, backing away. But there was one more thing.

"By the way," she added, just as she had rehearsed it. "Ron Jones suggested I look at what Tucker's up to. I'll tell you if I find anything else interesting."

"You do that," Mark said, turning away in his chair. In the heat of the moment, he didn't pay much attention to what she had said about Tucker.

As she walked back to her desk, Sarah reran the conversation in her mind. She didn't doubt Mark's sincerity. That was how he understood the rules of the game. And he may have had a point. What difference did it make where the information came from, or what a source's motives were, if the story was right?

The Republicans fought back against Susan Cameron through surrogates.

On the *Capital*'s own op-ed page the next day, Stewart Aiken, the conservative columnist who had made his reputation as an intellectual scold, condescendingly referred to Cameron as "a clueless novice on the national political stage." He wrote that it was "naïve" of her to castigate Warner Wylie for campaign contributions and junkets "routinely accepted by governors, as well as members of Congress, of both parties."

Aiken didn't tell his readers that he had benefited from the pharmaceutical companies' largesse himself, earning six-figure fees for speaking at industry gatherings. It was a fraction of the millions he made each year from his columns, books, speeches, and appearances on television.

"Perhaps Senator Cameron is still learning how to play with the big boys," Aiken concluded in his column, which was syndicated in hundreds of other newspapers across the country and reverberated through the blogosphere. "Or perhaps she and her handlers hope that baseless attacks on a good man will deflect the nation's gaze from her own inexperience. Senator Cameron would be wise to concentrate on offering some shred of evidence that she is ready to be only a heartbeat away from the presidency."

Crystal Malone was not so polite.

"How can this woman stand in judgment of anyone when her own husband systematically defrauded investors and taxpayers?" she asked disdainfully on her *Malone Report* on cable television. Her long, hot war on liberals had made the blond, model-thin, right-wing provocateur a wildly successful author, talk-show performer, and blogger.

"Susan Cameron benefited from her husband's ill-gotten gains. She shared his rich lifestyle. She was put into his seat in the United States Senate by his liberal political friends.

"Now, I realize that Senator Cameron is beautiful and charming and that her man cheated on her," Malone said, dramatically placing her heavily bejeweled hands on the stage-set desk and leaning toward the camera. "But she's running for vice president of the United States. And she has allowed the cynical liberals who run the Democrat party to exploit her, just as her husband did. There's a word for what you call a woman who allows herself to be used like that. I'm not going to say it on television. But it rhymes with 'more.' "

Other right-wing talk-show hosts and bloggers quickly piled on, while liberal commentators reacted with outrage.

"My mother always told me that if you couldn't say anything nice about somebody, don't say anything at all," the acerbic columnist Sally McGuire wrote in the *New York Herald.* "It appears that some of our friends on the right had a different kind of mother. Can you guess what that rhymes with?"

The controversy could have been one of

those Washington media flare-ups that burn brightly on op-ed pages, talk shows, and the Web for a few days before dying down as quickly as they ignited. But opinion polls showed that it left lingering questions in voters' minds about Wylie, while reinforcing Susan Cameron's political-outsider appeal. So the Democrats hit Wylie with a barrage of attack ads. After citing the pressing problems facing the nation, the first wave of television spots showed Susan rhetorically asking during her convention speech, "Where was Wylie?"

The second wave began with her refrain, followed by an announcer's answer to the question, voiced over photographs of Wylie, a sleek executive jet, and a picturesque golf course: "While you and your family were worrying about increases in the cost of prescription drugs and health care, Warner Wylie was enjoying the hospitality of his friends in the pharmaceutical industry. He was flying around the country in private planes and playing golf at exclusive resorts, all at the expense of the big drug companies. Who would he be working for in the White House — you or the big drug companies?"

From his spacious office on the top floor of a building just off Pennsylvania Avenue in downtown Washington, midway between the White House and Capitol Hill, Trent Tucker telephoned Susan at her parents' home in Palo Alto.

"How are you doing, Senator?" he asked.

"Well, my mother and father don't like what the opposition is saying about me," Cameron said, "and they don't particularly like what I've been saying either. They're clean campaign types. But I'm okay."

"Good," Tucker told her. "I'd like to keep you out front for a while. Your numbers are holding up. And you and the ads are hurting Wylie. That makes it harder for them to knock Senator Capehart off message."

"Mr. Tucker, I understand perfectly well what we're doing," Susan responded testily. She was putting him on notice about their relationship. "We're defining Wylie before they can define Monroe. I'm not as green as you may think."

"Sorry, ma'am," Tucker drawled. "Didn't mean any harm."

"I prefer 'Senator' to 'ma'am,' Mr. Tucker," she said. "It was nice of you to call, but I don't need coddling. I'll see you in New York."

7

"Listen, Susan, they're running you ragged," Amanda Peterson said in the gently scolding voice she still felt free to use with her old friend from California. "They're using you to protect Capehart."

"That's my job for now, although I do feel a bit overwhelmed sometimes."

It was women only in the bedroom of Susan's suite in the Waldorf-Astoria. Amanda, still resplendent in a silky black Versace dress, was reclining regally on a chaise longue in the bedroom. Susan, who had changed into old running shorts and a sleeveless top, was sitting cross-legged on the king-size bed. Alison Winters, who had carelessly tossed her shoes and suit jacket onto the floor next to the bed, was leaning back against a stack of pillows next to Susan. They were relaxing after a long evening of fund-raising receptions for rich New York Democrats in the Waldorf's ballrooms.

Penny Piper, who had left Cameron's congressional staff to work as her personal assistant during the campaign, was sitting on the floor in jeans, with pages of Susan's crowded schedule spread out around her. She had stayed in the suite to work on details of the week's remaining events. The rest of Cameron's Senate staff was still on Capitol Hill, leaving her dependent on campaign aides whom Trent Tucker had assembled for her.

"I had no idea what a national campaign would be like," Susan said. "Sometimes, when I hear myself talking to these crowds, it feels like I'm having an out-of-body experience."

Only two years earlier, while she was campaigning to keep her seat in the Senate, Susan had felt uncomfortable speaking to large groups of people. But she learned to focus on individuals in a crowd, talking to each of them as though they were the jurors she had once appealed to in courtrooms or the women she had recruited in suburban living rooms for her former husband's Senate campaign. When they appeared actually to be listening, she could feel an almost intoxicating surge of energy and determination.

"I'm feeding off the crowds, especially the women," she told Amanda. "I owe it to them to show I can hold my own, that I'm ready to become vice president. And, if that can happen . . ."

"A woman like you could be president," Amanda said, finishing the thought before the look on Susan's face stopped her from saying more.

Susan firmly avoided that subject, even though it was a central issue of her candidacy. She was more than content to follow Tucker's advice and leave it to Monroe Capehart to emphasize that he had complete confidence in her ability to serve as president.

Amanda was one of the few people to whom Susan could talk even this openly. After being thrust so suddenly into an intensely public life, she kept her guard up with almost everyone else.

The Camerons and the Petersons had known each other since their student days at Stanford. Like Michael Cameron, Woody Peterson had hit the jackpot in Silicon Valley, eventually selling his successful start-up computer-networking firm to a much larger company for an astonishing amount of money. Amanda ran an educational foundation the Petersons set up with part of their fortune, while Woody continued to dabble in the Internet world, serving on boards and investing in other start-ups. They had moved south to Carmel, on California's Monterey Peninsula, where Woody, obsessed with golf, could play regularly at Pebble Beach.

When scandal forced Michael Cameron out of the U.S. Senate, Amanda was among those who had urged Susan to accept the appointment to replace him. And she tirelessly raised money for Susan's successful election campaign two years later. Now Amanda was traveling with Susan whenever she could as an unofficial, unpaid adviser. She saw herself as something of a counterweight to the campaign professionals. She insisted on occasionally scheduling "girls' nights" when Susan could relax with the handful of women in her inner circle.

"Only the money stuff gets me down sometimes," Susan told them. "I don't mind fund-raisers like the ones tonight. I'm fine telling people why they should support Monroe and me. But I hate days when I have to dial for dollars. It's so demeaning to beg people for money, especially with one of Tucker's guys listening in on the other phone, taking notes. If Crystal Malone called me a whore for doing *that,* she'd be closer to the truth."

"Speaking of that witch," Amanda said, "going heavy against Wylie has exposed you to some pretty rough stuff. When's Tucker going to let up?"

"He says it's still pushing up Wylie's negatives without hurting me," said Susan.

Alison broke in. "Believe me, if the polls showed you should be talking about something else, Trent and Jeremy would have you change the subject."

"Jeremy?" Amanda asked. "Is that the young guy I see you with all the time?"

"He's the chief speechwriter," Alison said with a sheepish grin. "We have to work together to make sure we're on message."

"You seem to be doing a lot of that work in your room at night," Amanda said. "And what about you, Susan? Have you sworn off men during the campaign or are you sneaking them in when I'm not around?"

"I haven't seen any," Piper said, surprising the others. "I'm nearly always with her."

"It's almost impossible to have a normal relationship," said Susan. "Any man seen with me becomes a gossip-column item. And it draws attention to the fact that I don't have a husband. Who was the last person to run for president or vice president who wasn't married? I'm just not bothering with dating right now."

"I'd better go," Alison said, sliding off the bed and gathering up her jacket and shoes. "I've got work to finish."

"Me, too," Piper said, gathering up the papers around her on the floor. "If anything changes for tomorrow, I'll let you know when I come by in the morning."

The two young women left the suite.

"It's late," Amanda said. "I better get going, too."

"Wait," Susan told her. "I've got something to tell you that I couldn't say in front of them."

Amanda turned toward Susan, who flopped onto her stomach near the foot of the bed, with her head propped up on her hands to face her best friend.

"Michael's been in touch with me. He's made a lot of suggestions. He got his Hollywood friends to make the convention video. And he's pushed me to go after Wylie. We talk on the phone late at night. He reassures me. But it's beginning to feel like more than that."

"You don't really think you can trust him, do you?" Amanda asked. "There's so much at stake now."

"I know he hasn't changed. But we still believe in the same things. Everything I know about politics I learned from him. And I think he's really trying to help me now."

"Of course he is. It's the only way he'll ever get this close to the action again," Amanda said, trying to sound understanding. "And you wouldn't be telling me this if you weren't worried that it might get out of hand."

Alison Winters, carrying her jacket and shoes, had wandered down the hallway, past the rooms of other campaign aides. Most of their doors were still open, as they often were in the college dormitory atmosphere of the traveling campaign. No one needed to lock their doors because the floor had been secured by the Secret Service. Members of the campaign staff wandered in and out of one another's rooms without even knocking as they worked into the night.

When Alison came to Jeremy Cantor's room, she hesitated at the door, which was propped open with a suitcase. Jeremy was working on his laptop at the desk. On the bed next to him, surrounded by teetering piles of papers, was Rush Ripley. They were arguing over something Ripley wanted Jeremy to put into a speech for Susan. With their backs to the door, neither of them saw Alison come in.

"I don't want her saying that," Jeremy told Ripley. "It's too tough. It wouldn't sound right coming from a woman."

"Well, that's the problem, isn't it?" Ripley insisted.

"You still don't get it," Jeremy said. "It's

because she's a woman that she's gotten away with taking on Wylie in the first place. She doesn't look hard or mean doing it. We just can't go too far."

"What happens when the glamour wears off?" Ripley asked. "What happens when the Republicans and the press start treating her like a politician instead of a Hollywood star?"

"Aren't you supposed to scrub her first so there won't be any surprises?" Alison interrupted, startling both men. "I thought you guys were supposed to check out our candidates, too, so we're ready for whatever the enemy throws at us."

"How long have you been there?" Ripley asked, jumping up from the bed.

"Long enough to hear more of your misogynist bullshit," Alison said. "Monroe Capehart would look like a tired old man without Susan Cameron on the ticket. Instead, he gets to be the reassuring elder statesman while she takes the fight to Wylie. Maybe you don't recognize a strong woman when you see one, Rush."

"Why don't we finish this on the plane tomorrow," suggested Jeremy. "It's getting late."

The gangly Ripley shuffled uneasily past Alison. She pushed the suitcase out of the way and shut the door after him. Then she dropped her jacket and shoes, tossed back her long, curly hair, walked over to Jeremy's chair, and wrapped her arms around his head, burying his face in her bosom.

With his unkempt hair, mismatched clothes, and high-pitched laugh, Jeremy resembled an overgrown adolescent. But he lived and breathed politics, and he wrote with an innate feel for the spoken word. Just a few years out of college, he had been plucked by Trent Tucker from a rival campaign during the primaries and put to work writing speeches, first for Monroe Capehart and now for Susan Cameron.

Jeremy was immediately taken with Alison. Impressed by her relative maturity in politics and life, he became her devoted student in both. That gave Alison comfortable control over their campaign-trail relationship. Jeremy was available, attractive enough in his own way, and eager to please whenever she wanted him.

"I've got some things to go over with you for tomorrow," Alison told him. "But they can wait."

She began to unbutton her blouse. She was a big-boned woman, fleshy in the right places.

"Aren't we going to your room?" Jeremy

asked, glancing at the clutter on his bed.

"No, it's too close to Amanda Peterson. She's been spying on us." Alison unzipped her skirt and pulled Jeremy up from his chair. "From now on, I'm going to tell the RON to put her farther away."

They finished undressing quickly. They scooped the piles of campaign speeches and press releases off the bed and carefully placed them on the floor without mixing anything up. As Jeremy bent down with the last pile of papers cradled in his arms, Alison laughed out loud at how ludicrous he looked.

They jumped onto the bed like giggling teenagers, without bothering to pull back the covers. After directing him to do what satisfied her most, Alison thought about how it was never really romantic with Jeremy. It just felt good. With work still to be done for the next day's campaigning, she called room service for dessert and coffee.

"How was girls' night?" Jeremy asked idly, as they started putting their clothes back on.

"Oh, the usual. Amanda keeps worrying that Tucker and you guys are working Susan too hard. But Susan said she's okay. Penny and I left when they started talking about Susan's love life, or rather her lack of one."

"I guess it's kind of difficult when she's in the spotlight all the time," said Jeremy.

"I'd rather not talk about it," Alison said, straightening her skirt. "I want to know as little as possible about her personal life when I'm dealing with reporters."

"Can't you just lie?"

"I don't think I'd be very good at it."

"I guess we'll see. It's a long campaign."

In another hotel room a thousand miles to the south, Mark Daniels's insistently ringing cell phone finally woke him. As he fumbled for it on the night table in the pitch-black room, he felt the warmth and soft skin of Jeanne's body curved around his. They were in Miami at the Mandarin Oriental overlooking Biscayne Bay, unusually posh digs for the Capehart campaign. The presidential candidate had spent the day at poolside receptions in Miami, raising money from Florida fat cats. Then he had turned in early to rest up for a full day of campaigning around the state. Mark had nothing to file because the fund-raisers were closed to the press. So he and Jeanne indulged in a rare romantic evening of leisurely lovemaking before falling asleep, exhausted, without even calling room service.

"Mark, what the hell is this?" demanded the voice on the phone.

"What are you talking about?" Mark asked in a loud whisper. He recognized Trent Tucker's drawl.

"Don't you read your newspaper on the Web at night? That's what I'm doing right now in New York."

Tucker was in his room at the Waldorf, just down the hall from where Alison Winters and Jeremy Cantor were working on speeches and press releases for Susan Cameron. They had not yet seen the article on the *Capital*'s Web site.

"I'm in bed, Trent," Mark said. "You woke me up."

"Shit. You must be with some woman. Are you in your own hotel room at least? Get your ass out of bed and turn on your computer."

"Is this really so important?"

"Yes, it is. I'm royally pissed off."

Tucker lowered his voice and tried to sound more reasonable.

"Look, Mark, I know I'm probably bothering you at a bad time, but can you take a look at it?"

"I'll call you back. Give me a few minutes to get my bearings."

Mark eased himself out of bed, still trying

not to disturb Jeanne, and put on a robe from the bathroom. He turned on the desk lamp and clicked to the *Capital*'s Web site on his laptop.

"What's happening, honey?" Jeanne called over to him drowsily.

"I've got to check out something in tomorrow's paper. Trent Tucker just called. He's pretty upset. I'll just be a few minutes."

"How did he know where you were?"

"Don't worry, darling. He called on my cell. He could probably guess that I'm traveling with Capehart, but he doesn't know I'm with you. This is my room, remember?"

"Oh." Jeanne was up now, heading for the bathroom. Mark turned around to watch. He never tired of looking at her.

"Just do what you have to do," she told him, "so we can order something to eat. I'm starving."

Mark turned his attention back to his computer and immediately saw the story near the top of the newspaper's home page, under a provocative headline: "MAN FOR ALL POLITICAL SEASONS: Top Cameron Campaign Aide Paid to Lobby Politicians He Put into Office."

By Sarah Page

Although he is little known outside the nation's capital, Trent Tucker is the man to see in Washington. A combination of political consultant and lobbyist, he offers one-stop shopping for fund-raising, electioneering, and influence peddling.

If you are a politician, Tucker is the man to see if you need money to run for Congress. Or if you need someone to run your campaign and do your opinion polling and television advertising.

If you are a businessman, Tucker is the man to see if you need the votes of any of the many members of the House and Senate whom he has helped put into office.

At age 51, Robert Trent Tucker III, the son of a U.S. senator and grandson of a Georgia governor, has earned millions of dollars helping to elect congressmen and senators who are now influential on congressional committees and subcommittees that affect defense, oil, pharmaceutical, and other major industries. As a Washington lobbyist, Tucker is paid by big corporations in those industries to persuade the same congressmen and senators to use their influence in favor of Tucker's corporate clients.

Those clients are likely to be watching with interest as Tucker, who worked for Democratic presidential nominee Monroe Capehart during the primaries, helps shape the campaign of his running mate, Sen. Susan Cameron.

"It's an obvious conflict of interest when someone is paid both to elect a certain candidate and then to lobby that candidate after he or she is elected," commented Charles Whiteside, the chairman of Citizens for Good Government. "Senators Capehart and Cameron both have good reputations for integrity. But the prominent presence of Trent Tucker in the campaign raises questions about what influence he might exert on behalf of his business clients if they win the election."

One curious example of the potential conflicts involved in Tucker's work for both political and corporate clients involves the multinational pharmaceutical company Templeton Mannheim, which reportedly loaned company planes to the Republican presidential nominee, Vice President Warner Wylie, when he was governor of Missouri. Templeton Mannheim is a lobbying client of Trent Tucker, who has helped the firm secure valuable tax breaks from Congress. Yet Sen. Cameron has repeatedly criticized Wylie's ties to Templeton Mannheim and the pharmaceutical industry.

"That's Warner Wylie's problem, not mine," Tucker said in an interview. "Senator Cameron is simply trying to protect the interests of ordinary Americans, as she always does."

"My God, I've underestimated her," Mark said. "She's got balls."

"Who?" asked Jeanne, returning from the bathroom in a matching white robe.

"Sarah Page," Mark said. "She's done a tough story on Trent Tucker. I can see why he's so upset."

"Was she the one I saw you sitting with at the convention that night?"

"Yeah," Mark answered. "I told you I didn't have anything going on with her."

Jeanne was standing behind him now,

massaging his shoulders, as she tried to read the computer screen. Mark scrolled back to the beginning of the story for her.

"She came at me in the office about the story I did on Warner Wylie's free plane rides and golfing trips. I figured I had calmed her down. But now she's gone after Trent. She knows he's a source. She even threw in a little dig at me."

"What do you mean?"

"Look at this." Mark pointed to the word "reportedly" in the seventh paragraph. "That's bullshit. That's what you say about a competitor's story, not something that appeared in your own goddamned newspaper, something I fucking wrote."

"Calm down, sweetheart," Jeanne purred. She leaned over him and reached inside the folds of his robe to rub his chest. "This looks like trouble for Tucker, not you, honey. Maybe for Monroe and Susan, too."

She could feel Mark stiffen with anger.

"Don't patronize me. She's got her goddamned elbow in my ribs. I'm the chief political reporter. I don't have to take this."

"You'll figure out how to handle it, honey." Jeanne wrapped Mark in a long, calming hug. "She's no threat to you."

She handed him his cell phone.

"Call Tucker back and commiserate,"

Jeanne said, removing her robe and lying back down on the bed. "And then come here. I'll help you feel better. We can eat later."

In her bed at the Waldorf, Susan Cameron looked at the clock radio. It was after one in the morning. About ten at night in California. She pulled her purse from the floor, fished out her cell phone, and dialed a Los Angeles area code and number. She heard the recorded message on the first ring. Reaching back into her purse, she pulled out her little red phone book, looked up another, longer number and punched it into the phone carefully.

When Michael answered, he had to shout over the tumult of what sounded like heavy traffic.

"Where are you?" Susan asked. "I had to call your international phone."

"Tokyo. I just left a business lunch. I thought I'd take a walk around the Ginza. Sorry about the noise," he said, still talking loudly. "I've got a lot going on here, and in Seoul and Shanghai. They don't seem to care about my legal problems back home. All that seems to matter is what and who I still know. They pay me good money for that. They even think I might have some influence with you. The more I deny it, the more they believe it. They think I'm just being discreet. So, where are *you?*" he asked. "It's late there."

"I'm in New York and it is late. But I can't sleep. We did a bunch of fund-raisers here. And then we made time for girls' night. I finally told Amanda that you and I are back in touch."

"Did she say you were out of your mind?"

"Something like that. But she knows I don't really have anyone else to talk to, besides her. And she understands why I still trust you on politics."

"As opposed to everything else?"

"Yes, I guess so."

"I've been keeping up with the campaign on the Web," Michael said after an awkward silence. "It looks like the Wylie stuff is still working. Everything all right with Tucker?"

"He still thinks he's doing it all, that he's the one who's been refining my delivery and everything," Susan said. "Alison says he's been telling his friends in the press that I'm essentially his creation."

"Don't worry about that. It keeps him off your back. And if you make a mistake, the press might blame Tucker instead of you. At some point, you can establish your independence from him. You'll know when."

"Michael," Susan said, changing the

subject, "who's traveling with you?"

"Just a couple of my money guys."

"You know what I mean."

"Oh, that. No one, actually. But I've met someone here. She's a Japanese lawyer who works for one of my clients, still something of a rarity in this part of the world. It's nothing serious. I think she has a fiancé. We just spend a little time together here and there."

Michael paused before adding, "You knew a long time ago that this is the way I am. You just didn't want to believe it until everything hit the fan."

Susan was silent again.

"You knew I was a bad boy when we met at Stanford," he said with an audible laugh. "That was part of the attraction. You thought you could tame me."

"Are you saying this in the middle of the street with everybody listening?"

"They speak Japanese here, darling," Michael responded with another laugh. "And they're all busy talking and messaging on their own cell phones. I can't think of anyplace more anonymous than a crowded sidewalk in Tokyo."

"Well, look, Michael, since you're so far away in such an anonymous place," Susan said, after another nervous pause, "I guess it's a good time to say I've been missing you in some weird way. That's what I told Amanda tonight. The more you and I talk about the campaign, the more I want to talk to you about, well, other things. But I don't know where to begin."

Now Michael was silent.

"Are you still there?"

"Yes," he said. "Yes, I'm here. What do you mean, 'other things'?"

"Us. That's what I mean. All the unresolved things about us. What are we doing, anyway? We've talked on the phone almost every night since you called about the convention video. And we haven't even seen each other once?"

"We can't take that chance," Michael reminded her. "It would be political suicide for you even to tell anyone other than Amanda that you're talking to me, much less be seen with me. You're the anti–Michael Cameron. We have to stay in our separate universes. You'll just have to settle for phone sex."

Susan's forced laughter hid from Michael the embarrassment of starting to cry. Neither of them could tell what the other was really feeling as their voices bounced from their phones to satellites somewhere in space and back again. Susan only knew that she could not have felt more alone. What did Michael feel, she wondered, as he flitted from continent to continent and woman to woman?

"We're leaving in the morning for Boston and a little barnstorming in New England," Susan said, regaining enough composure to finish the conversation. "Where will you be?"

"Here for another day, and then Seoul before I go back to San Francisco. If you want to talk to me the next few nights, just call this phone again."

"Okay."

"Let me know how it goes in New England."

8

Sarah stretched out comfortably in her gray tank top and shorts on the dark blue mat. Nick, her personal trainer, bent down, took her right leg and pushed it back gently until it was perpendicular to the rest of her body. Then he put it down on the mat and stretched her left leg. This was the most relaxing part of Sarah's early morning workout. The treadmill and the weights were behind her for another day.

Membership in the well-appointed health club near Washington's Cleveland Park neighborhood was expensive. And an hour's workout several mornings a week with one of its muscular personal trainers cost considerably more. But it was worth the money. While Nick, an easy-going young man with an athletic physique, worked with Sarah, the two of them gossiped about his other clients, mostly wealthy middle-aged wives of Washington lawyers, diplomats, and businessmen. It was one of her few opportunities to enjoy a casual relationship with someone outside the newsroom.

Sarah had little time for much more than her morning workouts and runs and late night reading. In that way, she was not very different from other ambitious young journalists in Washington who put in long hours and were deeply absorbed by their work. They socialized mostly with colleagues and often wound up marrying them.

In her investigative reporting, Sarah didn't even have as much daily contact with other people as most reporters did. Many of her dealings with sources were necessarily furtive, and much of her research involved solitary searches of records on the Internet and in government offices and courthouses. She couldn't become too friendly with potential subjects of her stories, who were often hostile after the stories were published. Even some of her newsroom colleagues were wary that her reporting might alienate their sources.

When Nick was finished, Sarah got up from the mat and walked contentedly to the top of the wide marble steps leading down to the locker rooms. There, she was startled out of her reverie.

"Sarah, can I talk to you?" asked a pale, thin young man who was suddenly standing in front of her.

She remembered having seen him before at the club, lifting weights and running on the indoor track that encircled the gym. Once or twice, she had thought he might be watching her as she worked out with Nick. He had seemed creepy.

"I'm sorry," Sarah said. "Do I know you?"

"You've probably forgotten that you met me in Annapolis, where I used to work for Governor Tawney. I'm on the Hill now. There's no reason for you to remember me. People usually don't."

Wait for him to explain himself further, Sarah thought, so long as he's not trying to pick me up.

"I'm sorry to bother you," he told her. "I've resisted it up to now. But I read your story on Trent Tucker the other day."

He lowered his voice to nearly a whisper and looked around nervously. Sarah, suddenly intrigued, moved closer.

"It was a good story. But you've found only the tip of the iceberg. There's more, a lot more. And it gets nasty. Very nasty."

"When can we talk about this?" Sarah asked, all business now. "Let's go down to the front desk so I can write down your name and number."

"It's just as well that you don't know my name. Just call me Sam. Could we meet at the Taste of Bethesda this weekend? It'll be crowded and noisy there. Saturday afternoon would be good for me."

The Taste of Bethesda was one of Sarah's favorite street fairs, with plenty of good food and live music.

"When and where?" she asked.

"Two o'clock at the corner of Norfolk and St. Elmo."

He then hurried down the stairs and disappeared into the men's locker room.

Sarah was at work in the *Capital* newsroom a few hours later, searching the Internet for more information about Trent Tucker and his clients, when Mark came storming over to her desk.

"What the hell are you doing?" he asked. He had just come off the road with Monroe Capehart. "This campaign is my story, and that includes Trent Tucker. Besides, nothing you wrote was really news. Everybody in town knows how Tucker works. Are you trying to kill him as a source for me, some kind of revenge for the Wylie story?"

"This has nothing to do with you or that story," Sarah said, standing up from her desk to confront him. "I told you I was looking into Tucker. If he's got a problem with my story, he can call me."

"Who do you think you are? Trent Tucker is no statehouse hack."

"That's just the point." Sarah knew everyone around them would be listening by now. "Even though he isn't running for office himself, he should be held accountable for what he does behind the scenes. You political reporters don't do that because consultants and lobbyists are your best sources."

"Daniels!" shouted the national staff news aide. "Telephone."

The confrontation ended as Mark went to his desk to take the call.

Sarah sat back down at her desk. She sensed the icy stares of the other political reporters around her. She had hoped to fit in somehow, even though she knew her kind of reporting didn't always win friends, even among colleagues. Isolating herself could lead to potentially fatal errors.

Saturday was a beautiful, sunny early autumn day. In the nest of short streets crammed with restaurants in suburban Bethesda's old downtown, swarms of people on foot had replaced the usual car traffic. The curbs were lined with booths and tables where the restaurants served sample portions of their favorite dishes at the annual Taste of Bethesda. Bands sponsored by local radio stations played on temporary stages at the end of each block. Local politicians, trailed by entourages of supporters with campaign signs and T-shirts, snaked through the crowds like ceremonial dragons on the Chinese New Year.

No sooner had Sarah found Sam, somewhat disguised in a baseball cap and sunglasses, than they saw Elizabeth Tawney and her entourage heading straight toward them. "Oh, my God," Sam said, panicking, before Sarah grabbed his hand and pulled him away from the path of the governor, who had stopped to shake hands in the middle of an intersection filled with people.

"I don't think she saw us," Sarah reassured Sam, as they turned into a crowded side street. They bought some Thai food at one sidewalk stand and chocolate chip cookies at another, eating while they walked warily from one teeming block to the next. More than once, Sarah noticed a big man in blue jeans and a Redskins jersey, with an athletic bag slung over his shoulder. Was his presence among so many milling people just coincidental? Was it even the same man each time?

"Well," Sarah finally asked, "what do you have for me, Sam?"

"You have to find everything I tell you from other sources so nothing can be traced to me," he said.

"You're beginning to sound like Deep Throat."

Sam stopped abruptly and turned to face Sarah. "We're talking about big, powerful, well-financed people with tentacles deep into business and government who are doing nasty things. Are you serious about dealing with me, or not?"

"Yes," Sarah said.

Sam stood stubbornly in front of her as people pushed past.

"I'll protect your identity," Sarah insisted. "That's how I worked in Annapolis."

"I'll be in touch with you periodically to set up meetings like this one," he said. "I'll stay away from the gym so no one sees us there together."

"Okay. Where do we start?"

"You have to keep digging into Tucker's clients."

They were walking again, enveloped by families with children in strollers, packs of chattering teenagers, and middle-aged couples holding hands. Their gaiety and the bright autumn afternoon sun contrasted starkly with Sam's tone.

"Do you know about Palisar?" he asked Sarah.

"Yes, a bit," she answered tentatively. "Some of its companies are clients of Tucker's."

"Palisar's the sun," Sam said. "Tucker's just a planet, although an important one. Palisar's one of the biggest sources of money for Tucker's candidates. Palisar's companies are Tucker's biggest lobbying clients. Palisar has its own allies in Congress and the administration — Republicans and Democrats. It uses political muscle, money, fear — whatever works — to get what it wants."

"How do you know all this?" Susan asked. "It can't be that long since you were in Annapolis."

"When I started working on the Hill, I met an older guy who became a kind of mentor. Well, more, actually."

"That doesn't matter to me," Sarah assured him.

"He worked on a lot of committee staffs. He was a good investigator. Palisar kept turning up in things he worked on — foreign aid, defense contracts, campaign contributions. Even intelligence stuff. But he was never allowed to pursue it. No matter which committee it was, somebody always shut him down. He told me about it each time, even though he shouldn't have. And he said he knew a big secret. Something he couldn't tell me. But I could see it scared him."

Sam was walking faster now. His hands were balled into fists. Whenever Sarah pulled close to him, her face near his, he pushed farther ahead. She finally ran around in front of him, nearly colliding with a knot of people stopped in the street. They had walked right up to one of the performance stands. The beat of an oldies rock-and-roll band pulsed from speakers ten feet away.

"Sam!" she yelled into his face. "What?"

"I told him to go to the F.B.I.," he replied in a choked whisper that she could barely hear above the noise around them. "And then he just disappeared."

Sarah grabbed his hand again and pulled

him away from the bandstand, past a curb-side booth in front of an Italian restaurant, and into a little alley alongside the restaurant itself. I've never dealt with a source this frightened, she thought, as she held Sam by his shoulders.

"What do you mean disappeared? Have you called the police?"

"No, no, it's not exactly like that. He said he was going on vacation, to California, even though Congress was still in session. That was a couple of months ago, before the recess, and he never came back."

"Did you check with his family?"

Sam shook his head. "He told me his parents were dead and his brother, wherever he was, hadn't spoken to him in years, not since he came out of the closet."

"Where did he live?"

"With me."

Sam turned away toward the noisy scene in the street.

"When he moved in, he stored most of his own stuff. He said he was planning to retire someday to California. Somewhere around San Francisco."

"So, couldn't he have just stayed out there for some reason?"

"He would have told me. Maybe he did go to the F.B.I. and he's in some kind of protective custody, or he just went into hiding on his own, or . . .”

“What else did he tell you about Palisar? Did he give you any documents?”

“I can’t do this anymore today,” Sam said, cutting Sarah off. “Finish your records work on Palisar, all their investments and deals, everything they got from the government. The more you find on your own, the less I’ll have to tell you.”

I can push him only so far, Sarah thought. I have to play by his rules.

“Wait for me to call for our next meeting,” he said.

Sam slipped out of the alley, dodged people standing in line at the Italian food table, and disappeared into the crowd. Emerging from the alley herself, Sarah noticed that one of the people in line was the man with the athletic bag. She was certain now that it was the same man she had noticed during her walk with Sam. She started down the street before turning around quickly to look for him, but he was gone.

As she walked back toward the public garage where she had parked her car, Sarah took a notebook out of her purse and started scribbling down what Sam had said. When she next looked up, she found herself in a scrum of people around Governor Tawney.

"Sarah, what are you doing here? Are you stalking me?" the governor asked, laughing. "I see you're taking notes."

Sarah closed her notebook and shoved it back into her purse.

"That wasn't about you, Governor," she said. "Just something I'd remembered to write down."

Tawney pulled her aside.

"It looks like you're doing some interesting work at the paper these days," she said quietly. "I see you've taken on Trent Tucker."

"Yeah," Sarah said, trying to sound nonchalant. "Can I talk to you about that sometime?"

She thought the governor flinched slightly.

"I haven't seen him for a long time, not since he worked on my campaign." Tawney paused for a second. "I don't know that I can be much help."

Tucker was on Susan Cameron's mind, too. Reporters traveling on her campaign charter to the West Coast were asking about Sarah Page's story. Alison Winters tried to deflect their questions as she roamed the congested aisles of press seats. She kept Cameron in the front of the plane, away from the reporters. But they were getting restive.

Did the senator know about Tucker's conflicts of interest? Had her campaign accepted contributions from any of his lobbying clients? What influence did he have in her positions on the issues? How could she continue attacking Warner Wylie's ethics while Tucker was helping to direct her campaign?

Alison did not have good answers. She bought time by saying that Susan would answer all their questions as soon as she had enough information. Then Alison sought refuge in the front of the plane with Susan and Amanda Peterson. They spent the rest of the flight discussing what should be done.

"You've got to drop him right away," Amanda said to Susan.

"I agree," said Alison. "You need to stop it during this news cycle."

"All right," Susan said. "I'll think about it."

Later, as the three women rode together in the motorcade from the Los Angeles airport to the Four Seasons Beverly Wilshire hotel in Beverly Hills, Susan took her cell phone out of her purse and dialed a local number. As she waited for someone to answer, she said to Amanda and Alison, "What you're about to hear never happened, okay?"

They both nodded and looked out the window.

"Hi," Susan said into the phone. "We've landed. I'm in the limo on the way to the hotel. I'm not alone, so I'll talk to you later about tonight. But I need some advice right now. The Tucker story has blown up bigtime. The pack on the plane smells red meat.

"Yeah," she said after listening for a moment, "I think Aiken's column caught their attention, too. He was probably just waiting for something like this. Amanda and Alison think we have to move fast."

Susan held the little phone close to her ear, listening intently and nodding her head in agreement, as the limousine sped down the freeway, which had been cleared of traffic for her motorcade.

"Yes, Monroe should cooperate," she said at last. "He saddled me with Tucker in the first place. Thanks. I'll call you later."

She put the phone back in her purse.

"Alison, when we get to the hotel, I need to call Senator Capehart right away. And keep Tucker away from me for the rest of the day."

That afternoon and evening were filled

with lavish fund-raisers at the palatial Beverly Hills homes of entertainment executives. Susan and Amanda already knew many of the Hollywood stars, directors, producers, and lawyers, but Alison was dazzled. She couldn't wait to describe it all to Jeremy, who had been stuck in his hotel room reworking Cameron's stump speech for rallies the next day in downtown Los Angeles, Pasadena, and Santa Monica. But when she walked into his room that night, Alison found Jeremy worrying about something else.

"What's going on with Tucker?" he asked anxiously. "Rush says Capehart has ordered Trent back to headquarters. And Rush is supposed to go with him. Do you know about this?"

"I don't know," Alison said, as she sat down on the bed. It wasn't a problem lying to Jeremy.

"What's happening to me? Could you find out from Senator Cameron?" he asked with unusual formality.

"Sure."

For a moment, Jeremy looked so young and vulnerable that Alison felt uncomfortable about the way she used him. But the feeling quickly passed. She hoped he was staying on the campaign. It would be too much trouble to find a replacement.

As Alison started down the hall to ask Susan about it, she was surprised to see her leaving with her Secret Service detail in tow. Susan had combed out her hair and changed into something black and clingy, not what she would be wearing to another campaign event. There were none scheduled that night anyway.

Alison turned back to Jeremy's room, where she spent the night.

In the morning, after talking to Alison and Amanda Peterson, Susan surprised the rest of the traveling staff by calling an unscheduled breakfast meeting in her suite. Everyone crowded around a large table. Stragglers pulled in chairs from the adjacent parlor.

"I wanted you all to know about some changes that will be announced later today," she began. "Senator Capehart has asked Trent Tucker to move to campaign headquarters in Washington. He and Rush Ripley left last night on the red-eye."

Amanda, who was watching at a distance from a couch in the living room, heard muffled gasps at the swiftness of Tucker's exile.

"We will be joined in northern California tomorrow by Elliott Bancroft, who will be our new coordinator," Susan continued. "Some of you may remember him from Governor Drew's staff in the primaries."

Bill Drew of Massachusetts had gathered only a few convention delegates during the early primaries before he dropped out.

"Since the convention, Elliott's been working on issues for Senator Capehart, who has graciously loaned him to us," Susan said. "I've also asked some people from my Senate office to come into the campaign, including Emily Schwartz, who has been my chief of staff. That will free Alison to take charge of all of our communications. Since Jeremy Cantor was with Elliott in the Drew campaign, he'll stay with us."

Jeremy, sitting at the end of the table, didn't let on how relieved he was. Neither did Alison.

In Washington, Trent Tucker put a much different spin on these events when Carter Phillips called him. It was near twilight and Tucker took his cordless phone onto the little balcony outside his office. He could see the dome of the Capitol in one direction and the top of the Washington Monument in the other.

"Trent, why the hell did you let that woman fire your ass?" the general demanded. "What's happening to my investment in this ticket?"

"Don't worry," Tucker said in his most soothing drawl as he took in the view of government buildings lining Pennsylvania Avenue. Soon, he thought, he could be the master of almost all he saw. "I fired my own ass. It was about time, and that newspaper story gave me a way to do it."

"What the hell are you talking about?"

"That girl reporter created a little heat for me. And I was worried she might poke her nose into some of my other business connections, if you know what I mean."

Phillips said nothing.

"But I also saw it as an opportunity to get back to headquarters for the rest of the campaign," Tucker told him. "So I talked to some of Stewart Aiken's conservative Republican sources. I suggested he could capitalize on that newspaper story to force me off the Cameron campaign and take the pressure off Wylie. When Aiken called me about it, I practically begged him — off the record, of course — not to do it.

"That was all he needed," Tucker said with a chuckle. "He tore into me in his column. Aiken's so easy to manipulate, like all of them."

For both Tucker and Phillips, ideological

purity was folly. Tucker had worked mostly, but not exclusively, for Democrats because he had grown up with them and he knew they were more likely to achieve his populist goals. Phillips had served briefly in a Republican administration after retiring from the military. But Palisar had prospered with both Democratic and Republican administrations. If the White House changed hands, there would be some reseeding to do. Phillips was counting on Tucker to take care of it.

"I had already called Capehart to give him a heads-up about the Aiken column," Tucker said. "I told him he should protect Cameron by pulling me back to headquarters. It would make Susan look tough and decisive. Even better, Capehart agreed to replace me in Cameron's campaign with Elliott Bancroft."

"Who's he?"

"A guy I rescued from Bill Drew's sinking ship in the primaries. He's a Yankee lawyer who got bored with his Washington practice. He decided to try politics, dumped his family, and spent a lot of time on the road in one campaign or another. He knows the ropes. He's presentable in public and smooth with the ladies. Cameron will like him."

"What does that mean for us?"

"Bancroft's got some weaknesses. He pissed away his money partying and chasing women. I helped him out financially. So he'll do anything for me."

"Arc you going to win this thing, Trent? Will it pay off?"

"Trust me, General. We're right on plan."

As was Sarah. With Marge Lawson's help, she had started to do what Sam suggested — compile everything she could find about Palisar International's investments, government connections, and legal disputes. The list of Palisar-owned companies on its Web site was long, their contracts and financial connections with the U.S. and foreign governments myriad. Sarah had told Ron Jones just enough about her conversation with Sam for Jones to allow her to follow this lead while still covering campaign finance. But it was beginning to feel overwhelming.

"Don't you ever go home?" Lawson asked her one morning in the newsroom. "Whenever I come in, you're already here. And I get e-mails you've sent after midnight."

"This feels big to me, Marge. Sam was so scared."

"Well, the good news is the court stuff

didn't take too much time."

"And?"

"The bad news is how little I found," Lawson told her. "Except for the usual penny-ante stuff, almost every promising case was eventually dropped or settled. Either way, the records were sealed. No trial transcripts, no depositions, no affidavits, nothing but the bare-bones original complaint and a boilerplate answer. Palisar doesn't leave tracks in court."

"That certainly makes it harder."

"There's something else," Lawson added. "I was getting so frustrated by the lack of court records that I ran the names of people who sued Palisar through every filter I could think of. And I couldn't find many of them."

"What do you mean?"

"I found some obituaries. But others didn't show up anywhere. No home address. No telephone number. They just disappeared."

"Marge," Sarah said. "I want to find Sam."

She went to her desk to do her own search of online congressional and Maryland government directories. She discovered someone on the staff of the House Oversight Committee who had previously worked for Governor Tawney in Annapolis: Seth Alan Moore. S.A.M.

To be certain, Sarah phoned her health club. She said she was Seth Moore's assistant and asked whether he had been sent last month's bill. The desk clerk told her that Moore was never sent bills because everything was automatically charged to his credit card. Sarah knew she was bending, if not breaking, the newspaper's rule against impersonation, but she figured it was a meaningless transgression, and she had gotten what she wanted.

She went back to Marge Lawson and watched as Lawson clicked through databases on the Internet to find Moore's address, telephone number, driver's license, age, education, and family. Born in Washington, D.C., thirty-three years earlier, he had received his bachelor's degree in political science from George Washington University and his law degree from American University. He lived in a small house on Capitol Hill.

Sam may want me to wait for him to make contact again, Sarah thought, but I'm not going to wait that long.

9

Mark stumbled out the door into the glare of the early morning sun reflecting off

Chautauqua Lake on a chilly autumn day. An early walk along the lake would give him an opportunity to be with Jeanne briefly, a reporter chatting with a Capehart staff member.

In season, the lakeside Victorian village in western New York State was a bustling cultural camp for thousands of visitors who stayed in quaint guesthouses on leafy lanes and flocked to lectures, concerts, and discussion groups in neoclassical buildings and amphitheaters. All the visitors were gone by early October, making it an ideal place for Monroe Capehart to prepare for the presidential debates.

Jeanne was ensconced with Capehart and the rest of his entourage in the Athenaeum Hotel, a sprawling Victorian pile overlooking the lake. Mark was housed with a small group of reporters just across Bowman Avenue from the Athenaeum in the Wensley Guest House, where speakers and performers stayed during the Chautauqua season. Its communal parlors and porches made it impossible to bring Jeanne to his small room there.

Mark crossed the lawn between the Athenaeum and the lake to meet Jeanne, who came down the wide staircase from the hotel's veranda.

"If the old man turns in early enough tonight," he suggested to her, "maybe we can find some place around here to meet. It's pretty deserted."

Before Jeanne could answer, Mark noticed something in the distance along the lake. In the midst of a group of people walking toward them, an older man had stumbled heavily. Two others reached out to break his fall.

"My God, that's Capehart," Mark said. "The Secret Service guys are propping him up."

"I'd better get back to the hotel before he does," Jeanne said, grabbing Mark by the arm.

"I want to see what's going on with Capehart."

"I'm sure he's fine," Jeanne insisted. "This is his private time. You shouldn't be spying."

Mark pulled away roughly from her grasp. She had been holding something back from him.

"What the hell is going on?" he demanded.

"What do you mean?"

"There's something wrong with Capehart, isn't there? That's why they've had Cameron out front so much. Why didn't you tell me?"

"Look," Jeanne said, getting angry, "I'm not one of your sources."

Mark saw Capehart walking unassisted now as he came closer to them. Too bad about those ground rules, he thought. Mark had agreed with the Capehart campaign that he could watch the debate preparations and talk to the candidate's aides for a future profile of Capehart so long as what he saw and heard was off the record for now.

"You're right. I'm sorry," he told Jeanne as they turned back toward the hotel. His relationship with her was becoming as important to him as his work.

"But I'll have to tell my editor, so he can have someone else check it out," he said.

Jeanne looked at him plaintively. She knew that wasn't the end of it.

"What do you want me to say?" she asked.

"Just give me some idea of what's wrong with him."

"My God, Mark! This is hard for me."

They were back on the lawn in front of the hotel. Jeanne knew she should leave him there without saying anything more. But she couldn't do it.

"Okay, something's not right," she said. "He's having trouble moving. It's like his feet freeze up. He seems to stumble over nothing. Sometimes he loses his balance and has to hold on to whoever's nearby to keep from falling. I've seen some medicine he takes for it when I set out his pills. Nobody talks about it, so that's all I know. I've got to go in now and make sure his room is ready."

After she rushed off, Mark walked slowly toward the guesthouse, turning to watch Capehart and his Secret Service detail until they disappeared into a side entrance to the Athenaeum. As soon as he reached his room, Mark telephoned Ron Jones.

After Jones hung up, he called Sarah into his office.

"I want you to look into a tip from Mark Daniels about Monroe Capehart's health," he told her.

"I'm busy." One way or another Mark always seemed to be interfering with her work. "Why can't *he* check it out?"

"He's got a conflict," said Jones. "I need you to do this."

It was important, she knew, to gain as much of Jones's confidence as possible, whatever she felt.

"I'll see what I can do," she told him.

She grudgingly began working on it as fast she could. Summaries of Capehart's annual physical exams during his years in the Senate were posted on the campaign's Web site.

None of them showed any problems beyond slightly elevated blood pressure and cholesterol — not unusual at his age — for which Capehart took appropriate medication.

She started calling around town, as discreetly as possible, so as not to alert anyone else to the story, if there was one. She had been on her new beat long enough to know she didn't want to be attacked by liberal bloggers for spreading an unproven rumor about the Democratic candidate.

After getting nowhere, Sarah had no choice but to phone Mark.

"I can't tell you much because I've got a source problem," he said, further annoying her.

"What kind of source problem?"

"Do you want my help or what?"

"Sure," Sarah said. "I've got nothing else."

"Apparently, Capehart's unsteady at times, you know, balance problems, stumbling, something about his legs freezing up. He might be taking some kind of medicine for it. That's all I know."

Frozen limbs, loss of balance. It reminded Sarah of her grandmother, who had had Parkinson's disease. As it steadily progressed over the years, the disease eventually caused near-paralysis when she tried to walk, leading to sudden falls that had caused increasingly serious injuries. Sarah thought this could be something. She called Trent Tucker.

"Is there anything about Senator Capehart's health that you haven't disclosed yet?" she asked him matter-of-factly.

"What's this about?"

"Just checking on something we've heard."

Tucker didn't allow any hint of concern to creep into his voice.

"The senator had a clean bill of health at his last checkup," he told Sarah, as though she was just another reporter asking a routine question. "You can read it on the Web site."

"There's nothing else?"

"Nope."

Sarah had nothing firm with which to challenge him.

"By the way," Tucker added in an oddly formal way, "are you planning to write any more stories about me?"

Sarah was pleased he felt the need to ask.

"You're playing an important role in this campaign, and our readers should know more about you," she said in a similarly impersonal tone. "I'll be in touch when I'm further along."

That night, Mark took a long, lonely walk

in the deserted streets of Chautauqua. As he passed the darkened Refectory and other little shops along Brick Walk, he began questioning himself. Had he become a tired hack in the eyes of Sarah Page? Was he lost to his wife and sons, who sometimes seemed to be someone else's family? Would he and Jeanne ever be able to build a real relationship?

His cell phone rang.

"Okay, the old man did turn in early. Where are you?"

"Just walking around."

"Meet me by the lake in front of the hotel. I've found a room for us away from the others."

The rest of the night was consumed with almost desperate lovemaking, as though the tense encounter earlier in the day had never happened.

The next morning, after Jeanne had left early to resume her RON duties, Mark was awakened by his cell phone.

"You're the reporter covering Monroe Capehart, right?"

"Yeah," Mark answered groggily. "Who's this?"

"I've got something for you."

"Rush? Is that you?"

"Just listen for a minute," said the muffled

voice. "Capehart's got a secret in his past. He had an affair with one of his fund-raisers years ago, when he was first elected to the Senate. It nearly busted up his marriage."

"Who the hell is this? How did you get my cell number?"

"Write this down."

"Okay, okay. Just a second."

Mark fumbled for his notebook and pen in the pockets of the pants he had left on a chair near the bed.

"Karen Fitzgerald," the caller dictated impatiently. "She works for an environmental group in D.C., the Conservation Federation. She's younger than Capehart and still a looker. That's it."

Mark had no choice but to call Ron Jones again.

A little later, Sarah was back in his office.

"This is too much," she told him. "Why won't Mark do it himself?"

"He can't."

"Another 'conflict'? What's going on?"

"Look, this is just between you and me," Jones said, leaning toward Sarah. "Mark's got something going with one of Capehart's advance people."

"So that's who it is."

"What do you mean?"

Sarah hesitated, but then decided not to

trash Mark. That wouldn't make things any easier.

"Never mind," she said quietly.

Jones let it pass, too. He couldn't blame Sarah if she was upset about Mark getting away with something that could have meant trouble for her, but there was no point discussing it.

"The lady in question is not involved in the political part of the campaign, so Mark can still cover that," Jones told Sarah. "But personal stuff about Capehart is a problem."

"Do we have to do this? It doesn't sound like Bill Clinton's compulsive womanizing."

"We can't decide that until we have the facts. Find them and help us decide."

"Okay," she said. "I'll check it out."

It was relatively easy to locate Karen Fitzgerald, who reluctantly agreed to have lunch. After getting Sarah's assurance that her name would be kept out of the newspaper, Fitzgerald admitted that she had had a brief relationship with Monroe Capehart during a long-ago campaign.

"He was forty-one and a congressman running for the Senate. I was twenty-eight, working as a paid fund-raiser for his campaign," she said. "He spent more time with me than with his wife. It was good between us. But he really loved her, and he felt guilty.

He decided to break it off and tell her. He got me a job with somebody else on the Hill.

"I'm glad they stayed together," Fitzgerald added without any apparent regret. "He's a good man and he'd be a good president."

"Has anyone else talked to you about this recently?" Sarah asked.

"A young man called me a few weeks ago. He wouldn't identify himself, so I didn't tell him anything. But he seemed to know all about it anyway."

The caller could have been another reporter, Sarah thought, but then why wouldn't he identify himself? She guessed it was more likely an opposition researcher for one of the presidential campaigns. Was it one of Wiley's people, hoping to use the affair against Capehart? Or someone from Capehart's own campaign, who called Fitzgerald to see how likely she would be to reveal it? But then why tip off Mark?

Sarah confirmed the affair with two other women in whom Fitzgerald said she had confided at the time. She didn't need much more, except a response from Capehart. And she was surprised when her call to one of his press aides was returned by Trent Tucker.

"Why do you want an interview with the

senator? Doesn't Mark Daniels cover this campaign?" asked Tucker. Once again, his language was businesslike, but his tone was calculated to intimidate her. "What are you digging into now? More health questions? I've already told you where to go for that."

"My editors told me to talk only to the candidate about this."

"I handle this kind of inquiry for him," Tucker said firmly.

Sarah decided to deal with him. The more straightforward contact between her and Tucker, the better. She told him she knew about Karen Fitzgerald and wanted a response from Capehart. Tucker called back within the hour to say the candidate would not comment.

When Sarah started to write the story, she noticed that Fitzgerald and Capehart had been about the same ages at the time of their affair as she and Tom Evans had been. And Fitzgerald had not portrayed herself as a victim either. She had described two people thrown together in a close and intense working relationship, just as Sarah and Tom had been. Perhaps because of the passage of time, Fitzgerald didn't seem to blame Capehart for ending the relationship and staying with his wife. Sarah, however, was still angry at Tom for the way he had broken off their affair. But she was determined that that wouldn't affect the story she was writing.

When the story was finished, Ron Jones went to the paper's editor, Lou Runyan, who called a meeting. It was the first time Sarah had been in his office since Runyan interviewed her before she was hired.

Sarah, Jones, and a group of other reporters and editors, including the managing editor, Mary Sullivan, sat on chairs and couches facing Runyan, a rangy, graying man who loomed over his cluttered desk. Mark Daniels, who was still in Chautauqua for Capehart's debate preparation, was connected by speakerphone.

"Well, you all know the drill," Runyan told them. What to publish about the private life of a public figure, especially a candidate for president, was among the more difficult decisions an editor had to make. "Can we prove it?" he asked. "And why is it relevant to Capehart's candidacy?"

"Sarah's got it confirmed, airtight," Jones began. "Capehart did have an affair with a young campaign aide. But it was twenty-eight years ago, his wife forgave him, and we have no reason to believe he hasn't been clean since. We have the story, although we can't use the woman's name, which bothers me."

"What do you think, Sarah?" Runyan asked. Everybody in the room knew about her affair with Tom.

"I don't think it matters how long ago it was or what has happened since," she said. "Voters should know everything about his biography. They can decide what this means about his character."

"If we don't publish it," said Mary Sullivan, "we'd be deciding this was something voters didn't need to know."

"I put Sarah on this story and she's done a great job, so I feel a bit uncomfortable," Jones said. "But shouldn't there be some sort of statute of limitations for this kind of thing, even when you run for president?"

Why didn't he tell me this before the meeting? thought Sarah.

"Capehart's record since then should matter, too," said Jerry Fowler, the deputy managing editor, an older, professorial man. Runyan assigned great importance to what he said in situations like this. "Not a hint of scandal. And he's accomplished a lot on the Hill. He's respected by everyone up there, regardless of party. That has to count for something."

"Mark?" Runyan asked.

"Capehart isn't Gary Hart or Bill Clinton," Mark said over the speakerphone. "It's more like Bob Dole in '96. It came out that he had had an affair twenty-eight years earlier, too, at the end of his first marriage, before he married Elizabeth. The story never got traction. It didn't seem to matter to voters. Even Clinton's womanizing never mattered that much to *his* voters."

Sarah was surprised that Mark was arguing so strongly, given his own behavior.

"That's just the point, Mark," Mary Sullivan jumped in. "The voters decided for themselves in both those cases."

Having fought hard to become the newspaper's first female managing editor, at considerable cost to her family life, she was alert to signs of a double standard in how the newspaper handled these kinds of questions. And, as a former foreign correspondent who had risked her life under fire covering wars in Central America, Africa, and Eastern Europe, she was comfortable going toe-to-toe with her male colleagues.

"We're in the news business," she said. "We don't usually withhold news from our readers, especially news about someone running for president. It doesn't matter how long ago this was. As Sarah said, it's part of the development of his character. The voters have a right to know about it."

"It would be self-censorship," said Sarah, emboldened by Sullivan's support. She hadn't expected to fight so hard for the story. But Ron Jones's lack of support and Mark's intervention had fired her up.

Sullivan decided to wrap it up before anyone went too far.

"Lou's heard our arguments," she said. "He'll make the decision."

"I'll sleep on it," Runyan told them.

He didn't have to decide after all.

Early the next morning, Runyan got a call at home from Ron Jones. The Capehart-Cameron campaign headquarters in Washington had just informed the media that Susan Cameron would make an important statement at 10 a.m. at the National Press Club. Jones told Runyan he was sending several reporters.

Then he called Mark, who had already been notified in Chautauqua that the final debate rehearsal would be postponed until that afternoon. Just before ten, Mark went to the front parlor of the Wensley Guest House to watch Cameron on television.

"Something very disturbing has come to the attention of the Capehart-Cameron campaign," Susan began, soberly reading a statement into the television cameras from behind a lectern in the press club's wood-paneled auditorium. "Someone has been trying to plant derogatory stories in the media about Senator Capehart's private life. They concern an indiscretion committed by a young congressman going through the stress of his first campaign for the United States Senate in 1980.

"Senator Capehart quickly recognized that he had made a terrible mistake, and he confessed to his wonderful wife, Milly. They renewed their vows to each other and have now been married for forty-five years. Their love and respect for each other and their belief in the sanctity of family have never been greater.

"Perhaps no one understands the gravity of marital infidelity more than I do," Susan continued, her voice quavering. "But this does not in any way diminish my admira tion for Monroe Capehart. He is an outstanding leader with an unwavering commitment to honorable public service. Milly's forgiveness of this one private indiscretion more than a quarter century ago is all I need.

"Please join with me to help this loving couple protect their life together against whoever is trying to smear them for political gain," Susan said. Her eyes appeared moist in a close-up shot that would be repeated endlessly on newscasts over the days ahead. "I find this kind of smear politics beyond the bounds. Show Monroe and Milly Capehart that you agree."

Susan stepped back from the lectern and looked around the auditorium. She had no qualms about saying what she said because she believed it — and she had to protect the ticket.

"If you will pardon me," she told the reporters, "I do not think this is the time to take questions. Thank you for coming."

Mark left the guesthouse and walked toward the lake as Jeanne walked toward him from the Athenaeum.

"I had no idea," she said.

"I didn't think so."

"Did you know?"

"Yeah," he said. "Somebody called me a couple of days ago. I'm still trying to figure out who it was and exactly why. But I think I was set up."

That afternoon, Mark sat in the last row of the Chautauqua amphitheater to watch Monroe Capehart in his final debate rehearsal. Jeanne and the rest of the campaign staffers and volunteers seated below him were the only other spectators. On the stage, two aides, who were impersonating Warner

Wylie and the debate moderator, peppered Capehart with tough questions like those he would face in the debates. The man Mark had seen falter on the path along the lake stood steadily behind a lectern and handled everything thrown at him with ease.

Back in Washington, Sarah telephoned Trent Tucker after Cameron's dramatic statement.

"You took away my scoop," she said, testing him.

"Maybe now you'll leave Monroe Capehart alone," he responded, confirming what he had done. "And me, too."

"I told you, my beat is money and politics." It almost felt to her like their banter from another time and another place. "I can't ignore you, Trent."

"I'll just talk to Daniels."

"That's fine for now," she said. "I've got work to do."

Then, for the first time, Sarah called Seth Moore at the House Oversight Committee offices in the Rayburn House Office Building on Capitol Hill. She was told he had not come to work that day. She tried his home phone. There was no answer.

10

The day before, a man identifying himself as a *Washington Capital* reporter had called Seth Moore and told him that Sarah Page needed to talk with Sam. Rather than do it over the phone, the caller explained, Sarah wanted to meet Sam in the morning at a park near where she lived. To reassure Moore that he was speaking for Sarah, the caller made references to what Sarah and Sam had talked about when they met in Bethesda. He said Sarah had found out that Moore was Sam.

At dawn the next morning, after a sleepless night, Moore left his house and drove across town just past American University to Chain Bridge Road and the entrance to Battery Kemble Park. Crowning a hill in the Palisades, Battery Kemble was one of a ring of earthen forts built around Washington during the Civil War to protect the capital from Confederate attack. Its big guns, long since removed, had been aimed at the Virginia highlands across the Potomac River to protect the approach to nearby Chain Bridge. Now mostly wooded, the hilly park was popular with nearby residents who hiked and exercised their dogs there. A National Park Service historic marker at the park's entrance was the only sign of its military past.

Following instructions, Moore left his car in a small dirt lot near that marker. He stepped out onto Chain Bridge Road, which had no sidewalks, to watch for Sarah. He expected her to be walking up the road. He never saw the vehicle bearing down from behind him. With a dull thud that did not disturb anyone in the large homes across from the park, it knocked Moore into the air and, as he landed on the road, ran right over him, never braking.

By Joni Parker

Seth Alan Moore, a 33-year-old staff attorney for the House Oversight Committee, was killed yesterday morning in an apparent hit-and-run accident on Chain Bridge Road NW near Battery Kemble Park, police said.

A resident of a nearby home found Moore's battered body in the street shortly after 7 a.m., according to the police report. Officers investigating his death could not find any witnesses to the fatal accident.

A police spokesman said it appeared that Moore had been struck by a vehicle traveling at a high rate of speed that left no skid marks. Chain Bridge Road residents said they have complained to the police in the past about cars traveling dangerously fast down the winding, hilly road that borders Battery Kemble Park.

One resident said he told police that he saw a large black SUV speed by as he came out of his house to pick up his newspaper sometime before 7 a.m. He added that it resembled the black Ford Expedition SUVs used by officers who guard the home of the chairman of the Federal Reserve just down the hill from the scene of the accident.

A spokesman for the Federal Reserve Police said that none of their security vehicles had been involved in any accidents recently and that they are instructed to observe the speed limit unless they are using sirens and flashing lights in an emergency.

"We have good relations with the neighbors there," Lt. Adam Oglesby said. "They appreciate the extra security that our presence gives them."

Martin Wilding, staff director of the House Oversight Committee, confirmed that Moore had worked there. The committee monitors, among other things, the spending, travel, and campaign finances of House members.

"Seth was a quiet, pleasant colleague who devoted himself to his work," Wilding said.

Police found Moore's late model Honda sedan parked at the entrance to Battery Kemble Park, near the scene of the accident. They appealed for information from anyone who might have been at or near that location yesterday morning.

11

Sarah walked past the newspaper on her front walk early the following morning when she left for a run on the nearby towpath of the Chesapeake and Ohio Canal. When she returned home, feeling refreshed, she picked up the paper and flipped through the sections as she went inside. She had just reached the kitchen when she saw the story at the bottom of the front page of the local section.

As she read it, Sarah staggered to a chair at the little table by the back window and cried uncontrollably. She closed her eyes and saw again the fear contorting Seth Moore's face while she pulled information out of him on their walk in Bethesda. And she remembered the man in the Redskins jersey carrying an athletic bag.

My God, she thought, did being seen with me have anything to do with Seth's death? What the hell is going on?

Pulling herself together, she showered, dressed, and went downtown to the newsroom. Without discussing what had happened with anyone else, she phoned Martin Wilding at the House Oversight Committee.

"I had just started working on something with Seth," she told him, "and I'm really sorry about his death. Have the police talked to you?"

"They just called to confirm he worked here," Wilding said.

"Could I come by?" Sarah asked.

"I don't see why not."

When Sarah got to the committee's offices in the Rayburn House Office Building, she told Wilding again how distressed she was about Seth Moore's death.

"I'd only been working with him for a short time on some campaign-finance issues," she said. "We were, you know, trading information."

"Happens all the time."

"He seemed to be a nice guy."

"We all liked him, even though he was kind of shy," Wilding said, reaching for a piece of paper that he handed to Sarah. "His family has already scheduled a memorial service at a Catholic church here on the Hill."

A gay Catholic, Sarah thought. Moore must have been keeping a lot of secrets. She decided to take a gamble.

"I have kind of an unusual request," she said. "Seth had told me about his files on campaign-finance stuff." She was stretching the truth, she thought, but not too much. "Could I make some notes from them?"

Wilding thought for a moment. He had often helped reporters over the years. And he wasn't planning to do anything else with Moore's material.

"Sure," he said. "I'll show you his file cabinet. There's nothing classified here, so we don't keep them locked. Just put everything back."

Sarah spent the next hour rummaging through Moore's files. Most of them contained uninteresting information related to routine committee inquiries. There was nothing in them about Palisar, Trent Tucker, or the rest of what Moore had told her during their walk in Bethesda. But she found one dog-eared folder that intrigued her. It

147

was labeled "Pat." Inside were some scribbled telephone numbers, two addresses in California, and some unopened mail addressed to a Patrick Scully at the same address on Capitol Hill that she and Marge Lawson had found for Seth Moore.

"Did Seth know a Pat Scully?" Sarah asked Wilding.

"Yeah. He stopped by now and then. I think he worked for the Commerce Committee. But I haven't seen him around for a while."

With Wilding's permission, she called the staff director of the House Commerce Committee, who told her that Scully had worked there briefly as an investigative counsel before taking a leave of absence a few months earlier. He said Scully had not set a return date or left a forwarding address.

"We call it inoculation, General," Trent Tucker said with evident pride as he cut into his well-cooked steak. "We've inoculated Monroe against vulnerability on the character issue."

Sitting ramrod straight, Carter Phillips picked at his Dover sole. "Voters won't care that he cheated on his wife?" he asked.

"Now they won't," Tucker said. "We got

the story out first with our spin on it. Who would argue with Susan Cameron absolving him of adultery? She's given Monroe her seal of approval."

The two men were lunching in a private dining room at the King's Knight. Identified only by the small brass nameplate on its front door, the restaurant was located in a new office building just around the corner from Palisar's headquarters in a restored nineteenth-century stone relic on Pennsylvania Avenue. The offices of Tucker's political-consulting and lobbying firm were at the top of the building.

Tucker often found Phillips intimidating. But he believed Phillips had come to depend on his knowledge of politics and how Washington worked — and his ability to manipulate the system. He may have been fooling himself, but he also thought he knew enough about how Phillips did business to protect himself.

"Am I correct in understanding that this young woman reporter was making inquiries about the senator's health, in addition to his sex life?" Phillips asked Tucker. "How did she know about those things?"

"Actually, General, I had somebody plant the tip about Monroe's affair."

"Why would you do that?"

"Because, as you said, General, Sarah Page was fishing around about Capehart's health. Would you want everyone to know he'd been hiding the fact that he has a debilitating disease? It would ruin his reputation for integrity. And it would raise serious questions about his fitness to serve as president. So I decided to distract her and the rest of the media with an old indiscretion. Then I had Cameron neutralize it."

Tucker dug into his steak.

"You see, General," he explained with evident pride, "I steered the story to Sarah Page and then I took it away from her."

"Do you really expect her to leave the senator's health alone now?" Phillips had an unnerving habit of expressing himself through hostile-sounding questions, something he had cultivated in the Special Forces. It put subordinates on the defensive.

"I doubt she'd want to go through something like this again," said Tucker. "I hear most of her editors opposed publishing her story about the affair. And she doesn't seem to know that much about Monroe's condition. Besides, what she really wants to do is investigate me."

"Doesn't that concern you?" Phillips fixed Tucker with a hard look.

"Don't worry, General. I know her. I'm staying on top of it. She's barely scratched the surface."

That was as much as Tucker wanted to tell him or anyone else about himself and Sarah for now.

"By the way, Trent," Phillips asked, "did you see the story in this morning's paper about a nasty accident over your way? It was near that park. What's it called? Battery something or other?"

"Battery Kemble," Tucker answered with surprise.

"Well, some poor fellow got killed walking in the street near the park yesterday morning. Apparently, it was a hit-and-run. I'm surprised you didn't know about it."

"I've been busy since I got back to town. I don't spend much time at home."

"Well, you'll be careful, won't you?"

Getting up from the table abruptly, Phillips didn't wait for an answer.

Left alone in the small dining room, Tucker immediately asked for the check. Then he took the elevator up to his office, where he grabbed the *Capital* out of the stack of newspapers on his desk.

He read the story carefully. His house was near the end of a long, gated drive off Chain Bridge Road, just a few hundred feet from

151

the considerably more modest home of the Federal Reserve chairman. When he passed by it each morning, Tucker saw the big black Ford Expeditions parked in front, motors running, ready to escort the Fed chairman's chauffer-driven car downtown. But it would be absurd to think the Federal Reserve Police were involved in a hit-and-run accident. And why would someone who lived and worked on Capitol Hill be walking there at that hour of the morning? What really happened? Why?

Tucker read the story again, searching for clues to the answers. Phillips's veiled warning had its desired effect.

When Sarah got back to the newsroom that evening, she sought out Joni Parker, who covered the night police shift. Rookie reporters usually cut their teeth on that beat and moved on to other things. But Parker had stayed at her own request for nearly six years, becoming an unlikely newsroom star. Her reporting had helped lead police to the Fort Dupont Park serial killer. And a local priest who had murdered his lover had confessed to her in a teary interview.

An effusive black woman who still looked like a teenager, Parker had an easy smile that advertised to everyone her intention to be their special friend. She could get almost anyone to talk to her, even police officials and detectives who despised the press. She had forged a special bond with black police officers who felt white reporters looked down on them.

Her mother's brother was a cop who, in the absence of her long-departed father, had pushed Parker into Catholic schools. Her good grades and work on the student newspaper won her a scholarship to Georgetown University. She talked her way into a part-time news aide's job at the *Capital,* answering phones at night. She found time to write freelance feature stories for the paper, which helped her get into its summer intern program, filling in on the night police beat. She was hired full-time when she finished college.

Over the years, Parker had gotten some of her best stories by hanging around the newsroom long after her night shift ended, often until the dayside reporters drifted in to work, around ten in the morning. This also gave her first crack at breaking stories for the *Capital*'s Web site. That was how she wound up covering the hit-and-run accident near Battery Kemble. Wealthy neighborhood, congressional staffer, mysterious

153

black SUV — it had the elements of a good story.

"I need your help," Sarah told Parker. "I've got to find out what happened with that hit-and-run. The victim was a source of mine, or at least he was becoming one. I feel awful, Joni, just awful. He might have been killed because of me."

"Wait a minute," Parker said. "You think he was murdered?"

"I don't know. But he was beginning to talk to me about stuff that really scared him. Powerful, well-connected people. Corruption. Some big secret. A missing congressional investigator."

"Slow down, girl, you're losing me."

"Okay, don't worry about that other stuff. I'll keep working on it myself," Sarah said. "Could you just help me with the hit-and-run?"

"Of course. What do you need?"

"The autopsy results. Evidence from the scene about the vehicle that may have hit him. Anything the police found in Seth Moore's Honda. And everyone who rented or bought black Ford Expeditions here recently."

"This is D.C., girl. They won't have the manpower for all that. But I'll bug them for what they get."

"Thanks, Joni. I'll call around about Expeditions myself."

Back at her own desk, Sarah first tried dialing the phone numbers she had found in Seth Moore's file about "Pat." One was a hotel in San Francisco. Another was a motel in San Jose. Patrick Scully was not currently registered as a guest at either one. The third number appeared to be a private home, where the phone was answered by a man. When she asked if she could speak to Pat, she was met with silence.

"Hello?" Sarah repeated.

"He hasn't been here for weeks," the man finally said. "Who is this?"

Sarah identified herself and said she wanted to talk to Pat Scully.

"Well, he's not here and he's not coming back. I don't know how you got this number, but don't call again."

Against her better judgment, Sarah called her parents when she got home that night.

"It's good to hear from you," her father said.

"You could visit sometime," said her mother.

Her parents were on a speakerphone in their McMansion in Potomac, the most desirable address in suburban Maryland, where they had moved from Adams Morgan when they could afford it.

"What's wrong?" her mother asked. "You never call unless something's happened."

Sarah knew this wouldn't be easy. It never was when she called home.

"Did you see the story in today's paper about the guy killed in a hit-and-run accident near Battery Kemble Park in my neighborhood?"

"Were you involved, honey?"

"Thanks, Mom, but no."

"What happened then?" asked her father. At least he sounded concerned.

"He was a source of mine, Dad. I can't really go into it. But he was trying to help me with something I'm working on."

"In Maryland?"

"No. I'm on national politics now, campaign finance. Remember?"

"I hope it's nobody we work with," her mother said.

"I don't think that's the point," said her father.

"Exactly," Sarah said a bit sharply. "It's partly because of what you two do that I can't tell you any more right now."

She was already regretting that she called them.

"I'm having a very hard time dealing with

this guy's death," she said. "It might have something to do with his contacting me. He was real scared when we talked."

Sarah couldn't stop herself from sobbing audibly.

"That sounds far-fetched, honey," her mother said. "And you sound overwrought."

"I think that's why she called," her father said. "Sarah, have you talked to the police about this?"

"Not yet, Dad. I don't exactly know what I'd say to them. But I asked a friend of mine at the paper who covers the police to look into it."

"Then what can we do?" her mother asked.

"Just empathize a little for once, Mom."

The old anger welled up, drying Sarah's tears. As usual at this point in conversations with her parents, her father had fallen silent.

"Sorry, dear, we get busy," her mother said.

"Well, fuck, I'm busy, too," Sarah shouted into the phone. "I work all damn day almost every day of the week."

"No need to use that kind of language," her mother said. "Maybe you should work less. Maybe you should have a boyfriend. Or any kind of friend."

"You're doing a great job of making me

feel less sorry for myself."

"You know, dear, that your dad and I are proud of you. I thought that story about Trent Tucker was interesting. I noticed it got him moved from Susan Cameron's campaign."

"You want to come out here Sunday?" her father finally asked. "We could cook out."

"Thanks, Dad," Sarah answered. "But I'm kind of focused right now."

"Anything else we can do?" he asked.

"Actually," Sarah told her parents, "I really don't think so."

The next morning, Sarah asked Marge Lawson to search for information on the phone number she had called in California. Lawson found that it was listed to an Edward Borkin in Santa Cruz, whose address was one of the two Sarah had discovered in the "Pat" file. "According to the newspapers out there," Lawson said, "he's a local artist."

So Pat Scully appeared to have flown from Washington to San Francisco, stayed in a hotel there for a while, and then driven south, staying first in San Jose and then with an artist friend in Santa Cruz. But where was he now?

Lawson was also able to determine that

Patrick Scully was forty-eight years old and had valid driver's licenses in both D.C. and California. Maintaining dual licenses was not that unusual for someone who worked on Capitol Hill.

"The address on his California license is in Berkeley," she told Sarah. "But it doesn't look like he's lived there since he left the University of California. Its Web site shows he got both undergraduate and law degrees there. The address on his D.C. license is an apartment building in Foggy Bottom where he no longer has a phone number."

"Seth Moore told me that Scully had moved in with him," Sarah said.

Lawson had found that the other California address in the "Pat" file was a mail-and-package-service store in Berkeley. "He could have opened a post-office box there," she told Sarah, "and given the address to Seth Moore as a mail drop."

"But there's no other sign that Scully's been in Berkeley since leaving Washington," Sarah said. "He appears to have been heading away from the Bay Area."

A news aide found Sarah at Lawson's cubicle and told her that Joni Parker had been trying to reach her from home. Walking to her desk, Sarah glanced at the clock. It was nearly noon.

"Have you been up all night *and* all morning?" she asked Parker on the phone. "Don't you ever sleep?"

"I'd be fast asleep now, girl, if I had gotten through to you sooner. I got something from a detective friend of mine in homicide. They found a handwritten note on a piece of House committee stationery in the car that Seth Moore parked in Battery Kemble. It seems to be directions, beginning with your name: 'Sarah . . . Battery Kemble . . . AU . . . Chain Bridge Road . . . 7 a.m.' "

"Oh, my God!" said Sarah, nearly dropping the phone. She felt as though someone had punched her in the stomach.

"Why didn't you tell me that he went there to meet you?" Joni asked.

"He didn't. I mean I didn't." Sarah paused to think. "Somebody must have set him up. I told you he was just becoming a source. We had met secretly only once, in Bethesda."

"Well, whoever it was might have been following one of you. Be careful. You should talk to my detective friend. Sooner or later, the police will figure out it's your name on that piece of paper."

"No, not yet. I need time to get a better idea of what's going on. I feel really bad, Joni. He was so scared, and he trusted me."

160

On the verge of tears again, Sarah tried to steady herself as she looked around the newsroom.

"You can't blame yourself, honey," Parker told her over the phone. "Wait a minute. Do you still live in that little house in the Palisades? It's not very far from Battery Kemble, is it?"

"Yeah, I've already thought about that," Sarah said. "Whoever sent Seth there might have known where I live. If they thought Seth knew, too, they may have picked that spot to convince him that I would meet him there."

"Now I'm really worried," said Parker. "Promise me you'll be real careful, sugar, and you'll talk to the cops soon."

"Thanks, Joni. I promise. Get some sleep."

Sarah's sense of urgency was only greater now. Using an online directory, she started calling Washington area Ford dealers, identifying herself as a reporter and asking if they had sold any Expeditions recently. Encountering varying degrees of cooperation, she failed to find anything promising. She next tried car-rental companies operating in the city, but she was told they either didn't have Expeditions in their fleets or seldom rented them out. And most of them said they couldn't discuss individual

161

rentals with a reporter anyway.

It was now well past time for lunch. Sarah left the building, bought a sandwich and a bottle of water, and walked to Lafayette Square, where she found an empty bench. She studied the people around her. No one looked particularly suspicious.

She took an occasional bite of her sandwich and thought about what she should do next. A congressional staff member had been set up and probably murdered. His companion, who was investigating a corrupt relationship between a well-connected Washington business and the federal government, had disappeared. A prominent political consultant working for a presidential campaign, a man she knew too well, appeared to be involved in some way. And there might be something sinister behind it all that was too secret for Pat Scully to tell Seth Moore.

Sitting in the sunshine in Lafayette Square, staring blankly across the park and Pennsylvania Avenue, Sarah found it all deeply unsettling. But she felt both guilt and anger about Seth Moore's death, and she was determined to do something about it.

Sarah prided herself on being as self-sufficient as possible. She even regretted calling her parents, seeking comfort of some kind. But she knew she would have to take Ron Jones fully into her confidence soon. For now, she thought, she would do what she knew best: take the next step in her reporting and see where it led her.

She managed to eat only half of her sandwich before walking back to the newspaper.

12

Feeling a bit awkward in a gray pinstriped pantsuit she wore only to funerals, Sarah was not particularly hopeful when she took the Metro the next morning to Union Station and walked the few blocks to St. Joseph's Catholic Church on Capitol Hill. Inside its soaring nave, the mourners for Seth Alan Moore were scattered among the wooden pews.

Walking along an aisle on the far side, Sarah examined each person intently until she spotted a bulky man in a cheap blue suit sitting at the end of a pew. He was studying everyone in the church and writing in a small notebook on his lap. She retreated to the back of the church to watch and wait.

The music had started when she noticed

another man a few pews in front of where she was standing. She walked toward him and sat down across the aisle. He stood out from the young lawyers and congressional aides with his gray-flecked hair and beard, dark-tinted glasses, leather jacket, and corduroy pants.

As the service was about to begin, Sarah slipped across the aisle into the empty pew behind him. From there, she could see a small satchel-like traveling bag sitting next to his feet. The top of an airline-ticket folder protruded from its side pocket. Sarah had seen enough to take a chance. She leaned forward and whispered into the man's ear.

"Pat, you're a brave man and a good friend to come here. Seth would have been pleased."

The man stiffened slightly but did not acknowledge her.

"Pat, it's okay," she continued. "The person you might have to worry about is the goon in the shiny suit up there near the front. He's probably their spy. I'm a news-paper reporter. Seth was trying to tell me about what you were investigating. I want to do something about what happened to him. But I need your help."

The man remained silent and still.

"Look, Pat. When the service ends, if you

164

want to help me, go to Union Station and get a table for us in that restaurant above the big schedule board in the middle of the main concourse. I'll get there right after you. And I'll make sure we're not followed."

An hour later, after the priests, Seth Moore's family, and the pallbearers, carrying the casket, had filed down the center aisle and out of the church, Sarah hurried forward to confront the burly man as he shoved the notebook into his suit pocket.

"Listen to me," she said to him, "I'm a reporter for the *Washington Capital.* My name is Sarah Page. Write that down. Tell whoever you're working for that I'm going to find out what happened to Seth Moore. And I'm keeping my editors informed, just in case something happens to me."

The burly man said nothing. But his silence and hurried exit from the church told Sarah that she had guessed right. She followed him out and watched him walk down the street in the opposite direction from where she had told Pat Scully to go.

Then she walked quickly to Union Station, Washington's colossal neo-classical monument to the golden age of train travel. Kings, queens, and every president from Woodrow Wilson to Harry Truman had entered the capital through the station's triple-arched portico, modeled on Rome's Arch of Constantine. Rescued from decades of neglect and extensively remodeled with trendy restaurants and shops, it was still a bustling terminal for train travelers and subway riders — and an ideal place for a clandestine meeting.

Sarah walked into the central hall concourse with its vaulted ceiling and looked above the electronic board listing train arrivals and departures. She was relieved to see Scully sitting by himself in the circular upper level of the open-air Center Café, which seemed to float above the floor of the concourse. She climbed its staircase, went over to his table, and properly introduced herself.

Scully sat silently, sizing her up from behind his sunglasses, while Sarah told him what she knew about Trent Tucker, Carter Phillips, and Palisar. She repeated what Moore had said during their walk in Bethesda. And she told Scully about the note with her name and directions that the police had found in Moore's car.

"I never let Seth know where I finally holed up in California," Scully said at last, taking off his dark glasses to reveal dull blue eyes. "I was worried about dragging him too far into it. So I decided to hide out for a while. I didn't realize I might already have put his life in danger."

"I may have made it worse," Sarah said. "I feel terrible."

"There's no way to know."

"But we *can* find out what happened to Seth," she said. "I've got a colleague working on the police. And I can write about what Palisar is doing. But I need your help."

"I don't know whether I want to work with anyone, especially after what happened to Seth."

"He said you were talking to the F.B.I."

"He wanted me to. But I decided against it. Too many retired agents work for Palisar."

"All you have to do is tell me what you've found out about Palisar," she said. "Nobody needs to know you're working with me. I'll be more careful this time."

"The guy in the church was looking for me, wasn't he?"

"Probably. I told him to inform his employers that I was coming after them."

"You did what?" Scully's face betrayed some emotion for the first time.

"Harming a reporter would be too risky," said Sarah, although she wasn't sure she believed it. "I told the goon I'm keeping my editors informed about what I'm working on."

"What about me?"

"The paper can help keep our communications secure when you go back to California. We can pay for any computer stuff you need to communicate safely on the Internet. And we can use your post-office box in Berkeley."

"How do you know about that?"

"Sorry," Sarah said. "I found it with another address and some California phone numbers in a file Seth kept in his office on the Hill. I talked his boss into letting me see it. I used the phone numbers to trace your movements around the bay. Who's the artist named Borkin you stayed with in Santa Cruz?"

"Someone I knew from school."

"At Berkeley? I figured from your biography and the post-office box that you must have circled back to Berkeley to outfox anyone trying to follow you. Am I right?"

"You're good," Scully told Sarah. He smiled for the first time.

"So how are you living out there?"

"I'm staying with someone else I knew from school, a professor at Cal. He and his wife have a nice house in the Berkeley Hills. Their kids are grown, so there's plenty of room for me."

"What about money?"

"I don't spend much."

"So what aren't you telling me?"

"I want to write a book about Palisar," Scully told her. "I've got a lot of material. And access to people who were on the inside."

"So you help me and I'll help with your book," she suggested. "You'd have plenty of drama with all the cloak-and-dagger stuff and people disappearing."

"People disappearing?"

"Didn't I tell you what happened when we checked the court suits? We couldn't find the plaintiffs in cases where Palisar had something to lose."

"Yeah, I've been through those records, too," Scully said.

"Then why the disingenuous question?"

It was beginning to seem to Sarah that Scully was trying to maneuver her into something of his design rather than the other way around.

"I wanted to see if you had found any of them, because I did," he said, tantalizing her. "One's become a good source. He helped run a company owned by Palisar. He's living outside the country now."

"Sounds like you're ahead of me. Can you

help me catch up?"

Scully munched on his sandwich.

"Come on," Sarah said. "If you really want to accomplish something, you need the impact and immediacy of the newspaper. The book can come later. We owe Seth."

"Okay, okay, take it easy," Scully said. "I just want to make clear what it'll take to play this game. We're going to have to trust each other."

"Go ahead."

Scully reached down into his satchel on the floor and took out a cell phone.

"Here," he said. "It's got a long-lasting battery and can't be traced to either of us. I have more like it. I'll send you the numbers. But mostly we'll communicate on the Web."

He came prepared, Sarah thought as she shoved the phone into her purse. Who is this man?

"Where do the phones come from?" she asked.

"I said we're going to have to trust each other," Scully reminded her. His eyes told her not to ask any more questions.

Sarah had little choice. She had sought Scully out. She had asked him to help her. She had to play by his rules.

"I'll buy my computer stuff and send you the bill, along with instructions for what you'll need from your I.T. people," Scully said. "I'll send a list of e-mail names and addresses for us to use. Get your own post-office box. I don't want mail going to or from the newspaper. We'll start with how Palisar's companies get government contracts, loans, and grants. I'll send you copies of the documents. And I'll tell you where to look for others. Hold off on Freedom of Information requests until we're ready."

"Thanks, Pat." Sarah paused for a moment before trying once more to probe further. "Why are you doing this? I didn't think I was that persuasive."

"Seth sent a letter to the post-office box in Berkeley before he approached you. He told me how much he liked you and your work, going back to Annapolis. I couldn't answer him. But he sent one more note after he started talking to you. If you hadn't found me, I might eventually have contacted you."

Tears welled in Sarah's eyes. The more time that passed since Moore's death, the harder it seemed to hit her when she least expected.

"I wake up in the middle of the night and I see him again," she said to Scully. "I'm so sorry."

He reached out his hand to cover hers on

the table.

"I know. It really hurts. But I'm more responsible than you are. And we didn't kill him. They did."

He knows more than he's said about who that might be, Sarah thought.

"Somebody connected to Palisar, Pat?"

"I don't know yet," he said quickly.

Then Sarah remembered something. "Seth mentioned a secret he said you couldn't tell him."

"I still can't talk about it," he said, without explanation. "Look, I'd better go now. Do you mind if I leave ahead of you?"

Sarah shook her head. That touched a nerve, she thought.

Putting his sunglasses back on, Scully just smiled and got up from the table.

"Thanks," he said. "I'll be in touch."

It was the kind of beautiful early autumn day for which Washington was not well enough known, so Sarah decided to walk back to the newspaper. When she reached Pennsylvania Avenue, she paused for a moment to look back at the Capitol, its dome gleaming in the sunlight. She always found it inspiring, no matter what might be going on inside.

As she turned to walk up the avenue,

Sarah passed the fortress-like nineteenth-century stone building with arched windows and turrets where Carter Phillips presided over Palisar International. Thinking about its proximity to the nearby marble palaces of law and order   the federal courthouse, F.B.I. headquarters, and the Justice Department — she couldn't help wondering whether her reporting would eventually bring Phillips and Palisar to the attention of those who worked inside them. She then thought about the meeting she had requested with Ron Jones. It was time to tell him more about what she was doing.

Sitting on the leather couch across from Jones's desk a few hours later, Sarah was more aware than usual that everyone in the newsroom could watch through the glass wall of his office.

"Do you remember I told you that Trent Tucker was connected to Palisar International?" she began.

Jones nodded.

"I just talked to a confidential source who says he's got a ton of information linking Palisar to political corruption."

"What kind of source?"

"A former Hill investigator. He quit and went into hiding."

"So he's a whistle-blower?"

173

"He tried to be. But he was blocked from doing anything. And now he's too scared to talk to anyone in the government."

"So he came to you?"

"Well, sort of. I found him through somebody else."

Sarah still wasn't ready to tell Jones about Seth Moore or what she suspected about his death. Jones might worry about her safety and want to team her up with somebody else. She wanted to do this on her own.

She described the arrangements she had made for communicating with her source. The intrigue engaged Jones, who didn't usually direct this kind of reporting. He could hand it off to the paper's investigative editor. But he wanted to see what he and Sarah could do together.

"So who is he?" Jones asked. "Where's he now?"

"Can that wait until I see what I get from him? He's real skittish."

"I guess so, for now. But you'll have to tell me who he is before we can publish anything."

"Of course," Sarah said. "And I'll keep you informed about what he gives me. Will the paper pay for the logistics?"

"You trust this guy?"

Sarah knew there was a lot of emotion, if

not desperation, involved in the relationship she was establishing with Pat Scully, rather than a cold-blooded assessment of the identity and motivation of a confidential source.

"My gut does," she told Jones, even though she wasn't sure.

13

Before an audience of thousands of people in Duke University's Cameron Indoor Stadium and millions more on television, Monroe Capehart scored point after point against Warner Wylie in their first prime-time presidential-campaign debate. Looking fit, feisty, and far younger than his sixty-nine years, he blamed the Republican White House and Congress for everything from the sluggish economy to the war in Iraq and the continuing threat of terrorism. Wylie appeared unsure whether to defend or disassociate himself from his own administration.

Capehart's killing him, Mark Daniels thought as he wrote on his laptop. He was among hundreds of reporters watching the debate on large television monitors from long rows of tables in a makeshift press center in the Card Gym next to the Blue

Devils' basketball arena on the campus in Durham, North Carolina. They could see Wylie become increasingly frustrated as Capehart argued that his long experience in public office best qualified him to fix what was wrong in Washington.

"Perhaps you've been in Washington too long, Senator," the youthful vice president countered, in an obvious reference to the two-decade difference in their ages. "The next president of the United States will need new ideas and fresh energy."

"Excuse me, Mr. Vice President," Capehart interrupted. "I may be old, but I'm no fool."

His supporters in the audience erupted in cheers and applause before being silenced by the moderator.

"Have your handlers told you how interest rates work yet?" Capehart demanded, referring to one of Wylie's numerous gaffes during the campaign. "Do you know the difference between Sunni and Shiite Muslims? Which of your several positions on stem-cell research is the real policy?

"I may be old, Mr. Vice President," he repeated, looking directly at Wylie, "but I'm ready to carry out the duties of the president of the United States, which is more than I can say for you. And the voters know it."

"There it is," Mark muttered, recognizing that Capehart's rejoinder would be the memorable sound bite of the debate, reminiscent of "Where's the beef?" and "Senator, I served with Jack Kennedy, I knew Jack Kennedy, Jack Kennedy was a friend of mine. Senator, you're no Jack Kennedy."

Afterward, inside the curtained-off holding area backstage, Capehart thanked Trent Tucker, who had come down from Washington that morning, for suggesting the "I may be old" line.

"How did you know that Wylie would step right into it like that?"

"It's my job to anticipate all possibilities, Senator," Tucker responded with a shrug of false modesty.

When Monroe and Milly Capehart finally left the arena that night, they were taken to the nearby Washington Duke Inn on-campus, where they enjoyed a private victory dinner in its formal dining room. By the time Jeanne had settled them into their suite for the night and returned to her own room down the hall, it was nearly midnight. She pulled off her shoes, collapsed on the bed, and called Mark, who was staying with the rest of the press in a larger hotel off-campus.

"They're finally tucked in and I'm exhausted," Jeanne told him. "I'm leaving first thing in the morning for Los Angeles so I can have everything ready when MAC arrives at the end of the week for several days of campaigning and fund-raising. The other girls are doing his overnights on the way in Atlanta and St. Louis. Are you coming?"

"Only to Atlanta tomorrow," Mark said, stretching out on his own hotel bed. "Then I'm going to switch to Wylie for a few days to see how he handles the beating he took tonight. This could be a turning point in the campaign."

"You thought Capehart did that well?" Jeanne asked, trying to hide her disappointment at not being able to see Mark in Los Angeles.

"Oh, yeah." Mark was content to keep talking politics. "It wasn't just the 'I may be old' line. The old man totally thrashed Wylie. He certainly didn't look like there was anything wrong with him."

"I'm not going there."

"Sarah Page said she thought it might be Parkinson's."

"I told you I'm not talking about it anymore." Jeanne could feel herself spoiling for a fight. "Why are you doing this to me? We haven't seen each other since Chautauqua. We've barely spoken on the phone."

Mark felt trapped.

"I guess that's part of the problem," he said, his voice dropping.

"What problem?"

"Our relationship," he responded too quickly.

"What about our relationship?"

"Oh, God," Mark moaned, rolling over onto his side. "This is just what I wanted to avoid."

"Well, it's too late now. You better tell me what's going on."

"My editor told me to stay away from you until the election's over, so there's no appearance of a conflict of interest," Mark said nervously. "And he left me holding the bag on Capehart's health. I feel guilty because I'm not getting anywhere on it."

"And I suppose you want me to feel guilty about not helping you, even though you're dumping me."

"Come on, Jeanne, I'm not dumping you. It's only another month until the campaign's over. I hate not seeing you. But I don't know what to do. I'm starting to feel like a lousy reporter. And a lousy husband and father, too."

"So that's what you're really feeling guilty about."

Mark sighed. "What I'm really feeling

guilty about is that I may be falling in love with you."

His words hit Jeanne like an electrical charge. She had been comfortable within the boundaries of their relationship and wasn't prepared for any complications.

"I don't know what to do about Anne and the boys," Mark said. "And I'm really getting tired of campaign reporting. I feel like a pawn in the hands of the consultants. When I look at someone like Sarah Page, I see myself when I was a young reporter, and I wonder what's happened to me."

"Tonight is not a good time to do this," Jeanne interrupted, trying to calm Mark, as well as herself. "It's late and we've both had a long day."

"Are you dumping *me?*"

"No, of course not. I just don't want to talk about everything right now, especially not over the phone. Let's do what your editor ordered and wait until after the election."

Once again, she was setting the rules.

"You're still a great political reporter, Mark," Jeanne added soothingly before saying good night. "Just concentrate on the rest of the campaign."

That's what Mark tried to do. He hadn't told Jeanne he would be interviewing Monroe Capehart again on the flight to Atlanta the next day. It would be his best and last chance to pursue the question of the candidate's health.

In the morning, Mark rode the press bus to the Raleigh-Durham airport and boarded Capehart's charter aircraft, which was going first to an airport rally in Charlotte. Even with a number of women aboard, the candidate's plane resembled a flying fraternity house. Disheveled reporters, photographers, and radio and television technicians were sprawled in their seats in a sea of laptops, cameras, microphones, piles of paper, clumps of clothing, discarded paper plates and cups, and partially eaten food. An already picked-over breakfast buffet cluttered two carts parked against the partition that separated the media from the candidate's compartment in the front of the plane.

At the Charlotte airport, the plane taxied up to a large hangar overflowing with banners, balloons, high school bands, a few thousand invited Democrats, and the local media. The traveling press was shepherded into the hangar behind Capehart and his entourage. After the bands played and local politicians took turns praising him, Capehart delivered a rousing version of his stump

181

speech spiced with reminders of his strong showing in the debate the night before.

When everyone was back on the plane, Mark sat fidgeting as it took off for Atlanta. Capehart's press secretary came back and escorted him up front. Mark settled into a seat facing the candidate. The press secretary and another senior aide sat across the aisle, going over schedules and speech texts for Capehart's appearances the rest of the day.

After half an hour of routine questions and answers about the campaign and domestic policy issues, Mark asked about the candidates' differences in age and experience. When Capehart responded by repeating what he said in the debate, Mark pressed the point.

"Sir," he began gingerly, "last night, Vice President Wiley appeared to question the fitness of a man your age to handle the physical demands of the presidency. You parried that pretty effectively. But is there anything else about your physical condition that the voters should know?"

Capehart responded as though it were just another routine question. In answering it, he carefully avoided telling a lie.

"As I'm sure you know," he told Mark, "all my medical records are on the Web site.

Beyond that, you can judge for yourself. How did I look during the debate?"

Mark couldn't repeat what Jeanne had told him in Chautauqua. That left only what he had seen for himself that day on the walkway along the lake. But Capehart was too fast for him.

"I realize that I can seem a little like Gerald Ford," the senator volunteered. "I stumble sometimes when I'm not looking where I'm going or I'm thinking about something else. I've always been a bit clumsy that way."

As Capehart laughed, Mark joined in nervously. He was certain someone had scripted that response, just like "I may be old" during the debate. Did Capehart know Mark had seen him nearly fall at Chautauqua? Did Jeanne tell anyone? Did Sarah give too much away when she talked to Trent Tucker?

Capehart had successfully called his bluff. So Mark switched to foreign policy, nuclear proliferation, and terrorism before wrapping up the interview. He got enough good quotes for a front-page story that included what Capehart had said about his health. It was the best Mark could do.

The next morning, he went back to the Atlanta airport for a flight to Chicago, where he would pick up the Wylie campaign. He phoned Ron Jones in the newsroom and confessed his frustration in questioning Capehart about his health.

"I think there might be something there," Mark said, "but I can't get it."

"Maybe he was right when he told you we should judge his fitness by how he's performing during the campaign," Jones said, surprising Mark. "Runyan and I talked about it. There seems to be less concern these days about politicians' health, even things like heart or prostate surgery. We decided you can drop it for now."

Monroe Capehart completed the rest of the campaign without revealing that he was suffering from gradually advancing Parkinson's disease. A slow but steady loss of nerve cells and of the chemical dopamine in his brain had caused his limbs to stiffen and occasionally freeze up, making it difficult at times for him to walk or maintain his balance. He was fortunate to be among the one of every three people with Parkinson's who did not also have noticeable tremors in his hands or limbs.

Capehart had successfully hidden his symptoms from the doctor who did his publicly reported routine checkups, which never included neurological testing or brain scans. Instead, he was treated secretly for Parkinson's by a physician friend who prescribed medication that masked his condition most of the time. He had told the senator that the disease seldom resulted in major disability until a decade or two after its onset, so Capehart felt certain he was healthy enough for the White House. Pope John Paul II, whose initial Parkinson's symptoms were like his, continued to travel the world for years before the disease noticeably crippled and then killed him.

Not taking any chances, Trent Tucker confined the presidential candidate's remaining public appearances to one more debate, scripted speeches, choreographed rallies, and closed fund-raising receptions, with plenty of rest between them. Capehart consistently presented himself as a reassuring, conciliatory leader to voters weary of war, worried about terrorist threats, and wary of polarized Washington politics.

As Susan Cameron campaigned separately from Capehart, it remained her role to attack Wylie on issues like health care and Social Security, which mattered most to women, older people, and minorities. Elliott Bancroft, who was coordinating Susan's campaign under Tucker's direction, staged

185

scores of appearances in front of women's groups and senior citizens in communities where those voters were concentrated and the local news media were likely to give Susan uncritical celebrity coverage. Videos of her performances filled friendly blogs and the campaign's Web sites.

One morning in the crucial swing state of Florida, Susan spoke to several hundred retirees crowded into the multipurpose room of the North Broward Seniors' Center in Fort Lauderdale. Reporters and photographers lined the walls. Susan entered the room in a powder-blue pantsuit, took a microphone, and walked through the rows of seniors like a television talk-show host.

"How many of you are living on fixed incomes these days?"

Almost everyone raised a hand.

"Is it enough?"

"No," a few voices murmured.

"Is it enough for you?" Susan thrust the microphone toward one woman.

"Not really," she answered. "Especially with prescriptions costing so much."

"See," Susan said, glancing at the television cameras and her campaign's videographer. "It's the first thing on her mind, unprompted, the high price of prescription drugs, even with the changes in Medicare.

"How many of you still have that problem?"

Hands went up all over the room.

"Who is at fault?"

"Drug companies," someone said.

"Government."

"They both are," Susan said. "The drug companies and their high-paid lobbyists in Washington give a lot of money to members of Congress who vote against regulating the price of prescription drugs. Is that right?"

"No!" everyone answered.

"Of course not. And you can do something about it," Susan said, pausing to scan the faces in the audience. She loved the way people responded to her in these encounters. They took her out of the cocoon of campaign planes, hotels, and speeches to large audiences. "You can vote for me and Monroe Capehart. We'll stop profiteering by the drug companies."

The applause was loud and enthusiastic.

"Remember how the drug companies flew Warner Wylie all around the country? Remember how they paid for him to go to expensive resorts and play golf? Even as vice president, he's been working for them, not for you. Is that right?"

"No!"

"Well," Susan said, "you can do something

about that, too. You can send him packing."

As the campaign entered its final weeks, Pat Scully established contact with Sarah from California and e-mailed her organization charts and spreadsheets he had made for Palisar's companies, complete with financial details, lines of business, and names and thumbnail biographies of key people. Using Sarah's new post-office box, he sent packages stuffed with copies of government contracts, financing agreements, loan guarantees, and subsidy arrangements, along with page after page of relevant U.S. and foreign laws and regulations.

"pls familiarize yourself with everything before we take next steps," he told her in an exchange of messages after it had all arrived. "not to worry . . . will put pieces together in time"

"I'm still working here on what happened to Seth," Sarah said.

"what cops know?"

"Not much. They're still looking for the Expedition."

"they know you're sarah in note?"

"I haven't told them yet."

"good girl . . . don't know who you can trust"

"Not even you?"

"trust me . . . things not always what they seem"

14

"I know you feel strongly about gun control," Elliott Bancroft told Susan as they studied briefing books in her suite at the Fairmont Olympic hotel in Seattle. "But we need to add some nuance to your position. Couldn't you say that you understand the feelings of law-abiding citizens who enjoy hunting, but, as a woman, you feel a duty to all those mothers who have lost children to gunfire?"

"And my position, as a woman, would then be what?"

"We don't want you to be pinned down on a precise position," Elliott said. "We just want you to come across as sympathetic to legal gun owners. They're important swing voters. You can still say we need sensible gun controls, which is what our base wants to hear."

"But without saying exactly what those sensible gun controls would be."

"Exactly," he said. And they both laughed.

Weeks earlier, Elliott had given Susan several thick briefing books on issues and questions she would be likely to face in her nationally televised debate with the Republican vice presidential candidate, Ohio's Senator Harry Gans, in Sarasota, Florida, less than three weeks before the election. They had spent an hour or two going over them almost every day, wherever they stopped while campaigning.

Much of the material in the loose-leaf books was based on views that Democratic and independent voters had expressed in focus groups and opinion polls. Susan, who had become comfortable expressing her own feelings about issues that mattered to her, was not always a cooperative student.

It wasn't that she didn't like Elliott, who had been in charge of her campaign for weeks now. A former minor-league pitcher who had gone to law school after a shoulder injury sidelined him, Elliott still looked like an athlete, tall and lean, with an open face and sandy hair. He was attentive to Susan, appearing to take her seriously rather than treating her condescendingly as a relative political novice. In that way, he could not have been more different from Trent Tucker. Susan listened carefully to Elliott, even when she disagreed. But when she talked about Elliott's tutoring during one of her late-night phone conversations with Michael, he dismissed it.

"Don't worry about all that stuff," her ex-husband advised. "Ignore Harry Gans. Everybody knows he's just an old guy they added to the ticket because Wylie looks so young and inexperienced. Capehart easily trumps Gans in the political gravitas department, so you don't have to worry about that.

"This debate is all about you," Michael told Susan. "It's a television show. Most people will be watching just to see you. Make them feel comfortable with you as someone who could become their president."

On the day before the debate in Sarasota, Susan went with Elliott, Alison Winters, and Amanda Peterson to the city's Opera House to check on the arrangements. Susan immediately felt comfortable in the intimate atmosphere of the historic theater, where the Sarasota Opera performed for wealthy retirees who wintered in the surrounding resort communities on the Gulf of Mexico.

"We'll have plenty of our own people in the audience," Elliott assured Susan as she stood behind her lectern for a lighting check. "You'll be able to see familiar faces. Connect with them. Don't worry about everybody watching on television."

Technicians then tested the microphone Susan would be wearing on her suit jacket during the debate.

"We insisted on this mike because it lets you talk more naturally and move around," Alison explained. "You don't have to stay behind the lectern. You can be conversational, just like you've been at community events."

"Just be yourself," Amanda told Susan.

After returning to the Hyatt Sarasota, the three women retired to Susan's suite and invited Emily Schwartz and Penny Piper to join them. They ordered pizza from room service for their last girls' night of the campaign.

Susan, who had changed into shorts and a tank top, sprawled comfortably on her bed. The others relaxed in chairs pulled in from the adjoining sitting room. Through the open sliding door to the balcony they could see the lights on boats in the marina on Sarasota Bay.

"We've moved so fast it's become a blur of places," Susan said. "But tomorrow night I'll be able to show the whole country who I am. I'm nervous, but I'll be ready."

"I've got great spinners for the media afterward," said Alison. "Some governors. All the Democratic women senators."

"I've kept your schedule clear tomorrow," Penny said. "You can sleep late and relax until it's time to get ready."

"I asked Elliott to stop everyone from adding to the briefing books," Emily said, "in case you want to go over them again."

"Enough!" Amanda declared. "Let the girl alone. For the rest of the night, this is a politics-free zone."

They ate pizza and gossiped, ganging up on Alison.

"How's your favorite speechwriter?" Susan asked her playfully.

"He's there when I need him."

"Jeremy's just a boy," said Amanda.

"I'm not planning to marry him."

"Now, Elliott, he's a grown-up," Emily said. "I hadn't worked with him before. He knows how to make you feel appreciated."

"What do you think of him?" Penny asked Alison.

"Too old for me. But, like Emily says, he knows how to handle women. A lot of guys don't in this business."

Amanda noticed that Susan hadn't joined in.

"Well, he's a lot better than Trent Tucker," Amanda said and then changed the subject.

Late the next morning, Elliott telephoned Susan in her suite.

"Would you like to get out for a while?"

he asked her. "It's a nice, sunny day. I know a good bookstore downtown that has a sidewalk café. We could sneak over for some coffee. If the press shows up, we could always turn it into a decent photo op with local voters."

"You haven't already alerted the press?"

"C'mon, don't you trust me?"

"Bring Alison along, just in case we do have media."

The three of them, along with Susan's Secret Service detail, slipped out of the hotel garage in two cars and parked a few blocks away from Sarasota News and Books. With the agents following at a discreet distance, they strolled down the palm-lined street. At the bookstore, they bought coffee and pastries at a counter nestled among crowded bookshelves and found a table outside on the sidewalk.

For a while they were left to themselves to chat about books. Alison Winters, who had not seen Susan and Elliott alone together before, sensed chemistry between them. Elliott looked like one of those handsomely mature models in men's clothing catalogues in his black polo shirt, khaki chinos, and loafers.

"Did you ever read David McCullough's biography of Truman?" he asked Susan.

"I've been meaning to for years."

"I'll buy it for you. McCullough shows how Truman grew into the presidency after Roosevelt died without changing who he was."

Instead of bridling at a subject the rest of her staff had learned to avoid, Susan appeared to Alison to be flattered by Elliott's suggestion.

Eventually, people coming out of the bookstore began to drift over to shake Susan's hand and wish her well in the debate. That emboldened others who had been sitting nearby outside.

"I've been knocking on doors for you with my daughter," said a middle-aged woman in tennis whites.

"My wife told me to vote for you," added a weathered man in shorts, leaning on his cane. "But I might anyway. You and Senator Capehart look like a good team."

As if on cue, a camera crew from a local television station materialized, attracting a growing number of passersby. As the Secret Service agents moved in and Alison stage-directed, Susan stood to work the crowd and give the television reporter a short stand-up interview. She was soon surrounded by more cameras and reporters, which drew even more people. Looking relaxed amid a colorful swirl of humanity in the bright Florida sunshine, Susan cheerfully responded to the reporters' shouted questions while continuing to shake voters' hands. Elliott stood off to the side, out of camera range, smiling at how well it would play on the evening news just a few hours before the beginning of the debate.

That night, Susan still looked relaxed and confident in a new dark blue suit as she stood behind her lectern in the Sarasota Opera House. Paying little attention to Harry Gans or even the moderator's questions during much of the ninety-minute debate, she kept repeating dire warnings about the dangers that a Wylie presidency would pose to America's women, families, minorities, and senior citizens.

Asked about family values, she said, "Health care is a family value and too many Americans can't afford it."

Asked about abortion, she said, "Warner Wylie wants to take away a woman's right to choose. He wants to deny equal access to education and jobs. He wants to water down guarantees of affordable health care for the elderly and the poor. He would make government our enemy."

Asked about national security, she said, "You can't have national security without economic security. The last eight years have been difficult for everyone but the very rich. Warner Wylie wants to give the rich still more at the expense of everyone else."

When Gans eventually tried to stress his much longer experience in public service, Susan turned to talk to him directly.

"What kind of experience are we talking about, Senator?" she asked Gans. "All those years you've spent in Washington doing the bidding of your campaign contributors from big business? Is that better experience than working to improve our schools? Or finding child care for working women? Or legitimizing hard-working immigrants who contribute so much to our economy?"

She stepped out from behind the lectern and stood beside it, facing the audience and the nearest television camera, with her hands folded in front of her.

"I'll be honest with you," she said, looking directly into the camera. "I've only been a United States senator for a few years. My marriage failed. I've not had the good fortune to start a family of my own. I've been a working woman coping with life in the real world. And ever since my former husband took me to Washington, I've been working on what really matters in your lives. Child care. Public schools. Health care.

Good jobs and retirement security. I believe strongly in the values that have made this country great. Faith. Family. Education. Hard work. I am full of hope for our future. But we have to make changes to offer everyone real opportunity in the years ahead."

Ignoring the blinking red light on the moderator's table that signaled it was her opponent's turn, Susan took another step toward the camera.

"I can assure you that I have the experience and determination necessary to help Monroe Capehart make it possible for all hard-working Americans to achieve their aspirations. We want you to feel secure in living in the greatest country in the world."

"Well, I guess those were your closing remarks," the moderator said when Susan finished.

"What were you doing?" Elliott asked Susan during their postmortem back in her hotel suite. "You ignored the rules, our briefing books, your opponent, and the moderator."

"It was my chance to say what I pleased. I wanted to tell everyone who I was and what they could expect of me."

They had collapsed into comfortable chairs, sipping wine. Alison and Amanda had gone to the hotel dining room to arrange a late dinner for the candidate, staff, and spinners.

"I loved the freedom," Susan said with an ebullience Elliott had seldom seen. "No text, no talking points, and," she added with a smile, "no adviser at my elbow. In fact, I didn't see you there at all."

"I was in the press center to see how it played. Some of the reporters said you seemed to be following a script instead of answering the questions. I didn't tell them you were soloing."

"Good. If the polls are bad," she teased, focusing her eyes on his, "I can blame you for scripting me."

"The polls won't be bad," Elliott said. "The camera loves you no matter what you say. And most of it was right for our target audience."

"You just can't take all the credit for it, poor baby."

Exhausted but elated, Susan could feel the rush she remembered sharing with Michael during their early years together in politics. The prize was near at hand.

"We should go downstairs," she said to Elliott. "They're waiting for us."

It was well after midnight in Florida when

Susan returned alone to her suite and telephoned Michael in California.

"I've been waiting for you to call," he told her. "You were great. You stayed on message and really played to the camera."

"You, Amanda, and Elliott all helped."

"Elliott. He's all you talk about these days."

"I guess he makes me feel good about myself, the way you used to do."

"Oh, I get it."

"Don't jump to conclusions," Susan said firmly. "Nothing's going on. And it wouldn't be any business of yours anyway."

"So much for our little rendezvous."

"I told you, Michael. It felt good, but we could never do it again. Just add it to your long list of one-night stands."

"I guess I deserve that," he said. "But I'm still working hard for you. All my friends have contributed the max, and what's left of our old organization here will help get out the vote."

"Thanks," Susan told Michael. "I really appreciate our phone talks. They're the best way for me to deal with you right now."

In the days before the election, Trent Tucker worked the phones day and night from his command post in Capehart-Cameron headquarters. Susan's strong showing in the opinion polls after her debate had further buoyed the ticket in the home stretch of the race. She won approval from liberals, college students, women, the elderly, and minority racial and ethnic groups who had traditionally constituted the Democrats' base, while Capehart offered a reassuring alternative to Warner Wylie for many independent and moderate Republican voters.

Tucker even agreed to answer questions from Sarah for a story on the tactics being used to attack Wylie. Previously unknown "independent" citizens' groups with names like Working Americans' Alliance, Americans for Affordable Medicine, and Seniors to Save Social Security were paying for television ads suggesting that Wylie would endanger Social Security, cut taxes again for the rich, and do nothing about the cost of health care and prescription drugs. Computer-generated phone calls, mass e-mails, Weblog postings, and hand-delivered flyers were more pointed, suggesting, depending on the recipient, that Wylie would work to actually cut Social Security benefits or to outlaw abortion or to restrict the rights of immigrants.

"I can't monitor everything that's going out to voters, but there's nothing wrong with negative campaigning. It's a time-honored technique because it works," Tucker said to Sarah over the telephone. He loved this kind of inside baseball. "We're using databases to target individual Democrats and independents with messages to get them out and vote against Wylie."

" 'We'?" Sarah asked. "These are supposed to be independent expenditures. It would be illegal for you to coordinate them."

"Of course."

Tucker realized he had said too much. He didn't often make mistakes like that with reporters, but he hadn't slept much in weeks. And he had unguardedly reverted to his long-ago tutelage of Sarah about the mechanics of politics.

"Trent, on the record, are you coordinating the fund-raising and spending of these groups?"

"As you said, that wouldn't be kosher." He backtracked as best he could. "On the record, these are citizens exercising their free-speech rights, independent of the Capehart-Cameron campaign. They just happen to have the same objective: to put Democrats who'll protect working Americans back into the White House."

"Nice spontaneous quote," Sarah said, proud of herself for winning a battle of wits with Tucker. "I'll be sure to put it in my story."

"That little girl is sticking to you like glue, isn't she?" Carter Phillips observed pointedly in a phone call to Tucker after Sarah's story appeared.

"Not to worry," Tucker told him. "The Federal Election Commission won't catch up until long after the election is over."

"Do you think that was my point?" Phillips persisted in a bullying tone. "When are you going to get that girl off your back? I don't want her coming after me. There's a lot at stake, more than I've told you."

What does that mean? Tucker thought. He was still confident he could manage Sarah. But he was worried about his relationship with Phillips. He knew the general could be ruthless in confronting his enemies and, if necessary, in cutting his losses. People had disappeared. And there was that still unsolved hit-and-run on Tucker's own street that Phillips had called to his attention as some kind of warning.

"I'll work on it after the election, General," Tucker promised nervously. "Right now, I'm 24/7 on getting across the finish line first."

"My Republican friends are getting anxious, and I've told them I can't help," Phillips told him. "I've ordered our people to stay on the sidelines. I can't be seen doing anything for you either."

"But you'll keep the money coming?" Tucker asked. "I need it for the ground war at the end."

"Nobody will know where it's coming from?"

"That's why we're putting it into the independent groups. And we're moving it around from one account to another before it reaches them," Tucker said. "Nothing can be traced to you."

He didn't tell Phillips that there was a detailed record of the complicated laundering of these illegal campaign contributions. Tucker had put it away for safekeeping.

15

By midnight on election day, as the vote counts flashed on computer and television screens in the crowded *Capital* newsroom, the emerging electoral majority for Capehart and Cameron had become clear. The Democratic ticket won most of the states in an arc from New England and New York to Iowa, Wisconsin, and Minnesota, plus the West Coast, Nevada, New Mexico, and Florida.

With Ron Jones hovering over him anxiously, Mark was able to write a definitive story in time for most of the paper's Wednesday editions.

By Mark Daniels

Monroe Capehart was elected president of the United States yesterday, reclaiming the White House for the Democrats in a historic election in which Susan Cameron was chosen as the country's first woman vice president.

As the vote count continued early this morning, Sen. Capehart appeared to be winning more than 300 electoral votes, well over the 270 needed for victory. In the popular vote, he was leading Republican Vice President Warner Wylie by 51 to 47 percent, with the rest going to third-party candidates.

Vice President Wylie conceded just after midnight.

"I regret that I will no longer be able to serve my country in Washington," he told disappointed supporters gathered at the Hyatt hotel in Kansas City. Wylie made no reference to Sen. Cameron, who frequently criticized him by name during the campaign.

Minutes later, Capehart and Cameron, who had returned to Washington after voting in their home states, thanked their campaign workers at a boisterous celebration in the ballroom of the Washington Hilton.

"This is a great victory for you, for our party, and for our country," Capehart told the loudly cheering crowd. "And it is a historic victory for the women of America.

"Susan Cameron is writing an overdue new chapter in American politics and government," Capehart added, holding her hand high as the crowd roared. "She has been a great running mate and a great campaigner. And she will be a great vice president of the United States."

The newsroom filled again by the middle of the next afternoon with reporters and editors working on postelection stories. Sarah was assigned to analyze the exit polls. She was just starting to write her story when Joni Parker called from police headquarters.

"I know you must be up to your eyeballs, but I've got to tell you right away what I heard from one of my sources," said Parker. "They may have found the Expedition, or at least what's left of it, in a boarded-up housing project in Southeast. The one they're going to tear down. The Expedition looked like just another stripped, stolen SUV, so nobody reported it. Eventually, the housing authority asked the police to take it away. The tow-truck guy remembered that one of my homicide detectives had asked him to let him know if he ever found a black Expedition on the street. They've moved it to the lab for tests, which will probably take a few weeks."

"My God, Joni, that's great."

"Don't get your hopes up too high, sugar. They may not find anything. But I'm staying on their butts."

"You're wonderful. Call me if you hear anything from the lab."

Sarah somehow managed to finish the exit-poll story. And she was still there after the last edition closed and everyone else had drifted away. She knew she wouldn't be able to sleep, so she decided to stay and go through the files of material on Palisar. What was the secret, she wondered, that Pat Scully wasn't ready to tell?

At dawn, Sarah forced herself to go home, shower, change clothes, and eat breakfast. She was back in the office before eleven and went to see Ron Jones.

"My source on Palisar has been sending me lots of good stuff. It fits with what Marge and I had already found," she said. "We're beginning to understand how Palisar works. We're going to find big-time corruption."

Still exhausted from election night himself, Jones had difficulty following everything she said. But he heard the last part.

"Okay, that's enough for now," he said, waving his hand wearily. "I don't know how long I can give you. But the election's over, so you can stay on it. When I'm not so damned tired, I'll buy you lunch and you can tell me more."

16

"I'm freezing," said Mark Daniels, stamping his feet on the hard marble. "Inauguration day always seems to be one of the coldest of the winter."

"It wouldn't be so bad if they hadn't made everyone come through security so early," Jeanne said. "At least the sun's shining. And my thermal underwear's working."

"I'd like to see you in long johns."

"Wait until you see the dress I'm wearing tonight. That'll raise your temperature."

They were bundled up in parkas on metal

folding chairs in a corner of the friends and family seating area just below the inaugural stand on the steps of the west front of the Capitol. Mark had accepted the ticket from Jeanne so he could sit with her. It freed up a place in the press section behind them for Sarah, who was assigned to help Mark for the day.

"With all the inaugural balls tonight," Mark said to Jeanne, "I'm not expected home before morning."

"Your editor's okay with you seeing me again?"

"He's watching how it goes. He'll send somebody else on trips you advance."

Half an hour before noon, the Marine Band struck up "Hail to the Chief" for the outgoing president for the last time as he arrived on the inaugural stand. A few minutes later, Monroe Capehart followed him down the steps from inside the Capitol and sat next to his wife, Milly, in the front row.

After a musical interlude, Speaker of the House Charlotte Ames administered the oath of office of the vice president to Susan Cameron. It was the first time the oath had been both administered and taken by women. Taking advantage of the heaters built into the floor of the inaugural stand,

Susan defied the cold by wearing a blue wool suit without a coat or hat. The stiff breeze ruffled her long blond hair. Susan's parents, bundled in heavy coats, held their family Bible as she took the oath.

At precisely noon, Monroe and Milly Capehart joined the chief justice of the United States at the front of the platform. Milly, wearing a warm gray coat and matching hat, cradled their Bible in her gloved hands. Monroe Capehart, bareheaded but wearing a dark overcoat, placed his left hand on it, raised his right hand, and repeated the oath of office. He shook hands with the chief justice and embraced first Milly and then his vice president. A staccato salute boomed from four artillery pieces positioned on the Capitol grounds nearby.

Sarah, looking up from the press section, thought about Trent Tucker, sitting proudly on the inaugural stand. He would now be working in the White House as the president's political director. Palisar would have direct access to the seat of power.

"The American people expect their leaders to work together to protect our democracy from the threat of terrorism, to revive our economy, to educate our children, and to strengthen the safety net for the less fortunate," President Capehart said in his inaugural address. "It is time to end the polarization of politics in Washington. It is time to replace ideological rigidity with pragmatic progress on the nation's agenda. It is time to put the needs of all Americans ahead of the narrow interests of political parties."

Mark turned to Jeanne when the ceremony ended. "I need to find Sarah. Ron has her working the parade for me," he said. "Are you going to watch it?"

"I have to go to the White House to help supervise the unpacking," Jeanne said. "The moving vans should already be there."

After Mark found Sarah and told her what he needed, she plunged into the sea of excited people filling the sidewalks and temporary viewing stands along Pennsylvania Avenue. Passing Palisar's building once again, Sarah remembered the last time she had walked the length of the ceremonial avenue after her meeting with Pat Scully at Union Station. As she looked up, she wondered whether Carter Phillips was among the parade watchers she could just see through the small windows in the thick, gray stone walls.

After interviewing people along a dozen blocks of the parade route, she positioned herself in front of the Hotel Washington at

Fifteenth Street, where Pennsylvania Avenue zigzagged around the Treasury Building. It felt like an eternity in the deepening chill before the military honor guards finally appeared at the head of the parade. Then came formations of police cars and motorcyles, followed by several open-backed trucks filled with photographers.

The armored black Cadillac limousine bearing the president and the First Lady came next, slightly ahead of the car carrying the vice president. Secret Service agents walked alongside both vehicles. Black battle-wagon SUVs filled with more agents, heavily armed, followed closely behind. Then came the first marching band, its booming drums and blaring horns mixing with the cheers of the crowd as Capehart waved from inside his bulletproof car. As the vehicles passed by Sarah and turned onto the pedestrian-only portion of Pennsylvania Avenue, which was lined with reviewing stands in front of the White House, she could hear the cheering grow louder.

At the back of the presidential mansion, Jeanne climbed up a few steps of the South Portico to look out on the winter tranquillity of the South Lawn. Members of the White House domestic staff bustled below her, supervising movers who were unloading trucks parked on the South Drive. They were taking the Capeharts' possessions to the family quarters on the second and third floors of the White House. Relatively little of it was furniture, because the presidential couple would be using furnishings accumulated by previous tenants over the past two centuries.

When Jeanne spotted movers carrying boxes labeled "bedroom," she hurried down to lead them through a door under the portico and up an elevator to the presidential bedroom suite at the west end of the main hall on the second floor. The bedroom contained a large Victorian bed, selected by the Capeharts from the White House collection, and an antique couch and accompanying chairs arranged around a fireplace that faced the bed. On the far wall, tall windows opened onto the South Lawn, filling the room with sunlight. Adjoining the bedroom were a bathroom, a sitting room, and a small study.

One of the White House ushers, a veteran of presidential moving days, was waiting when Jeanne reached the bedroom. The two of them supervised the housekeepers who put the Capeharts' clothes into closets and dresser drawers. Jeanne herself arranged their toiletries and personal items in the bathroom and the sitting room. And she showed the butler the clothes the Capeharts would be changing into for the inaugural balls that night.

It was little different from what Jeanne had done for several candidates in countless hotel suites along the campaign trail over the years. But, although she was trying not to show it in front of the White House staff, Jeanne was thrilled to be arranging things for a president and First Lady inside the family quarters of the White House, where every president since John Adams had lived.

Darkness had fallen in the late afternoon by the time Jeanne could go outside and find the seat reserved for her on the presidential reviewing stand in front of the White House, where she watched what remained of the inaugural parade. When it was over, she followed the Capeharts back to the mansion as far as the pillared North Portico. Standing under its huge lantern, she watched while the president and the First Lady went through the front door into the Grand Foyer, where one hundred ushers, butlers, housekeepers, cooks, and gardeners lined its long red carpet. As she turned to walk back down the driveway to the security gate on Pennsylvania Avenue, Jeanne could not have anticipated that her first day inside the White House would also be her last while Monroe Capehart was president.

Of the many inaugural balls held by the Democrats that night, the largest was the California ball in the Great Hall of the National Building Museum. The redbrick building had been erected a few blocks north of Pennsylvania Avenue in the 1880s to honor Civil War soldiers and dispense military pensions to them and their widows and orphans. A century later, it was emptied of government offices and turned into a museum.

On inauguration night, the hall's soaring interior space, as long as a football field and interrupted only by two rows of seventy-five-foot-tall Corinthian columns, was bathed by spotlights that shone down on potted palm trees and a stage festooned with red, white, and blue bunting. A multitude of Hollywood celebrities and Silicon Valley moguls — big contributors to both the winning campaign and the Inaugural Committee — were there in tuxedos and ball gowns to see the first female vice president of the United States at her home state's inaugural ball. They waited for hours while she and the Capeharts made the rounds in separate motorcades.

Mark and Sarah arrived at the National Building Museum together in a taxi. They had worked until the night's first deadline and changed clothes in bathrooms in the newsroom. When they found Jeanne in the crowd, Mark surprised both women by introducing them to each other. Sarah was wearing the snug, sleeveless black sheath she still relied on for most dressy occasions, while Jeanne looked stunning in a new low-cut red dress that clung to her body.

"I'll excuse myself now," Sarah told Jeanne after a few minutes of small talk. "I'm working for Mark tonight. Have fun."

"So we finally meet," Jeanne said to Mark, as Sarah disappeared into the milling crowd. "She's cute."

"We've worked together now and then. She and Ron Jones have secret meetings about what she does the rest of the time. I guess she doesn't trust me."

"But you trust her to know about us?"

"She figured it out a long time ago."

"So we're no longer a big secret?"

"I don't really care anymore," Mark said. "Let's just enjoy ourselves tonight."

Shortly before midnight, an hour after the Capeharts had come and gone, Vice President Susan Cameron finally arrived with

Elliott Bancroft. Now her chief of staff, he stayed in the background while Susan, wearing a dazzling golden gown, stepped onto the stage. She spoke briefly to the huge crowd before trying a few dance steps that would be seen again and again on television news shows and Web sites. Then she came down from the stage, escorted by Secret Service agents in black tie, and plunged into the crowd filled with stars of entertainment, business, and politics. Although she had been in Washington for years, as Michael Cameron's wife and then as a United States senator, this was her debut, and she was a huge hit.

The weeks ahead turned out to be disorienting and frustrating for Susan, as she encountered the unique isolation of the office of vice president.

Her new home, the white Victorian "Admiral's House" on the tree-filled grounds of the Naval Observatory just beyond Embassy Row on Massachusetts Avenue, looked appealing, with its turret, dormers, and spacious porches. But the 1893 house, first designated as the vice president's residence in 1974, felt empty and lonely inside its security perimeter of fences and guardhouses on Observatory Circle. Susan felt like a prisoner of the household staff and Secret Service. She could no longer walk alone or drive her own car. She missed her old house and neighbors, only a mile away.

Susan also missed setting her own political course. As he had signaled in his inaugural address, President Capehart was moving cautiously, seeking consensus in the new Congress for his agenda. On the issues Susan cared about most — health care, prescription drug benefits, child care for working mothers, federal aid for education, and the future of Social Security and Medicare — he set up Cabinet committees and bipartisan presidential commissions to suggest what to do.

Elliott Bancroft had started building a domestic-policy team for Susan. But its members had little influence in interdepartmental meetings. Sometimes they weren't even invited. Everything of substance that Susan wanted to do had to be cleared with the president's staff.

"Dammit, Elliott, who do you work for, me or Tucker?" Susan asked one afternoon in her sunny corner office in the West Wing of the White House. The coveted office, which looked out onto the South Lawn, was usually given to the president's chief of staff, but Capehart had insisted that Susan have it. "What good does it do me to be down the hall from the Oval Office," she continued, "if everything has to go through Tucker's cubbyhole upstairs?"

"His job is to get you and Capehart reelected in four years," Bancroft said, "and that starts as soon as you get into the White House."

"Then why am I having such a hard time clearing a speech about air and water pollution? That would play well with our base. But Tucker's holding it up."

"It's probably just buried under everything he has to do."

"Elliott, don't treat me like a child. I'm the vice president. Tell Tucker I want this to stop, or I'm going to the president."

An hour later, Elliott was sitting next to a teetering pile of papers on a worn sofa facing Tucker's cluttered desk in a small office on the second floor of the West Wing. There was little sign that Tucker was one of the most powerful people in the White House, reviewing every appointment, decision, and speech in advance for its political impact.

"What are you doing with her environment speech?" Elliott asked. "Checking it first with some of your clients?"

"Former clients. I've got somebody else running the firm now. And I don't like that kind of talk," Tucker said with a scowl. "Tell Susan I cleared her speech. I just got behind. I'm busy getting our people in place. Everybody in the Cabinet is waiting for me to decide who'll run their shops. Some will be Capehart's people. Some will be helping us get reelected. And the rest will be mine."

"Anyone I know?"

"Arnold Fox, the energy lobbyist, for one. He put a lot of his clients' money into the campaign. He's going to run public lands at Interior. It does mining regs and hands out gas and oil leases."

"Who else?"

"Archie Winthrop, who lost his seat in the House, is going to Homeland Security. They're still spending a lot of money. George Burros, the senator's son, will be at Commerce. He'll handle overseas business deals. And Jennifer Hartman finally agreed to do the export-loan guarantee job in the Pentagon."

"I know her," Elliott said. "That's a big pay cut. She was doing well with the defense contractors."

"That's why she isn't happy about this," Tucker said. "But I got her husband elected to the Senate. And I got Jennifer her first lobbying job. I even bailed them out of debt when they moved here. They bought too big a house and partied all the time. She was even supporting some . . ."

A big smile spread across Tucker's face as he saw Elliott's face flush. "I forgot you worked on that New Jersey race."

"She wasn't 'supporting' me. Just giving me some help here and there," Elliott insisted. "It was my first real political job, so I wasn't paid much, and my divorce was expensive. It was a campaign, for Chrissakes. Her husband was never with her. And I was in charge of her appearances. We just hit it off."

"Take it easy," Tucker said. He was already thinking about how this could increase his leverage with both Elliott and the Hartmans. "I've taken my own pleasures where I could find them."

"Susan wants to do more than give speeches," Elliott said, changing the subject.

"Then create a task force for her to run. Something like child care or the space program," Tucker said. "Susan's your account. Just keep her out of my hair."

Mark took Jeanne to dinner on a Friday night in late February to tell her that he could no longer lead two lives. He began with small talk about the White House, which grew into an argument.

"How can you say the president is off to a slow start?" Jeanne asked testily.

"You know the first hundred days are the most important time in any new administration," Mark told her, "and he's in danger of wasting them. He hasn't set any priorities. I should find out what Susan Cameron thinks. I bet she wants him to move faster."

"A typical journalist, always looking for conflict. You're not going to get any help from me," Jeanne said.

They fell into gossiping. Jeanne told Mark about a well-known married client of her travel agency sneaking off with his male lover to the Caribbean. And he told her about the married network-television reporter who, when he did stand-ups on camera at the White House, always wore a tie given to him by the one of his many girlfriends he was planning to see that night.

"It's like one of those flags that ships fly," Mark said. "He's signaling who's coming aboard."

"All right," Jeanne said when they stopped laughing. "I guess I'm ready for you to come aboard. Pay the check and take me home."

The wine and the sex were soothing. They slept soundly until Jeanne turned over and noticed the time in the large, luminous numbers on her clock radio.

"Mark," she said, shaking him. "It's nearly three-thirty. You've got to go home. What are you going to tell your wife?"

He slowly raised his head and propped it up with a second pillow. Then he nervously smoothed the covers over their naked bodies.

"I don't have to go home," he said. "I've left Anne."

"What?" Jeanne bolted upright, tugging at the sheet to cover her bosom. She was furious. He had changed everything about their relationship without giving her any warning or any say in the decision.

"When were you going to tell me?"

"At dinner, actually, but we didn't get to it," Mark said sheepishly. "I moved out yesterday. Most of my things are still in the house."

Jeanne's mind raced as she fought to regain control. "Where are you living?"

"I checked into a hotel near the paper downtown. But I could stay here."

"Are you out of your mind?" Jeanne shouted at him. "This is my apartment. And you're not my husband."

Although she had given him fair warning about how she felt when he first confessed his love for her during the campaign, Mark was dumbfounded.

"I thought this was what you were waiting for," he said to Jeanne weakly.

"We had rules."

"Because I was married."

"Men just don't get it." Jeanne slid back down under the covers. "I never, ever asked you to leave your wife. What's going to happen with your kids?"

"We'll work something out."

"Who's 'we'?" Jeanne asked. "You're responsible for children I've never even met. Everything was fine when we kept the rest of our lives separate. I'm not ready for this."

She fell silent, resenting the pressure he had put on her.

"So now what do we do?" Mark asked.

"I really don't know," she said, closing her eyes and rolling over, away from him. "I'll have to think about it. No more talking now."

It took Mark longer than Jeanne to go back to sleep. When he awoke, well after eight, he found her in the kitchen, making coffee and breakfast. He put his arms around her from behind and kissed the back of her neck.

"I could get used to this," he told her.

"Forget it, buster," she said, shrugging out of his grasp. "We're not going to make a habit of it."

Mark took a seat at the table, while Jeanne poured juice and coffee. When the eggs and toast were ready, she sat down next to him.

"We're just going to have to start over," she said. "If you're serious about this, you'll have to find a place to live and figure out what you're going to do about getting a divorce and taking care of your kids. When you've done that and I've gotten over the shock, maybe we can try again."

"So I have hope?" Mark asked, risking a smile.

"We'll see," Jeanne said. "I have to think about it."

17

Across the continent from the Washington winter, Sarah Page rose with the sun in her beachfront hotel room to take an early morning run along the Pacific Ocean. She had only a few hours before joining Pat Scully and his secret source at a clandestine meeting on the nearby La Jolla campus of the University of California at San Diego. It was Scully's idea to ask his source, who was living in Mexico, to drive to San Diego, while Scully flew in from San Francisco and Sarah from Washington.

Apparently with the help of the Cal professor he was living with in Berkeley, Scully had arranged for the use of the secluded office of a U.C.S.D. faculty member who was away on leave. It came with a powerful computer on the university's broadband network, untraceable to any of the three of them. Sarah had decided to stay at the La Jolla Shores Hotel, a low-rise, Spanish-style inn right on the ocean, and take her daily exercise on the La Jolla Shores beach.

As she ran along soft sand between the hotel and the Scripps Pier, a mile to the north, Sarah thought about what she had learned so far. With the help of Scully and Marge Lawson, she had identified dozens of American and foreign companies owned by Palisar. And she had discovered how dependent they were on the largesse of the U.S. and foreign governments.

Some of the companies had huge contracts with the Pentagon to provide services to U.S. military forces around the world. Others had benefited from subsidies, loans, and guarantees from federal agencies in building airports and power plants, mining valuable natural resources, and selling civilian and military technology in the Third World. Scully had sent Sarah evidence that much of it was authorized by special provisions put into appropriations bills by members of Congress, who received campaign contributions and other favors from Palisar companies and investors. Sarah now needed to find specific examples of where Palisar might have crossed the line from political favoritism to real corruption.

That would make a great story, she thought. But would it explain why someone would kill Seth Moore or cause a man like Pat Scully to go into hiding? What about the secret that Scully had refused to tell her or Seth? And Carter Phillips. Why had Trent Tucker been so eager to get her away from him that night in Chicago? Sarah was convinced that this was not just another case of corruption in Washington.

Later that day, Sarah drove up Torrey Pines Road between the ocean and the tree-covered campus of U.C.S.D., which sprawled across the scenic hills of La Jolla. As Scully had directed, she turned into a parking lot between Muir and Thurgood Marshall Colleges, took a faculty space at the back, and walked uphill through a grove of eucalyptus trees to a long gray building. She took an elevator to the third floor, found the office number, and knocked on the door. Scully opened it.

Although she hadn't seen him in months,

he looked comfortably familiar in a checked flannel shirt and corduroy pants. His hair was longer and his beard needed a trim. A large window behind him distracted Sarah at first with its view of the ocean in the distance. Then she saw the other man rising from his seat at a table across the room.

He appeared to be much younger than Scully, although he turned out to be almost the same age. He was tall and fit-looking, with short-cropped hair and a deep tan. Sarah correctly guessed he was a veteran of one of the military service's special forces.

"Hi, I'm Andy Foster."

As Foster extended his hand, Scully mumbled an apology for not introducing him.

"I met Andy when I worked on the Hill and he was thinking about becoming a whistle-blower," he explained as they sat down around the table. "Then he decided it would be healthier to get out of the country."

"Everything's cheaper in Mexico, even in a place like La Paz," Foster said. "I can afford to live well and be protected there. We have a house with a great view and lots of American friends. They think my security guys are servants and drivers, just like theirs."

"Andy was the chief financial officer for Smith and Hawley, a Pentagon contractor that Palisar bought in the late nineties," Scully said. "He was recruited from the Special Forces in the Army and moved up pretty fast."

"What did you do in the Green Berets?" Sarah asked Foster, who still had the steely-eyed look of a commando.

"I still can't say much about it, but I made lieutenant colonel in the first Persian Gulf War. I commanded an Operational Detachment Charlie — about the size of a regular Army battalion — in the Fifth Special Forces Group. What we did was supposed to be secret, although the media reported we were hunting for SCUD missiles Saddam had hidden in the desert. It was hard on my home life, even without children, so I decided to get out after the war. I was offered a good job by some S.F. vets who worked for Smith and Hawley."

"Because you could help them get Pentagon contracts?"

Sarah wanted to take Foster's measure.

"At first, that was all right with me," he said straightforwardly. "Before Palisar bought it, Smith and Hawley had a good reputation providing the Army with logistics for overseas deployments. With the military stretched so thin, the Pentagon had to out-source things like camp construction, trans-portation, food service, communications, even security and intelligence. I was work-ing with people I knew in the Army. It felt like I was still serving my country.

"But I have to admit, by the time I became number two in the company, I was also motivated by money. You don't get six-figure bonuses in the Army."

Sarah was impressed by what seemed to be candor.

"Did you know Carter Phillips?" she asked.

Foster appeared to flinch at Phillips's name.

"I knew he had been a commanding general in S.F. I only met him once, when he visited Smith and Hawley for some ceremonial occasion. But I had heard about him. He scared people. We dealt mostly with his subordinates at Palisar. We had to hit their profit targets or else."

"Tell her what happened, Andy," Scully prodded.

"It was during the war in Iraq, when the Pentagon got all that money for the occupa-tion and reconstruction. I noticed we were getting a much bigger share of the contracts for base services, supply, and security. Nothing like Halliburton, of course, but big for us. Things that didn't add up. I started staying late to go through the records. I found what looked like a ghost company."

"What do you mean?"

Sarah could have guessed. But it was usually more productive to ask what might sound like uninformed questions.

"Contracts with different terms than the ones I'd seen. No-bid contracts for things I thought had been competitively bid. Excessive markups over what subcontractors and suppliers were charging us. Subcontractors whose names I didn't know. Payments to them that looked way too high."

"What did you do?"

"I copied it all on computer disks and took them home. And I questioned employees I thought I could trust. They told me about unexplained payments that had been sent to people and places in Washington that I didn't know about. They said the C.E.O. ordered the payments and instructed them not to tell anyone."

"So you couldn't go to him."

"I went to Baghdad instead, just before it got really dangerous. I wasn't surprised to find that cash had been spread around to get things done and keep our people safe. But I found that a lot more money had been skimmed off in kickbacks to us and our subcontractors.

"By the time I got back to the office, the C.E.O. had figured out what I was up to. Somebody had ratted me out. I was naïve. I should have realized Palisar had the company wired, including the C.E.O."

"He fired you?"

"He offered me a skimpy separation agreement," Foster said, slumping in his chair. "If I didn't take it and leave quietly, he said they'd sue and get the government to prosecute me for contract fraud."

"But you were the one exposing the fraud," said Sarah.

"He told me that I didn't know what I was up against. Palisar's people could manufacture records and witnesses to prove anything they wanted. They had friends in government. I'd be helpless."

"What about your own records?"

"They couldn't save my job," Foster said. "But I thought someone else might use them to expose what was going on. So I nosed around on the Hill and found Pat."

"I was excited," Scully said to Sarah. "I figured I finally had Palisar red-handed. But a senior member of the committee pressured the chief counsel to stop me from going further. By the time I moved to another committee, it had become too hot for Andy."

"What do you mean?" Sarah asked.

"They were spying on me," Foster said. "I've been in covert ops myself, so I knew they were following me and tapping my phone. The last straw was when they searched my house. I had trip-wired my file drawers and silent-alarmed my computers. Fortunately, they couldn't find anything because I had given it all to Pat."

"Was that the end of it?"

"I had gone to a lawyer who filed suit to get a better separation agreement," Foster told Sarah. "But I was worried about what they might do next. I had heard about people who crossed them disappearing. And there were rumors about Palisar companies being mixed up in some rough stuff with the military that nobody wanted to talk about. They might have thought I was getting too close to that."

"What do you mean, some rough stuff with the military?" Sarah asked.

Foster shot Scully a look that told Sarah he had made a mistake.

"I never found out," he said quickly.

"First I've heard of it," Scully added. "Nothing about Palisar would surprise me."

Sarah could tell that he and Foster were hiding something important. But if she pursued it now, it might interfere with what they were ready to tell her.

"I told them I was moving out of the country," Foster continued. "I offered to drop the suit if they paid me some more money, which they did. I'm ashamed about it, and I've been trying to figure out how to make it right ever since."

"I kept everything he gave me," Scully said. "But I promised Andy I wouldn't do anything until he was ready."

"When Pat told me he was working with you," Foster said to Sarah, "I decided to help."

"You'll have to take us through this slowly," Scully told Foster. "We'll look at your records and see what else we can find on the Web. It'll probably take a few days."

"I've got nothing but time," Foster said.

"Are you ready to go on the record?" Sarah asked him.

"You mean I'd be quoted by name?"

"That would make the story more powerful. The fact that you had to leave the country and everything. But we wouldn't say where you went."

"Why don't I start by just telling you what I know," Foster said. "We can decide later about using my name or quoting me."

"It's a deal," she said quickly. Foster

seemed to be the genuine article. "I'll probably need to file Freedom of Information Act requests, but I'll keep your name out of it."

"Good," Foster said, sitting at attention. "Let's get started. I've waited a long time."

18

"Did you see Martin Sheen?"

"I didn't realize he was so short."

"Why's he still coming to these things? Does he think he really was president?"

"I saw Catherine Zeta-Jones and Michael Douglas at the *Newsweek* reception. She looks even better in person."

Sarah overheard snatches of starstruck conversation as she navigated the clogged streams of tuxedos and evening gowns in the narrow spaces between tables in the Washington Hilton ballroom. She was heading for her newspaper's table up front, facing the head table, where President Capehart would be sitting at the first White House Correspondents' Association dinner since his inauguration three months earlier. Feeling a hand on her bare shoulder, Sarah turned and saw Mark.

"Is this your first time?" he asked, noticing she was wearing that black dress again.

"Kind of amazing, no?"

"Really," Sarah said. "What's the deal?"

"Mutual admiration is the nicest way I can put it. Washington and Hollywood get off on each other."

For decades, White House reporters had invited government officials and politicians to their annual dinner. The star of the evening was the president, who usually entertained them with an amusing speech. But, beginning in the Clinton years, the president had been sharing the spotlight with movie and television celebrities invited by an increasing number of news organizations in an escalating competition for the hottest stars. The show-business guests were attracted to power on the Potomac, just as their hosts had been seduced by the glamour of Hollywood. Actors played politicians and journalists in movies and television shows, while journalists and politicians had become media personalities.

"So why do you come?" Sarah asked Mark. She felt his hand back on her shoulder as they pushed through the crush of people.

"It's still good for cultivating sources, if you invite them instead of celebrities," he said. "I asked Trent Tucker to come tonight. I hope that doesn't bother you."

"Not at all," she said. "That's why I came."

Tucker was already standing near the newspaper's table, one hand in a pocket of the black velvet vest he wore under his tuxedo jacket, holding court for a steady stream of supplicants, both journalists and politicians. He made a point of turning away from them when Mark and Sarah approached.

"Hello, my dear," he said, grinning and taking Sarah's hand in both of his. "You look most attractive this evening. I believe I remember that lovely dress from Chicago."

"You have a good memory, Trent. You chased me away as soon as you saw me there that night."

Sarah studied Tucker as he greeted Mark. A few years had passed since she first met him in Maryland, but he had the same pot belly, craggy face, and lopsided, leering grin. What had she seen in him then? Was it the Southern charm that now appeared so affected? Or what had seemed then to be a wicked sense of humor? Or his notoriety as a quick-trigger political gunslinger?

"Didn't I apologize for that?" Tucker asked Sarah with mock indignation when he turned back toward her.

"Was Carter Phillips the reason you had

to get me out of there?"

"Oh, he didn't matter," Tucker lied unconvincingly, his smile gone. "That event was closed to the press, which was the way our guests wanted it. I don't like to offend people who give us money."

"Well, I was hoping you'd sit next to me tonight so we could chat," Sarah said, trying to be charming herself.

"Always a pleasure, my dear."

Mark was clearly surprised by Tucker's familiarity with Sarah, but his attention was diverted as their tablemates were arriving. Alison Winters, now the vice president's press secretary, walked up with Ron Jones, to whom Mark had introduced her at a reception before the dinner. Lou Runyan and the *Capital*'s Justice Department reporter escorted the new attorney general, who had been chairman of Capehart's presidential campaign.

"I figured you'd lose interest in me again, now that the election's over," Tucker said to Sarah after they sat down.

"You're even more important now."

"I just do what I can to help the president."

"And your clients?"

"The president is my only client. I'm not running my business now. And I'm staying away from anything that might affect its clients."

Sarah didn't believe that either.

"Including Palisar?" she asked.

Tucker finished his last mouthful of salad before answering.

"I've never done much for it," he said, not mentioning the numerous Palisar-owned companies he represented. He figured Sarah would have checked his lobbyist registration forms.

When the main course of filet mignon and lobster was served, Sarah chatted with Tucker about his daily routine in the White House.

"How's that big house of yours?" she eventually asked.

"I don't do much more than sleep there. I haven't had a social life worth mentioning since I started with Capehart before the primaries. How about you?"

"Pretty much the same."

"Now that's a real shame. A waste of beauty and brains."

"Speaking of your house," Sarah said, "do you remember that hit-and-run accident on Chain Bridge Road last year? The congressional aide who was run over and killed?"

"It was at the other end of the road," Tucker said. "I didn't know about it until I saw a story in the paper."

"The police don't think it was an accident. The reporter covering it is a friend of mine."

She leaned over and spoke so quietly that only Tucker could hear. From across the table, Mark wondered what was going on.

"The cops told her that someone apparently lured the guy over there," Sarah said. "A couple of months ago, they found the SUV that hit him. A new black Ford Expedition. Bought with cash. It was abandoned and stripped before the police found it. They aren't giving us much more, so it hasn't been in the paper yet."

Tucker listened intently.

"The victim was some kind of investigator on the Hill," Sarah said. "We don't know if that had anything to do with his getting killed, but we're looking into it."

"You're working on it, too?"

"On the Capitol Hill angle."

She figured she had her fish on her line. But just then, the Marine Corps Band struck up "Hail to the Chief."

"Ladies and gentlemen," a voice announced, "the president of the United States and First Lady Milly Capehart."

Everyone rose and applauded as the Capeharts emerged from behind a heavy blue curtain and took their seats at the head table. Sarah noticed the vice president standing at the head table to applaud the president. Susan Cameron looked as beautiful in her long, fitted gown as any of the Hollywood stars.

When he got up to speak, Monroe Capehart made light of both his age and how deliberately he had been moving on his administration's agenda. He retold a joke from a White House Correspondents' dinner sixteen years earlier about the elder President Harrison, who had died on his thirty-second day in office in 1841.

"As Bill Clinton said when he spoke here at the beginning of his presidency," Capehart told his audience, "I'm not doing so bad. At this point in his administration, William Henry Harrison had been dead for sixty-eight days."

Then, departing from tradition, he started speaking seriously.

"We Americans are a people in a hurry, impatient with nagging problems that stand in our way," Capehart said. "But we need to take the time, beyond the honeymoon period that the press and Congress usually give a new president, to find better ways to solve those problems. On behalf of the American people, I ask you tonight to give me that time."

"The President sounds very sincere," Sarah said to Tucker after Capehart finished and was ushered out of the ballroom with the First Lady.

"He's a good man. He's going to be a great president," Tucker responded, getting up from the table. "I hate to leave you, my dear. But I've got to hurry to make the motorcade."

The president was in a good mood when he and Milly returned to the White House. "I think I got my point across," he told her as their limousine drove up the South Drive.

When they went inside, instead of taking the elevator, as Secret Service procedures normally dictated, they walked up the grand ceremonial staircase to the second floor. As had become their habit before turning in, they strolled alone, hand-in-hand, through the wide, furnished "sitting halls" that ran the length of the second floor, past its most historic rooms.

Like tourists, they looked into the pink Queen's Bedroom, where at least five European queens had slept in its nineteenth-century four-poster bed. Winston Churchill had stayed there for several weeks while consulting with President Franklin D. Roosevelt during the darkest days of World War II.

They sat for a moment in the Lincoln Bedroom, which had actually been Lincoln's office. The nine-by-six-foot bed had been bought by Mary Todd Lincoln, but it was never used by her husband. Before leaving the room, a favorite of White House guests, the Capeharts looked once again at Lincoln's handwritten copy of the Gettysburg Address.

They went next to the Treaty Room, which had also been used as a presidential office. They walked through the Yellow Oval reception room, where presidents met privately with official guests, and out onto the Truman Balcony. They stood with their arms around each other in the cool night air, gazing out at the floodlit South Lawn.

"I still can't believe this is where we live," Milly told her husband.

Coming back inside, they walked through the last sitting hall, filled with fine furniture and priceless paintings, which served as their living room. That brought them to their own bedroom, where so many presidential couples had slept. Shortly after notifying the usher on duty that they were turning in, the Capeharts were asleep in their bed.

Hours later, in the middle of the night, the president got up to go to the bathroom. Half asleep and not wanting to disturb Milly, he felt his way through the dark. He was still groggy when he had finished and turned to leave the bathroom.

Suddenly, his legs froze.

Oh, that again, he thought vaguely. I'll have to tell the doc about it.

As he tried to move, his momentum carried his upper body beyond his immobile lower limbs. He lost his balance and started falling forward, as though in a dream. Not fully realizing what was happening to him, he didn't reach out his arms to break his fall. As he crashed to the tile floor, his head hit the side of the porcelain bathtub, smashing his brain against the inside of his skull.

Neither his wife nor the Secret Service officer stationed across the hall heard him fall. Perhaps nothing could have been done to save him if they had. But the bizarre reality was that the president of the United States, one of the most closely attended and tightly protected people in the world, was left alone to die.

Milly slept soundly until nearly five in the morning, when she realized that her husband was not in bed beside her. Not hearing any answer to her quiet calls for him in the dark, she turned on the light and got out of bed. When she found him on the bathroom floor, his head lying in a pool of blood, she screamed hysterically for help.

Suddenly the residence was filled with Secret Service agents, military officers, and medics. Orders were shouted and the president was put onto a stretcher and carried downstairs.

He still had a faint pulse when he was taken out of the White House by the medics and, attended by a doctor in the ambulance, rushed eight blocks to George Washington University Hospital in the middle of a makeshift motorcade of black Secret Service battlewagon SUVs and the presidential limousine, with Milly inside. The hospital's emergency room was cleared of other patients and sealed off by the Secret Service. Doctors and nurses worked on him frantically.

But it was too late. President Monroe Arthur Capehart was pronounced dead in the emergency room shortly after dawn.

Within an hour, Susan Cameron was sworn in as the forty-fifth president of the United States in a parlor of the vice president's house on the Naval Observatory grounds. She had been awakened by the Secret

Service when Monroe Capehart was rushed to the hospital. And she was notified immediately when he died.

Susan had put on a simple black dress and summoned Alison Winters and Elliott Bancroft to join her at the vice presidential residence. The chief justice was driven there with a police escort from his home in suburban Maryland. Minutes after arriving, he administered the oath of office. As Elliott stood nearby, Alison held out a Bible she had found on a bookshelf in the parlor. Susan put her left hand on it and raised her right hand and solemnly swore that she would uphold the Constitution of the United States of America.

Several Secret Service agents and the members of a small news-media pool, alerted by the White House, were the only other witnesses to the passing of power. The video record made by the press pool's television cameraman would be broadcast around the world on every television network and countless Web sites for days.

In the blink of an eye in historical time, Susan Cameron had gone from Washington wife to U.S. senator to vice president to president of the United States.

While the chief justice was being driven

back home, the newsroom of the *Washington Capital* was filling with journalists who rushed in from their homes on a Sunday morning. Amid what looked like uncontrolled chaos, they quickly organized to cover the story. Mark, who had gone straight from his new apartment to the press room in the West Wing of the White House, wrote one version of the story after another, first for the Web site, then for a rare afternoon "Extra," and, finally, for Monday morning's edition of the newspaper.

By Mark Daniels

Monroe Capehart, the 44th president of the United States, died suddenly today of massive head injuries suffered in an early morning fall in the family quarters of the White House. The 70-year-old president was pronounced dead at 6:22 a.m. at George Washington University Hospital.

Vice President Susan Cameron, 43, was sworn in as the 45th president by the Chief Justice of the United States at 7:20 a.m. in the vice president's residence on the grounds of the Naval Observatory.

Monroe Capehart was the ninth president to die in office. His administration lasted less than 100 days.

19

"Good afternoon, ladies and gentlemen," Susan said from behind the lectern in the White House press briefing room. "Thank you for coming — and for your patience during these difficult days."

The new president had last been seen speaking at Monroe Capehart's funeral in Washington's National Cathedral. It was Elliott Bancroft's idea that she next appear talking to reporters at a midday briefing, rather than a formal, prime-time press conference in the East Room of the White House.

"It is time to move ahead with the domestic agenda of our administration," Susan told them. "I'm removing all federal restrictions on family-planning assistance and a woman's right to choose. To the extent that I can through executive orders, I will require federal programs and regulations to treat people joined in civil unions in the same manner as married spouses.

"I will step up enforcement of anti-discrimination laws," she continued, looking down at handwritten notes, "and I will take action to increase the participation of minority firms in federal contracts. On the environment, I will strictly enforce the clean air and water acts and limit destructive logging, mining, and oil drilling on public lands."

"Madam President, have you consulted with Congress about all this?" asked the Associated Press reporter in the front row.

"No," Susan said with a firmness that seemed to signal a new approach. "I'll be meeting with congressional leaders later today. I want them to work with me on Social Security and Medicare."

"What happened to the 'new era of cooperation in the national interest' that President Capehart promised in his inaugural address?" Mark asked when she called on him.

"I'm only doing what he and I promised during the campaign," Susan answered. "It's what the voters elected us to do."

"Madam President, what have you decided about a vice president?"

"That's a perfectly reasonable question, Ms. . . ."

Susan looked down at the seating chart to find the name of the White House correspondent of the *New York Herald*.

"Ms. Sterling," she said. "With all due

respect to Speaker Ames, we need to select a new vice president soon. We've just witnessed the importance of an orderly transition of power. I've asked my chief of staff, Elliott Bancroft, to lead the search and make a recommendation as soon as possible.

"You all know Elliott, don't you," she added, gesturing to where he was standing alongside Alison near the doorway behind her. Taken by surprise, he tried to replace the look of irritation on his face with a modest smile.

After the press conference, Alison and Elliott walked with Susan back into the West Wing, past the office Alison now occupied as press secretary and down the hall. When they reached the Oval Office, the afternoon sunlight was streaming in through its tall windows. The three of them stood wordlessly for a few moments in front of the president's massive oak desk, an 1880 gift from Queen Victoria made from the timbers of H.M.S. *Resolute,* a wrecked English sailing ship recovered by American whalers in the Arctic and returned to the queen. The front of the desk, the ceiling above them, and the carpet on which they were standing all bore the seal of the president of the United States.

"Well," Susan finally asked, "how did it go?"

"You certainly made news," Alison said.

"I didn't know you were going to do all that today," Elliott complained. Without warning him, Susan had announced policy initiatives that Elliott hadn't staffed out or run by congressional leaders.

"We have to move quickly," Susan told him. "I don't know how long we'll stay this high in the polls."

Although she hadn't thought twice about making Elliott her chief of staff, Susan didn't always depend on his advice. She continued to consult Michael, but she mostly trusted her own instincts. She was determined to be more than a caretaker president.

"I'd better get back," Alison said, sensing the tension between them. "I'm going to have a desk full of callbacks."

Catching herself as she turned to leave, she added, "Thank you, Madam President."

"We're still getting used to that," Elliott told Susan, fully conscious of the double meaning, as he followed Alison out the door. "Thank you, Madam President."

Susan was still getting used to it, too. Looking around the Oval Office, she noticed a bowl filled with small candy boxes bearing the presidential seal. She remembered slipping some into her purse when she first visited the White House as a senator's wife. Now she could dispense an endless supply of presidential pins, cuff links and tie clips, autographed photos, seats in the presidential boxes at the Kennedy Center, rides on Air Force One, even tennis games on the South Lawn court. Not to mention highways and bridges, water projects, and national parks, so long as Congress went along.

Then Susan thought about the ever-present military officer carrying the "football," a briefcase with codes and secure satellite communications for ordering a nuclear attack. She knew he would be just outside her office, a sobering reminder that she was indeed the president of the United States — POTUS, in the bureaucratic jargon of the White House.

Sitting down behind the Resolute Desk, she went back to work.

In luminescent green letters, the electronic locator box in the Secret Service command post flashed: POTUS–Oval Office.

That evening, Elliott walked across Pennsylvania Avenue from the White House to Lafayette Square in the spring twilight. He strolled through the square along one of its semicircular walks, savoring the trees' fresh green leaves and the beds of red tulips in full bloom, before crossing H Street to the historic Hay-Adams hotel. He went in through its small, formal lobby and down the back stairs to the Off the Record lounge.

Trent Tucker was waiting for him in a red velvet–lined alcove hidden behind the bar. Its walls were filled with framed black-and-white caricatures of famous politicians.

"You may want to stop phoning me from the White House," Tucker told Elliott as he sat down. "They keep logs of all your calls."

"Even though Susan tossed you out, you're not exactly persona non grata," Elliott said. "How are you doing?"

"I'm fine. I don't have to be inside to get things done. Our people are already in place."

"She's moving awfully fast."

Elliott knew he wasn't controlling the flow of business in the White House the way Tucker had.

"It plays well with the party's base," Tucker told him. "And it won't get in our way."

Tucker took a drink of Scotch. He was hiding from Elliott how he really felt. He had had just enough time in the White House to put people into the administration who could help him get what Carter Phillips wanted. But he was no longer in charge. And he had been unable to start what he had waited years to work on himself, the big issues facing the country, rather than just what his clients wanted. Susan Cameron would now be doing that without him.

"What about Stetson?" Elliott asked.

"As a senator, he'll sail through confirmation. And we've taken good care of him."

"I guess he'd match up with Susan the same way Capehart did — experienced, mature, strong on defense," Elliott said. "Can she trust him?"

"He doesn't want to be president. He's too old." Tucker gulped down the rest of his Scotch and studied Elliott's face for a moment. "Are you going soft on her?"

Elliott laughed out loud. "You're going to have to get used to a little ambiguity," he said, getting up to leave. "Susan and I have a country to run now."

"What's the hurry?"

"I've got to get ready for tomorrow morning's staff meeting. You know what that's like."

"Not anymore."

Elliott thought he noticed an uncharacteristic vulnerability.

"I left you on the WAVES list, in case you

want to visit," he told Tucker, referring to the roster of people regularly allowed into the White House without a prior background check. "Of course," he added in an attempt at witty irony, "they keep a log for that, too."

A half hour later, it was dark but still balmy outside when Tucker found his way to the door that led directly up a flight of steps to the sidewalk. He peered wistfully across Lafayette Square at the brightly lit White House before turning up Sixteenth Street. Suddenly, he remembered something. He stepped into the street and hailed a taxi, telling the driver to take him across the Potomac River to an address in suburban Arlington.

When he arrived at the stately house, enclosed by a high brick wall, Tucker was pleased that he could still remember the numbered entrance codes for the gate and the front door. The evening's activities had not yet gotten under way, so he had time to sit outside on the pool deck and sober up a little. When it began to fill with noisy, naked men and women, he went back inside, hung his own clothes in the big walk-in closet and headed upstairs to a room where there would be people who shared his particular tastes in sexual gratification.

He knew he might be recognized by some of the other visitors. But granting complete anonymity to any guest who wanted it was one of the most strictly enforced rules of the house. Exposure of any one of them could lead to mutually assured destruction.

After the first-edition deadline in the newsroom, Mark and Sarah drifted into Ron Jones's office.

"It looks like Cameron's going to be moving a lot faster than Capehart," Mark said to Jones. "I wonder how that's going to affect her numbers."

"The voters knew they were getting her, too," Jones said, "even if they didn't expect her to become president now."

"That's our fault," said Sarah, poised on the arm of an old leather chair. "We didn't tell them Capehart had Parkinson's."

"We didn't get the story," Mark said curtly as he flopped down on the couch. Sarah's moral dilemmas continued to get on his nerves. "We tried, but we couldn't nail it down."

"Well, your friend knew about it."

"Look," Mark responded even more sharply. "She didn't really know. She only saw symptoms. And, anyway, she isn't that kind of friend anymore."

"Oh," Sarah said. She wondered what had happened.

"Listen, that buck stops with Lou and me," Jones said. "We called you off. Now we've got Cameron. Let's see what she does."

"Can I get back to my project?" Sarah asked. She had been helping out on coverage of the White House transition ever since Capehart's death, and it felt like she was losing momentum on Palisar. She wanted to check out what Andy Foster had told her.

"Sure," Jones said. "And let's have that lunch so you can tell me more about it."

Sarah bolted from his office.

"Don't ask," Jones said to Mark. "You've got enough on your hands. Susan Cameron is the best story you'll ever have."

When Mark returned to his desk, he was surprised to find Sarah waiting for him.

"I'm really sorry," she said. "I never should have said that about your friend, or whatever she is. And I heard that you and your wife split up. What are you going to do?"

Mark considered telling Sarah to mind her own business. But he had kept so much bottled up that he gave in to the opportunity to talk to someone about it.

"I've got an apartment a few minutes from

the house," he said. "And it wasn't far from where Jeanne lived. She was a travel agent who did advance for Capehart."

"Past tense? Where'd she go?"

Mark eased himself onto the edge of his desk. "She's gone off to Italy for a while. Her sister's running their travel business."

"She just left?"

"She took Capehart's death really hard. She'd gotten close to him. And he died not long after she and I had sort of broken up. She wasn't happy that I left my family. I should have talked to her about it first."

"I guess so," Sarah told him. "Men take women so much for granted that you never realize how much it pisses us off until it's too late."

"It's been a long time since I've lived alone," Mark said.

"It's not so bad once you decide to make the best of it," Sarah heard herself say. "Maybe we could get something to eat one night when we're both here late."

"Sure," Mark said carelessly, looking up at the clock. "That reminds me. I'm being interviewed about Cameron on CNN tonight. I'll see you later."

His perfunctory response left Sarah deflated. Why did she say that to him anyway? Was it because he now seemed lonely, too?

■ ■ ■ ■

A dozen blocks away, Susan Cameron was herself alone in the family quarters of the White House. She was one of the relatively few presidents to live there without a spouse for any period of time — she had asked one of the ushers. Thomas Jefferson, Andrew Jackson, Martin Van Buren, and Chester Alan Arthur were widowers before moving into the White House. John Tyler and Woodrow Wilson were widowed in office but later remarried while they still lived there. James Buchanan was a lifelong bachelor. And Grover Cleveland lived alone in the White House for a year before being married there.

Plenty of people were still around in the evening in the 132-room mansion: ushers, housekeepers, telephone operators, Secret Service agents, military personnel running everything from the Communications Office on the first floor to the Senior Staff Mess in the basement, and everyone working late in the West Wing. But Susan had made clear to the staff when she moved in that she would take care of herself outside working hours whenever possible. She sent the cook and housekeeper home when she was in the family quarters at night.

Somehow, being surrounded by staff made her feel even more isolated than when she was alone. She had been happy enough as the only child of university professors who doted on their daughter but often left her in the care of a nanny. And she had managed as the wife of a businessman and politician who was away more than he was home. As president of the United States, she had legions of people attending to her from the time she awoke each morning. But there was no one in the White House with whom she could share her most intimate thoughts and feelings, much less her life and bed.

On this evening, dressed in gray sweats, she made lamb chops in the little kitchen just off the dining room on the second floor. Afterward, she went upstairs to what already had become her favorite retreat, the third-floor solarium.

Ever since Mrs. Coolidge had christened it "the sky parlor," the octagonal aerie atop the South Portico had been beloved by White House women, all of them First Ladies before Susan. Its comfortable couches and chairs faced three adjoining walls of glass that afforded a spectacular view over the South Lawn to the Washington Monument, the Jefferson Memorial, and the

Potomac River. The memorials were illuminated at night, and a red aircraft-warning lamp blinked dependably at the top of the Washington Monument.

Susan stretched out on an overstuffed couch and sampled the cable news shows to see how they were portraying her day. She worked on papers she had brought from the Oval Office. And she tried to read more of Gore Vidal's *Lincoln,* which vividly brought to life the White House during the Civil War. But she couldn't concentrate.

Finally, Susan used her cell phone to call Michael in Los Angeles. She had told White House operators that she would dial her own personal calls, but she avoided the switchboard altogether when phoning Michael.

"You were great with the press," he told Susan. "I like the agenda and I like the energy."

"Elliott's worried I'm doing too much too soon. And the leadership was grumpy. Ames was particularly cool."

"Better put the Secret Service on high alert until you have a vice president."

"That's not funny," Susan said, curling up on the couch. "But Elliott will have names for me soon."

"You're not letting this guy do your job,

are you?"

"I had no one else to run the search for me. Otherwise, I pay as much attention to him as I do to you. I'm doing it my way."

"That's my girl."

"Not anymore, Michael," Susan said, gazing out at the monuments. "Just think. If you hadn't fucked everything up, you might have been here with me. You'd be president and I'd be First Lady."

"Watch your language on the phone, darling. Remember what happened to Nixon."

"It's my cell."

"The spooks are probably listening anyway. It's easier than on landlines. Better say good night, Gracie. I've got to give another speech. Defense contractors for a hundred grand. Can you believe it?"

"I'd believe anything about you."

"Do you really wish I was there?"

"Sometimes," Susan answered. "But not as president. I'm starting to like the job. And I don't know whether people are ready for a First Husband."

"Are you thinking about a second husband?"

"I'm too busy."

"I'm always here when you need me."

"You mean to talk to? That's all I want

right now."

"I don't believe that," Michael told her. "But you're the boss now. And I've got to go."

Susan made her way downstairs, taking Gore Vidal with her to bed. And he quickly put her to sleep.

20

At the sound of gunfire, the convoy of dust-covered Chevy Suburbans and Jeep Cherokees clattered to a stop, bumper against bumper, on the cratered dirt road. The mostly middle-aged men who had been riding inside the four vehicles jumped out and took cover behind them. They aimed their automatic rifles at the plywood façades of buildings by the side of the road and started shooting back at their attackers.

"I know they don't look like much," Derek Stevens shouted at Sarah over the din of gunfire. "They're all retired military. They'll shape up."

From Sarah's perch alongside Stevens on a wooden observation deck across the road, the training exercise looked like a scene in a low-budget action movie. The paunchy good guys, dressed in mismatched fatigues and baseball caps, were the trainees. The fitter-looking bad guys, who wore khaki Falcon Services uniforms, were the instructors. Darting out from behind the fake buildings, the instructors suddenly stormed the vehicles from several directions, easily overwhelming the trainees.

"Good thing they were firing blanks," Stevens said, shaking his head. A compact man with short-cropped, graying hair, he stood ramrod straight in neatly pressed pants and his own uniform shirt, imprinted with FALCON SERVICES on the back and C.E.O. on the left breast pocket.

"We've got it all on tape," he said to Sarah, pointing to instructors standing near them with video cameras. "We'll go back to the classroom and work on their mistakes."

The two of them climbed into Stevens's Cadillac Escalade for a short ride through the woods. The exercise had been taking place in a remote corner of the Fort A. P. Hill military reservation in the northeastern Virginia countryside. The instructors' vans and the trainees' convoy followed behind.

"It looks peaceful right now with all the trees and little streams," Stevens said, gesturing at the bucolic spring scene through the windshield. "But when the military's got a big exercise going, it's full of smoke, especially if they're using heavy artillery. All the services come here for specialized training — hand-to-hand combat, urban warfare, cross-country infantry assaults, even aerial landings, you name it."

"Special Forces, too?"

"Yeah. I was here a couple of times. That's why I came when Falcon got this contract."

"Wasn't Falcon one of Smith and Hawley's subcontractors on Pentagon contracts in Iraq?"

"Yes, ma'am." Stevens knew Sarah wasn't just making conversation. "I worked for Smith and Hawley after I left the military. They hired a lot of S.F. guys when the Pentagon began outsourcing things like supply and security for overseas deployments. I trained a lot of the security people."

"Was that before Palisar bought Smith and Hawley?"

"Yes, ma'am. Palisar took it over after 9/11, when the Pentagon stepped up its spending in Afghanistan and Iraq. I figured it was time to go into business for myself. So I started Falcon to provide security for Smith and Hawley and other big contractors. Later, I added things like interrogation, but most of that's classified. We lost some guys in Iraq," Stevens added matter-of-factly, "but we mostly stayed out of trouble. We train well."

"Is that why you stopped subcontracting for Smith and Hawley? Because you wanted to stay out of trouble?"

"You know," Stevens said, "when you came to see me in Crystal City, I didn't think you really wanted to watch us play soldier."

"I'm looking into Smith and Hawley," Sarah said, not yet sure how much to tell him. "And I thought we'd be able to talk more freely if we got away from your office."

Andy Foster had told Sarah that Falcon Services appeared to be clean. She found nothing to contradict that in the records she got from Foster or with Freedom of Information Act requests from the government. She had met Stevens at his company's headquarters in Crystal City, a cluster of office buildings filled with defense contractors near the Pentagon and Reagan National Airport just across the Potomac in Virginia. And he had driven her down Interstate 95 to Fort A. P. Hill.

"You don't really need to see the after-action stuff," Stevens said to Sarah as they approached an Army classroom building on the base. "Why don't we start back to Washington, and I'll tell you what I know. Nobody can overhear us in the car. I get it

266

swept regularly."

Was that a normal precaution in his business, Sarah wondered, or was Stevens concerned about someone in particular overhearing his conversations?

As the Escalade sped down a country road leading to the highway, he said, "Smith and Hawley's been gaming the system. It's wrong, and it's unfair to the rest of us."

"How?" Sarah asked, taking a notebook and pen out of her purse. To get the most out of him, she didn't want to let on how much she knew.

"They got no-bid contracts. The worst are the LOGCAPs."

"What are those?" Sarah asked, although Andy Foster had already told her about them.

"Long-term logistical-support contracts," Stevens said. "It stands for 'logistics civil augmentation program.' They're open-ended. Smith and Hawley got a huge one for Iraq and Kuwait. The government reimbursed all their costs for overhead, in addition to the supplies and services they provided the military. On top of that, they got a fat fee. The Pentagon didn't have enough people to audit them, so Smith and Hawley did its own performance evaluations. That left the door open for unchecked cost overruns and expense padding. At best, it was corporate welfare. At worst, it was fraud."

Sarah took notes rapidly, trying not to betray her excitement. Andy Foster had been a gift from Pat Scully. But Stevens was hers.

"When we were shut out of Iraq," he went on, "I had to subcontract with Smith and Hawley for security work they couldn't do themselves. I had to accept their terms. And I had to pay kickbacks."

"What do you mean?" Sarah asked as calmly as she could. This could be pay dirt, she thought, confirmation of what Foster had first told her.

"We were instructed to write checks every month to strange-sounding places in Washington. We had to write 'for services rendered' on the checks, even though nobody rendered us any services."

"Was 1776 Pennsylvania Avenue one of the addresses?" Sarah asked.

"Yeah, a couple of places there, different suites," Stevens said. "I don't recall the names, but that address is easy to remember. How'd you know?"

"I've got a source who used to work for Smith and Hawley." She thought there was no harm in revealing that much to him. "I went through some of their old records and saw payments sent to that address. Can I look at your records?"

"Okay," Stevens said. "But you can't tell anybody."

"I thought you weren't working with Smith and Hawley anymore."

"I'm not. I'm contracting directly with the Pentagon now. But they could still make trouble. Do you know Carter Phillips? He runs Palisar International, which owns Smith and Hawley."

Sarah smiled and nodded.

"Then you know he's well-connected," Stevens told her. "He probably rigged things for Smith and Hawley. And I hear he keeps score. I don't want him as an enemy."

That afternoon, Elliott Bancroft went to see Susan Cameron in the Oval Office.

"Madam President," he said, standing in front of her desk, "I'm ready to give you a recommendation for vice president. We've consulted extensively here and on the Hill."

"Come on, Elliott," Susan said in the familiar way she often spoke to him. "Out with it."

"Sam Stetson."

"Are you serious? He's old. He's to the right of me on almost everything except entitlements. And he hasn't done anything in the Senate for years."

"Exactly," Elliott said, leaning forward and putting his hands on the edge of her desk. "He'll never be your rival. He'll balance the ticket next time out. And confirmation's a certainty."

"No nasty surprises?"

"I'll show you the background stuff. He's been on Armed Services for years and has every security clearance you can get. I can arrange for you to interview him."

"Let me see it all, and I'll think about it."

"Thank you, Madam President," Elliott said, backing away from the desk.

"Elliott," Susan called after him. "Thanks for this."

"Thank you again, Madam President."

When Sarah returned to the newsroom, she found an e-mail from one of Pat Scully's coded addresses: "get in touch . . . pronto"

"What's up?" she messaged him.

"andy's missing"

"What do you mean?"

"went out for run without security . . . never came home"

"When?"

"couple weeks ago . . . just heard about it . . . called his wife"

"What are the authorities doing?"

"we're talking mexican police"

"That's all you know?"

"wife blames me . . . didn't want him meeting us in la jolla"

What about me? Sarah thought. Did I help put someone in danger again? She was almost overcome by the anguished ache deep inside her that she had so frequently felt since Seth Moore's death.

"sarah???"

"What do we do now?" she managed to type.

"we can still use interview transcript and records"

"I know that." Even for Scully, she thought, it seemed cold-blooded, and it jolted her. "I meant about Foster."

"nothing we can do . . . wife won't talk to me anymore"

"Should we contact F.B.I. or State Department?"

"not good idea right now"

"Why? You think Palisar's involved?" Sarah remembered that Foster had said he moved to Mexico because he had heard about people who had defied Palisar disappearing. Scully himself had left Washington because of Palisar. And they both thought

Palisar had something to do with Moore's death.

"good working assumption . . . means more extensive surveillance . . . bigger threat to you and me"

"Me?" Despite everything that had happened Sarah hadn't really thought of being in danger herself.

"they watched you and moore . . . must have watched andy if they snatched him"

"You're scaring me."

"how was a p hill trip"

"Now you're really scaring me. How do you know about that?"

"sources . . ."

This unnerved Sarah. Although Foster had approvingly mentioned Falcon Services in passing during their discussion with Scully, Derek Stevens's name hadn't come up. How did Scully know about her trip into Virginia with him?

She decided to limit what she told Scully about it.

"Another source corroborated what Foster told us."

"good"

Sarah just couldn't leave it there.

"Does this have anything to do with the secret you wouldn't tell Seth or me?"

"just forget that for now . . . best for all of us"

This doesn't feel right, Sarah thought. She would have to reevaluate her relationship with Scully.

"Okay," she told him.

"be careful"

Sarah took that seriously. That night, she found herself looking purposefully around her as she parked in front of her little house in the Palisades. As usual, her housemate, the lawyer, Caroline Long, was not yet home. With their long and erratic work hours, the two women seldom saw each other.

As she picked at the take-out chicken she had warmed up in the microwave, Sarah wondered whom she could talk to about Andy Foster's disappearance and Scully's warning about her own safety. She was still worried that Ron Jones would pull her off the story if he thought she was in danger. Joni Parker would want her to go to the police. And her parents would be no more help than they were after Seth Moore was killed.

For now, at least, she had no one to rely on but herself.

21

It was one of those special late spring mornings in Washington. The air was still fresh, even though the penetrating warmth of the bright sunshine foretold the stagnant heat of summer. Sarah went out of her way to cross leafy Lafayette Square, savoring the contrasts of light and shade. She walked down the pedestrian-only portion of Pennsylvania Avenue in front of the White House, past the ornate Old Executive Office Building and onto the sidewalk in the next block.

She searched without success for a building with the address of 1776 Pennsylvania Avenue until she noticed the MailServices store. She had to walk right up to the door to make out the worn numerals above it. Of course, she thought, mail drops. Just like the ones she and Pat Scully were using.

"Can I help you?" asked the olive-skinned woman behind the counter inside. She spoke with a South Asian accent. On the wall just over her shoulder, Sarah saw a framed photograph and certificate identifying the woman as the store manager.

"I'm looking for Redwing Associates in Suite 720," Sarah said earnestly.

"This is a mail-and-package store," the manager responded curtly. "We don't have any suites here."

"How about Security Services Partners? I think that's Suite 555." Sarah pulled out her notebook and flipped through its pages. "Or American Guardian in Suite 610. Eagle Consultants, Suite 933. Overseas Security Services, Suite 484 —"

"Look, miss," the manager interrupted. "I don't know who you are, but I'm not supposed to discuss our clients."

"I'm a reporter for the *Washington Capital*," Sarah told her. "What you're not supposed to do is allow your customers to refer to their mailboxes as 'suites' to make it look like they have real offices here. If you want, I can call the postal inspectors and talk to them about it. Or you can help me."

"You'll leave me out of your story?"

"I just want to verify which names on my list have mailboxes here. And how long they've had them."

It didn't take long. They all had mailboxes there.

The next address on Sarah's itinerary was a real office building a dozen blocks east on a side street just off Pennsylvania Avenue. Next to its entrance, Sarah noticed what appeared to be an expensive restaurant with a small brass nameplate on the door: King's Knight.

Inside the office building's marble-lined lobby, Sarah went to the directory, in a glass case on the wall, where she found several more names on the list in her notebook: American Freedom Alliance, the National Center for a Better Congress, Malin Associates, Public Relations Solutions, RT2 Group. And one she hadn't expected: Tucker and Associates. Sarah chided herself for being sloppy. She had always phoned Tucker without bothering to look up the address of his office.

It was clear from the lobby directory that Tucker and Associates took up the entire top two floors of the building. The names on her list all seemed to be located in Suite 1000 on the floor below them.

Sarah convinced the building guard that an assistant to Trent Tucker was expecting her, signed the visitors' log, and took an elevator to the tenth floor. There were no names on the glass doors for Suite 1000. Inside, she found herself facing an empty receptionist's desk in front of a blank gray wall. Corridors led off to the left and right to places unknown. A middle-aged African-American woman in a business suit materialized from the corridor on the left, apparently on her way to the elevator. Sarah stepped in front of her to ask the location of

Malin Associates.

"What can I do for you?" asked the woman, who seemed dismayed to be confronted by an unannounced visitor.

"I'd like to see Mr. Malin, please."

"I don't think he's here this morning."

"Is there anyone else I can talk to from Malin Associates? Or the American Freedom Alliance or Public Relations Solutions? They have offices here, too, don't they?"

"Who *are* you?"

Sarah decided to play it straight.

"My name is Sarah Page. I'm a reporter for the *Washington Capital*."

Just then, Sarah heard the glass door open behind her. The woman's expression turned from panic to relief.

"Bob," she called to a man walking quickly past them toward the corridor on the right. "There's someone here you should talk to. She says she's a newspaper reporter."

The man turned immediately toward Sarah. Everything he wore was expensive, right down to his tassled loafers. His dark gray wool trousers and unbuttoned vest were obviously part of a well-tailored suit. His blue shirt had a white collar and looked as if it might have been handmade in London or Hong Kong. It was perfectly complemented by a silk tie in several shades of blue. His silvery gray hair was carefully combed back in waves, framing his tanned face.

"Thanks, Lucilla," he said. "I'll handle this."

The woman hurried away through the glass door to the elevators.

"How did you get up here?" the man asked Sarah. "This is a secure building."

"I'd like to talk to some of the people who have offices here," she said. "Should I go upstairs and speak to Trent Tucker about it?"

"And I suppose you know Mr. Tucker?"

"I'm Sarah Page," she said, holding out her hand, which he ignored. "I've written about Mr. Tucker in the newspaper. We've talked often."

"I recognize the name," the man said coldly. "I think it's time for you to leave now. I'll let Mr. Tucker know you stopped by."

He escorted her into the elevator, then through the lobby to the front door. As Sarah was leaving, she heard him sternly address the security guard.

"Stephen," he told him, "when your relief arrives at lunchtime, I want you up in my office immediately."

She held the door open just long enough

to hear the security guard's reply.

"Yes, sir, Mr. Malin."

Sarah paused on the sidewalk outside to jot down some notes, including his name and "King's Knight."

When she got back to the newsroom, Sarah asked Marge Lawson what she had found for the names of recipients of money from Smith and Hawley's Pentagon contracts in the records supplied to Sarah by Andy Foster and Derek Stevens. There was nothing on Redwing Associates or any of the others with mailing addresses at the MailServices store on Pennsylvania Avenue. But Malin Associates, American Freedom Alliance, and Public Relations Solutions all turned up with phone numbers at Suite 1000 in the office building Sarah had just visited.

"Robert Malin," Marge told her triumphantly. "He and Malin Associates actually exist."

"I know. I just met him," Sarah said, "although he didn't exactly introduce himself. He threw me out of the building. He's quite the dandy. Dresses like a rich preppy."

"Makes sense," Marge said. "He's the son of a local developer. Went to St. Albans and Harvard. He knew Tucker in school. You can see them together in pictures in the St.

Albans yearbook. And they were in the same house at Harvard.

"Malin inherited his father's real-estate business. Office buildings downtown and in the suburbs. The federal government alone pays him millions in rent. He's got a big old house in Georgetown and a big new one near Annapolis on the Severn River."

"So what's Malin Associates?"

"It appears to be a kind of personal holding company for Malin, Trent Tucker, and Carter Phillips," Marge said. "It's the end of the line for a bunch of complicated transactions, including mortgages on their homes and titles to the buildings where their offices are located. And something called the King's Knight."

"It's a restaurant in Tucker's building."

"For some reason, they've put all that stuff into Malin Associates. It could be a money-laundering operation."

"Anyone else involved in it?"

"On paper, just Malin's wife, Elizabeth, and a woman named Lucilla Brown. She's a real-estate lawyer who works for his property company. A lot of the transactions pass through her at some point."

"Oh, great," Sarah said. "I just met two-thirds of Malin Associates and didn't know it when I was talking to them. What about the others in Suite 1000?"

"The National Center for a Better Congress is a nonprofit that Tucker apparently uses for junkets for members of Congress on behalf of his clients. Congressmen and senators are allowed to take money for trips from nonprofits for so-called educational purposes, but not directly from lobbyists or special interests. So Tucker has his clients pass the money through the National Center for a Better Congress. To figure out who's really paying for which trips, I'll have to check its I.R.S. filings and the travel disclosure forms of Tucker's friends in Congress."

"Thanks, Marge. You're great. And the rest of them?"

"You're a greedy girl. But I do have more. A lot of money goes back and forth between American Freedom Alliance and political action committees for candidates who are Tucker's clients. It's not a PAC itself and it's not a registered nonprofit, so I can't find anything more about it.

"Public Relations Solutions appears to be Tucker's primary piggy bank. Just about all the campaigns he's run have paid fees to it, besides what they pay to Tucker and Associates for the actual work. I bet Public Relations Solutions collects from his lobbying clients, too. I can't get access to those records, but you found payments to it from some of your Pentagon contractors."

"And RT2?" Sarah asked.

"Not a trace," Marge said. "I can only guess that its name comes from the initials for Robert Trent Tucker."

Sarah headed back to her desk. She was feeling hungry. She noticed Mark hard at work at his computer, with a half-eaten sandwich and cup of coffee on a cafeteria tray next to him. She knew he hated the cafeteria.

"Are you actually eating at your desk?" she asked him. "Must be a big story."

"As a matter of fact, it is," Mark said, without looking up.

"What's it about?"

"It's exclusive."

"I won't tell Matt Drudge," Sarah said.

"Okay. Cameron's going to pick Stetson for vice president."

Mark kept typing.

"I think it'll keep for the rest of the day," he told Sarah. "I won't call the White House for comment until after the evening news. Just before the first edition goes to press, we'll break it on the Web and cable."

"Where did you get it from? Trent Tucker?"

Mark stopped typing and swiveled to face

Sarah. His face was a mask of tension and anger.

"Look, I cover the White House, and I've got good sources. I don't need to explain myself to you all the time."

"For God's sake, Mark. It's just that I'm impressed," Sarah said. "Like you told me, if the information's good, that's all that matters."

Mark looked at her for another moment before deciding there was nothing else to say. He turned back to his computer, and Sarah continued on to her desk.

Her mind filled with questions. Why would Tucker leak it to Mark? And why Stetson?

Sarah's musing was interrupted by the telephone ringing on her desk.

"Hey, girl. Are you fussing with Mark Daniels again?"

"Where are you, Joni?"

"Just across the newsroom. I came in early to find you. But I don't want to talk here. It's nice outside. Let's meet at the Iron Gate Inn."

After taking a few minutes to check her e-mails, Sarah walked the half dozen blocks to the open gate of a covered cobblestone walkway next to a white nineteenth-century house on N Street not far from Dupont Circle. She loved this row of historic town houses, which had been restored over the years as offices. The General Federation of Women's Clubs occupied the white stone house at 1734.

Sarah walked alongside it to the Iron Gate Inn's intimate outdoor courtyard in back. Enclosed by stone and brick walls, one adorned by a small lion's head fountain, and shaded overhead by latticework laced with wisteria, it was a secluded oasis in bustling downtown Washington.

At a table in a far corner of the courtyard, Sarah found Joni Parker sitting with an older man in a white shirt and plain blue tie. His suit coat was draped over the back of his chair. As Sarah approached, he rose slowly and extended a dark-skinned hand.

"Sarah, this is Lieutenant Charles Langford," Joni told her. "He runs the homicide squad and he's interested in the Seth Moore case. I've told him everything I know. We think it's time for you to tell him the rest."

We? Sarah could have been angry with Joni for setting her up like this, but she knew the timing was right. As they ate, the story of Sam spilled out of her, tears and all.

"So who's this friend of his in California?"

asked Langford, who was taking notes.

"He's a confidential source of mine," Sarah said. "And he's afraid of the authorities."

She decided not to tell him about Andy Foster. She didn't really know what had happened to him or whether it had anything to do with Seth Moore. Besides, she didn't want to do anything that might jeopardize the information she had from Foster until she finished her story.

"Tell your source he can trust me," Langford said. "This is an investigation of the murder of an employee of the United States Congress. I'm not proud of how slowly we've moved on this so far. But I'm not pleased about what you've withheld from us either."

Sarah picked at her curried chicken salad.

"Don't worry," Joni told her. "Charlie's not going to arrest you or anything. That's his serious face. It gets him confessions. But he's okay. I've known him since I was a little girl."

Langford stayed focused on Sarah.

"I won't interfere with your reporting," he added. "But you've got to cooperate fully with this investigation."

"It's not all up to me," Sarah said. "My newspaper has policies about confidential sources and what we can share with the police. I'll have to talk to my editor — and maybe our lawyers."

"I understand. But tell them what I said."

After they finished lunch, Sarah and Joni parted company with Langford and walked back to the newspaper together.

"Sorry to blindside you," Joni told Sarah. "He didn't know if you'd meet with him otherwise."

"We had to cross this bridge sometime," Sarah said. "But I'm going to have to figure out how to tell my source. And Ron Jones, too."

Only a few blocks away, Elliott Bancroft was leaving a lunch at the Oval Room. He took a detour on his way back to the White House, turning west on Pennsylvania Avenue. He looked around on the crowded sidewalk before slipping into the MailServices store. The manager must have been at lunch, because a younger woman was behind the counter. Just as well, Elliott thought, as he turned his key in the box assigned to Redwing Associates. He was still new to this.

Back out on the sidewalk, Elliott couldn't resist opening each of the envelopes to peek inside. He smiled at the numbers on the checks, drawn on bank accounts in Panama and the Bahamas, before putting them into his inside suit pocket.

At the northwest gate to the White House grounds, Elliott flashed his security pass, exchanged greetings with the uniformed Secret Service officers on duty, and walked up the long driveway to the West Wing.

22

Sarah was standing in Ron Jones's office, wanting to explain everything. But she was distracted by Seth Moore and Andy Foster, who were sitting motionless on a leather couch. When she realized she wasn't wearing any clothes, she ran out into the newsroom, trying to get to her desk.

She found herself facing her mother, who was wearing a long formal dress. Her hair was done the way it always had been for Washington dinner parties.

"You see, I told you," her mother scolded. "You work all the time. You never go out. You won't find a husband that way. And you'll never have children."

Sarah could hear the phone ringing on her desk.

"It's probably your father."

Sarah wanted to talk to him. But she

couldn't get past her mother. She tried and tried, but her feet wouldn't move. The phone kept ringing.

Then she woke up.

The phone was still ringing on the table next to her bed. When Sarah opened her eyes, she saw the display on the clock radio change from 4:00 to 4:01. She reached out and picked up the phone.

"Hello."

Silence.

"Hello?"

"Miss Page? Miss Sarah Page?"

"Yes."

"Are you the *Washington Capital* reporter?"

"Yes. Who's this?"

"Miss Page, I have a question. Is the security of our country important to you?"

"Who *is* this? And why are you calling me at four in the morning?"

"A patriot, Miss Page. I help protect our country."

His voice had no accent or affect. Sarah thought he might be in the military.

"Where did you get my home number?" She was wide awake now. "Call me later in my office."

"We don't all work the same hours you do, Miss Page. We protect our country around the clock. And we're concerned about what you're doing."

Listening carefully now, Sarah could hear other, indistinct voices in the background. She thought he might be calling from an office of some kind.

"What are you talking about?" she asked.

"You're a political reporter, Miss Page. You should stay away from defense matters. You could make mistakes, serious mistakes."

"I really don't understand." She tried to draw more information out of him. "Where are you calling from? You sound too polite to be making crank calls."

"This is not a crank call, Miss Page. This is serious business. It's about the security of our country."

"What about it?"

"Your reporting, Miss Page. Whom you've been talking to. What you've been asking. You need to return to politics, Miss Page."

"Has someone been conducting surveillance on me? That would be illegal."

"Not necessarily, Miss Page. Not when it involves national security."

"Bullshit." Instinct told her to push back. "If you really want to know what I've been reporting on, it's corruption. Are you involved in that?"

"Please, Miss Page. You should watch your

language. And your accusations. You don't know what you're getting into."

Sarah wasn't getting anywhere with him, so it was time to end the conversation for now.

"I'll decide what I'll do or won't do," she said. "If you want to have a real conversation, call during working hours at my newspaper."

After Sarah hung up, her heart was pounding and her mind was racing. She went over what the man on the phone had claimed to know about her reporting and what he kept repeating about national security. She focused on what he sounded like: disciplined and vaguely threatening. Did he have anything to do with the secret that Pat Scully wouldn't tell her? Or what Andy Foster had said about rumors of Palisar companies "being mixed up in some rough stuff with the military"?

"Sarah?" It was Caroline out in the hall. "Is everything all right?"

"Just a friend on the foreign staff. Got the time difference wrong. Sorry it woke you up. Good night."

Using a deep-breathing technique she had learned in yoga class at the gym, she eventually relaxed and fell back to sleep for a few more hours.

23

"Who leaked it?" Susan had come out from behind her desk to confront Elliott in the middle of the Oval Office. Wearing one of her tailored, skirted suits, she looked every inch the chief executive, brightly lit by the early morning sun off the South Lawn behind her.

"It wasn't me, Madam President," Elliott answered. "I don't talk to reporters."

He wasn't about to admit discussing Sam Stetson with Trent Tucker. His double game was becoming increasingly difficult for him to manage, serving the president while remaining dangerously indebted to Tucker.

Susan stood facing him, silent in thought. The newspaper story that morning was forcing her hand.

Her own conversations with Stetson had gone well. He had been cleared by the F.B.I. after a quick investigation that drew extensively on his security clearances. The White House aides and congressional leaders she consulted had been generally positive. And Michael had reassured her during one of their late-night talks on the telephone.

Susan knew it could be her biggest decision as president. But more time would not necessarily offer more information or better advice. Once again, she would have to trust her instincts.

"Okay," she said finally as she turned back toward her desk. "Set it up for noon today in the Rose Garden."

Mark had scooped everyone, but there were still plenty of stories for the newsroom to produce about the president's announcement. Sarah volunteered to help on a detailed profile of Stetson. Discovering more about him might help her figure out whether Trent Tucker had played a role in his selection, and, if so, why.

In between calls to members of Congress and staff members who knew Stetson, she tried to contact Pat Scully. She was surprised when "AC/DC60" messaged back immediately.

"bingo . . . great minds and all that . . . sending printouts of stetson stuff from files . . . started digging when story broke"

"What do you have?" Sarah asked him.

"campaign $$$ from palisar companies, execs, employees . . . quo for the quid are earmarks in spending bills — senators and reps put line items into appropriations bills specifying govt spending for pet projects . . . easy way to pay back contributors"

"Thanks. I know that."

Whatever Scully was up to, Sarah thought, he was still helpful. She wondered about mentioning the 4 a.m. phone call. But she had already decided to be more careful about what she shared with Scully until she knew more about his game.

"Anything on Andy Foster?" she asked instead.

"nada . . . still a mystery"

"By the way," she typed, "cops here are finally focusing on the Sam investigation. They found his connection to me and I told them my story. I left your name out of it as a confidential source. But a senior cop wants to talk to you. Joni vouches for him."

"no . . . no . . . no"

"Why?"

"stall him"

"Okay."

"stetson package overnighting"

When Marge Lawson arrived at her cubicle the next morning, Sarah was waiting with a pile of papers from Scully.

"Sorry to dump this on you," she told Marge, "but could you verify these campaign contributions?"

"Stetson?"

"Yeah, my source has connected him with Palisar."

"I'm already on the case," Marge said.

"Remember when I told you Tucker used the National Center for a Better Congress to launder money from his clients that paid for trips for senators and congressmen? I thought I'd check whether the Honorable Sam Stetson took any of those trips."

"And?"

"He did. Trips to Europe, the Middle East, China, Australia. All through the National Center for a Better Congress. All around times the center received contributions from companies owned by Palisar: Mammoth Mining; Dorsey Energy; Stinson Thorpe Engineering; Braxton and Cox, the big construction company; Smith and Hawley, the defense contractor. Oh, and one other thing. Stetson also flew back and forth between Washington and Texas on corporate jets owned by some of the same companies."

"He flies for free?" Sarah asked.

"His PAC usually pays, using campaign money, some of which also comes from those companies," Marge told her.

"The ethics rules allow that?"

"They're full of loopholes."

When Sarah was ready to write her story, Stetson's staff said he couldn't talk to her before the confirmation vote. Spokesmen for the various Palisar companies would only confirm the contributions to the National Center for a Better Congress, which they called "an educational foundation." When Sarah tried its phone number, she was referred to the executive director, who turned out to be Lucilla Brown.

"Didn't I meet you a few weeks ago in Trent Tucker's building?" Sarah asked her. "Aren't you an officer of Malin Associates? Doesn't it have the same offices as the National Center for a Better Congress?"

"Malin Associates is a private organization that I won't discuss," responded Brown, who sounded as though she had been expecting Sarah's call. "The National Center for a Better Congress is a registered non-profit educational foundation that assists members of Congress in their work. I trust you are familiar with our Internal Revenue Service filings."

"I am," Sarah said. "They show that several companies that are lobbying clients of Trent Tucker made contributions to the center at the same times as it sponsored foreign trips for certain members of Congress, including Senator Sam Stetson."

"There is absolutely no connection between the generous support some businesses give the center and the trips we sponsor for members of Congress," Brown told her.

Sarah enjoyed the combat of confrontational interviews. She sometimes thought of it as fencing, a sport she had tried with some success in college. Thrust and parry, thrust and parry.

"What about Senator Stetson's trip to the Persian Gulf with Smith and Hawley executives after they made a contribution to the center?"

"The senior senator on the Armed Services Committee was inspecting American forces," Brown said stiffly. "Smith and Hawley has been a consistent supporter of the center, so it would be misleading for you to single out any particular contribution."

"And Indonesia, Australia, and Hawaii. Stinson Thorpe Engineering. What was that delegation doing for nearly two weeks?"

"It was a fact-finding trip. It was some time ago. I don't recall the details."

As Brown retreated, Sarah lunged forward.

"Nothing to do with Senator Stetson's earmarks in appropriations bills that gave government subsidies and loan guarantees to Stinson Thorpe's Indonesian airport and power-plant projects?" she asked. "Doesn't Stinson Thorpe also contribute —"

"That's quite enough," Brown interrupted. She was resigning the match. "The assumptions implicit in your questions are absolutely false. I would strongly suggest you consult your lawyers before publishing anything so reckless."

Sarah did exactly that before showing a draft of her story to Ron Jones. He read it quickly at his desk while she stood waiting.

"I didn't know you were working on Stetson, much less talking to our lawyers about it," he said when he looked up. "Our guys on the Hill are covering the confirmation process."

"I'm way ahead of them." Sarah had prepared herself for this. "None of it has come out on the Hill."

"Who assigned you?"

"You did. It's part of my reporting for the Stetson profile. And it fits with my project. All the companies are Trent Tucker clients, and all of them are owned by Palisar. It's all tied together."

"All tied together," Jones repeated. "Are you telling me that a respected senator who has been nominated to be vice president of the United States is at the center of some kind of conspiracy?"

"No," Sarah said quickly. She realized she had gone too far. "I'm just laying out the facts about his relationships with these companies."

Sarah knew Jones had to play devil's

advocate on a story that could damage a public official's reputation. Doubly so, as he suggested, when it involved the very rare congressional confirmation of a nominee for vice president. And she had tried to rush it past him. But it was a solid story, so she was disturbed by his reaction.

Jones was uncomfortable, too. The story could plunge them both into deep water, jeopardizing a reporting project he still didn't fully understand. But he remembered how vulnerable he had felt whenever editors failed to back him over the years. Having committed himself to Sarah's Palisar investigation, he knew he needed to be as supportive as possible.

"Let me read it more carefully," he told her. "I'll get back to you tomorrow."

24

"What's this meeting with Lou Runyan?" Sarah asked Ron Jones the next day. "Did you show him the story?"

"He asked me for it," Jones told her. "Some people from the White House are coming in."

"Who?" Sarah was puzzled. "I hadn't called them for comment yet."

"How about the press secretary and the

chief of staff?"

"You're kidding me. For this story?"

"Some of Stetson's people will be at the meeting, too," Jones said. "Did you talk to them?"

"Of course. Several times," said Sarah. "I ran everything by them."

"Well, someone must have called the White House."

"Did Runyan like the story?"

"Don't know," Jones said. "I guess we'll find out."

When the two of them walked into the editor's office that afternoon, everyone attending the meeting was already there, including the managing editor, Mary Sullivan. Elliott Bancroft and Alison Winters stood to introduce themselves, as did Sam Stetson's press secretary from his Senate office.

"We've agreed that this meeting will be off the record," Lou Runyan said, looking at Sarah, as everyone sat down on couches lining the glass walls of his office. "Our guests want to discuss your story with us before we make a decision about publishing it."

Your story, Sarah noticed. *Make a decision about publishing it.* Remembering that Runyan had been reluctant to print her story about Monroe Capehart's affair, she didn't like what she was hearing.

"Mr. Bancroft," Runyan said. He pulled his chair up to the desk, leaned his elbows on it and put his hands together in what appeared to be thoughtful concentration. "The floor is yours."

"I want to thank you for having us here today," Elliott began. "The president appreciates the opportunity for us to share our thoughts with you. It seems that Miss Page has done a good job of gathering information about aspects of Senator Stetson's record in Congress. But her story, as I understand it, lacks context, so it appears to be saying there's something wrong with that record."

"I've reviewed the current draft of the story carefully," Runyan told him. "What do you mean by context?"

Current draft, Sarah noted. Was he offering the possibility of changing it?

"Well, to begin with, everyone in Congress receives campaign contributions from many sources," Elliott said. "And it's not unusual for members to seek a fair share of federal spending for their constituents. Dorsey Energy, for example, is a Texas company. Senator Stetson did put a provision into an appropriations bill a few years ago to increase tax incentives for research into alternative energy sources, which would benefit Dorsey, among other firms. But it also would benefit all Americans if it helped reduce our dependence on imported oil.

"I believe the story also cites legislative action by Senator Stetson to establish a ceiling on fees the government could charge the Mammoth Mining company for mineral rights on federal lands. This could produce long-term benefits in natural-resources exploration.

"And it goes without saying that we should all be grateful for the senator's efforts on the Armed Services Committee to keep American defense firms financially sound in competing for contracts that support our forces overseas."

This guy's good, Sarah thought. She hoped Runyan wouldn't be completely snowed by him.

"What about all his flying around on corporate jets?" Runyan asked.

At least that seemed encouraging to Sarah. He *had* read the story.

"Every single trip and its reimbursement complied with Senate rules at the time and was completely and properly accounted for in the senator's filings," Elliott said. He had briefed himself thoroughly on the details. "As for trips sponsored by the National

Center for a Better Congress, many members of Congress have taken advantage of similar opportunities for educational travel offered by nonprofit foundations. In fact, members of the other party did a lot more of this kind of traveling."

"We've written about that," Jones said. He had been involved in many meetings like this over the years, as both reporter and editor. To him, it was all spin. Sarah had the facts cold.

"I know you have," Elliott told him. "And that's just the point. What you've got here is just a little more of the same old stuff. That's why it needs context. Sam Stetson should not be portrayed as an exceptional case."

Stetson's press secretary silently nodded his head in agreement, while Alison Winters sat stone-faced.

Sarah had no way of knowing the president's press secretary had been reluctant to accompany Elliott to this meeting. If everybody on the Hill did this, Alison thought, why make a fuss? The story wouldn't hurt Stetson's chances of being confirmed as vice president by his colleagues in Congress.

"Well, thank you all for coming," Runyan said, rising impatiently from his desk. "We'll take what you told us very seriously."

"Could I ask a few questions?" Sarah said as everyone stood up.

"We didn't come here for an interview," Elliott told her, turning to shake hands with Runyan. "Your editor agreed to an off-the-record meeting for the sole purpose of listening to our concerns."

There was an awkward silence as Sarah looked first to Runyan and then Mary Sullivan, but neither said anything. Stunned by what she considered their lack of support, Sarah considered pressing the issue anyway. Then Alison Winters put a hand on her shoulder.

"We really can't be speaking publicly while Congress considers the senator's nomination," she told Sarah. "Why don't you and I get together for lunch after it's over."

"That sounds like a good idea," Elliott added, before Sarah could say anything more. He then led the group out of the editor's office and through the newsroom to the elevators. Heads turned as everyone wondered why they were there.

"I don't like being patronized," Sarah said to Ron Jones as they walked back to his office.

"By Bancroft or Winters?"

"Runyan," she said sharply. "He never

really stuck up for the story."

"He didn't make any promises to them either," said Jones. "He just listened and shooed them out."

"So, now what?"

"We'll confer later with Lou and decide what to do."

That turned into another meeting in Runyan's office the next morning. Sarah was surprised to see Mark there, along with Jones and Mary Sullivan. It quickly became clear that the meeting had started before she was asked to join them.

"There's nothing in here that's different from what everyone in Congress does," Mark said, pointing to a copy of the story in his lap. He enjoyed a special relationship with Runyan, who relived his own days as a political journalist through conversations with Mark. "Singling this out as some kind of scandal would be a distortion."

"Like you did with Warner Wylie?" asked Sarah. She resented Mark's intervention and wondered why he had a copy of her story in the first place.

"Wylie was running for president, and that was during the campaign," Mark responded, impatient that he had to explain this to her all over again. "His connection with Big Pharma was an issue. His trips were all boondoggles and vacations. And he never reimbursed the drug companies for them."

"The point is the same," Sarah said, undeterred by his condescending attitude. "Wylie was in the pocket of the drug companies, and Stetson is beholden to these companies who've been flying him around. You know the National Center for a Better Congress is just a front for" — she decided not to throw Trent Tucker in Mark's face — "some of those companies. And then Stetson puts earmarks that benefit them into appropriations bills."

"That's a perfectly legal, common practice on the Hill. It would be fine in a legislative profile of Stetson or a story about members of Congress and their campaign contributors," Mark said. He actually was impressed by Sarah's grasp of it all. "But this story, standing on its own, wouldn't look fair in the middle of his confirmation process."

"He may have a point," Runyan said quickly. It appeared to Sarah that he had heard all this from Mark before she got there. But she wasn't going to be outmaneuvered easily. She steeled herself to challenge the editor.

"Look," she said. "Stetson could be another Gerald Ford, a president who wasn't elected president or even vice president.

This confirmation process may be the only opportunity to thoroughly examine his fitness for the presidency."

"Susan Cameron is young, healthy, and not involved in any scandal like Watergate," Runyan said. "But I get your point." He liked this young woman. He was impressed by her moxie. "We should probably put this in the paper. The question is how.

"Mary," he said, turning to Sullivan. "Why don't you work with Ron and Sarah to soften this a bit, so it doesn't look like the guy is breaking the law. Make it a story about Stetson's record in Congress, like Mark suggested. Include what he's done on Armed Services. That'll balance it out."

"Okay," Sullivan said, looking surprised.

"We'll get it done right away," Jones added.

No one asked Sarah what she thought.

"Here," she said, storming into Ron Jones's office a few minutes later, dropping a pile of printouts onto his desk. "You and the managing editor can rewrite the story any damn way you want."

"Hey, calm down," Jones said firmly. "We'll work this out. Lou doesn't expect us to do exactly what he says. Just find a way to shape the story so it's not so much of an indictment. Put what you've got against the background of Stetson's Senate career. I'll get memos from Mark and our Hill people. You do the rewrite. I'll edit it and show it to Mary."

Sarah was still angry about the way the meeting had gone.

"What was Mark doing in that meeting?" she asked.

"After our meeting with the White House people, Runyan gave him a copy of your story. Mark took it home to read and dropped in on Lou this morning to talk about it."

"What?" Sarah couldn't believe it.

"Lou trusts Mark's judgment on political stuff," said Jones. "If anyone's nose should be out of joint, it's mine. When I saw what was going on in his office this morning, I told Lou that you and I needed to be there. And he brought in Mary."

"Okay," Sarah said. She just wanted to get the story in the paper. "I'll try it the way you want. People should know about this before Stetson's confirmed."

"Agreed."

"And please let me stay on Tucker and Palisar. I know I'm on the right track now."

"Oh, don't worry about that," Jones said. "I'm convinced you're on the right track, too."

"Why?" Sarah asked with surprise.

"You'll excuse me, but your story should not have brought those high-powered folks in to see us," Jones said, leaning back in his chair. "It's not going to affect Stetson's confirmation. So I don't think it's Stetson that worries Elliott Bancroft. It's got to be what's in the story about Tucker and Palisar. Someone must want us to back off. So keep going. And take Alison Winters up on her luncheon invitation."

25

This time, when the phone rang at precisely 4 a.m., Sarah was not taken by surprise. She had guessed, even hoped, that the mysterious caller might react to her story about Sam Stetson, which had gone up on the newspaper's Web site at midnight. It would give her an opportunity to fish for more information.

"Hello," she answered, after giving herself a few seconds to wake up. "Did you like the story?"

"Senator Stetson is a great man, a real friend to the people who protect our country. He'll make an outstanding vice president."

It sounded to Sarah like the same voice.

"You called at four in the morning to tell me that?"

"I'm reminding you not to go too far down the road you're on. Turn off before it's too late."

Then he hung up.

Sarah sat up in bed. In his brevity, he had seemed more menacing this time. And he hadn't given her a chance to find out more about him or why he was calling. Remembering something she hadn't done last time, she checked her phone for the list of numbers of previous callers. Not surprisingly, for his call, it was blank.

The warning that Carter Phillips gave Trent Tucker over lunch at the King's Knight was more direct.

"I'm not happy," he said as he sat down. His right hand was clenched around a rolled-up copy of the front section of the *Washington Capital.*

"It's just a newspaper story, General," Tucker said, too nonchalantly for Phillips.

"She wrote that you helped my companies buy favors from the future vice president of the United States." Phillips put the paper on the table, where it sat through lunch like an unwanted guest. "Don't expect any more money for the National Congress Center, or whatever that phony foundation of yours is called."

"I can handle this," Tucker said.

"That girl's been in your building, for God's sake, looking for things she shouldn't even know about."

Phillips was speaking quietly. But Tucker could hear the simmering anger in his voice, which frightened him more than loud threats would from anyone else. And he saw the cold fury in his eyes.

"I didn't know she was," Tucker said timidly.

"Malin told me."

"Why didn't he tell me?"

"When I heard about that girl calling our people to ask about plane trips and contributions to your . . ."

"National Center for a Better Congress."

" 'Better Congress.' Right. I like the irony." Phillips smiled thinly. "Anyway, I called Bob. He told me she had been there. So I gave him instructions for what Lucilla should say if that girl called her."

"He didn't tell me that either."

"I'm telling you now."

Tucker tried to understand what he was hearing. Phillips and Malin had gone around him, as though he couldn't be trusted. What was going on?

"Everything in that story can be found in public records," he said.

"How did she know what to look for? Somebody must still be helping her."

Still? Tucker gave him a questioning look. But Phillips didn't elaborate.

"You need to do something," he told Tucker. "How about your friend Daniels?"

"I'll try, General."

"You do that."

"Sarah Page?" This call came to her in the newsroom, and she didn't recognize the voice. "I'm Representative Chris Collins. You don't know me, but we have a mutual friend in California. He worked with me on the Hill."

"Did he tell you to call me?"

Sarah looked at the caller ID and saw it was a congressional office. Then she started an Internet search while they talked.

"Not exactly," Collins told her. "I've been reading your stories. Especially the one in today's paper about Sam Stetson and those Palisar companies. What are you going to do next?"

Sarah's antennae went up. Even if he was a congressman, she was suspicious about the question.

"Why do you want to know?"

"I think I can help. Could we talk in person?"

By now, she had the bio for Representative Christopher Collins on her computer screen. Democrat. Ohio. Age thirty-four. Widowed. No children. Political science and law degrees from Ohio State. County prosecutor. State legislator. Army Reserve. Wounded in Iraq. House Appropriations Committee.

If this really was Collins and Pat Scully had worked with him, Sarah thought, the congressman could help her learn more about who Scully was and what he was doing.

"Have you heard much from Pat?"

"You're testing me, which is probably a good idea," Collins said. "He only called me a couple of times from those disposable phones he's using. The second time he told me about you. I had already noticed your Trent Tucker story during the campaign."

"What did he say?"

"He told me the two of you were working together. Today's story showed me that you were making good progress. But I could still help. I know it's hard to pick out the good guys from the bad guys in this town, so I'd understand if you were wary of me."

Sarah figured there'd be no harm in meeting him.

"How do you want to get together?"

"Someplace we won't be noticed. I love the F.D.R. Memorial at night. Very inspirational. And full of people at all hours."

"Tonight?"

"Eight o'clock?"

"Fine."

"Let's meet in the first big open area. Next to the waterfall, there's a bronze frieze of F.D.R. being driven down Pennsylvania Avenue after his first inauguration. Above it is the famous quote from his inaugural address."

"I've seen it."

"Oh, and I'm kind of a little guy," Collins said. "I'll be wearing a red-and-gray Ohio State T-shirt with red shorts."

"Doesn't sound very inconspicuous."

"That's the point. Nobody will take me for a member of Congress."

The setting sun had painted the Potomac in shades of orange and red by the time Sarah found a parking space on Ohio Drive along the river in West Potomac Park. Wearing white walking shorts, a sleeveless red knit top, and sneakers on a warm, humid early summer evening, she walked away from the water and across a softball field to the entrance of the Franklin Delano Roosevelt Memorial. Set in the trees on the southern edge of the Reflecting Pool, the sprawling outdoor memorial for the nation's longest-serving president was designed as a series of granite-walled open spaces filled with tumbling waterfalls, life-sized sculptures, and F.D.R.'s words carved into the stone.

Christopher Collins was standing beneath an inscription: THE ONLY THING WE HAVE TO FEAR IS FEAR ITSELF. His face was immediately recognizable from photographs. But, just as he had said, in his T-shirt, shorts, and running shoes, he blended in with the milling tourists. He was only a little taller than Sarah, just as trim, and even younger looking. He was sweating, as though he had been running. Yet his thick sandy hair looked barely ruffled.

"Congressman Collins," she said quietly, trying not to draw attention.

"Chris, from now on." He took her hand in both of his, just as Trent Tucker always had, and fixed his brown eyes on hers in the way politicians like to do. "Pat told me you were pretty, even though that doesn't really matter to him, as I'm sure you know."

Sarah wondered if he intended the reference to Scully's sexual orientation to be a kind of secret password.

"How do you know Pat?" she asked in a businesslike tone, taking back her hand.

"He came to me for help investigating Smith and Hawley, even though he was on the staff of another committee," said Collins. "Pat said he checked me out and knew I'd been a prosecutor and served in Iraq. He thought I'd be interested in what he had found."

"What happened?"

They strolled past a sculpture depicting a breadline during the Great Depression. Tourists took turns standing behind the last man in line to be photographed by their relatives.

"I got Pat detailed to the staff of my subcommittee," Collins told Sarah. "He came up with a plan to hold hearings. But my chairman told me it was a nonstarter. And I had to dump Pat."

"Was that the end of it?"

"More like the beginning. I was outraged by what Smith and Hawley had done. And curious about why it was off-limits on the Hill. I sneaked Pat onto the staff of another committee and told him to keep his head down. He kept digging into Smith and Hawley and the rest of Palisar."

In the space devoted to F.D.R.'s leadership during World War II, they stopped to watch happily screaming children play in a waterfall splashing over huge rocks arranged as though they had been scattered by a large bomb.

"Did you know about Pat's friend Seth?" she asked.

"Sure. They lived together before Pat left for California. I read that he was killed in some kind of car accident."

Sarah thought a moment about that. Had Scully not told Collins what happened to Seth and that Scully had sneaked into town for his memorial service? Or was Collins hiding how much he knew?

The congressman led Sarah into the memorial's last large open space. On one long granite wall behind a still pool of water was a bronze bas-relief of Roosevelt's funeral cortege moving down Pennsylvania Avenue. In a niche in a stone wall nearby stood a statue depicting Eleanor Roosevelt as the first American delegate to the United Nations. Beyond a final waterfall, on a wall that opened onto a dramatic view of the brightly lit Jefferson Memorial and the Tidal Basin, were F.D.R.'s Four Freedoms chiseled in massive letters: FREEDOM OF SPEECH. FREEDOM OF WORSHIP. FREEDOM FROM WANT. FREEDOM FROM FEAR.

"When I first came here," Collins told

Sarah, "that reminded me why I've been serving my country in one way or another most of my life."

They walked out of the memorial onto a path that continued around the Tidal Basin.

"You were wounded in Iraq?"

"I was a lawyer and served in the State Legislature, so I was put into a civic reconstruction unit to advise the Iraqis on how to do local government," Collins told her, as though he had expected the question. "We were in a convoy that hit an I.E.D. It went off behind the Humvee I was in. I caught shrapnel in my back and rear end. It was pretty messy. But I didn't lose any limbs like other guys. Some of them in the other Humvee didn't make it. I knew them all from home."

They walked across a bridge where river water flowed into the Tidal Basin. On the other side of the bridge, the water slapped up against rocks along the path to the Jefferson Memorial.

"That's why I agreed to run for Congress when I got back," Collins said. "I know it sounds corny, but I figured I had a responsibility to do it because I was spared. I was asked to run when the incumbent announced his retirement. My military service didn't hurt. The local papers made me look like some kind of hero. It helped me get a seat on Appropriations when I expressed an interest in defense spending."

Collins fell silent as the path opened up onto the esplanade of the Jefferson Memorial. They stopped to look up at the enormous statue of Thomas Jefferson standing inside the rotunda and then out at the Tidal Basin and the other monuments and federal buildings beyond it.

"I grew up here," Sarah said, "and I'm still impressed by all this."

"Me, too. But it's getting late. I've got an early breakfast in the morning. It'll take me a while to run back up the Mall. I've become a fitness freak since recovering from my wounds."

"You live on the Hill?"

"I rent a little town house with another bachelor congressman."

"I could drive you home," Sarah said. "The walk back to my car will give us some exercise."

"You live there, too?"

"No, but it's not a problem."

After they had retraced their steps to the still-crowded F.D.R. memorial, Sarah suggested a shortcut. "We can go across the ball fields," she told Collins, leading him toward the river.

Without saying more, Sarah broke into a jog. Collins joined her. She sped up. He caught her. She started running flat out. He quickly pulled ahead. But Sarah had tricked him, running away from the shortest distance to her car. At the last moment, she veered off toward it before Collins could recover.

"Another misleading journalist," he joked, breathing heavily while she unlocked the car. "Don't you have one of those clicker things?"

"I think its battery died or something and I haven't gotten it fixed," she said between gasps. "It's probably a metaphor for how I live."

"I'm not much better," Collins told her. "My part of our house is a mess. And my roommate's a neat freak. I'm not allowed on his floor. He's a very conservative Republican from Utah."

As Sarah drove east on Independence Avenue, she probed further.

"I'm sorry you lost your wife, Congressman. Would you mind if I asked how she died?"

"Please call me Chris," he repeated, turning to look out the window on his side of the car. Again, he seemed ready for the question. "It was an automobile accident

319

during my first term. She was still in Ohio. We couldn't afford two houses.

"She'd been drinking," he said softly. "It was my fault. I'd left her alone too much. Legislative sessions in Columbus. Reserve training. Nine months in Iraq. Living apart most of the week after I came to Washington because she didn't like it here. Even at home on weekends, there were events and campaigning."

He was quiet for a moment.

"I'll never, ever forgive myself for losing her."

He gave Sarah directions to his town house, which was near the House office buildings just north of the Capitol. When Sarah pulled up in front of the house, he turned toward her. His eyes were moist.

"I'm really sorry," Sarah said as he opened the car door. "I shouldn't have asked."

"No, no, it's fine," he said, waving his hand. "I need to be able to talk about it.

"Call me when you're ready to talk about Palisar," he added, swinging his legs out of the car.

"Sure," Sarah said. "Good night."

She watched Collins walk quickly up a short flight of steps to his front door. Then she found her way to Massachusetts Avenue and started home. She turned the radio on and then switched it off again.

That had been too easy, she thought, even though they had Pat Scully and suspicions about Palisar in common. The congressman had opened up completely to a total stranger, a reporter, no less. In Sarah's experience, politicians were usually much more cautious, often duplicitous, in their dealings with the press. Collins had appeared to be as transparent as Scully had become opaque. It didn't compute.

26

Smith and Hawley's headquarters turned out to be an unmarked glass-and-steel building in a fenced office park near Dulles Airport. It looked to Sarah like a high-security government installation. A uniformed guard at the gatehouse checked her identification and wrote down her license-plate number before letting her car pass. Smith and Hawley's press person, Cathy Adams, was waiting for her in the visitors' parking lot.

She handed Sarah an encoded visitor's pass that she showed to another guard at the building's entrance. Once inside, under the watchful eyes of more security personnel, Sarah pressed it against an electronic reader that opened a gate at the checkpoint in the lobby. Adams then took her through automatic glass doors and down a short hallway to a windowless, wood-paneled room.

"Mr. Allenby will meet with you here in the visitors' conference room," Adams said. "Have a seat while I go up to get him."

Sarah sat down in one of the black leather chairs arranged around a long table and put her briefcase on the floor beside her. Studying the room, she noticed a small square of dark, opaque glass on the back wall. She guessed that it concealed a video camera for taping what occurred there. Sarah had brought along her own audio recorder, which she placed in the middle of the conference table.

"Welcome, Miss Page."

Sarah turned around to see George Allenby, a compact, crew-cut, middle-aged man with a confident stride leading a small delegation into the conference room. In shirtsleeves without a tie, he appeared to have spent even more time in the gym than she had. Sarah knew he had served two decades in the Special Forces before joining Smith and Hawley and eventually becoming its C.E.O. She could easily imagine him in fatigues leading Green Berets on a mission.

"I'm George Allenby," he said, shaking her hand firmly. "Thank you for coming out to see us."

He introduced the others, including Smith and Hawley's general counsel and its vice president for corporate relations.

"You've already met Miss Adams, and this is our outside counsel for media matters, Clay Lowell," he said, presenting a patrician-looking, expensively suited older man with well-coiffed silver hair.

Flanked by the others, Allenby sat down opposite Sarah.

"Do you mind if I record our conversation for accuracy?" she asked him.

"Of course not. We have nothing to hide, despite what I hear you may believe."

"I'm not in the belief business," Sarah said. She assumed Allenby had been briefed on the questions she had asked others at the firm and its subcontractors over the past several weeks, as well as government documents she had obtained under the Freedom of Information Act. "I'm gathering information for a story I'm doing about Smith and Hawley's contracts with the military in Iraq."

"Go ahead," Allenby told her. "Fire away."

Sarah leaned over, took several thick file folders from her briefcase, and spread them out on the table. She wanted to impress Allenby with what she already knew.

"These are the contracts I want to focus on," she said. "There're all LOGCAPs awarded to Smith and Hawley by the Pentagon. Long-term, no-bid, open-ended, cost-plus logistical contracts for everything from tents and food service to supplies and security."

She pointed out the extraordinary inflation over the original cost estimate for each contract, the large markups for services supplied by subcontractors, and the numerous payments that could not be accounted for in the few audits of the contracts. "The fairest way to approach this," she said, "would be to ask you about each of these issues one at a time."

"That won't be necessary," Allenby said, leaning back in his chair. "You've gotten answers to your questions from people in our organization. They should be sufficient. I want to tell you that this is a good company, a patriotic company that has been providing essential services to our men in arms in wartime.

"Yes, we've made a good profit. After all, this is not a socialist country. And, yes, we and some of our subcontractors have made mistakes along the way. War is not a tidy business. But, on balance, we've served our country well."

It was clear to Sarah that he had decided to stonewall her.

"Am I to understand, Mr. Allenby, that you're not going to respond to questions about your contracts and what the taxpayers got for their money?"

"We think you should reconsider some of your questions, Miss Page," Clay Lowell broke in. "From what I understand, you're erroneously seeing overruns in the legitimate costs of fulfilling the Pentagon's requirements for these contracts. You're wrongly assigning responsibility to Smith and Hawley for what some subcontractors may have done without its knowledge. I've heard that you've even been using the word 'fraud' in questions you've put to people in this company. That, young lady, is libelous on its face."

Allenby looked on passively while Lowell leaned across the table and looked directly at Sarah.

"This is a private company, Miss Page, even though it is engaged in government business," he said. "We have recourse if you print lies about it or ask questions with false premises."

"It is not my intention to do either." Sarah recognized the language Lowell was using to intimidate her, with its implied threat of legal action. She had steeled herself for a confrontation and was determined to keep her composure. Turning back to Allenby, she pressed on.

"I came here to make certain my information is accurate and to get your side of the story."

"But this is not a story with two sides," Allenby said with a smile. "This is a patriotic company serving its country well. Write that story."

"Mr. Allenby, I appreciate what you're saying. But not everyone sees it that way. Government auditors have raised questions about what the Pentagon has paid you. Some people in Congress have raised questions about travel and other favors you've provided members of the leadership and the Armed Services committees."

"That's just politics," Allenby responded. "And I've already told you war is untidy and expensive. Look at the equipment lost over there in accidents and roadside bombings alone. Regrettable but unavoidable in war."

Sarah took another file folder from her

briefcase and played her last card.

"Let me ask you this, Mr. Allenby" — she pulled several sheets of paper out of the folder — "I've documented a series of questionable payments from subcontractors in Iraq to subsidiaries of Smith and Hawley and other entities here in Washington, including some that appear to be only post-office boxes. What are those payments for?"

"What are you implying, Miss Page?"

"I'm just trying to find out what these payments are."

"Why?"

"I'm wondering whether they're legal," she said, trying to provoke him. "I'm wondering if they're kickbacks."

"That's quite enough!" Clay Lowell thundered. "For the record, Miss Page, that demonstrates a reckless disregard for the truth. It is proof of your bias in this matter, which I will be discussing very soon with your editors. This meeting is over."

Sarah looked questioningly at Allenby.

"I'm sorry, Miss Page," he said, rising from his chair. "But I have to listen to my lawyer. I hope you will, too, before writing your story. Thank you again for coming."

As Sarah gathered her files and put them back into her briefcase, everyone but Cathy Adams filed out of the room.

"Well, that was not what I would call an interview," Sarah told her as they walked out into the lobby. "Why do I have the feeling it was going to end that way no matter what I did?"

"They don't like the company coming under fire."

"Come on, they didn't give me a chance to mount much of an attack."

"They don't want a negative story. That's why they brought in Clay Lowell," Adams said, once they were outside. "They call him 'the story killer.' He's been retained to stop your story from being published. Like he said, your editors will hear from him soon."

"What do you think about that?"

Sarah sensed something about Adams that made her think she might eventually be able to work with her.

"My job is to handle the media the way Smith and Hawley wants me to. I don't ask questions. These are military people and they run a tight ship. I was an Army public-information officer, so I know what they're like."

Sarah took note of Adams's military background, as well as the references to her own company as "they."

"On weekends," Adams added as they reached the parking lot, "I go sailing with my husband over on the Chesapeake. I look forward to that all week long."

When Sarah got back to the newsroom and logged on to her computer, she found an e-mail from Pat Scully. It had been several days since she had messaged him about Chris Collins and her progress on Smith and Hawley.

"collins ok . . . helped me on hill . . . found job for me before I split"

That tracked with what Collins had said, she thought. But why hadn't Scully told her about Collins in the first place?

"by the way," Scully's message ended, "got in touch with your police lieutenant . . . told him what seth knew about my work . . . gave him some leads . . . figured I owed seth"

Sarah was baffled. Scully had resisted her telling Langford who he was or how to find him. And he had "owed" Seth Moore all along. What made him change his mind? How did he know to call Langford? She hadn't told Scully his name.

Sarah decided next to ask Derek Stevens what he knew about George Allenby.

"Smith and Hawley," a woman's voice answered.

"I'm sorry," Sarah said, checking the number in her notes. "I was calling Falcon

Services."

"It's now part of Smith and Hawley," the voice said. "Would you like the number of our headquarters?"

"No, I have that, thank you. Could I just talk to Mr. Stevens?"

"Who?"

"Derek Stevens." Sarah was feeling frustrated. "He runs Falcon Services."

"I'm afraid there's nobody here by that name. I just transferred from headquarters myself. Is there some other way I can help you?"

"Well." Sarah tried to think. "Who took Mr. Stevens's place?"

"I'm not able to give out that information. You should call headquarters."

So Sarah called Cathy Adams.

"Did Smith and Hawley buy a company called Falcon Services?"

"They buy lots of things, and I don't do all the press releases," Adams told her. "Wait a sec while I look through this stuff. What's Falcon Services?"

"A little security contractor in Crystal City. It has some contracts with the Pentagon."

"Oh, here it is," Adams said. "They bought it a couple of weeks ago. Not sure whether its people will stay in Crystal City or be moved here. Looks like the old owner took his money and left."

"Do you have a name?" Sarah asked. She didn't know yet how much she could share with Adams.

"Derek Stevens. No mention of where he went."

Worried now, Sarah hurried across the newsroom to ask Marge Lawson for help. Together, they scoured cyberspace for Derek Stevens. A local telephone number had been disconnected. Sarah found a neighbor near the address for that number in Arlington, who said over the phone that someone had just moved out of a house down the street, a former military man and his family. The neighbor thought the man did some kind of work for the Pentagon, but she didn't know where he went.

Another source had disappeared.

Sarah went back to her desk to think. Should she tell Scully? Was it time to tell Ron Jones everything, whatever the consequences might be? She felt more precariously on her own than ever. Then she remembered Chris Collins. She wasn't sure what to think about him either, but she needed a favor.

A few desks away, Mark Daniels got an

unexpected phone call from Trent Tucker.

"Can we talk?"

"Sure," Mark said. "What about?"

"Remember during the campaign when Sarah Page wrote that story about me?"

"How could I forget? You called me in the middle of the night to complain."

"She's after one of my clients."

"You mean the story about Stetson before he was confirmed? Every company in it was a client of yours."

"She's targeting Smith and Hawley."

"Never heard of them."

"They do contracting for the Pentagon. They flew Stetson to Iraq a couple of times."

"So? That's not unusual."

"Which is why I called," Tucker said. "You understand how these things work. She doesn't. She's looking for scandal."

"What are you talking about, Trent?"

"She met with Smith and Hawley's C.E.O. today and made a lot of reckless accusations about their contracts in Iraq. Cost overruns, kickbacks, you name it. They brought in a lawyer who said it's all libelous. He's going to warn your paper about it."

"Then why call me? I'm not an editor. And I haven't the slightest idea what Sarah's working on. I'm not in that loop."

"She'll listen to you."

"I told you it doesn't work that way, Trent. Your client and their lawyer should talk to Lou Runyan. He'll give them a fair hearing."

Mark hung up the phone and looked over at Sarah, who was typing away at her computer. He thought Tucker's call would just upset her. So he went to see Runyan himself.

27

Sarah met Chris Collins for lunch the next day at B. Smith's restaurant in the East Hall of Union Station, a short walk from the Capitol. Its high-ceilinged Beaux Arts dining room had once been the station's Presidential Suite, through which heads of state passed on their way to and from trains.

"I haven't seen anything by you in the paper lately," Collins said. In a tan summer suit, indigo shirt, and red-and-blue striped tie, he still didn't look to Sarah like a congressman.

"I've been working on a story about Smith and Hawley's contracts in Iraq," she told him. "I met with their C.E.O. yesterday."

"George Allenby?"

"How'd you know who he was?"

"I've been catching up, waiting for you to get in touch," said Collins. "How'd it go with Allenby?"

"Not well," Sarah said. "He didn't really answer my questions. His lawyer's coming to the paper this week for a big meeting with me and my editors."

"What are you going to do?"

"Fight for my story and hope the editors don't cave."

"What can I do?"

Collins seemed genuinely eager to help. And there was something Sarah wanted from him. Maybe that's why she had decided to wear her favorite black dress to lunch.

"What happened to everything Scully gave you on Smith and Hawley?"

"It's all in a couple of file cabinets," Collins said.

"That's not exactly what I meant. Is your investigation still technically open, even though you never held hearings?"

"Oh, I get it." Collins smiled knowingly. "You want to be able to say that a congressman is investigating Smith and Hawley's contracts."

"Would that be a problem for you?"

"Do you have to say which congressman?"

"Not yet."

When their food came, Collins took a big bite out of his pulled pork sandwich, leaving barbecue sauce dripping from the bottom of his nose. Sarah tried not to laugh as he sheepishly wiped it off with his napkin. For a moment, she was distracted by how cute he looked.

"Look," he said after thinking about it. "I'll be your unnamed congressman. And, if the story has enough impact on the Hill, I'll come out of the closet and announce hearings in my subcommittee."

"Thanks, Chris. That's all I could ask for."

Although it was common practice for investigative reporters to work with congressmen and their staffs on investigations of what they revealed in their stories, Sarah felt a little uncomfortable about it. But Collins had offered to help. And it would keep them in touch.

After lunch, they walked out of the restaurant, through the East Hall shops and into the station's main concourse, going right past the Center Café, where Sarah had first met with Pat Scully.

"Is this stuff hard on you?" Collins asked in a way that tempted Sarah to tell him everything. The disappearing sources. The 4 a.m. phone calls. Her uneasiness with Mark, even her uncertainty about Scully. But she wasn't sure about Collins either, although she found him quite likable.

"Sure, it's hard sometimes," she told him. "But I like doing journalism that matters."

"I got into politics because I thought it mattered, too," Collins said. "Sometimes, now, I'm not so sure. Too often, you feel like a pawn of the interest groups."

"What do they want?"

"It's not as simple as it sometimes seems. A lot of their money comes your way simply because you're the incumbent or you're on a committee that affects their interests. They hedge their bets. The problem comes when an issue is so important to them that you know they'll be spending money to defeat you if you don't vote their way."

"What do you do then?"

They had gone upstairs, where they strolled past fashionable clothing shops along the elevated walkways overlooking the concourse. Collins was beginning to sound like one of the political-science professors Sarah had had in college, rather than the instinctive, crassly cynical politicians she had covered in Maryland.

"I pick and choose when to risk it," Collins said. "For example, gun ownership matters in my district. I might be able to sell some restrictions on assault rifles as a public safety issue. But I can't vote for any really meaningful gun controls, or the N.R.A. will kill me. Taxes are a big concern for my people, so I'm careful on votes that might stir up antitax groups. My military record gives me enough credibility on defense spending that I can take on that lobby."

"But you don't want to get out front of my story," Sarah said.

"That's because it involves Palisar, which could mean taking on some of the most powerful people in Congress. If your story makes it possible for me to say Smith and Hawley is wasting taxpayers' money and weakening our defense, then I can buck them."

They went back down to the floor of the main concourse, where they stopped to say good-bye. Collins looked into Sarah's eyes and gave her hand an extra squeeze.

"Well, this was certainly different from walking around the Tidal Basin in our shorts," he said. "You look great in that dress."

Sarah felt herself blushing. It had been a while since a man had treated her this way.

"You look quite presentable yourself, Congressman," she said. "I look forward to doing business with you."

"Let me know how your meeting comes out."

Collins pushed through a door to the street. Sarah turned and walked briskly toward the West Hall and the escalator down to the Metro. She thought again about the rules, pushing aside her doubts about who she could trust. Was Chris Collins interested in more than helping with her story? Was she?

The next morning, when Sarah walked into the dining room of the Hay-Adams hotel, Ron Jones was already waiting at a table by a window looking out onto Lafayette Square.

"I've read your story carefully," he said after they had ordered breakfast. "I've looked at all the records you gave me. Now I need to know everything else, including your secret source in California. I don't want any surprises at the meeting with the company and its lawyer tomorrow."

Sarah decided she had no choice but to tell him the whole story, from the beginning.

Jones was furious.

"A source of yours is killed. You and our police reporter start playing detective. The police question you and another one of your sources, who's in hiding because of some kind of threat. Two more sources vanish into thin air. Somebody's trying to scare you away from the story and may even be watching your every move. And you make a deal on your own with some congressman who sought you out. But you don't tell any of this to your editor?"

"I was afraid you'd pull me off the story."

"Take you off the story?" Jones paused for effect. "I should fire you on the spot."

Not without some fear, Sarah fought for herself. "But the story's right. I can back up everything in it."

"Can you really, Sarah, when one of your sources is hiding out somewhere and the others have disappeared?"

Her voice started to quaver as she pleaded with him. "I've got the records. So does a member of Congress. Punish me in some other way. But don't kill the story."

She looked vacantly out the window, ignoring her egg-white omelet.

Jones pushed what was left of his scrambled eggs around his plate while he tried to sort it all out in his mind. Sarah had made a serious mistake in not keeping him informed. The paper could be mixed up in investigations of a murder and who knows what else. And one of its reporters could be in danger.

But Sarah had not done anything unethical. Her story could be saved, a story that might have far-reaching implications. This could be a defining moment in *his* career.

"Sarah, look at me."

She braced herself.

"You should have told me all of this a long time ago. You need to trust me as much as I have to trust you. From now on, there can be no more secrets. Understood?"

"Understood."

"When we get back to the office, I'm going to talk to Lou and our general counsel. You're going to have to do whatever they say about cooperating with the police. And looking after your own safety. Okay?"

"Okay."

"I'm also going to tell Lou that I think we can save the story."

Sarah slumped in her chair with relief.

"That doesn't mean he's going to let us do it," Jones said. "The story still needs work. We'll have to go over it with our lawyers. And it's going to have to survive tomorrow's meeting with the people from Smith and Hawley."

Not long after they returned to the newspaper, Jones took Sarah to see the general counsel, Anna Wentworth. She questioned

Sarah about both her sources for the story and her own safety. Sarah started to cry when the lawyer pressed her for details about Seth Moore and his suspicious death.

"I'm sorry. I know this must be painful for you," Wentworth said. "The police are still investigating, and you've talked to them?"

"Yes," Sarah said, composing herself. "Lieutenant Charles Langford in homicide. He seems very interested in the case."

"I'll get in touch with him right away. I'll tell him about these sources of yours who've disappeared. What about this man who called you at four in the morning?"

"He sounded like he could be in the military," Sarah said, "and he talked about national security."

"Did he threaten you?"

"No, but he made it clear he's warning me."

Telling the lawyer about the phone calls made them feel more menacing to Sarah.

"I'll need to know if he calls again," Wentworth said. "And I'd like to know more about Patrick Scully. Could you and Marge give me everything you've found about him? It sounds like you've got plenty of independent documentation for your story, which I'll also have to see, but he's kind of an unusual source."

The reservation that afternoon at the Bombay Club, a block away from the White House at the northwest corner of Lafayette Square, was in Sarah's name. But, as soon as the maître d' saw Alison Winters, he found a better table for them in the middle of the wood-paneled dining room dotted with potted palms.

Sarah had taken Ron Jones's advice to have lunch with the president's press secretary. Like the Oval Room across the street, the Bombay Club was a favored meeting place for journalists and White House officials. Their conversations might sound casual to an onlooker, but the subtext was often more meaningful.

"We're still feeling our way over there," Alison told Sarah after they had both ordered curry dishes. "But she'll be a great president."

Sarah tried to probe a little. "Why did you and Elliott Bancroft come to the paper to argue against the Stetson story?"

"It wasn't my meeting," Alison said. "And I didn't argue against the story. It seemed fair to me. No offense, but it wasn't going to influence the confirmation vote anyway."

Rather than being offended, Sarah was

impressed by Alison's candor.

"So what was Bancroft up to?"

"That's what I wondered while we were sitting there."

Sarah was intrigued.

"Don't the two of you work closely together?"

Alison didn't answer right away. Sarah guessed that her hesitation meant Alison might have said too much already.

"Elliott's my boss," she finally told Sarah. "I hadn't met him before he joined our campaign. Now he works more closely with the president than I do."

"And Trent Tucker?"

"He's long gone," Alison said firmly. "It was the first thing the president did when she moved into the Oval Office."

"No contact at all?"

"None," Alison said, but she looked puzzled. "Why?" she asked Sarah. "What are you working on?"

"Just more about money and politics."

"Like the Stetson story?"

"Yes."

"It seems like very lonely work," said Alison. "A few confidential sources and all those records."

"At times." Sarah figured Alison had no idea what it was like and might just be fishing for information. But it was worth trying to be empathetic. "Your job has to be kind of confining, too. And the hours must be brutal."

"Sure," Alison said. "I realize this could be the only chance I ever have to do something like this. But it's been totally demanding, just like the campaign. There's not much opportunity to socialize outside the people I work with, and that's kind of incestuous."

"It's not just the hours," Sarah said, unintentionally talking about herself more than Alison. "It's pretty difficult to have normal relationships when almost everyone you deal with has an agenda and you can't get too close to them."

Both women sensed that that was the situation they were in now, until they knew whether they could really trust each other. They finished their curries, split the check to satisfy the ethical rules of both the newspaper and the government, and then set off in opposite directions.

28

Ron Jones came by Sarah's desk to walk with her to the conference room across the newsroom, where the editors held their front-page meetings each afternoon.

"Why aren't we going to Runyan's office?" Sarah asked him.

"Lou uses the conference room for meetings like this so he can leave when he's had enough," Jones told her. "If this lawyer comes on too strong, he'll lose Lou right away."

Mary Sullivan was waiting with their visitors. It was the same group Sarah had faced at Smith and Hawley, except George Allenby was missing. Sullivan introduced Jones to Smith and Hawley's general counsel; its vice president for corporate relations; its press spokesman, Cathy Adams; and their outside lawyer, Clay Lowell.

"Where's Mr. Allenby?" Sarah asked Adams.

"He's got a company to run and this could be a long meeting." Adams, using a somewhat formal tone, seemed to be speaking for the benefit of her delegation. "Mr. Lowell is representing him today."

"Good to see you again, Miss Page," Lowell said, smiling broadly as he extended a well-manicured hand. "Where's *your* big boss?"

"He's on his way," said Sullivan. Her expression made it clear she was not pleased that Lowell seemed to be minimizing her significance.

A moment later, Lou Runyan ambled in, shook everyone's hand and took his usual seat at the end of the conference table. Everyone in the Smith and Hawley delegation sat on one side of the table, leaving Sarah and the other two editors facing them.

"Miss Page," Lowell began, as he took several files out of his briefcase and piled them on the table. "I hope you brought a copy of your proposed story with you, so we can discuss it in detail."

"I assume Miss Adams told you that we couldn't do that," Ron Jones answered for Sarah. "Miss Page e-mailed Miss Adams a memo detailing the story's significant points, along with a list of questions." Looking at the file folders, Jones added, "I hope you brought those answers with you."

Sarah was reassured by his aggressiveness.

"I have the memo, as unsatisfactory as it is," Lowell said, opening the folder at the top of the pile. "Almost every statement in it contains an error or worse."

"We're prepared to listen to everything you have to say," Jones said. He and Sarah put legal pads onto the table and took out pens, ready to write. Sarah stole a glance toward Runyan, who was fiddling impatiently with the chain he wore around his neck for his security pass.

"There's so much to say," Lowell told them. "To begin with, you can't connect the awarding of Pentagon contracts to Smith and Hawley with the firm's contributions to political campaigns or these other entities, much less any air travel it made available for congressional fact-finding missions in war zones. You can't characterize normal expansions of LOGCAP contracts as overruns or inflated charges. You can't say that routine transfers of funds to and from subcontractors are questionable or suspicious. You can't rely on partial audits of contracts, especially when we have shown the audits to be flawed. And you certainly can't repeat unfounded accusations by disgruntled former employees."

"Hold on," Runyan interrupted. "Is there anything in there that you don't find fault with?"

"I'm glad you asked that," Lowell said with a self-satisfied smile, "because the answer is no. Judging from this memo, your story would be libelous on its face, from beginning to end." Turning to face Runyan at the end of the table, he added, "You would be putting your newspaper in jeopardy by publishing this story."

The room fell silent.

Then Runyan calmly rested his hands on the edge of the table and, looking directly at Lowell, spoke: "Well, that's interesting, because Mary here told me our lawyers went over the story carefully with Miss Page. They think it's okay. We just need responses from your clients. Of course, if we don't get any, we can go ahead and publish the story anyway."

Sarah could feel Ron Jones nudging her with his elbow.

"Perhaps your in-house counsel hasn't handled a story like this before," Lowell said to Runyan.

"Our general counsel is a crackerjack libel lawyer," Runyan responded. "She also reviewed the story with our own outside counsel. You might remember Dudley Willis from that news magazine case some years ago. He beat your ass. That's one of the reasons we retained him."

Mary Sullivan leaned slightly forward to watch how this was registering on the Smith and Hawley side of the table. Jones allowed himself a hint of a smile. Sarah sat motionless, riveted by the drama playing out in front of her.

"Well, sir, I hear you," Lowell said, gathering his thoughts. "How do you suggest we proceed?"

"Get used to the fact that we're going to run this story whether you like it or not," Runyan said, backing his chair away from the table. "I suggest you and your clients may want to answer Miss Page's questions. And you can give her any other comments and explanations you wish. Take your time. I'll leave Mary in charge. She can bring in our lawyers if you want them."

Runyan got up and walked out the door. Sullivan moved over to his chair. She had brought along her own legal pad and a file folder, from which she took copies of Sarah's memo to Smith and Hawley and distributed them around the table.

"If you're ready," she said to Lowell and his clients, "we'll go through this carefully now. It'll save time if we refrain from speeches and focus on the facts, so we can get them right."

Lowell initially disputed many of the facts and most of Sarah's interpretations of them. But, under patient questioning from Sarah and her editors as the hours dragged on, he gradually conceded point after point. He even confirmed information based on the records Sarah had obtained from Andy Foster and Derek Stevens, making the sources' unavailability irrelevant. Lowell agreed to disagree on other aspects of the story. And he promised a written statement from Smith and Hawley by the end of the day. The company's executives said little during the meeting.

"Okay, I think we've covered everything," Sullivan said after several hours of work. "We're going to need this room soon for our front-page conference, and I'm sure all of you want to get back to your offices. I'm sorry you've missed lunch. Mr. Jones and I will work on the story with Miss Page. We'll take into consideration everything we've discussed here, as well as the statement you've promised. Thank you for your time."

Clay Lowell rose from his chair and stuffed files back into his briefcase without saying another word. He nodded curtly at Sarah and Ron Jones as he and the others followed Mary Sullivan out the door. Only Cathy Adams paused to tell Sarah, "I'll call you later."

Jones stood and stretched his long arms and legs. Sarah remained in her chair, drained of her usual energy and amazed at what had taken place. She looked up at Jones and asked, "Did you expect Runyan to do that?"

"No," he said, "although I've seen it happen when he gets his back up. He clearly had listened to what Mary and I and the lawyers told him about the story. I think he knew exactly what he was going to do when he walked in here this morning."

They worked into the evening in Jones's office, Sullivan sprawled comfortably on the couch and Sarah sitting patiently next to Jones while he edited the story a line at a time. At one point, a phone call from Cathy Adams was put through to Sarah.

"Mr. Allenby wants you to know that he can't believe you're going to publish that story," Adams told her in that formal tone of voice again. "But he agreed to give you a short statement that Mr. Lowell has approved. I'm faxing it over to you."

Sarah and the two editors continued working until after eight, when Sullivan decided they should break for the night. On her way back to her desk, Sarah was intercepted by Mark Daniels. He had just gotten back from a daylong trip with the White House press corps to Chicago, where President Cameron had made a speech on health care.

"What happened in your big meeting?" he asked.

"How do you know about that?"

"I've been keeping tabs on your story ever since Trent Tucker called me about it."

"What?" Sarah's exhaustion gave way instantly to a familiar anger.

"Take it easy," Mark told her. "I didn't like Trent's call. I knew he was trying to use me to stop the story."

Sarah took a few steps to her chair and sat down.

"So I went in and warned Runyan about the hotshot lawyer Trent had mentioned." Mark perched himself on the edge of Sarah's desk. "I told Lou you're a damn good reporter. He said Sullivan and Jones had already vouched for the story and the lawyers were fine with it. He just wanted to read it himself."

"Why didn't you tell me about Tucker?"

"Because you would've gotten pissed off. Would you have wanted to go into that meeting today spitting fire without Lou's backing?"

Leaving his office, Ron Jones seemed surprised to see Mark there.

"You're back from Chicago?" he asked, striding toward them. "What's up?"

"He's just telling me what a drag these one-day trips are," Sarah said. "No dinners at great restaurants. No overnights in five-star hotels. You know, the miserable life of a White House correspondent."

Jones joined them in laughter and moved

on toward home.

"That was impressive," Mark told Sarah.

"I wouldn't want Ron to know you went over his head again. So you read my story, too?"

"Yeah, last night, with Lou."

"And?"

"It's a hell of a story. I couldn't begin to do that kind of work."

"Thanks," Sarah said softly. That surprised her.

"I believe in good stories and playing it straight with readers," Mark said, "in spite of what you may think."

Sarah felt uncomfortable with his defensiveness.

"I've got to get some rest," she said. "We have to finish the editing and go over the story with the lawyers again tomorrow. I'm going home."

Later that night, after she had settled into bed, Sarah was surprised to get a phone call from Mark.

"Sorry to be bothering you at home, but it's personal," he said. "I got your number from the National desk. Is this a bad time to talk?"

"No, not for a little while anyway. I'm trying to read, but I'm having a hard time staying awake."

"I'll make it quick. I need advice."

Sarah was surprised. "What about?"

"One of the advance girls on the press plane told me today that Jeanne's home from Italy and back on advance, this time for Cameron."

"That's good, isn't it?"

"But Jeanne hasn't told me she's back."

"Didn't you two keep in touch?"

"On and off. A few postcards and letters. Phone calls when I could get past the housekeeper there, who didn't speak English. Jeanne called me a few times, but she never gave me the number of the international cell phone she took from the travel agency."

"But she stayed in touch with the White House?"

"Apparently, they kept calling to ask her to come back," Mark said. "She was the old hand for overnight advance. She did their training sessions. She had said she'd like to work with a woman president. But I had no idea she was doing it."

"She probably hasn't decided about you yet," said Sarah. "When did she get back?"

"I'm not sure. The girl on the plane today said Jeanne's in L.A. doing hotel advance for the president's trip there next week."

"Aren't you going?"

"Sure."

"Then you'll see her there."

"She'll be busy at Cameron's hotel. Should I try to get in touch with her anyway? Or should I wait until we're both back here?"

Sarah couldn't believe that she, of all people, was being asked for relationship advice.

"You're still serious about her?"

"I'm afraid so. My divorce is moving along, but I haven't really been with anyone else. That's never happened before."

"Then call her in L.A. right now," Sarah told him. "Say you want to see her when you get there and you want to talk about where the two of you stand. The worst that can happen," she added from her own experience, "is she'll tell you it's over for good. Then at least you can get on with your life."

Now that she was wide awake, Sarah decided to call Chris Collins on the cellphone number he had given her.

"It looks like they're going to publish the story on Sunday," she told him. Hearing a cacophony of voices and music in the background, she wondered where he was. But she decided not to ask.

"So the meeting went well?"

"The editors were great," Sarah said, pleased that he had asked. "Lou Runyan went after their lawyer right away. We fought over details for hours, but it worked out."

"Did you bring up the unnamed congressman?"

"I didn't have to, except in private with my editor. But I'd like to use you in the story."

"What do you want to say?"

"That the House Appropriations Defense Subcommittee has been studying audits of questionable charges in Smith and Hawley's contracts as part of its oversight of Pentagon contracting."

"That has the virtue of being true," Collins said. "But our staff does stuff like that all the time."

"And that at least one member of the subcommittee is considering a formal inquiry into contract irregularities based on those audits."

"According to an unnamed congressman?"

"According to a member of the House Appropriations Committee," Sarah said.

"Sold," Collins told her. "You drive a hard bargain. What other business would you like to do with me?"

Sarah wondered whether he meant personal business. But, once again, this wasn't the time to pursue it.

"All I can think about right now is this story," she told Collins. "It's the biggest one of my life."

"I understand," he said, in a way that made her regret that she had to say good night.

29

Trent Tucker read Sarah's story shortly after midnight Sunday on his home computer.

Carter Phillips was at his country house on the St. Mary's River at the southern tip of Maryland when Tucker called to tell him about it.

George Allenby saw the headline when he picked up the newspaper on Sunday morning from the circular driveway in front of his house in Great Falls, Virginia: THE SPOILS OF WAR: How One Defense Contractor Profited from Iraq.

When Cathy Adams was awakened by a phone call from Allenby, she hurried to pick up a paper in the lobby of her Alexandria apartment house.

Representative Chris Collins bought the newspaper at a Capitol Hill coffee shop, where he underlined parts of Sarah's story and wrote notes to himself in the margins.

President Susan Cameron was told about it during her Sunday morning briefing at Camp David, the rustic presidential retreat in Maryland's Catoctin Mountain Park. She asked an orderly to bring a copy of the story to her in Aspen Lodge. Then she called Signal, the White House military communications system, to locate Elliott Bancroft.

Alison Winters, who, along with Elliott, had been given a rare weekend off by the president, took several newspapers with her when she walked from her basement apartment in Georgetown to Dean & DeLuca on M Street to eat breakfast outdoors. When she saw Sarah's story, she took out her cell phone and called Signal herself.

Elliott was contacted by Signal in a McLean mansion where he had spent the night with an old acquaintance whose husband was in China on business. He pulled on his clothes and drove to the White House.

It was a long story that got right to the point at the beginning.

By Sarah Page

A politically connected Northern Virginia defense contractor inflated the costs of Pentagon contracts to provide support for the U.S. military in Iraq by hundreds of millions of dollars annually for several years, according to internal company records, interviews with former employees, and Pentagon audits.

Smith and Hawley Inc., headquartered near Dulles Airport, used influence in Congress to obtain billions of dollars in open-ended, no-bid contracts to supply American troops in Iraq with construction, food service, communications, delivery, security, and other services.

Most of the work was done by American and foreign subcontractors hired by Smith and Hawley at exorbitant markups, according to documents and interviews. In addition to large profits it made from each contract's management fees, Smith and Hawley charged the Pentagon several times as much money as it paid subcontractors to do the work.

According to interviews and records, some of its subcontractors sent unexplained payments to several addresses in Washington, a number of which are actually post-office boxes at a MailServices store on Pennsylvania Avenue near the White House, whose owners could not be determined.

Other recipients — Public Relations Solutions, American Freedom Alliance, and Malin Associates — are linked to Washington lobbyist and political consultant Trent Tucker, a former campaign aide to President Susan Cameron and White House political adviser to her predecessor, the late Monroe Capehart.

Tucker's lobbying firm, Tucker and Associates, shares offices on the top three floors of a downtown Washington building with these groups and the nonprofit National Center for a Better Congress. The center has financed expensive domestic and foreign travel for members of Congress who helped Smith and Hawley obtain Pentagon contracts.

Smith and Hawley is owned by the Washington investment firm Palisar International, whose principal partner is Gen. Carter Phillips, retired U.S. Army Special Forces commander and former director of the Central Intelligence Agency.

In a statement, George Allenby, the C.E.O. of Smith and Hawley, said the firm's contracts in Iraq were "performed well and according to the Pentagon's specifications and at a fair price. Any suggestion that Smith and Hawley or any of its subcontractors overcharged the government would be false and misleading."

30

The clock radio woke Sarah just before seven on Monday morning, giving her time for a quick run before work. Wearing a white T-shirt, black shorts, and a fanny pack, she jogged a few blocks to Potomac Avenue at the edge of the Palisades bluff on the Washington side of the Potomac River Gorge. She ran along the narrow strip of parkland overlooking the river until she reached the chain-link security fence around the sprawling Washington Aqueduct, where the U.S. Army Corps of Engineers pumped water for the city from the river.

There she went down a steep dirt path behind the fence to the paved Capital Crescent Trail, which ran along the river and the Chesapeake and Ohio Canal from Georgetown. At the Washington Aqueduct, it turned away from the river into Maryland. It was the route of an abandoned single-track rail line, the Georgetown Branch of the old Baltimore and Ohio Railroad, which carried coal to Washington from 1910 until 1985.

Only a few bikers passed by as Sarah followed the curve of the trail through the fenced-off Washington Aqueduct grounds. In the early morning sunlight, no one could be seen around its manicured lawns, interconnected water-storage ponds, and scattered redbrick buildings. Sarah ran by a small rest area with a water fountain, benches, and a glass-covered notice board displaying a map of the trail and a history of the old rail line. Then the trail straightened and went into the woods. Sunlight gave way to shadow inside a cathedral of leaves formed by the top branches of the tallest trees.

A few hundred yards ahead, Sarah could see the even darker interior of the Dalecarlia Tunnel. Several stories high, eighteen feet wide, and 341 feet long, the century-old brick tunnel had taken the coal trains under MacArthur Boulevard. At staggered intervals inside the tunnel were five-foot-high "step-ins," two on each side, into which track workers could escape an oncoming train.

Except for a fast-disappearing biker, the damp, musty tunnel was empty when Sarah ran into it. Then she heard the heavy footsteps of a runner gaining on her from behind. She was just about to pass the first step-in on the right when she felt the powerful arms of a large man grab her. He forced her into the step-in, pushing her face and body roughly against its cold, dirty brick wall.

Panic paralyzed Sarah and pain radiated along the front of her body as the man pinned her more tightly against the brick. She felt his face close to her.

"Don't scream," he said, "or I'll smash your face in."

"What do you want?"

"This is your last warning." Although he was gasping for breath, his voice sounded rough and convincingly threatening. "Stop now. We know where you live. We know everywhere you go."

He gave her one last shove, buckling her knees, before releasing her. Sarah sank into the wet mud at the bottom of the step-in. When she heard him running away in the same direction from which he had come, she turned her head and saw the back of a burly man in a dark blue jogging suit.

Sarah stayed on her knees long enough to catch her breath and take stock. She was alive, and nothing seemed to hurt so much that it might be broken. She touched her face and found dirt but no blood. Grabbing on to the brick framework of the step-in with both hands, she slowly pulled herself up and looked around.

She saw another bike approaching from out of the sunshine at the far end. She felt her heart pounding until she realized the rider was a woman. She straightened up and tried to brush herself off. The cyclist, wearing sunglasses and earphones, paid no attention as she flashed by.

Sarah decided not to go back home. She started toward the far end of the tunnel instead. She tried to run, but it was too painful. She walked as fast as she could until she was out of the tunnel. She continued along the trail, wondering whether she should walk all the way to Bethesda.

Then, suddenly, someone appeared out of nowhere, climbing up from below onto the railing of a small bridge just ahead of her on the trail. Sarah froze. It was a scraggly-haired, middle-aged woman, who appeared to be homeless. The woman was thin and barefoot, wearing rolled-up blue jeans and a dirty long-sleeved shirt. She was carrying two plastic grocery bags. Without acknowledging Sarah's presence, she pulled herself with surprising agility over the rail and onto the little bridge as Sarah walked by.

A few yards farther along, Sarah saw another paved path that veered off to the right. She remembered that it curved down, went under the little bridge the woman had just climbed onto, and continued up a hill and out of the woods at MacArthur Boulevard. She decided to take it, holding her breath as she walked under the bridge.

She followed the winding path up the tree-covered hill, criss-crossing over a gurgling stream and then passing a bench and a picnic table. She had rounded its last bend, with the opening to the street in sight, when she saw the homeless woman again, walking just ahead of her before turning onto a connecting path. How had she gotten there?

Then Sarah was back out in the sunshine on a sidewalk along MacArthur Boulevard in Maryland, only a mile or so from her neighborhood in the District. Commuters raced by in their cars. She felt safer there.

For the first time since the attack, Sarah thought about her fanny pack. She reached back, pulled it around her and unzipped it. She still had her wallet and keys — and her cell phone.

Ron Jones wouldn't be in his office yet, and Sarah didn't know his home number. Then she remembered she had taken down Mark's number from her caller ID when he telephoned a few nights earlier. And she had programmed it into her cell phone the next morning.

She almost ended the call after several rings, figuring Mark had already left for the White House. But, in the lethargy passing over her, she let it continue to ring. And Mark finally answered.

"Who's this?" he asked drowsily.

"Sarah," she said. "Why are you still sleeping on a Monday?"

"Well, if you must know," he responded, yawning, "I'm not working today. They gave me three days off because I'll be in L.A. with the president next weekend."

"Oh, yeah, sorry," Sarah said, her voice trailing off as she lost concentration. Feeling faint, she sat down in the grass near the curb, crossing her legs in front of her.

"I can barely hear you," Mark said. "Why are you calling me?"

"I was out running, I mean I'm still out," she responded aimlessly. "This man, he came up behind me . . ."

"My God, Sarah. Has someone attacked you?"

"Yes. Attacked me. In the tunnel."

"What tunnel? Where are you now?" Mark was now alert and concerned. "Did this man, you know, hurt you?"

Dealing with his timidity helped Sarah take stock.

"No, he didn't rape me," she told Mark. "He pushed me into the wall of the tunnel. He said he was warning me. I'm okay, but it hurts. And it scared the shit out of me."

She started crying.

"I'm still scared," she said, sobbing. "Can you come help me?"

"Of course." Mark was already out of bed, putting on clothes. "Just tell me where you are."

"MacArthur Boulevard just over the Maryland line. At Sangamore."

"I know where that is. I've been there on my bike coming up from the Crescent Trail."

"That's just what I did, but without the bike."

Sarah smiled at that, even though her eyes were still filled with tears.

"I'm sitting in the grass," she told Mark. "I don't think I can move."

"Then stay there," he instructed. "Stay in sight of the traffic. Keep your cell phone out. Call 911 if anyone comes near you. I'll be right there."

"I still don't understand why you didn't call the police right away," Mark said an hour later. Sarah had just emerged from the bedroom of his apartment. After showering, she was dressed in one of his shirts and a pair of his running shorts. She had pulled the drawstring of the shorts as tight as she could to keep them from falling off. The shirt came nearly to her knees.

"I feel like Katharine Hepburn in one of those old movies with Spencer Tracy," she said. "Or was it Bacall and Bogart?"

Mark appraised Sarah from an overstuffed chair in the middle of his sparsely furnished living room. She had sat down on the couch opposite him, folding her legs under her. During the ride to the apartment building on Connecticut Avenue, Sarah had told Mark in tearful detail about everything she could remember until the time she called him. But she hadn't responded when he asked why she didn't contact the police or ask a passerby to do it.

"So why haven't you called the cops?"

"What happened was because of my work," she said. "So I wanted someone at the paper to help me decide what to do."

"Then you should talk to Ron right away. He'll tell security about it. And he'll probably want you to report it to the police."

"Okay."

Sarah had already told Ron Jones and Anna Wentworth, the newspaper's general counsel, about the goon at Seth Moore's funeral and the 4 a.m. telephone calls. Wentworth hadn't yet gotten back to her after saying she would talk to the police. The rough voice of the man who attacked Sarah hadn't sounded like the crisp military cadence of her early morning caller. The goon in the church hadn't said a word, but Sarah remembered he was big and rough-looking.

"I could write about it, too," she said. "Putting it in the paper would show whoever it was that I'm not intimidated."

"I don't know," Mark told her. "That might make them even more determined to stop you."

Sarah could tell he was really concerned.

"I appreciate this, Mark," she told him. "And it meant a lot to me that you supported my story with Runyan."

She unfolded her legs and stretched out on the couch.

"And then I bothered you about Jeanne," Mark said. "I can't believe I did that."

"If you hadn't, I wouldn't have had your phone number. By the way, did you call her?"

"She said she was too busy to talk much, but she sort of apologized for not letting me know she was back," Mark said. "She told me to try her again when I got into L.A. with the president."

"Hang in there."

"Isn't that what I should be telling you?"

After Mark showered and dressed, he drove Sarah to her house and then downtown, leaving her car behind. He told her that he had plenty to do in the newsroom until she was ready for him to take her home.

They went into Ron Jones's office together and told him what happened. He sent for Mary Sullivan and they all went to see Lou Runyan.

After Sarah repeated the whole story, Runyan called the newspaper's head of security, who arranged with the police to have a squad car cruise by Sarah's house regularly. She turned down Lou's suggestion that she be examined at a hospital but agreed to visit the nurse if anything still hurt later in the day.

"Your story embarrassed a lot of folks," Runyan mused aloud. "And it may get some of them in trouble with the law. But that's happened before in this town, and I don't remember a reporter being harassed this way. Not to mention what's happened to some of your sources."

Sarah couldn't decide which worried her

more: the danger she might be facing or the possibility that Runyan might stop her from doing more reporting.

"Do you think we should pull her off?" Mary Sullivan asked him. "For her own safety?"

Sarah was about to protest. But Runyan anticipated her.

"I doubt she would listen to us," he told Sullivan, as though Sarah weren't there. "Just as you wouldn't have when you were running around the world covering wars. And I sure don't want her off on her own. Just make sure we're doing everything we can to protect her."

Sullivan and Jones nodded.

"And you have to help us keep you safe," Runyan said to Sarah. "Listen to what your editors and the police say. Don't do anything foolish. Or I will take you off the story."

"Okay," Sarah responded meekly. She recognized this was a huge vote of confidence.

"If you don't mind," Runyan said, "I'm going to talk to some people I know about how your stories could be putting you and your sources in danger. I'll let you know if they tell me anything."

Then, without Sarah asking, Runyan

called the Metro editor and ordered up a story about the attack on her.

When Sarah got back to her desk, the phone was ringing. It was Chris Collins.

"Where've you been?" he asked in an excited voice. "I've got clearance to hold hearings. Your story blew everything wide open. We're making the announcement at a press conference at noon in Rayburn."

"That's great," Sarah said. She was pleased and relieved. And she decided not to spoil the moment by telling him what had happened to her. "I'll make sure our House reporter is there."

"It'll be on C-SPAN."

"I'll watch. I hope you're wearing that nice suit you had on at lunch."

"I do have more than one," he told her, sounding downright flirtatious. "You know, I'll need your help with this."

"That might be a little tricky," Sarah said, becoming more businesslike, another opportunity missed because of her work. "I'll have to get guidance from my editors."

"Fair enough," Collins said. "We'll work it out."

While Sarah was on the phone, a news aide brought her a pile of phone messages. Sorting through them, she noticed the name "Kit Morgan" and puzzled over why she recognized it. Then she remembered the brassy woman from Washington she had met at the fund-raising reception during the Democratic convention in Chicago. She dialed the number.

"Miss Morgan, this is Sarah Page returning your call."

"Sarah, please call me Kit," Morgan said in an overly familiar way. "I saw your story. It's a real blockbuster."

"I'm glad you liked it, if that's what you mean."

"I might be able to help you understand the business of those kinds of defense contractors," Morgan said. "I work with a bunch of them here."

Sarah still wasn't quite sure what Morgan meant. But she thought she should find out.

"I'd like that," she said. "I'll give you a call."

At noon, Sarah watched Chris Collins's televised announcement with Mark and Ron Jones in the political editor's office. She was excited: her story had made a difference. But she wished she had found a way to be more friendly with Collins on the telephone that morning.

Jones just leaned back in the chair behind his desk to enjoy one of those rare times when a momentum shift could be felt in

Washington. "Sarah," he said to her, "your story has legs."

"Breakfast or lunch? I'm buying," asked Joni Parker, who had materialized outside Jones's office as Sarah was leaving it.

"What are you doing here?" Sarah asked her.

"The Metro editor woke me up. He asked if I wanted to write about your little adventure. What was I going to say? You're my girl. He filled me in on what you told Runyan. And I called Langford. He wants to talk to you. The Montgomery County cops will, too, since it happened in their jurisdiction. Langford's pulling strings to put more security on your house. Drive-bys aren't enough."

"Is all that necessary?"

"Langford said you should be taking this very seriously," Joni said to Sarah as they walked across the newsroom. "How are you feeling?"

"Okay, I guess. Some scrapes and bruises. Nothing serious."

"Where's your head at?"

"I'm kind of numb, but staying on the story will keep me going, especially with a congressional investigation starting."

They stepped into an elevator.

"I admit I was really scared at first. I wandered around for a while before I called Mark to come get me."

"Why Mark?"

"I had his number in my cell. I was sort of out of it, and I didn't think about calling the operator at the paper to reach Ron Jones."

Seeing the skeptical expression on Joni's face, Sarah added, "Mark was terrific."

"Well, that's a nice change," Joni said as they left the elevator.

"You're not being fair to him."

Joni laughed. "I only meant that the two of you were finally getting along. Have you told your roomie what happened?"

"No. I'd better call Caroline. It's going to freak her out."

"The weather's nice," Joni said when they emerged from the building. "Let's walk up to my neighborhood. There's a place that saves a sidewalk table for me on days like this. We don't have to hurry. I've arranged for the cops to talk to you this afternoon."

"Sometimes, Joni, it seems like you run the world."

"Only my little part of it, sugar."

That night, after calling first, Sarah showed up at her parents' house in Potomac. Joni had persuaded her to go. If Sarah couldn't turn to them now, Joni had asked her, when could she? Never, Sarah had thought. But she went anyway.

"Is that a bruise on your face?" her mother asked when they and her father were under the track lights in the high-ceilinged living room.

"It's possible." Sarah doubted her mother would be very sympathetic. "I haven't looked at it for a while."

She and her parents sat down facing each other on matching couches in front of a massive brick fireplace. She told them what had happened.

"That's horrible," her father said when she had finished. Turning to her mother, he added, "Now does it sound so far-fetched that someone may have killed that source of hers because he talked to Sarah?"

"I'm so sorry, dear," her mother said to Sarah, ignoring her father. "Are you all right?"

"Just bruised, I think. The paper told the police about it. They're going to watch my house."

"That's good, dear," her mother said.

"I hope you do what they tell you," her father said. "We saw your story on Smith and Hawley. Did you get my e-mail about it today?"

"Yes, but I was somewhat distracted," Sarah said. "I thought I'd hear from you yesterday."

"We were at the club and didn't look at the paper until we got home," her father said. "It was pretty late, so I sent you an e-mail this morning."

Couldn't they have just picked up the phone no matter how late it was? Sarah thought.

"Why didn't you tell us the story was coming?" her mother asked.

"You knew what I was working on. And you know why I couldn't tell you more about it."

"Don't worry," her father assured Sarah. "Nobody in it is a client of ours."

"Good to know."

Her parents' preoccupation with themselves continued to amaze Sarah and annoy her. Didn't she at least rate a hug after being mugged?

"I saw Congress is going to investigate Smith and Hawley's contracts," her father said matter-of-factly. "What's next?"

"I don't know, Dad." Sarah didn't want to be drawn into a detailed discussion. "I'll just keep plugging away."

"Please take care of yourself," her mother told her. "Let the police do their job."

"Sure, Mom."

Sarah got up to leave.

"Do you want a bite before you go?" her mother asked. "We ate downtown. But I'm sure there's something in the fridge."

"That's okay," Sarah lied. "I ate downtown, too."

On her way home, she stopped at the McDonald's on River Road. Sarah normally avoided fast food, but she had suddenly felt a craving for a Big Mac with fries and one of those sickly sweet chocolate milk shakes. She knew the feeling would wear off if she waited to eat it at home. So she sat alone in the yellowish light in the nearly empty McDonald's to have her dinner, watching the traffic flash by outside.

31

Aboard Air Force One, Alison Winters was besieged by the handful of pool reporters during a routine "gaggle" briefing.

Q.: Will the president be talking to us in Los Angeles?

MS. WINTERS: As we briefed in Washington, she's giving three speeches, including the one on national security at U.C.L.A.

Q.: No other events?

MS. WINTERS: Just the fund-raisers, which are closed.

Q.: No press availability?

MS. WINTERS: You've had plenty of access in Washington.

Q.: Not since the Smith and Hawley story.

MS. WINTERS: We've covered that in briefings. The Defense Department's looking into it.

Q.: Is the president speaking on national security without mentioning a major defense-contracting scandal?

MS. WINTERS: The president is waiting to see what Defense tells us.

Q.: We understand the Pentagon is only reviewing existing audits of Smith and Hawley's contracts. Does the president think that's enough? Will she order a wider investigation?

MS. WINTERS: If the Department of Defense discovers criminal activity, it will make a referral to Justice. As you know, there will also be hearings on the Hill.

Q.: Trent Tucker appears to be in the middle of this. He ran the Capehart-Cameron campaign. And he worked in the White House as President Capehart's political adviser. Does this create a conflict for the

White House? Might it become necessary to appoint a special prosecutor?

MS. WINTERS: Slow down. As I've said before, Trent Tucker no longer works for the White House. He has no connection with this administration.

Q.: Alison, campaign-finance and congressional records confirm that Vice President Stetson received campaign contributions and free travel when he was a senator from companies owned by Palisar International, including Smith and Hawley. And he put earmarks into defense appropriations that guaranteed no-bid contracts for Smith and Hawley. Has the president asked the vice president about this? What did she know before she selected him?

MS. WINTERS: Mark, I'm glad it was your turn to be in the pool so nobody would think we're trying to cut off the *Capital. (Laughter)*

MS. WINTERS: The president has not discussed your colleague's story with the vice president. As I've said all week, I'm not going to speculate about its contents. The vice president can speak for himself.

Q.: So the president is distancing herself from the vice president because of this story?

MS. WINTERS: I said nothing of the kind,

Mark. The president has full confidence in the vice president.

"Why *did* you let Mark Daniels into the pool?" Elliott Bancroft demanded when he and Alison reviewed the transcript with the president in the front compartment of Air Force One. "A little favor from the old days?"

"Fuck you," Alison blurted out. "There were no old days. I wasn't one of his girls. Or yours, for that matter."

"Remember who you work for," Elliott said.

"It would help if you both calmed down," Susan told them. "It's been a long week."

"Sorry about my language," Alison said to Susan. She knew she should probably apologize to Elliott, too. But she was irritated by his reluctance to help her deal with the media firestorm ignited by the Smith and Hawley story.

"It was his paper's turn," she told Elliott. "If we skipped Mark, it would look like the story and the reaction to it has hurt us."

"Has it?" Susan asked. "The press isn't letting up, never mind the bloggers. Should I be saying something?"

"I don't think so," Elliott said quickly. "It's not about us, and we shouldn't make it look like it is."

Alison gave him a sharp look. She was the one the president had asked.

"The longer we avoid it, the more it looks like we're hiding something," she said to Susan. "After all, Tucker *did* work for you."

"But that was during the campaign," Elliott said, turning to Susan. "And you kicked him out."

"Everything went through Tucker before Monroe died, and I didn't like it," Susan reminded him. "It felt like there was a burglar in the house. We still don't know exactly what he did."

"I'll ask the counsel's office to look into it," said Elliott, who was careful not to react to what she said about Tucker. "And I'll monitor the Pentagon and Hill investigations."

"Okay," Susan told him. "We'll start there."

"Can you leak that to Jane Sterling at the *Herald*?" Elliott asked Alison. "And make it clear the president is personally concerned."

"You mean, so we can screw the *Capital*?"

She was feeling liberated by this conversation.

"So we can make sure Sterling does a story, because she's getting an exclusive," Elliott told Alison, ignoring her sarcasm.

382

"And take Sally McGuire out to lunch. Her columns have been very supportive. Remind her that the president wants to make this a clean administration, especially after all the Republican scandals. Tell her the president's determined to get to the bottom of the defense contracting problem, which she inherited from them."

"A little manipulative, aren't we?" Susan asked. Alison noticed that it was a serious question, not a playful comment.

"Just some preliminary damage control until you can get a handle on this, Madam President," he said.

"All right, go ahead," Susan told Alison. "But don't lay it on too thick."

The three of them sat quietly for a while, looking out the windows of Air Force One at the vast expanse of the American west. Then Susan turned back to Elliott and asked, "Did we make a mistake with Stetson?"

"He didn't really do anything wrong," Elliott answered. "It was all business as usual on the Hill."

His words reminded Alison about the day she had gone with Elliott to the *Capital* newsroom. She never could figure out what that was all about, unless he had hoped to head off something worse that might be coming, something like the Smith and Hawley story.

"You can trust the vice president," Elliott added. "He'll stand by you."

Susan said nothing more about it. But Alison thought she could discern doubt in the expression on the president's face.

Hours later, Mark was hoping he might run across Jeanne as the presidential motorcade formed for the trip from the U.C.L.A. campus in Westwood to the Century Plaza hotel in Century City. He thought she might slip away from her advance chores to watch Cameron's national security speech. He waited as long as he could before getting on the bus. Back in the temporary pressroom set up in the Century Plaza ballroom, he wrote and filed his story before trying to contact her in the hotel.

"Hi," Jeanne said when he called her room. "She's gone to some fund-raisers, and I was just about to catch a nap."

"Could I talk you into dinner instead?"

"I'm more tired than hungry. And I don't want to change clothes. But I guess we could sit somewhere and get a snack."

"You could come to my room."

"Not a good idea," Jeanne said. "I don't want to be a mess when the president returns. Let's meet by the pools in the garden out back."

Even in the wrinkled pinstriped pantsuit she had been wearing all day, Jeanne looked more beautiful to Mark than ever. They strolled around the garden on a perfect southern California evening. Lit from underwater, the swimming pools glowed in soothing shades of green. The fronds on the spotlighted palm trees fluttered gently in the breeze. Mark let his fingers brush against hers as they walked. She didn't draw away.

"It's not Tuscany, but it beats Washington," Mark said. "Do you miss Italy?"

"I found what I needed there. It was beautiful, relaxing, and far away. It was like wiping the slate clean."

"That's sort of what I did, except I've been working, too."

"What do you mean?"

They sat down next to each other at a small table on the lawn.

"I'm living alone — for the first time in my life, really. We're getting the divorce done. I'm working on my relationship with the boys. And I'm thinking about the rest of my career. Politics doesn't turn me on the way it used to, even covering Cameron. I don't know what I'll do next, but it feels good just to start thinking about it."

"That does sound like a fresh start." Jeanne put her hand over his on the table.

Mark looked into her eyes. He felt the way he had in high school.

"Could we?"

"What?"

"Make a fresh start."

"Well, you still have children who need a father. And we both have to make a living."

"Why did you come back?" Mark asked.

"I realized I couldn't run away from my life. I missed you. My sister was getting overwhelmed at the agency. And the White House said they needed me."

"You didn't talk to me much while you were gone," Mark said. "You didn't even tell me you were coming back."

"I hadn't decided what to say to you yet. I figured we'd see each other again on a trip like this. And then I'd take it step by step." She paused and smiled. "I guess you could consider that a fresh start."

He leaned forward and kissed her.

Only a few hours later, after Susan had dismissed her for the night, Jeanne rejoined Mark in his room.

In the wood-paneled parlor of the presidential suite of the Century Plaza, Susan Cam-

386

eron relaxed with Alison and Amanda Peterson, who had decided to come after watching the Smith and Hawley scandal become Topic A in the media. It was almost like one of their girls' nights during the campaign. Susan was stretched out on a couch in jeans. Alison was slumped in an easy chair, still wearing a businesslike blue blouse and skirt, her jacket in a heap on the thick rug. But Amanda was pacing near a large window against a backdrop of the lights of Los Angeles, with the Hollywood sign visible in the distant hills.

"I think you should be careful with Elliott," she said after Susan and Alison had recounted their discussion on Air Force One.

"You were never comfortable with him," Susan said. "You thought he was an intruder."

"Will you at least admit you were sweet on him?"

"What a quaint expression, especially coming from you, Amanda. The answer is that I didn't go to bed with him. I'll admit to being a bit turned on by the excitement of the campaign, like the old days with Michael. But it passed. We've been all business in the White House. This job creates a strange space around me. Only the two of you and my family still treat me like an ordinary person."

"And you trust Elliott?" Amanda persisted.

"I trust myself. He's just one of the people I listen to."

"I worry that he has an agenda of his own," Alison said. "I just haven't figured out what it is yet."

"What are you talking about?" Amanda asked with interest.

"Well, for one thing, he seemed very eager for the president to pick Sam Stetson. And he's been protective of him ever since. Even today, when we were talking on the plane."

"The vice president's helping us on the Hill," Susan said. "He got the Medicare prescription bill unstuck. He's going to run the Social Security task force. And he has the Armed Services committees taking seriously what we want to do with the Pentagon budget."

"I've got no problem with all of that," Alison said. "It's just something about the way Elliott's been trying to protect him."

"I'll watch Sam," Susan said. "We have lunch every week."

"Fine," Amanda said. "But Elliott's the one you should really watch."

When Susan called Michael later that

night, he was in Hawaii to make another big money speech. She knew from the blogs she checked regularly when she was alone that he was staying in an exclusive resort with an attractive heiress he met some months earlier.

"Is this a good time to talk?" she asked.

"If you're referring to Marsha," Michael said, "she's at the other end of the suite taking forever to get ready for dinner."

"How's that working out?"

"Fine. No strings. What do you need? Worried about the contracting scandal? Are you putting up a firewall?"

"Elliott's asking the White House counsel's office to investigate. And he's monitoring the Pentagon and the Hill. But Alison and Amanda don't think I should trust him."

"I never thought you should."

"Why?"

"Didn't he suddenly materialize when you dumped Trent Tucker during the campaign?"

"Monroe sent him to me."

"Did you talk to him about it?"

"Briefly. I told Monroe I wanted Tucker out. One of his people called back to recommend Elliott. He seemed to fit in right away."

"Too well, I thought at the time. And you seemed sweet on him."

Susan laughed out loud.

"What?"

"That expression. Amanda used it tonight, too. You're both usually more plainspoken."

"My dear, we're talking to the president of the United States."

"So what are you driving at?"

"Capehart's people wanted to keep you in line because you were so popular on your own. So they gave you someone they could trust, but less obvious than Tucker. And he ingratiated himself with you. Now you're the president, and he's still there. The question is, where's his real loyalty?"

"What do you think?"

"I don't know enough. But you need to find out. You should ask someone you really trust to help you."

32

Trent Tucker was waiting on the sidewalk when the big silver Mercedes pulled up in front of the King's Knight. He opened the back door and slid in next to Carter Phillips.

"We've got a problem," Tucker said.

"Not now," Phillips said firmly, nodding

toward the driver.

The car weaved through traffic, crossed the Fourteenth Street Bridge, turned north onto the George Washington Parkway, and climbed up the Virginia side of the Potomac River Gorge. Just past Chain Bridge, the driver took the turnoff for Fort Marcy Park and followed a curving drive into an empty parking lot ringed by low, tree-covered hills.

"Let's get out and take a walk," Phillips said. He led the way up a steep, short path into a clearing in the trees.

Tucker looked around uneasily as they waded through ankle-high grass in their expensive suits and shoes. He wondered why they were there.

"Did you know, Trent, that this was one of the Union forts encircling Washington during the Civil War?" Phillips didn't wait for an answer. "This was farmland then, and it had a commanding view of the river. Fort Marcy guarded this side, while Battery Kemble did the same on the other side."

All Tucker could see around him were trees. But he remembered that, a year earlier, when the two of them were talking at the King's Knight about the hit-and-run on Chain Bridge Road, Phillips didn't seem to know the name of Battery Kemble. Why was he going on about this now?

"Did I ever tell you that I read everything I could about the Civil War when I was at West Point? It was brutal and bloody. Neither side gave quarter."

Tucker was growing impatient. He was facing a crisis. For the first time in all his years of political combat and influence peddling in Washington, he felt vulnerable.

"You know, Trent, I come from a military family."

"Yes, General, you've told me. Third generation."

"Just like you and politics."

"Yes, General."

"My father died in Korea before I really got to know him. I had a couple of close calls myself in 'Nam. In the Special Forces, it was either kill or be killed. You couldn't always play by the rules. Know what I mean?"

"I think so."

"I was raised to fight and never back away. My grandfather put gloves on me when I was a kid and beat it into me, day after day."

Tucker had never heard Phillips talk this way.

"You remember Vince Foster? He was a friend of the Clintons."

"Yes, General."

Where was this going? Tucker wondered.

"He shot himself right over there. It was the summer of '93, after I left Langley. Foster had come to Washington with the Arkansas crowd as Clinton's lawyer. They said he suffered from depression and couldn't stand the pressure here. He was being hounded by the press for some mess of Hillary's. I think he just gave up."

Phillips stopped abruptly and turned to face Tucker.

"I don't give up." His fists were clenched. "I fight."

"I understand, General."

"I don't think you do. This isn't just about Palisar or you or me. There's a lot more at stake."

"I guess I don't understand."

"You have no idea," Phillips said. "But it's all classified."

Tucker couldn't contain himself any longer.

"I've got problems of my own," he blurted out, without taking in what Phillips had just said. "What happens when that subcommittee starts sending out subpoenas? What if the Feds want to talk to me?"

"I told you, we'll fight. I'll find you a good lawyer."

They started walking in circles again. Tucker had steeled himself for this conversation. He knew how scandals usually played out in Washington. People like Carter Phillips eventually escaped unscathed, while people like himself were left exposed.

"I don't think that's such a good idea for either of us, General," he said with some trepidation. "We're each going to have to deal with it in our own way."

Phillips turned to face him again. Tucker didn't like the look in his eyes, but he couldn't stop now.

"It's starting to unravel, General. The White House has begun an internal investigation. It's only a matter of time before they find our people in the administration."

"So cut our losses. What about Bancroft?"

"I don't know where his loyalty is right now."

"Tell him that if one of us goes, we all go," Phillips said forcefully. "Time to circle the wagons. I don't know who's still feeding that reporter. You haven't been able to stop her. And my people have been clumsy about it."

"You mean what happened the other day?"

Tucker had read about Sarah Page's mugging in the newspaper.

"Under the circumstances, the less said the better," said Phillips. "But I'm going to want to know where your loyalty is, Trent."

That frightened Tucker, but he said nothing.

Phillips led him back down the path to the parking lot, where the Mercedes was waiting. The two men rode back downtown in silence.

Chris Collins came to meet Sarah at the security checkpoint at the entrance to the sprawling Rayburn House Office Building. In shirtsleeves, with his tie loosened, collar unbuttoned, and hair tousled, he looked like another reporter. He guided her through a maze of marble corridors and stairwells to the basement offices of the staff he had assembled for his subcommittee's hearings.

They walked past cramped cubicles to a small conference room, where young men and women crowded around a table piled high with papers. When Sarah got near the table, she saw among them copies of documents that Pat Scully had sent her.

"Did our source give you these before he left town?" she asked Collins.

"Those and others he sent recently."

Sarah grabbed the congressman's arm and pulled him out of the room.

"When did he contact you?"

"Don't worry," Collins said. "You know Pat. He e-mailed me after I announced my hearings. He wanted to make sure I had everything. My staff doesn't know who he is. We've even given him a code name: Deep Files."

They stepped back into the conference room and sat down at the table with his staff.

"This is a little uncomfortable," Sarah said. "But the congressman was kind enough to invite me to meet you. I'll be interested in what you find."

"And we're interested in any guidance you can give us," Collins said to Sarah.

"Everything I know so far was in the story." Sarah was being careful not to break any rules in dealing with sources. "You could subpoena the records of those post-office boxes. And you might persuade Robert Malin or Lucilla Brown to tell you more about where the money went."

"Not too fast, please," Collins interrupted. "We have the authority to look into Smith and Hawley's contracts and how they got them." He seemed to be talking to his staff as much as to Sarah. "If we build a record that points to others, we'll need approval to take the next step."

Sarah was puzzled. Why was Collins still being so cautious?

As they left the meeting, the congressman

put on his suit jacket and tightened his tie before showing Sarah out of the Rayburn Building, avoiding the elevators again.

"Justice checked in with me," he told Sarah cryptically while they were walking alone up the stairs. "They wanted to know where I was heading. But they wouldn't tell me what they were doing. They said they'd get back to me."

"Justice?"

"Your story would be reason enough for them to open a preliminary inquiry. That doesn't necessarily mean there'll be a full-scale investigation."

"Should I call them?"

"They'd just put you off. Why don't you wait till I can find out more?"

"Thanks, Chris." As comfortable as Sarah felt with Collins, that seemed somehow inappropriate inside the Rayburn Building. "I mean, Congressman."

"You were right the first time. I thought we'd settled that."

They had reached the main floor.

"Want to go back to B. Smith's for lunch?"

Collins seemed to throw out the invitation casually, but Sarah guessed he had been working his way up to it. And she liked that.

"Not today," she told him. "I have to meet someone downtown. And I'm late."

"Rain check?"

"Absolutely." Despite her best intentions about their relationship as reporter and source, she could feel herself becoming drawn to him.

"When I find out more, I'll call you," Collins said. "I should get your cell number, just in case."

"Hand me your phone, Congressman," she said almost too eagerly, "and I'll put it in."

As she walked quickly from the Rayburn Building to the subway station, Sarah thought carefully about Collins. She found him attractive. She liked his values and was moved by his life story. He was the right age and, notably, unattached. But she had to keep those feelings separate from a sober assessment of him as a source and a player in the story she was reporting. She remembered Ron Jones's warning, as well as her own bitter experience. Be careful, she told herself, as she reached the subway station.

After taking the Metro to Dupont Circle, Sarah raced up the long escalator to the street and hurried several blocks through an early November chill to the Tabard Inn. With the garden of the Iron Gate Inn across the street closed for the season, she had chosen N Street's other historic restaurant for a clandestine rendezvous with Cathy Adams. Occupying forty rooms in three Victorian town houses, the Tabard Inn was Washington's oldest continuously operated hotel. The cozy restaurant off its quaint lobby was usually crowded at lunchtime, and Sarah had reserved a table in a back corner where she and her guest were less likely to be noticed.

Smith and Hawley's lanky spokeswoman, wearing a black sweater that set off her blond hair, was waiting at the table when Sarah arrived.

"Thanks for coming into town," she said to Adams. "I thought you might feel safer here."

"I called in sick so I wouldn't have to rush. To tell the truth, coming here has made me a bit sick to my stomach."

"Well, let's get some wine to help you relax."

Sarah recommended the salmon, and they ordered a bottle of Chardonnay.

"Tell me again why I'm doing this," Adams asked after her first sip of wine.

"Because you're still an Army P.I.O. at heart who believes in her country and the people who wear its uniform. And you know your employer's been ripping them off."

"What will happen to me?"

Sarah tried to balance empathy for Adams with a dose of harsh reality to win her co-operation.

"I'll keep your identity confidential. But congressional investigators are already on the case. And probably the F.B.I. and federal prosecutors, too. You're so close to Allenby that you'll probably have to become a cooperating witness, whether you help me or not."

"What do you want?"

"Only two things, really. Allenby's relationship with Carter Phillips and Palisar. And who's getting the kickbacks."

"Oh, the easy stuff." Adams laughed nervously and took another sip of wine. "I don't know that much about Palisar or those payments. George said they're ordinary business transactions."

Sarah set down her own glass and leaned toward her guest.

"Payments to post-office boxes? To fronts for Trent Tucker and his friends? You know better than that, Cathy."

"So what do you need from me?"

Sarah waited until the waiter had finished serving their food.

"There must be someone in your shop who's still keeping track of the payments," she said. "Whoever it is will get caught up in the investigations sooner or later. I'd like to talk to that person first."

"I'm going to have to think about it. And talk to my husband. It sounds like we may need a lawyer."

When she returned to the newsroom, Sarah went straight into Ron Jones's office to tell him about her meeting on the Hill and her lunch with Cathy Adams. Now, she wanted him to be informed about everything.

"Shut the door for a minute," he told her.

Jones had never done that before. Sarah reached back to close his door and then sat down in a chair facing his desk.

"What's up?"

"Lou had a conversation with the vice president. They were at a big dinner somewhere, and he got Stetson off alone for a couple of minutes."

Sarah was excited. This meant Runyan was invested in the story.

"What did he find out?"

"Lou said it was weird. Stetson didn't dispute anything you'd written. But he warned there could be trouble down the road."

"The kickbacks?"

"No, Stetson said it was fine with him that you were nailing the corruption. He insisted that he hadn't done anything illegal. But he told Lou that it was the tip of a very dangerous iceberg."

"What does that mean?"

"Something about national security. He said we shouldn't go there."

"Just like my anonymous caller. It sounded phony to me."

"This could be, too," Jones said. "Stetson, the president, and members of Congress would all have political reasons to limit the scandal."

"What does Lou think?"

"Stetson got his attention. He'll try to talk to some of his friends in the intelligence community."

National security, Sarah thought as she left Jones's office. *The intelligence community.* That's serious stuff — and unfamiliar territory.

Sarah next stopped by Marge Lawson's cubicle.

"What have you found on Kathleen Morgan?" she asked. "I got nowhere in Google. And nothing in our own database, which really surprised me. She said she was well known in Washington."

"I didn't do much better," Lawson said. "Just her driving records. An address from her license and registration for a condo across the river in Arlington. Upscale building, pool, and all the amenities, according to real-estate listings. Her unit's owned by something called the Anglo-Saxon Trust. Doesn't look like there's a mortgage."

"That's it?"

"She drives fast, and sometimes while drunk. Bunch of traffic tickets. But no suspensions or court appearances. She must have a good lawyer or friends in the right places."

"Nothing in lobbyist reports or campaign-contribution records?"

"Nada," Marge said. "If there had been, I would have told you that first. Your girl's kind of a ghost."

When Sarah checked her e-mail, she found something from OLDNATSFAN that said only: "hope you're okay"

She didn't know much about baseball, but she recognized another of Pat Scully's handles.

"It's about time," she wrote back. "I'm fine. Just a few bruises left."

After an hour, he was back in touch.

"great . . . btw great story"

Sarah ignored the compliment. "You didn't tell me you were feeding Collins."

"old stuff . . . you're past that . . . what's next"

403

She wondered why Scully was being evasive about Collins. But she needed his help.

"Kickbacks."

"i'm looking . . . did you get inside smith and hawley"

Sarah had never told him she was trying. Did he know something he was holding back? She decided not to tell him about her approach to Cathy Adams.

"I'm working on it."

"good . . . what's latest w/langford"

That reminded Sarah about something else that had been bothering her.

"He interviewed me again," she typed. "Cops are working on the assumption that the guy who attacked me is connected to the goon at Seth's funeral and whoever was watching Seth and me in Bethesda. Maybe even the same person. They're looking for the guy who bought the Expedition. His ID was bogus, but the dealer gave them a description. Langford's looking at Palisar. Did you send him stuff, too?"

"everything . . . same as you have . . . hang in there"

Before Sarah could ask him anything else, Scully vanished again into cyberspace, leaving only his words on her computer screen. She read them all again. Who else might he be working with, besides her, Collins, and now Langford? He always seemed to leave her with more questions than answers.

33

After a long day in the White House press office, Alison Winters was surprised to be summoned early that evening to the solarium in the residence.

"Take the couch," Susan suggested, "so you can see the lights and monuments."

Alison kept her eyes on the president.

Susan was wearing jeans and a sweatshirt, but she didn't look relaxed.

"I need to know what's going on," she told Alison. "Congress has scheduled hearings. Justice is doing something that nobody will tell me about. The Pentagon still hasn't reported back. And I haven't heard anything from the White House counsel's office. I don't like it."

"Have you asked Elliott?"

"You told me I shouldn't trust him."

Alison didn't know what to say.

"I want you to help me with this. I don't know who else to trust right now."

Alison was completely unprepared for this.

"Theoretically, I report to Elliott," she said.

"You're also an assistant to the president,

and you'll be reporting directly to me," Susan responded firmly. "I want to know what's going on. You already have access to everybody in the White House and the rest of the administration. It's normal for you to ask questions."

"You're sure about this?"

Alison wanted explicit authorization.

"I'm ordering you to do it," Susan told her.

"Thank you, Madam President."

A little later, Alison told Jeremy Cantor to meet her on Pennsylvania Avenue in front of the White House. They walked across Lafayette Square and up Sixteenth Street to Olives. The popular restaurant was crowded and noisy, just the way Alison wanted it.

"I need your help," she told Jeremy. "But you can't tell anybody, especially Elliott."

"Okay, but my boss works for him."

"I'm reporting directly to the president on this," Alison told him with a tone full of authority. "She doesn't want Elliott to know."

Jeremy's eyes widened.

"Okay. What's my assignment?"

"Are you still in touch with Rush Ripley?"

"Touch football every Sunday morning. Then beer and the Redskins game at Champs."

"And he still works for Tucker?"

"He's sort of his personal assistant."

"Try to find out who Tucker's in touch with in the administration. And what his relationship is with Elliott." Alison hoped she wasn't making a mistake. Sometimes it felt too easy getting what she wanted from Jeremy without giving him much in return. "Ripley can't know what you're doing. And nothing can get back to Tucker. Can you handle that?"

Jeremy leaned forward and lowered his voice to a whisper. "This is an assignment from the president?"

"Straight from the president."

"That's serious," Jeremy said solemnly. "I won't let you down."

"I know it's kind of cold, but do you mind taking a walk?" Alison asked Sarah when they met on the Ellipse behind the White House the next day.

"Sure." Sarah was intrigued. She and Alison had not yet established a real rapport.

"Can we be on deep background?"

"Okay."

Wrapping their coats tightly around them, they braved a stiff autumn breeze walking across the Ellipse toward Constitution Avenue.

"I need help," Alison said, surprising Sarah. "The president wants to find out what Trent Tucker did when he worked in the White House."

"I had been hoping to find that out from you," Sarah said. She wasn't sure what Alison was asking, but she was willing, up to a point, to trade information. "What does Bancroft know about it?"

"Well, that's another issue."

It took Sarah a moment to realize what Alison meant. This was about the White House chief of staff.

"The president's worried about Tucker *and* Bancroft? That's a real problem."

"And that's why I'm talking to you," said Alison.

They crossed Constitution and started up the slope of the Monument grounds.

"Let's see if I have this straight," Sarah said. "The president of the United States has asked her press secretary to investigate her own chief of staff because she doesn't trust anyone else."

"I have to go completely off the record."

Sarah nodded her agreement.

"The president doesn't know I'm talking to you. But I'm looking for information wherever I can get it. And I may find out things that would be useful to you."

"What does the president suspect?"

"Let's establish what we know," Alison said. "Bancroft was sent to her campaign to replace Tucker, and she kept him on when she became vice president. Until Capehart died, Tucker virtually ran the White House. When she became president, she kicked out Tucker. Bancroft was the logical choice for chief of staff. He pushed Stetson for vice president. And Bancroft tried to stop your story about Stetson."

They walked around the Washington Monument, avoiding the lines of tourists. The flags on the tall poles encircling the Monument snapped loudly in the wind.

"Then came your story about the contracting scandal and its connections to Tucker," Alison continued. "Bancroft tried to deflect the president's concern about both the story and the investigations."

"You mean the House subcommittee and whatever Justice is doing?"

"Yes. I heard you were up on the Hill, so you know what Congressman Collins is doing," Alison said. "I've been told it's routine for the Public Integrity Section to look into media reports of possible criminal activity by public officials."

Sarah guessed Chris Collins must be talking to Alison, but she didn't ask.

"So you're wondering whether Bancroft has his own agenda or may even be working with Tucker," she said instead. "You want to know whether Tucker put his own people elsewhere inside the administration, possibly including the vice president."

"That's about right."

Sarah had had her own suspicions about Bancroft and Stetson, of course, but she never expected that the president would have them, too.

"Well, it's likely that Tucker got some of the kickback money from Pentagon contracts," she told Alison. "And he's probably not the only one. I haven't found any connection to Bancroft yet. But I bet Tucker wired at least part of the administration while he was in the White House. That's what he and Carter Phillips did in Congress."

As they walked back down the Monument grounds, Alison prodded her further. "What are you working on now?"

Sarah wouldn't answer that question under normal circumstances, but now it seemed worth building trust with the president's press secretary.

"I'm concentrating on who got kickbacks from Smith and Hawley's contracts. And I'm interested in what Palisar may be getting out of your administration."

"Then we're working the same ground," Alison said. She had once been a reporter herself at the *Des Moines Register* before she was bitten by the political bug while covering the Iowa caucuses.

"Let me know what you find," Sarah told her, implicitly setting the rules for their information trading. "I might be able to help you evaluate it."

"Good," Alison said. They were nearing the White House. "We'd better split up here. Let's stay in touch."

Sarah shoved her hands into her coat pockets as she walked back toward the newspaper. She decided she had underestimated Alison.

Joni Parker first saw the flashing emergency lights as her car rounded a bend on Beach Drive in Rock Creek Park. When she got closer, she noticed fire trucks among the police cars and smoke hovering over the creek. After she parked her car just outside the police line, Charlie Langford walked over.

"Come with me," he said brusquely.

Joni didn't like this. Langford had summoned her by telephone without an explanation. On the police radio in the newsroom, it sounded like a routine car crash on Beach Drive, which snaked alongside Rock Creek through the heavily wooded park that bisected the city from north to south.

Bundled in overcoats, they made their way among idling emergency vehicles toward a small bridge where Beach Drive turned sharply to cross over to the other side of the creek. Joni sometimes biked there on weekends, when the road was closed to motor vehicles. From the bridge, she could see police and fire personnel inspecting the charred remains of a car lying on its side among the boulders in the water.

"She got out just in time," Langford told Joni in his laconic way. "She's in the hospital. They told me she'll be okay."

She? Joni felt a sharp stab of fear. "Who?"

"The woman who lives with Sarah Page. Her name's Caroline Long. That Jetta in the creek belongs to Page."

"Oh, my God."

As worried as she had been about Sarah, especially after the attack on the Crescent Trail, Joni had never imagined anything like this.

"Long identified herself before the ambulance took her away. She said she borrowed the car," Langford said. "We were able to read the license plate to confirm it."

"How did it happen?"

"We're guessing some kind of explosive device. Fortunately, it must not have been that powerful. The car crashed into the creek, but she was able to climb out before the gas tank blew."

"Have you called Sarah?" Joni asked.

"I thought you might want to do that. Then I'll have to talk to her again. We've got to figure out what the hell is happening. This has gone too far. Someone tried to kill your friend."

34

"The F.B.I. will be calling you," Charlie Langford said to Sarah in her living room. He had pulled his chair as close as he could to the one in which she was curled up in sweat clothes.

"The local field office was surprised that I hadn't contacted them sooner," he told her. "We'll set up a joint task force. The officers at the hospital said Caroline's going to be fine. No serious injuries. Her parents are there."

Sarah didn't respond. Overwhelmed by what had happened, she had said little since Langford, Ron Jones, and Mary Sullivan arrived, one after the other, to check on her.

"I thought you had her under surveillance," Sullivan said to Langford.

"This house was," Langford told her.

"That obviously wasn't good enough," said Jones, who was sitting with Sullivan on the couch.

"I understand your concern," Langford said. "We didn't see anybody tamper with Miss Page's car. But when Miss Long drove off this evening, an officer noticed another vehicle pulling away at the same time. He took down the make, model, and license number."

"He didn't follow it?" Sullivan asked.

"His responsibility was to watch the house, and Miss Page was still inside. We're trying to locate the owner of the other vehicle. The officer's description resembled a dark-colored Jeep Cherokee that a witness saw behind Miss Page's car just before it crashed in Rock Creek.

"I didn't tell that to Joni Parker," Langford warned everyone. "I don't want it in the paper yet."

Sarah was listening impassively to what were unmistakably the details of an apparent attempt to kill her. It had put her housemate in the hospital. She knew this was one more person her reporting had endangered.

"You've just been doing your job," Langford said to Sarah. Understanding her distress, he was trying to reassure her. "Some sonofabitch has been trying to stop you. We'll do everything we can to get whoever it is."

The doorbell rang, startling everyone but Langford.

"I'll get it," he said, getting up and moving to the front door in a few strides.

"Mr. and Mrs. Page?" He ushered in Sarah's parents. "Thanks for coming so quickly."

It was hard for Sarah to believe her parents were there, rushing toward her. Her father was in black tie and her mother in a long dress with her hair done the way it always was for Washington dinner parties.

"My poor dear, it could have been you," her mother said. "It could have been you."

Her father practically lifted Sarah out of the chair and held her tightly in a way he hadn't done in years. Sullivan and Jones stood up and started toward the door. Langford motioned for them to stay.

"We were at the French embassy," her father said to Sarah, who was sobbing in his arms. "Joni called on my cell. She gave me Lieutenant Langford's number. He asked us to come."

Sarah pulled back, humiliated. Everyone

415

in the room had just heard that her parents had to be told by a police detective to visit their daughter after someone tried to kill her — and that Sarah had not contacted them herself.

"I'm all right," Sarah said, wiping her eyes with her hands. She introduced her parents to her editors. The unexpected encounter had brought her back to life.

"Your daughter's an outstanding reporter and very brave," Mary Sullivan told them. "We and the police will do everything we can to protect her. The newspaper will put her in a hotel until it's safe for her to return home."

"She could come home with us," her father said. "Her mother would like that."

Seeing how shaken her mother still was, Sarah realized it would be cruel to turn her parents down flat, even though she didn't expect real comfort from them.

"That's fine for tonight," she told them. "If you could loan me one of your cars, I'd like to stay downtown after that so I can be near the newspaper." Looking over at Jones and Sullivan, she added, "I want to stay on the story."

"We thought you would," Sullivan said, allowing herself a smile. "I told Lou that on the phone coming over here, and he agreed.

He just wants you working it from the newsroom as much as possible for now so we'll know you're safe."

It didn't take long for Sarah to stray from the newsroom, however. After Cathy Adams called on her cell phone early in the morning two days later, she hurried from her hotel downtown in her borrowed car to Dulles airport. She thought this could be big.

Sarah turned into Parking Garage One and found a space on the second level. She took an elevator down to the brightly lit underground passageway to the terminal and waited by the elevators for Adams to emerge.

"Your car or mine?" Sarah asked.

"Yours, if that's okay," answered Adams, who was holding a large brown envelope against her cloth winter coat. "After what I read in the paper, I'm happy to see you in one piece."

They went into the elevator.

"How's your housemate doing?"

"Former housemate," Sarah said. "As soon as she got out of the hospital yesterday, she moved into one of her law firm's corporate apartments. They sent people out to the house to get her stuff."

On the second level of the garage, Sarah led the way to her car.

"You were right," Adams said, laying the envelope on her lap after settling into the front passenger seat. "The House committee sent a staff lawyer over to talk to George. The F.B.I.'s been in to question him, too."

" 'George'?"

Sarah was becoming suspicious of everyone.

"I've worked closely with the man for nearly five years," Adams said. "I feel very differently about him now, of course, but I don't dare show it. It's like I'm some kind of spy."

"Sorry," Sarah said, shaking her head. She had put still another source into a difficult position. "This can't be easy for you."

"George said everything they asked about came from your story," Adams said. "They didn't seem to have talked to anyone else yet. But word's gotten around the company. People are scared. Especially the accounting supervisor who oversaw the subcontractor payments."

"How did you find out?"

"I've been sneaking around asking questions. She told me she had her suspicions, but your story really shook her up. She's planning to get a lawyer and go to the authorities."

"Who is she?"

Sarah wasn't doing a very good job of being patient. She knew it was always best to let a source like Adams, who was putting her neck on the line, set her own pace.

"You'll find out later," Adams said. "Right now, she's worried about what's going to happen to her."

"What about you?"

"I'm meeting with a lawyer tonight. I decided to wait until I brought this to you." She held up the envelope. "After all you've been through, I didn't want the lawyer to talk me out of it."

"What's in there?"

Sarah resisted the urge to reach over and grab it.

"Ground rules first?" Adams asked.

"Okay."

"You can't use any of this until our lawyers talk to the F.B.I. and the House committee. We want to get immunity."

"Fine."

Sarah was willing to agree to almost anything.

"Just say you obtained copies of the documents. Nothing about your source."

"Okay."

Finally, Adams opened the envelope and

pulled out a small stack of papers. She handed the ones on top to Sarah.

"You'll recognize these as the most recent monthly payments from Smith and Hawley subcontractors to the places listed in your story."

Sarah read the names aloud.

"Malin Associates, American Freedom Alliance, Public Relations Solutions — and, look at that, RT2 Group — all in Suite 1000 of Tucker's building. Redwing Associates, Security Services Partners, American Guardian, Eagle Consultants, and Overseas Security Services — all still at post-office boxes at the MailServices store on Pennsylvania Avenue."

Remembering the lists from Derek Stevens and Andy Foster, Sarah noticed that the size of the payments had grown larger. More than one payment had been sent to each destination by subcontractors using different offshore bank accounts, which would make the money more difficult to follow.

"Look where the checks came from," Adams said. "Banks I'd never heard of in the Caribbean and Panama and the Persian Gulf."

"What was the accounting supervisor's role?"

"She contacted the subcontractors and

420

authorized the payments from a list George gave her each month. He told her Smith and Hawley had contracted for support services from these places in Washington and the subcontractors were sharing the costs," Adams said. "But when your story came out, George told her to stop the payments until further notice."

All of that was valuable confirmation of what Sarah already knew.

"What else do you have?" she asked.

"This is really interesting," Adams said. "Remember, George personally brought her a new payment list each month — always in an unmarked file folder. Well, one month, she found some handwritten notes inside the folder. She waited for George to remember he had left them there, but he never said anything. So she put them away for safe-keeping."

Adams handed Sarah photocopies of what appeared to be sheets torn from a legal pad, each with a date scribbled at the top, each date roughly a month apart for twelve months. The notations were in three columns, initials on the left, numbers in the middle, and what looked like the destinations for the payments on the right.

"The numbers appear to be denominations of thousands of dollars," Adams said.

"They match the payments on the computer list for that same month."

"TT has to be Trent Tucker," Sarah said. Adams was right. This was really interesting. "RM must be Robert Malin. And GA is probably Allenby. My God, could CP be Carter Phillips? I don't recognize the others."

"This might help you."

Adams reached back into the envelope and handed Sarah photocopies of several more legal-pad pages. Handwritten phone numbers were scattered all over them.

"I stole it," Adams said sheepishly. "George's secretary keeps his phone numbers in Rolodexes and her computer. She places most of his calls. But I had seen these on his desk near his phone. He looked through them once when I was with him to find the number of a congressman he called himself about a subcontract we were announcing for someone in his district."

Sarah was impressed by how far this loyal soldier had gone to help her.

"How'd you get them?"

"I stayed after he left yesterday and told his secretary I had to copy something in his office for a press release. I smuggled them out in a file folder and put them back on his desk after I copied them. It looks like he jotted down the numbers while talking on the phone. Sometimes, he used initials, other times first or last names."

"I'll ask our researcher to find the full name for each number. Then I'll compare their initials to those on the payment lists," said Sarah.

"Would it be easier for the F.B.I. to do that?" Adams asked.

"They'd have a legal problem until they could subpoena this. But I don't."

"I think you might have some congressmen here," Marge Lawson told Sarah later that day. She had spent several hours mining databases for information that could help decode the documents from Cathy Adams.

"This number for 'Mike' is the direct dial into the office of Mike Mahoney, the congressman from New York," Lawson said. "He could be the 'MM' next to American Freedom Alliance on Allenby's list of payment notations."

"Sounds like a reach."

Sarah hadn't expected to find anything like that.

"But look here," Lawson pointed out. "This phone number is Congressman Jerry Stanton's home in California. It's got both 'JS' and 'Jerry' written next to it on Allenby's phone list. And there's a 'JS' for American Freedom Alliance on the payment list.

"How about this? 'Tom and Jen' next to the home number of Senator Tom Hartman in New Jersey. His wife, Jennifer, handles export licenses at the Pentagon. She was a defense-industry lobbyist. Smith and Hawley is a Pentagon contractor. And 'TH' is on the list of payments from the American Freedom Alliance."

Sarah just listened. It was sinking in that she might have evidence of outright bribes to members of Congress.

"Am I the only one seeing a pattern here?" Lawson asked. "Remember when I found money going back and forth between the American Freedom Alliance and the political action committees for Tucker's consultant clients? Tom Hartman, Jerry Stanton, and Mike Mahoney all have been clients of his. Their PACs got money from the American Freedom Alliance."

"What about 'GB'?"

"Almost too easy. The number for 'George' on the phone list is the office of George Burros in the Hart Senate Office Building. There's a 'GB' on the list for the American Freedom Alliance. Burros has been a Tucker client. The senator's son, George, Jr., turns up in the Commerce

Department, also involved in export stuff."

" 'MT'?"

"More of a wild guess," Lawson said. "Congresswoman Margaret Thompson from Illinois is on House Armed Services. She's taken a few rides on Smith and Hawley corporate jets. But that's all I can find."

"And 'SS'?"

"Vice President Stetson's old Senate office number is on the phone list next to 'Sam.' That's logical for Allenby, since Stetson was Mister Senate Armed Services. And Smith and Hawley took him on trips to the Middle East."

Sarah was beginning to think their speculation had gone too far.

"C'mon, Marge, do you really think the vice president's been getting cash payoffs?"

But Lawson had more to say.

"Congressman Sanford Smith is also on House Armed Services. He's flown on Smith and Hawley corporate jets. His Hill office number is on Allenby's phone list for 'SS,' along with his home phone in Florida, next to 'Smith.' And his PAC got money from the American Freedom Alliance, even though he's never shown up as a Tucker client."

"So you think the American Freedom Alliance may be laundering what amounts to bribes from Palisar to members of Congress?"

Sarah had finally said it out loud. And it seemed believable.

"Couldn't have put it better myself," Lawson said. "I'll keep working on the other payments. 'GA' and 'CP' have to be Allenby and Phillips. But 'EB,' getting payments from Redwing, is a mystery to me."

"RT2 must be another piggy bank for Tucker," Sarah guessed. She was getting caught up in it.

"And 'LB' is in Allenby's notes as a recipient of money sent to Malin Associates," Lawson pointed out. "I'll bet that's your friend Lucilla Brown."

"She'd be at the bottom of the ladder." Sarah thought aloud about the next steps to take. "That makes her vulnerable when the Feds move in. Maybe I can get her to talk to me now."

"Do you really think that's what's going on?" Ron Jones asked after Sarah went over the documents with him later that day. "It would be pretty blatant corruption."

"My sources inside Smith and Hawley think it's possible." Sarah had been looking forward to laying it all out for him.

"Who besides Cathy Adams?"

"An accounting supervisor who handled the payments. She gave most of these documents to Adams."

"Who is she?"

"I haven't met her, and Adams hasn't told me her name yet. They want to make deals with the Feds first."

Jones looked skeptical. He knew shadowy sourcing and guesswork conclusions were typical of investigative reporting, but they always needed to be challenged.

"I don't think you're there yet," he told Sarah. "You've still got more reporting to do."

Sarah had gone to him too soon. There was no dependable evidence for what Adams had told her or what Marge had deduced from it. She couldn't be sure the accounting supervisor existed. And anyone could have used information from her Smith and Hawley story to fabricate documents like those Adams gave her.

The next morning, Sarah decided to confide in Mark about where things stood and seek his advice. There was no one else with his experience whom she felt she could trust.

"I've slept on it," she said over coffee in the cafeteria, "and I believe in Cathy Adams and the documents."

"Then do what Ron said. Keep reporting." He thought for a minute before adding, "I might be able to help you with Trent Tucker."

At noon the next day, Sarah stood outside the King's Knight, looking as though she were meeting someone for lunch. When she saw Lucilla Brown bundled up in a fur coat and matching hat emerging from the office building next door, Sarah walked up quickly alongside her.

"Ms. Brown?"

"Not you again, Miss Page."

"You recognize me?"

"We have pictures," Brown said, "so you can't sneak in again."

"I'm flattered." Sarah didn't think to ask where the pictures came from. "But I really need to talk to you."

"I don't want to talk to you." Brown walked faster in long strides, and Sarah practically ran to keep up.

"You might be able to help yourself."

"If you don't leave me alone," Brown said, pulling a cell phone from her coat pocket, "I'll have to call the police."

"I could go to the F.B.I. instead." Sarah had planned what she would say. "I could ask them what they know about kickbacks you've been getting through Malin Associates."

Brown suddenly stopped to face the smaller woman. "Are you threatening me?"

Sarah had decided to confront Brown with how much trouble she was in, hoping to convince her to cooperate, even though that risked further alienating her.

"I can ask you about the money or I can ask the F.B.I.," Sarah said. "They've already been given the payment records. So has the House subcommittee. Are Malin and Tucker going to protect you?"

Brown thought for a moment.

"I'm going to talk to my lawyer," she said. "I'm sure he'll be in touch with your editor."

That actually sounded like progress to Sarah.

"Fine with me," she said to Brown. "And you may not want to tell anyone in your office about this. Just for your protection."

Brown turned and hurried down the street.

35

"How are you?" Chris Collins asked Sarah when she called him the next morning. "I was worried when I couldn't reach you."

"Sorry. I'm fine. I've been swamped with calls, even after the paper put out a statement for me. And I've been trying to concentrate on my work. Did Cathy Adams talk to you?"

"She and the accounting supervisor at Smith and Hawley came yesterday with their lawyers and a bunch of documents. Have you seen them?"

"I've got copies. Do they look legit to you?"

"Enough to issue subpoenas when we're ready."

That was helpful, but Sarah needed more. "Could you give me the name of the accounting supervisor?"

"For once, I have something you don't?"

He sounded almost flirtatious again. But Sarah was all business. "You wouldn't have her or Adams if it wasn't for me."

"And I'm grateful," Collins said quickly. "Her name's Monica Saunders. Age forty-seven. Lives in Arlington."

"Are you giving them both immunity?"

"Are we off the record, as usual?"

"Of course, Congressman."

"I'll need committee approval. And we have to coordinate with Justice. Adams and Saunders are going there, too. The investigation is beyond the preliminary inquiry stage now. Justice has formed a task force with the F.B.I. and the I.R.S."

That meant the F.B.I. was now part of two investigative task forces Sarah wanted to monitor.

"You know anybody at Justice or the F.B.I. who could help me?" she asked. She knew she was running the risk of becoming more indebted to Collins.

"That could be tough. But let me check and get back to you."

"I really appreciate that," Sarah said in a softer voice.

"Anything for you," Collins responded in that flirting way again.

But Sarah remembered something else she wanted to ask. "So, how are you and Alison Winters getting along?"

"She called to fish for information. We've been talking. She thinks the president's got a problem."

"Do you?" she asked.

"Let's not get ahead of ourselves."

"Congressman, is there something more going on here?"

"What do you mean?"

"I've been hearing this might involve much more than contract fraud and kick-backs."

"You mean the money going to people

here on the Hill?"

"That's not what I'm talking about." Sarah thought Collins was being evasive. "I mean national security. Something apparently very secret."

"You're getting out of my league," he said, almost curtly. "I've got all I can handle. The biggest corruption scandal in this town in a long time. Bigger than Abramoff. And you've got a helluva story."

Now she was sure he was putting her off. But, for the moment, she decided not to push further.

"You'll work on that source for me?" she reminded him instead.

"Whatever I can do. And, Sarah, please, please be careful." He couldn't sound more sincere or caring. "Someone did try to kill you."

She wasn't prepared for how much that moved her.

"Thanks, Chris," was all she could manage before quickly saying good-bye.

Later in the morning, Pat Scully messaged Sarah.

"relieved they missed you . . . roomie ok?"

"We're both fine. Have you found anything more about the payments?"

Scully's answer took her by surprise.

"hear you got captured enemy documents"

"Did Chris tell you that?"

"we're still in touch"

"How about me?"

"seem to be doing great on your own . . . regular woodward . . . underground garage and all"

Sarah couldn't believe it.

"Aboveground garage," she corrected him. "How did you know about that?"

Nothing more appeared on her screen for a minute.

"How did you know?" she repeated.

"your source told chris"

If that was true, Sarah would have a problem with Collins passing along such sensitive information, considering the danger she and her sources faced. If it wasn't true, how could Scully know where she had met with Cathy Adams?

Sarah still didn't know much about this mysterious man beyond the few details he, Seth Moore, and Marge Lawson had given her months ago. Since the day she and Scully had talked in person at Union Station, their contact had been limited to the Internet and mail drops. He hadn't called her on the cell phone he gave her, which was still in her purse.

"Nothing more on the payments?" she persisted.

"working some lines . . . will let you know"

Sarah decided to test him.

"Have you started work on the book?"

During a long pause before he responded, she thought he might have disappeared again.

"getting my thoughts together . . . your stories help . . . maybe we should collaborate when it's over"

"When will it be over?"

"after you put everyone in prison"

"What about the national security problem?"

Sarah waited out another, longer pause.

"what?"

"My editors and I are hearing things about where this may lead."

"what things"

He was sniffing the bait.

"National security secrets."

"don't know anything about that"

"Chris hasn't told you?"

Another pause.

"no . . . what's he told you"

That was as far as Sarah could take it for now.

"Don't want to get him in trouble," she told Scully.

"right . . . keep eye on ball . . . stay in touch"

"Meet Josh Samuels," Ron Jones told Sarah after calling her into his office that afternoon. "He's an old source of mine. He managed to keep several politicians I covered out of jail."

When Samuels rose from his chair to shake her hand, Sarah noticed Lucilla Brown sitting next to him. She acknowledged Sarah only with a slight nod of her head. Her fur coat was draped over one end of the couch. Sarah sat down next to it.

"Josh tells me, Sarah, that you were rather rough with his client the other day," Jones began. "He said you threatened to tell the F.B.I. on her."

Sarah readied herself to respond. But Samuels spoke first.

"Ms. Brown is grateful, in a way, for what you told her," he said. "She didn't know about the Justice investigation or what the F.B.I. and Congressman Collins have been doing. She has decided to come forward. It seems that certain people misled her and took advantage of her good name."

"Are you negotiating with Congressman Collins or the Justice Department for immunity?" Sarah asked.

She was addressing Brown. But Samuels answered.

"Yes, we are in discussions, and I'm confident of a reasonable outcome. We believe you are monitoring these investigations and plan to write about them. So we'd like to give you some guidance from Ms. Brown's point of view."

"Josh likes to get his client out in front of the story," Jones said.

"Ground rules," Samuels said. "Background, with attribution to sources, plural — that's Ms. Brown and me — who have knowledge of what she has told the F.B.I. and the House subcommittee."

"Fine," Jones said.

Sarah took a notebook and pen out of her purse.

"Let me give you the outline," Samuels said to her. "Then you can ask questions.

"Ms. Brown has worked for Robert Malin for more than thirty years. She started as a secretary in his real-estate business. She subsequently earned her law degree and did management and legal work for Mr. Malin's various enterprises. She met Carter Phillips when he invested with Mr. Malin. She met Trent Tucker when he and Mr. Malin moved into offices together. Mr. Malin set up some entities involving all three men.

Ms. Brown was asked by Mr. Malin to assist them, just as she had over the years with his real-estate subsidiaries. She occasionally acted as a straw party in property deals. All legal and aboveboard.

"Until she saw your stories," Samuels continued, "Ms. Brown had no reason to disbelieve what Mr. Malin had represented to her. Malin Associates, of which Ms. Brown was an officer, was a holding company for certain assets of Mr. Malin, Mr. Tucker, and Mr. Phillips. Public Relations Solutions and American Freedom Alliance, for which Ms. Brown performed legal work, were among the organizations Mr. Tucker used for what appeared to be legitimate lobbying and political consulting. The National Center for a Better Congress, with which Ms. Brown was also associated, appeared to be funded by public-spirited corporations to provide educational travel for members of Congress."

"But what about the payments?" Sarah wanted confirmation of everything she had gotten so far.

"I was getting to that," Samuels said. "Ms. Brown was told by Mr. Malin that the payments she received monthly through Malin Associates, in addition to her salary, were compensation for the added work she did for these entities. When she asked about the names on the checks and the banks on which they were drawn, Mr. Malin told her the payments were part of complicated transactions involving Mr. Tucker's and Mr. Phillips's businesses. Ms. Brown had no reason to doubt Mr. Malin's explanation."

Sarah glanced at Brown, whose somber expression was unchanged.

"However, when you began making inquiries," Samuels continued, "Ms. Brown decided to check the records for herself. She was puzzled by what she found, including payments to what appeared to be members of Congress through the American Freedom Alliance. After your stories appeared, Mr. Malin restricted access to those records, despite Ms. Brown's legal responsibility for them. But Ms. Brown had already taken the precaution of making careful notes about what she had found. We've turned those notes over to the F.B.I. and the House subcommittee."

The room fell silent until Sarah, writing furiously, finished taking down everything Samuels had told her.

"Can I ask some questions now?"

"Certainly," Samuels said.

"Ms. Brown, when I first called to ask about the activities of the National Center

438

for a Better Congress, did you answer me in your own words?"

Brown looked to Samuels, who nodded his permission.

"No, not entirely," she said slowly. "Mr. Malin had given me talking points."

"Did you know where they came from?"

"No, I did not."

"Did you ever see Carter Phillips in your offices?"

"No, although I saw him a few times at the King's Knight when I was there for luncheon meetings."

"With him?"

"No, with Mr. Malin and others."

Sarah hoped she had successfully set the stage for the next question.

"Could you please tell me the names of the members of Congress who received payments through the American Freedom Alliance?"

"Attribution to sources with knowledge of the investigation," Samuels broke in. "And you need to get at least one more confirmation."

Sarah looked to Jones.

"That's fine," he said.

"Senator Tom Hartman," Samuels answered for Brown. "Congressman Mike Mahoney. Senator George Burros. Congressman Jerry Stanton. Congresswoman Margaret Thompson."

Sarah listened with mounting anticipation for "SS."

"And Congressman Sanford Smith. Both Republicans and Democrats."

Sarah stayed outwardly calm. But she knew this was a very big moment. Marge had gotten a perfect score.

"I must caution you," Samuels added, "that my client is unable to draw any conclusions about these payments. But she has supplied investigators with the names of the recipients, as well as the sources of the payments."

Sarah decided to push her luck.

"Can I ask about something else?"

"Certainly," Samuels said.

"Ms. Brown, have you heard of Redwing Associates, Eagle Consultants, American Guardian, Overseas Security Services, or Security Services Partners?"

"Only from the newspaper," Brown said.

"Mr. Malin never mentioned them?"

"No, he did not."

"You never saw any paperwork or records for them?"

"No, I did not."

"So you have no idea what they are?"

"None whatsoever."

"Does Mr. Malin know what you are doing now?"

"Ms. Brown has severed all ties with Mr. Malin," Samuels interceded. "After doing her duty as a citizen in these investigations, Ms. Brown will be seeking other employment. I am confident she will still be eligible to practice law."

"Do you know," Sarah asked him, "what Mr. Malin is doing now?"

"I believe he has retained counsel," Samuels said. "You might try Hobart Glassman at Hanson, Thompson and Glassman. If Mr. Malin were my client, however, I wouldn't talk to you."

"That means," Jones told Sarah, "Josh thinks Malin is in really deep doo-doo."

"I'm not talking to the press," Trent Tucker told Mark Daniels when Mark called him.

"Listen, Trent, I want to help you. Meet me at Smith & Wollensky's at eight. I'll buy you a big steak."

"People know me there."

"Me, too. That's the point. Anybody asks, we're talking about the midterms."

Even though Mark had reserved an isolated table at the restaurant, Tucker appeared more nervous than he had ever seen him. So Mark made political small talk until their sirloins were served.

"The train's leaving the station," he told Tucker as they started eating. "The Justice task force already has several witnesses and boxes full of documents. They'll be getting subpoenas out soon. We hear half a dozen members of Congress are targets, along with Smith and Hawley. All clients of yours. The House subcommittee is heading in the same direction. Sarah will have another story soon."

Tucker didn't say anything.

"I hope you've lawyered up," Mark said. "Has the F.B.I. contacted you yet?"

Tucker picked up his knife and fork and sawed determinedly into the thick steak. "You said you were going to help me."

"You have to trade up, Trent. That's what we hear Lucilla Brown is doing. You better move fast. She won't be the only one."

Tucker took another bite, and then another, chewing faster and faster. He didn't know whether he was more frightened or angry. Was Lucilla doing this on her own? She hadn't said a thing to him about it. Or was someone — maybe even Bob Malin or Carter Phillips — setting him up to be the scapegoat?

"Don't take my word for it," Mark said. "Ask your lawyer. You could help them land big fish and get a good deal. But if you don't, well, you're a pretty big fish yourself."

"This is how you're going to help me?"

"If you want to trade up, you could signal it in Sarah's next story. Justice and the House subcommittee would be bidding for you."

Tucker stopped eating. He hadn't come up with a strategy yet, but he might as well play out this hand.

"What does she want?"

"A source with your knowledge of the American Freedom Alliance to confirm payments to Burros, Hartman, Mahoney, Smith, Stanton, and Thompson. I memorized them in alphabetical order, the senators first."

"A source with knowledge of the records of the American Freedom Alliance," said Tucker. "Just like Lucilla Brown and that bastard Malin."

"Fine."

"Those are the six. Three Democrats and three Republicans. It's about the only thing left in Washington that's bipartisan."

"That's a good first step, Trent."

"What else?"

"Well, you could identify the person with the initials 'EB' who received payments sent to Redwing Associates at that mail store on

Pennsylvania Avenue."

"Where did you get that?"

"Those initials are on lists of payments from government contracts, along with the six members of Congress. Yours are there, too, next to the payments you got every month through Public Relations Solutions and something called RT2."

Tucker pushed back his chair, yanked the napkin out of the vest of his three-piece suit, and walked out of the restaurant.

"I hope I'm not waking you," Sarah said to Alison Winters when she called from her hotel room just before midnight.

"Are you kidding? I didn't get home until an hour ago. I've been taking people out to dinner almost every night to pump them."

Sarah needed to know if she was going to get anything helpful from Alison.

"How's it going?" she asked.

"Not that great. But I heard Elliott talked to people in some of the Cabinet departments a while ago about things like contracts and loan guarantees."

That encouraged Sarah.

"Was he asking about specific companies?"

"Madison something or other. One with two names — something and Cox. Dorsey

444

Energy, which I recognized. And Smith and Hawley, of course."

"Could it have been Madison Partners? And Braxton and Cox?"

"Sounds right."

"Those are all Palisar companies," Sarah said, "and clients of Trent Tucker."

"Tucker and Bancroft have been talking," Alison said, surprising Sarah. "And Tucker hasn't been too happy lately."

"How do you know?"

"I've got a source who has a source close to Tucker."

Sarah laughed. "You sound like me talking to my editor."

"I told you I was a reporter once, too."

"Has Chris Collins been keeping you up on his investigation?"

Alison didn't answer right away.

"It's okay," Sarah said. "He told me the two of you were talking."

"His investigation is moving fast," Alison said. It sounded as though she was choosing her words carefully. "I'm just trying to keep up."

Sarah let it go at that for now.

"Then you know about the lists of payments," she told Alison. "The initials of one recipient were 'EB.' "

The phone went silent again for a moment.

"Alison?"

"Jesus. The president's chief of staff is taking bribes?"

"All I have so far are those initials and a few other hints," Sarah said. "But I thought you'd want to know."

"Thanks."

"My next story should be ready in a day or two. I expect to name six members of Congress who've been receiving payments. I'll call you for comment. But don't tell anyone until I do."

"Of course."

"Not even Chris."

36

"Great story," a network television reporter said to Sarah as they waited in line at the East Entrance to the White House for the first of several holiday receptions for the news media in the weeks before Christmas. "Is there more coming?"

"You never know," Sarah said. She couldn't let her guard down, even with a fellow reporter who didn't really compete with her.

She was with Mark and Jeanne, who were

holding hands. Their closeness reminded her that she would be spending the holidays alone again, and she wished she wasn't. She had turned down her parents' invitation to their annual New Year's Eve party because she couldn't face her mother without a date.

When they reached the front of the line, Mark, Sarah, and Jeanne were checked off the social secretary's list and cleared by the Secret Service to enter the East Wing lobby. They left their coats with ushers at the presidential movie theater, walked through the East Wing colonnade, and climbed the stairs to the main floor of the White House. A Marine Corps string ensemble was playing Christmas carols in the entrance hall, which opened onto the red-carpeted Cross Hall. Brightly decorated Christmas trees, wreaths, and garlands filled the mansion, where there would be similar holiday parties for the White House staff, administration officials, and members of Congress.

Mark had attended so many of them over the years that he knew the tallest tree would be in the Blue Room and the most ornate decorations, along with a brimming buffet table, in the State Dining Room. He decided to take Jeanne on a tour.

"Everything's so beautiful," she said as they started down the wide hall. "It's the first time I've been here since I helped the Capeharts move in."

Sarah stayed behind in the Cross Hall until she found Alison, just as they had arranged over the phone. Alison took her through a door into the Blue Room. They were alone with the large Christmas tree, decorated, like the room, in royal blue and gold, until a lone man came in and stood on the other side of the room, facing them.

"We're on background," Alison told Sarah. She seemed nervous. "Stetson came to see the president today. He said he read your story this morning and wanted to tell her that Tom Hartman had asked him for a favor."

That took Sarah's attention off the man across the room.

"What was Hartman after?"

"He wanted Stetson to intercede at the Ex-Im Bank for some deal Hartman's wife was working on in the Pentagon. Stetson said he stiffed him. He told the president he thought the Hartmans were in Tucker's pocket even before he saw your story."

When a large group of people walked in, talking loudly while admiring the tree, Alison took Sarah next door to the State Dining Room. With everyone there crowded around the long buffet table, the two women were able to find a quiet spot in front of one of the tall windows on a far wall. Sarah noticed the same man among the people nearest them.

"What did the president say?" she asked Alison, turning toward the window.

"She told him she was getting rid of any Tucker people we found in the administration, and Hartman's wife would be among them. I had already told her what I heard about Elliott, so she asked Stetson about it."

"And?"

"All he knew was that Elliott had seemed close to Tucker before he went to work for her."

"Did he say anything about himself?"

Looking at the window's reflection of the lights and people behind them, Sarah saw the man was still there.

"He told the president he wasn't one of Tucker's people, even though Elliott had recommended him to her," Alison said. "He said the trips and contributions he accepted from Tucker's clients were perfectly legal, and he'd be happy to cooperate with the investigations. He even offered to resign if she wanted him to."

Sarah just nodded her head, her expression unchanged, but she thought this was a lot more than she had expected from Alison.

"What did the president say to that?"

"She told me she went with her instincts. She had come to trust him. And she needed his help."

"Why are you telling me all this?"

Whenever any source spoon-fed Sarah so much information, it made her wonder.

"I trust you not to burn me," Alison said. "And I want you to trust *me* when I say everything you've written has been news to the president. She's going to make sure her White House is clean. And she's already taken the first step. She replaced the White House counsel with someone she trusts from California. He's going to report directly to her."

"Cutting out Bancroft?"

"The new counsel is starting an official internal investigation," Alison said, without directly answering Sarah's question.

"When are you announcing this?"

"Tomorrow, but I'm giving it to you first."

The offer of a leaked scoop made Sarah uncomfortable.

"Mark's here," she said to Alison. "Would you mind telling him?"

"Sure."

"I know this sounds silly standing in the

White House," Sarah said, nodding back toward the middle of the room, "but I think that man has been following us."

"Of course he has," Alison said, smiling. "I'm sorry. I should have told you right away. He's part of my new Secret Service detail."

Sarah was relieved, but mystified.

"Since when does the press secretary have Secret Service protection?"

"This has to be completely off the record," Alison said. "I was awakened at home the other morning by a call from somebody who warned me to stop talking to you. He seemed to know what we had said on the phone the night before about Elliott. I went straight to the president about it. She called in the Secret Service. They said my home phone was tapped."

"By whom?"

"I can't tell you anything else," Alison said sheepishly.

"What the hell is going on?" Sarah asked in a loud whisper. Despite what Alison had already given her in a clearly authorized leak, the president's press secretary appeared to be still another source holding out on her.

"All I can say is, you've opened a real Pandora's box. And they want to close it behind Elliott Bancroft."

"Who's 'they'? What's this all about?"

"I'm sorry. I really can't tell you anything more. I don't want to go to jail." Alison seemed quite serious. "I'd better get back to the party."

Now Sarah felt compelled to meet Susan Cameron, if only for a few moments. So she went downstairs and joined the line leading into the Diplomatic Reception Room on the ground floor. Military aides ushered in guests, one by one, to be photographed with the president. Resplendent in a dark red suit for the occasion, Susan was waiting in the middle of the oval room filled with antique furniture, where presidents received the credentials of new ambassadors to Washington. When Sarah's name was announced, she walked in and shook hands.

"Finally, we meet," Susan said, holding on to Sarah's hand to slow down the line. "You're doing important work."

"Thank you, Madam President." Sarah had little to lose by being bold. "I want to follow the story wherever it leads. I just talked to your press secretary about it."

Letting go of Sarah's hand, Susan acted as though she didn't know what Sarah was talking about, her face a question mark.

"Let's get our picture taken," she told Sarah.

After leaving the Diplomatic Reception Room, Sarah wandered back upstairs to think about what had just happened with Alison and the president. Startled to see Elliott Bancroft coming toward her in the Cross Hall, she practically jumped into his path to confront him.

"Are you a member of the White House press?" Elliott asked archly, even though he knew perfectly well who she was.

Sarah tried a bluff.

"I've been trying to reach you, Mr. Bancroft. Your initials are on the list of payments being investigated by the Justice Department and the House subcommittee. What can you tell me about that?"

"How dare you." Elliott looked around to see if anyone had overheard.

"I doubt that I'll be the only one asking, Mr. Bancroft," Sarah said. "And the others will probably be armed with subpoenas."

"I think we're done now."

"Do you have a lawyer I could contact?" asked Sarah.

"You won't have to contact him," Elliott told Sarah as he started to walk away. "He'll be calling you."

■ ■ ■ ■

Ron Jones was still in his office when Sarah got back from the White House that evening. Before she could tell him what had happened there, he asked her to close his door and sit down.

"Lou finally got a call back from one of his intelligence friends," he said. "Lou says he's somebody who was high up in the agency. He's supposedly retired now but still plugged in. He called about your story. He told Lou we're playing with fire."

Sarah remembered Alison, with her own Secret Service protection after being told her phone was tapped, saying she could go to jail if she said anything more to Sarah.

"He told Lou that all six of those members of Congress are key players in the black-budget process," Jones said.

"The black budget?"

"Appropriations for the intelligence agencies. Billions of dollars. All classified."

This was a subject Sarah knew nothing about.

"What does that mean?"

"Lou was told that revealing why they were getting that money could create very big problems in the spook world."

"Why?"

"Lou's friend said he absolutely can't get into that," said Jones. "He said we should be happy with the scandal you've uncovered. He predicted it would be walled off quickly."

It was essentially the same message Sarah had gotten from Alison, Chris Collins, and Pat Scully.

"What should I do now?"

"That's what I asked Lou. He said to keep reporting. He figures that if you get too close to whatever it is somebody will let us know and we'll decide how to handle it."

Sarah left his office and stopped by her desk to get ready to leave the newsroom when her phone rang.

"Can we talk off the record, Ms. Page?"

"It depends on who you are and what you want to say."

"My name is Norman Reilly and I represent Elliott Bancroft."

Sarah clenched her fist in silent triumph and sat down at her computer to take notes.

"Why are you calling, Mr. Reilly?"

"My client has reason to believe he is under investigation by the Justice Department, a House subcommittee, and the White House counsel," Reilly said. "He believes from what you told him today that you know why."

"I doubt you called just to tell me that."

"What if my client was prepared to provide detailed information about a bribery and influence-peddling conspiracy involving officials of this administration, Trent Tucker, and Palisar International, in addition to the members of Congress you wrote about?"

"Then he would want to get to the Justice Department before the others do."

"But he wouldn't necessarily know who may already have done that or what they might be saying."

"So you want everyone to know what your client could deliver?"

"I've been told you're a smart young woman."

"Then let's put this on background," Sarah said, "with attribution to a source familiar with what your client would tell investigators."

There was a long pause, during which she thought she heard muffled conversation.

"Yes," Reilly said. "We can proceed that way."

"Inside the White House," Sarah asked, "does this end with your client?"

"He has no reason or evidence to implicate anyone else currently in the White House, including the president and the vice president."

"But he can testify that Trent Tucker furthered this conspiracy during the time he worked there?"

Sarah had been brushing up on the kinds of crimes that Justice and the F.B.I. might be investigating.

"That's correct," Reilly said. "When he worked in the White House, Mr. Tucker put people into positions in the administration to do his bidding on behalf of his clients, especially companies owned by Palisar International."

"Which departments?"

"Defense. State. Commerce. Interior. Homeland Security. Labor. F.D.A. And others that I cannot discuss at this time."

"Okay," Sarah said, typing furiously. "Who are we talking about? And what did they do?"

"I've got a list," Reilly said. "Arnold Fox, Interior Department: mining, gas, and oil leases for Mammoth Mining and Dorsey Energy. Jennifer Hartman, the senator's wife, Defense: export loan guarantees for Smith and Hawley. Archie Winthrop, Homeland Security: contracts for Madison Partners. George Burros, the senator's son, Commerce; and Connie Solerno, State: export assistance for Stinson Thorpe and Braxton and Cox. Tucker also put a lobbyist named Duffy Johnson into F.D.A. for his pharmaceutical clients."

"What about the payments to members of Congress?" Sarah asked.

"My client has no specific knowledge of them. But he wasn't surprised."

"Because he was getting similar payments himself?"

"You already know that," Reilly said. Sarah stopped typing long enough to pump her fist again.

" 'EB' at Redwing Associates?"

"That's right. We're saving the details for the Justice task force. Bargaining chips. And issues of national security."

There it was again.

"What does that mean?" Sarah asked.

"All I can say is that my client is still legally obligated to keep classified material secret, even though others may be trying to scapegoat him."

"Who might that be?"

"I shouldn't say right now. But if you talk to Mr. Tucker about this, as I imagine you will, tell him Mr. Bancroft remembers the message he relayed from his friend Mr. Phillips."

"What's that, Mr. Reilly?"

" 'If one of us goes, we all go.' "

37

When Mark called this time, Trent Tucker sounded almost despondent. But he agreed to meet Mark at the National Cathedral, where they were unlikely to be noticed among tourists wandering through the cavernous, medieval-style Episcopal cathedral on the Monday before Christmas. After finding each other at the back of the long nave, the two men, wearing suits and open overcoats, walked down the center aisle and took seats in a row of empty chairs.

"It's time, Trent," Mark said, turning to look Tucker in the eye. "Sarah's working on another story. Elliott Bancroft's telling her and the authorities that you put people in the administration to do favors for Palisar. And Lucilla Brown's getting immunity to testify against you and Malin."

"Oh, my God."

"And Bancroft wanted us to remind you that you told him: 'If one of us goes, we all go.' "

Tucker looked nervously around them.

"I was just passing it along from somebody else," he said to Mark. "But that seems to be what's happening."

Tucker had been trying to decide what to do for weeks. And that had meant trying to understand just what he had done. So much of it had seemed to him to be business as usual in Washington: doing whatever was necessary to win elections and buy influence with the politicians he helped get elected.

"You do have a lawyer, don't you, Trent?"

Mark was there primarily to help Sarah. But he also had some sympathy for a man he had known and worked with as a journalist for so many years.

"Yes," Tucker said. "He's been feeling out Justice, but they won't tell him anything."

"That's because you're a target. I said you had to trade up. What can you tell them about Carter Phillips?"

At the mention of the name, Tucker slumped in his chair. He knew he had allowed Phillips to gain too much leverage in their relationship.

"I'm boxed in," he told Mark. "The general has so much on me."

"You mean the money?"

"Sex. Drugs. I have appetites." Tucker lowered his voice to nearly a whisper. "He has pictures and tapes." He paused before going further. "And he knows about me and Sarah. I'm surprised he hasn't used it against her already."

"What the hell?" Mark blurted out, looking around anxiously. "Let's go somewhere more private."

They walked out of the cathedral and headed a few blocks north on Wisconsin Avenue toward a cluster of restaurants and shops at Macomb Street in Cleveland Park.

"Over there." Tucker pointed to a wine bar on the next corner. "I could use something alcoholic.

"You know," he told Mark while they crossed the street, "that used to be the Zebra Lounge. It became famous a long time ago. A Speaker of the House came out of there drunk as a skunk one night and wrapped his car around a telephone pole right across the street. He was lucky he didn't get killed. It was the first time a congressman's alcoholism had become public. Nobody had reported it before. Just like nobody had reported what Kennedy or Johnson were doing with women in the White House."

"The good old days," Mark said sarcastically. He himself had looked the other way at times while covering campaigns.

"Booze, women, influence peddling. Most of it never hit the papers back then."

"We're talking bribery here, Trent. Cash-money bribes. Like what Spiro Agnew got in envelopes before he was forced to take a plea and resign."

Tucker knew Mark was right. It just hadn't seemed that way at the time. Paying to play the game in Washington took so many forms that were arguably legal or close to the line. He had ignored or rationalized the times he was involved in crossing that line, while being paid well for it.

The two men fell silent until they walked into the nearly empty Enology Wine Bar, took off their overcoats, and sat down at a table. Tucker ordered a glass of Pinot Noir. Mark asked for a cup of coffee.

"Okay," said Mark. "What were you saying about Sarah?"

"We had a fling when she was working in Maryland. The governor was one of my clients," Tucker said. "It didn't last long. But the general knows."

"Shit."

"She hasn't told you? Or her editors?" Tucker perked up a bit. "Guess she didn't want to get taken off the story."

If Mark was going to help Sarah, he had to finish what he came to do.

"No matter what Phillips has on you," he said, changing the subject, "you sure as hell better beat him to the Justice Department. What can you tell me?"

Tucker raised his hand for another glass

of wine. No matter what he did now, he would be the scapegoat. So he decided to do it his own way.

"Okay. This has to be attributed to a source familiar with what I've told my lawyer. His name is Morgan Whitaker."

"Fine," Mark said. "We know American Freedom Alliance was the laundry for the payments to six members of Congress. What about Public Relations Solutions?"

"That's how I got my money from the Smith and Hawley contracts. I used it to pad my clients' bills, too."

"And RT2?"

"Same thing."

"Malin Associates?"

"That's how fucking Malin got his money."

"From the same Smith and Hawley sub-contractors."

"Yeah. It's also the holding company for our real estate."

"Another way to launder money?"

"Government money that neither Malin nor the general ever explained. It's apparently real secret. The general said something the other day about it all being classified. It's the only time he's ever seemed scared."

With his work for Sarah done, Mark once again felt a measure of sympathy for Tucker.

He was about to take a huge fall.

"Sounds like you'd better get moving to take care of yourself as best you can," he said to Tucker.

"Don't worry about me. I know just what I'm going to do now."

38

"A fling? Is that what he called it? Getting me drunk so he could have sex with me?"

Sarah was angry, embarrassed, and frightened. As soon as Mark started telling her about his conversation with Tucker, she took him into Ron Jones's office. She knew she should have told Jones about it long ago.

"Thanks," Jones said, when Mark was finished. "I need to talk to Sarah. Please shut the door on your way out."

Sarah was determined not to cry.

"I'm really sorry, Ron."

"Why don't you tell me your version?" he asked her calmly.

"I met him when I was covering Tawney's campaign for governor," Sarah began. It was surprisingly easy to get it out.

"He was doing her message and media, so he became a source. I'd never covered a campaign before, all that traveling and everything. The best time to talk was usually at night in a hotel bar. He told me a lot about politics that I didn't know. We drank and talked for hours and hours night after night.

"I guess I was taken in by the attention he paid to me. He was glamorous in a weird way. The Maryland pols were awestruck around him. National politicians and reporters were calling him all the time. I drank more with him than I could handle. I told him my life story, the distance I felt from my parents and almost everyone else, the difficulty I had getting to really know anybody in my work. He said I was attractive and smart and talented, and I deserved better."

The next part was harder for her. Jones waited while she found the words.

"One night, in a kind of haze, I realized we were having sex in his hotel room. I let him take advantage of me, although I was certainly no virgin. We wound up doing it a few more times when we got drunk. We never talked about it. And he disappeared right after the election."

"And after that?"

"I didn't see him again until last year, when you gave me the political money beat and told me to check him out. It turned out he lived in my neighborhood. I've kept everything completely businesslike this time."

"You should have told me this at the very beginning," Jones said sternly.

"I know." Sarah felt drained. "I almost did, but . . ."

"And you should have told your editors on Metro before that."

"But I never saw him after Tawney became governor."

"You were covering the governor of Maryland after sleeping with her campaign consultant."

"That sounds pretty bad," Sarah said.

"And now you're accusing him of corrupt behavior, and you could be holding a grudge against him."

"That sounds worse."

Sarah knew Jones was right. She had had plenty of time and opportunity to tell him about Tucker.

"For what it's worth," she said. "I really didn't think I was biased against him."

She had long ago written off what had happened with Tucker as her own fault. But she hadn't wanted it to limit what she could report on.

"When did this happen?" Lou Runyan asked, after Jones and Sarah had gone to his office and told him everything.

"About five years ago," Sarah said.

"Let's see," Runyan mused. "In proportion to your age, that's just about the slack we cut for Monroe Capehart."

"Lou," Jones said. "This is serious."

"So am I. After all that's been done to Sarah and some of her sources by whoever wants to get her off this story, I'd say she has much better reasons to be biased than a few rolls in the hay five years ago.

"Look," Runyan told Jones. "If anybody brings it up, I'll handle it. Let her do her job."

Sarah left his office drained and relieved. But, as she walked through the newsroom with Jones, he delivered one more warning.

"Any more surprises like this and you're out," he said. "Lou likes being on the brink. But if we go over it, he won't even bother to look for your body — or mine."

39

Christmas Eve is normally one of the quietest news days of the year. But not after Sarah's front-page story implicating the White House chief of staff and other administration officials in the growing government-contracting scandal. President

Cameron postponed her departure for Camp David, where she was planning to spend Christmas with her parents. The White House promised big news at the noon briefing.

Alison Winters had said that Mark should feel free to invite Sarah to the briefing. "I think they want to be seen taking your story seriously," Mark said as he walked with Sarah through Lafayette Square, where the leafless trees swayed in a chilly wind.

Inside the White House press-briefing room, Mark and Sarah sat down in the second row of royal blue seats. When Alison came to the podium, Sarah was surprised to see Elizabeth Tawney standing next to her.

"Good afternoon and happy holidays," Alison said to begin the on-the-record briefing, which was being televised live on cable and the Internet. "I have some announcements. This morning, President Cameron requested and accepted the resignation of Elliott Bancroft as White House chief of staff. The president thanked Mr. Bancroft for his service and told him she appreciated his decision to cooperate fully with the ongoing investigations. I will not be able to comment further on those investigations at this time."

The reporters clamored to ask questions

about it anyway, but Alison raised her hands for quiet.

"I have a related announcement," she said. "Effective immediately, the president's new chief of staff will be Elizabeth Tawney. She resigned today as governor of Maryland so she can serve the president and the nation at this important time. Governor Tawney brings to the White House a well-earned reputation for effective management, good judgment, and unblemished integrity."

When Alison called on Sarah to ask the first question, Tawney gave her a little wink. It should have made Sarah feel uncomfortable, but she was still caught up in the experience of participating in a White House briefing about her own story.

"Is any action being taken in other parts of the administration?"

"Welcome, Ms. Page," Alison replied with a slight smile. "We expect announcements of significant personnel changes later today at State, Defense, Commerce, and Homeland Security."

"Can I follow up? Did the president know about what Mr. Bancroft is expected to tell investigators? And did she know about Mr. Tucker's activities when he worked in the White House?"

Alison's smile vanished. Tawney stretched

to whisper something to the taller woman. Except for the rapid-fire clicks of camera shutters, the crowded briefing room fell silent.

"I'll let my new boss handle this," Alison said, standing aside.

"Ms. Page, I discussed this matter fully with President Cameron before accepting this job," Tawney said. "I'm personally convinced she knew nothing about any irregularities anywhere in her administration before your stories appeared. She has since moved decisively to dismiss anyone under suspicion. She has cooperated fully with all investigations and will continue to do so."

"And Vice President Stetson?" asked Sarah.

"He told the president that your earlier reports concerning his activities as a senator were accurate," Tawney responded. "He said he did not knowingly break any laws, however, and he joined the president in promising full cooperation with all investigations. He even offered his resignation, which the president refused."

Pandemonium broke out in the briefing room, while Sarah sat contentedly, and perhaps too smugly, in the *Washington Capital* seat in the second row.

"The president believes he has done a

good job since becoming vice president," Tawney continued over the uproar. "She welcomes his continued support and wisdom in the White House."

40

Trent Tucker awoke to his alarm well before dawn on the first work day of the new year. He dressed in his favorite three-piece suit. Switching on lights ahead of him, he walked downstairs to the dining room, his favorite place in the house. He had lavished money on making it into a miniature medieval banquet hall, complete with hammer-beam ceiling and leaded windows.

He went over to the long dining-room table, where he had left several cardboard boxes filled with files he had meticulously organized and labeled. One by one, he took them out of the boxes and distributed them around the table, as though preparing for a meeting.

Checking his watch, Tucker walked out of the house, leaving the lights burning brightly and the front door unlocked. He went down the long cobblestone driveway, through the iron front gate and onto the road. He stood there in the dark and waited.

Just down the hill, the engines were already running in two black Ford Expeditions and a Lincoln Town Car parked on a gravel-covered drive next to the Victorian home of the chairman of the Federal Reserve. Several minutes passed before he emerged from his house, carrying his customary stack of newspapers, official documents, and economic reports. He eased himself into the backseat of the Town Car, where the reading lamp was already lit. He fastened his seat belt and opened one of the newspapers.

With the two Expeditions driven by Federal Reserve Police officers taking the lead, the three vehicles pulled out onto Chain Bridge Road. They accelerated as they ascended the hill, their headlamps burrowing a tunnel of light into the darkness.

When he saw the light bouncing off the trees in Battery Kemble Park across the road, Tucker braced himself. As the vehicles raced toward him, he lunged into their path. He was hit by the left front side of the first Expedition. The driver of the second SUV was able to swerve just enough to avoid Tucker's tumbling body. The Town Car remained on course.

It would never be determined whether Tucker was still alive when he landed on the hood of the sedan and slid back against its windshield. Despite being blinded by Tucker's body and the blood oozing from it, the driver managed to skid safely to a stop, leaving the Fed chairman shaken but unhurt.

A short time later, Mark arrived at the newspaper to check his mail before going to the White House for the morning briefing. A young news aide greeted him as he entered the mail room.

"This box was delivered for you over the weekend," she said. "The return address is a UPS store on MacArthur Boulevard. We put it through the scanner and it looks okay."

Mark pried open the box. It was filled with papers in file folders. On top was a hand-written note:

Mark,
By the time you get this, the police should have found everything on my dining-room table. I made it easy for them. I copied the best stuff for you. You were always straight with me, even when I wasn't with you.

Trent

The note left Mark puzzled. He carried

the box upstairs, where he found early arrivals in the newsroom standing in knots around the overhead television screens.

"What's going on?" he asked.

"It's that lobbyist, Trent Tucker," said an editor on the Web site news desk. "He was run over in front of his house by the Fed chairman's motorcade. Joni Parker called to say she's on her way."

"Do you have her cell number?"

"Sure."

Mark punched it into his phone.

"When you get there, could you check on what the police find in Tucker's house," he asked Joni. "I think he's committed suicide in a rather bizarre way."

"Slow down, honey. What are you talking about?"

"Tucker sent me a box of documents. He left the same stuff for the police on his dining-room table."

"I'm almost there," Joni said. "I'll call back when I know something. Should I tell my cop friends what you've got?"

"Better wait till I check with Ron Jones."

"Look at these," Mark said, holding up a sheaf of documents and a computer disk he had taken from one of the file folders. "Lists of illegal campaign contributions from

474

companies owned by Palisar that were funneled through labor-union PACs. Trent put a memo in the file explaining how it worked."

Mark, Sarah, Ron Jones, and Mary Sullivan were all in Jones's office, examining copies of the contents of the box Tucker had sent to Mark. At the direction of the newspaper's general counsel, everything in it had been copied. After conferring with Lou Runyan and the publisher, the general counsel had put the originals back in the box and turned it over to the police.

Mark had shocked Sarah when he woke her a few hours earlier with word of Tucker's death. While she showered and dressed in her hotel room, she wrestled with the news. Tucker had been a target of the biggest investigative story of her life. Her history with him had been painfully exposed to her editors just a few days earlier. But she certainly hadn't sought or expected anything like this.

It didn't feel good that her journalism might have led to another person's death, especially someone she knew that well. But she believed in what she was doing, and she *knew* Tucker had ultimately brought this on himself. He had become so deeply involved in corruption with Carter Phillips that it could not have come to a good end. Proof of that was his own painstaking stockpiling of evidence that could pull Phillips down with him.

Now, in the newsroom, where her devotion to her work had often displaced other emotions, Sarah concentrated on the documents she and her colleagues were sorting through.

"There are master lists of the payments from Smith and Hawley's Pentagon contracts, just like the ones from my sources," she said, leafing through another file. "This shows that Carter Phillips *is* the 'CP' who got the payments sent to the other post-office boxes at that place on Pennsylvania Avenue. Why would he do that when he could pay himself as much as he wanted from Palisar?"

"Maybe he wanted to hide the money from his partners," Jones said.

"He might have gotten in the habit of diverting money when he was in the Special Forces," added Sullivan, who had written about covert military operations as a reporter. "They used lots of untraceable cash for black projects in places like Iraq and Afghanistan."

Black projects. Black budgets. Sarah guessed that she would find the answer to the mystery in that shadowy part of Washington. She just had to figure out how to do it.

"Let's get as much as we can into tomorrow's paper," Jones said.

After the meeting broke up, Sarah lingered in his office, a stack of the documents in her arms, looking as though she had something to tell him.

"It must be tough for you," Jones said. "First Seth Moore, then the bombing of your car, and now this. Is there somebody you can talk to about it? Your parents?"

"Are you kidding? You've met them."

Sarah felt more alone than ever. But that was not what she wanted to discuss with Jones.

"Ron, can I ask you about something else?"

"Sure."

"Remember Michael Cameron's mistress, the one who outed him on television?"

"Yeah, but I've forgotten her name."

"Catherine Nichols. She called me. She'd read my Bancroft story on the Web. She wants to talk to me about Susan Cameron. But it has to be in L.A."

"You're pretty busy here."

"I know," Sarah said. "But I think it might be worth it. Marge and I checked her out. I could make the trip in a day and take the red-eye back."

"sorry about tucker . . . know you didn't want it to end that way"

Sarah wondered what Pat Scully's real reason was for contacting her.

"He left lots of documents showing who got payments, including Carter Phillips. We'll have a good story for tomorrow."

"payments to phillips . . . what kind . . . who from"

"From Smith and Hawley's subcontractors, just like the others. Laundered offshore and sent to the mail drop on Pennsylvania Avenue. We don't know why. Do you?"

"not really . . . you must be pleased . . . he's your big fish"

"Not sure anymore. Maybe he's the key to the national security stuff. Have you found out anything about that?"

"nope . . . maybe smoke screen to protect corruption"

Once again, Scully was holding out on Sarah.

"We're past that, Pat," she typed. "I need to know what you know about black projects and budgets."

There was no reply. He had disappeared again.

Sarah spent the rest of the day, with help from Mark, reporting and writing stories about Trent Tucker's documents. She wondered why she hadn't heard from Chris Collins. So, that night, when her cell phone rang at the hotel, she thought it might be him.

"I'm sorry to call so late," said a woman who identified herself as Lois Engle, the head of the Justice task force. "Congressman Collins gave me your number."

"I asked him to."

Sarah was pleased that Collins had come through for her.

"I have to be honest. I wouldn't have called if you hadn't come into possession of documents pertinent to our investigation."

"How did you know?" Sarah asked her. "We're keeping our stories off the Web until later tonight, so the competition can't rip us off."

"You interviewed a lot of our targets' defense lawyers today, and they called us in a panic. They thought we leaked the documents. But we haven't seen them yet."

"On what basis are we talking?"

Sarah took a notebook and pen from her purse. Establishing a relationship with a new confidential source was always tricky, but she knew this one would be particularly sensitive.

"Completely off the record," said Engle.

"And you can promise that there won't be any subpoenas of me or investigations of leaks based on our conversations?"

Ever since the Scooter Libby case, the newspaper's lawyers had been warning everyone about those risks. Sarah had convinced herself that she was willing to go to jail to protect a confidential source if it became necessary, but she hoped it never would be.

"Not while I'm in charge of this task force," Engle said.

"Okay. Tucker sent us a box containing copies of some of the documents he left in his house. We made our own copies before the newspaper's general counsel gave the box to the police. You'll see some of the stuff in our stories. But I could go over the highlights now, if you can help me with the status of your investigation."

"I was expecting that. I can tell you that Robert Malin is negotiating a plea deal, although it's complicated."

"Laundered payments from Pentagon contracts to Malin are in the records we've got," Sarah said. "It'll be in the paper."

"Good. That could speed up negotiations."

"We found payments to Carter Phillips, too," Sarah said. "But we don't understand them."

"I can't discuss anything about that."

Still another source avoiding something secret, Sarah thought.

"Could it have something to do with covert intelligence operations? Is that why the Malin negotiations are complicated? Are you trying to wall off something that affects national security?"

"I'm sorry. I just can't discuss it," Engle said. "Chris was right."

"About what?"

"You're persistent."

41

In Sarah's dream, she was running from Trent Tucker down Main Street toward the City Dock in Annapolis. She was awakened suddenly at precisely 4 a.m. by the telephone in her downtown Washington hotel room.

"How did you find me here?" Her annoying anonymous caller was back.

"We always know where you are, Miss Page — the hotel, the newspaper, your parents' house, even the parking garage at the airport."

Sarah sat up in bed and tried to think clearly. Pat Scully had also alluded to the garage at Dulles where she met with Cathy Adams. But she hadn't actually spoken with Scully since their meeting many months ago at Union Station. Could he be the man on the phone? She didn't think it sounded like the same voice, but she couldn't be sure.

"Miss Page?"

"I'm getting tired of this," Sarah said. "Why do you keep calling me?"

"You know why, Miss Page. We have warned you repeatedly that your reporting could jeopardize national security. I admit that your recent stories have actually been helpful. But you must stop there. Don't put anyone else in danger."

The caller's calm, even tone never changed, which only added to Sarah's irritation.

"What do you mean by that? Who killed Seth Moore? Who blew up my car?"

"Those are matters for the police, Miss Page. But I do worry about your safety."

"Is that a threat?"

"Please, Miss Page. I'm only saying, once again, that you must stay away from national-security activities whose exposure could cause great harm."

"What activities? Why don't you tell me

what you're talking about?"

"I've made myself perfectly clear, Miss Page. Just stop now. Stop before it's too late."

Sarah seldom ended a conversation with a potential source prematurely, no matter how unproductive or maddening, but the caller had delivered his message and, once again, she wasn't getting anything more out of him. So she hung up.

When she got to the newsroom later that morning, Sarah found a surprise in her e-mail:

FOR IMMEDIATE RELEASE

Palisar International announced today that its managing partner, Gen. Carter Phillips, has resigned. His investment in the Washington-based firm has been liquidated.

Ronald Moffett, chairman of Moffett Carlson, the New York–based investment firm, and a former president of the Federal Reserve Bank of New York, has agreed to a request by the remaining Palisar partners to serve as interim managing partner for an indefinite period of time.

Mr. Moffett has secured outside counsel, Thad Ferguson, former Attorney General of New York State and a partner of Ferguson, Lyon and Wells. He will investigate any allegations of illegality involving personnel of Palisar International or the firms it owns.

Mr. Moffett said that any active personnel found to have engaged in illegal activity will be terminated and referred to the proper authorities. He also pledged full cooperation with all ongoing government investigations.

When she tried to contact Pat Scully, Sarah was surprised that he messaged her back almost immediately, despite the early hour on the West Coast.
"already saw it . . ."
"What happened?"
"phillips flew the coop . . . probably left the country"
"How do you know?"
"good source"
"What source?"
"can't say"
"What aren't you telling me?"
"nothing . . . why"
"You didn't respond last time when I

asked about national security and black projects."

"sorry . . . can't help on that"

"Can't or won't? What's going on, Pat?"

"really can't say more now . . . trust me"

Sarah set about fleshing out a story from the bare-bones Palisar press release. Among other calls, she tried repeatedly to reach Chris Collins, leaving messages at his office and on his cell phone. She finally heard from him late in the afternoon.

"I was on my way back from my district. I spent the holidays there," he said. "I was sorry to hear about Trent Tucker."

"He was in pretty deep. But it's still a horrible way to go."

"You okay?"

"I think so." She was pleased he had asked, but she was determined to get what information she could from him. "Did you know Carter Phillips is on the run?"

"Really?"

Sarah couldn't tell whether he was surprised or being coy.

"I still have to confirm it."

"I'll check," Collins said. "That would change the hearings."

"Speaking of the hearings, are you going to question any of the six senators and congressmen who took the money?"

"That's a matter for the House and Senate Ethics committees, if there's anything left to do after Justice finishes."

"Were all six involved in defense spending in some way?" asked Sarah.

"I'm not sure they were all on those committees. But they could do it through earmarks anyway."

"How about authorization and appropriations for intelligence operations?"

"I wouldn't know," Collins said quickly. "That's black-budget stuff. You know, secret."

Sarah had come up against that barrier again, and she wanted badly to break through it.

"Congressman, can I talk to you in person? Maybe lunch later in the week?"

"Why not dinner tonight?"

As off-handed as Collins had made it sound, Sarah sensed an eagerness. And that brought back the conflicts she felt each time she saw or heard from him.

"I have a story to finish."

"Whenever you're ready will be fine for me," Collins said. "How about the Monocle here on the Hill?" The restaurant had a reputation as a clubhouse for members of Congress.

"I'll let you know when I'm done," Sarah said.

She then got a call she had been expecting from Joni Parker.

"You were right," Joni said. "The Feds told the cops that Carter Phillips has disappeared. But they may have the guy who killed Seth Moore. He's one of the security people Phillips had at Palisar. The local task force is rolling up a bunch of them on weapons and other charges before they can get away."

"Can I write that?"

"If you get it confirmed someplace else."

Sarah dialed the cell phone of her new Justice source, Lois Engle.

"I hope you aren't going to make a habit of this," Engle said. "I gave you this number for emergencies."

"I'm working on a story for tomorrow. Can you confirm that Carter Phillips has fled the country?"

"How do you know that?"

"I have other sources, too."

"Then why call me?"

"I want to make sure it's right."

"Well, he hasn't been charged. So I don't think traveling outside the country constitutes fleeing. But we're looking for him."

"Is he a target of your investigation?"

"I believe the right term at this stage is 'person of interest.' You've seen the documents."

That was just the confirmation that Sarah needed for her story.

"What about the local task force of police and the F.B.I.?" she asked.

"We're working together now."

"Have they begun arresting Phillips's security people?"

"That's what I hear, but you'd have to talk to them about details," Engle said.

"One more thing. Did the six members of Congress who took bribes have anything to do with the black budget for the intelligence services?"

"You know I can't talk about that."

"Would you wave me off?"

There was a long pause.

"I can't say anything more."

42

The Monocle looked much as Sarah had imagined — a whitewashed, two-story Federal-style relic with green awnings just a block from the nearest Senate office building and within sight of the Capitol. Inside, the wood-paneled walls were covered with framed photographs of the countless members of Congress who had dined and dallied in the restaurant during its half century in business.

After taking her coat, the maître d' guided Sarah to a far corner table where Chris Collins was waiting. Dressed in a blue blazer over an open-necked checked shirt and tan slacks, he looked as boyishly appealing as ever.

"You're wearing that dress again," Collins said as he stood to greet Sarah. He reached for her hands with both of his and pulled her so close she thought he was going to kiss her, but he didn't.

"I don't have a lot to choose from," Sarah said. She had stopped at the hotel and changed into her sleeveless black sheath, despite the winter cold outside. "I never seem to have time to shop."

"Well, if you don't mind my saying so, you look great."

Sarah didn't mind, but she didn't say anything.

"Would you like some wine?" Collins asked as they sat down. "They have my favorite Chardonnay here. Believe it or not, it's called Fat Bastard and it comes from France. I'm afraid I have common tastes — in wine, I mean."

Sarah laughed. If Collins had intended to

put her at ease immediately, he had succeeded.

"I actually know Fat Bastard," she said, repeating the name with relish. "And I like it."

Collins nodded to a nearby waiter, who soon reappeared with a chilled bottle.

"Here's to us," Collins said, raising his glass before adding with a sly smile, "in the spirit of cooperation between Congress and the press."

Sarah didn't respond in words, but her eyes met his as their glasses touched.

"Thanks for the source at Justice," she said as she put down her glass.

"Did you finish your story?"

"It says the Feds are looking for Carter Phillips as a person of interest."

"Because he paid off members of Congress?"

"Wouldn't you know?"

Even in a mellow mood, Sarah's instincts as a reporter took over.

"You've been ahead of me every step of the way so far," he told her.

"That's flattering, Congressman, but . . ."

"C'mon. It's Chris."

"That's flattering, Chris, but I have questions that you and Pat Scully and our Justice friend won't answer."

"Try me," he said, leaning toward her with his hands folded on the table.

"Okay." Sarah had prepared for this. "Why was Carter Phillips, who could take all the money he wanted out of Palisar, getting kickbacks from Pentagon contracts? Was he bribing those people on the Hill just to get defense contracts for his companies? Or was he also trying to influence appropriations for black intelligence operations? Is that the connection between the contracting scandal and national security?"

"You ask good questions."

"Is that a hint?"

As the waiter refilled their wineglasses, Collins looked intently into Sarah's face.

"I'm buying time while I figure out how to answer," he said. "I'm legally prohibited from disclosing classified information, especially when it could endanger national security."

"Now you sound like the guy who's been waking me up with harassing phone calls."

"What guy?"

"He won't identify himself, but he sounds military," Sarah said. "Very polite but kind of scary, especially at four in the morning."

Collins looked concerned. "He's calling you at four a.m.?"

"He keeps warning me to stop my reporting before it gets involved in national security. He's very insistent."

"Well, I don't like that, especially with everything you've been through, Sarah." Collins reached his hand toward hers without quite touching it. "I'll see if there's anything I can do."

Sarah moved her hand to take hold of his.

"Chris," she asked, "are you going to tell me what's going on?"

"I'll try," he said. "But it has to be off the record, just between you and me, for now."

"For now."

The waiter came to serve their food, and Sarah let go of his hand.

"The military outsourced a lot of work to private contractors because they were stretched so thin by Iraq and Afghanistan," he said after the waiter had left. "The Pentagon spent billions on tens of thousands of contract employees in Iraq alone. They became a private army of military retirees, mercenaries, and adventurers. They ran supply convoys. They guarded American bases, protected diplomats and dignitaries, and provided security for the Army Corps of Engineers on reconstruction projects. And they gathered and analyzed intelligence."

"What about the intelligence agencies?"

"They couldn't expand fast enough after

9/11, so they hired a lot of contractors, too. Half the work of the clandestine services was outsourced to big defense contractors like Booz Allen and SAIC. Recruiting and running spies. Managing important stations like Baghdad and Islamabad.

"The covert-ops jobs went to smaller companies. Some of them turned out to be owned by Carter Phillips. I'm guessing he hid the covert work from his partners at Palisar so he could skim money off the top."

"But he already had plenty of money."

"Some guys measure winning and losing in life by how much they accumulate, whether they need it or not."

"If this is just about intelligence contracts, why is everybody covering it up?"

"Not my preferred choice of words."

"Sorry. But you know what I mean."

"Look, I'm playing way outside the lines here," Collins said with a seriousness Sarah had not seen before. "This covert work is critical to our counterterrorism efforts. We and Justice have agreed to leave it out of our investigations, no matter what Phillips has done."

In the silence that followed, Sarah carefully considered what Collins had said.

"Are you satisfied with that?" she asked him.

"You're really idealistic, aren't you? It's not something I've seen that much of in Washington."

"I'm just doing my job, Chris. I believe in holding people with power accountable for how they use it."

"And I believe in the oaths I've taken to protect our country."

They emptied their wineglasses.

"So can I report that Congress and the Justice Department have put limits on their corruption investigations to protect covert operations being carried out by some of the contractors?"

Collins shook his head and laughed. "That was off the record for now, remember?"

"What if I pursued it elsewhere?"

"You can, but you won't get any answers." He laughed again.

"You really are persistent, Sarah."

"That's what you told our Justice friend."

"I did warn her. But I said it would still be better to talk to you so she'd know what you're doing."

"Thanks a lot. Have you been keeping tabs on me?"

"I'd like to do more than that."

"Excuse me?" Sarah asked, although they both knew what he meant.

"I'm sorry," Collins said, reaching out for

her hand again. "You're just so attractive in so many ways, like the passion you bring to your work. That's what I meant by persistent. I guess I was avoiding what I really wanted to say."

Sarah looked into his eyes. He was a congressman. He was a source. But not that much of a source anymore. She had already gotten into trouble twice for sleeping with the wrong men. But it just felt right, at least for now.

"Tell me what you really wanted to say, Chris," she said, once more putting her hand into his.

"It's been such a long time, it feels like high school," he said sheepishly. "I want to get to know you better."

"I'm a reporter, Chris."

"Not just any reporter, Sarah. And you don't cover the Hill anyway."

"Then I bet a smart guy like you already has his next move in mind."

Collins actually blushed. "My housemate won't be back in town until late tomorrow."

His childlike expression at being caught out closed the deal for Sarah.

"Let's pay the check," she said.

43

With Sarah and Ron Jones in the backseat and Lou Runyan riding shotgun, Mary Sullivan drove out to the heavily wooded, three-hundred-acre campus of the Central Intelligence Agency just across the Potomac River in Langley, Virginia. They stopped first at the gatehouse on the entrance road, where a guard checked their identification and phoned ahead for clearance.

"Tell me again why we're doing this," Sullivan asked, turning toward Runyan while they waited.

"I'm not sure myself. Like I said, the director of national intelligence called me and asked us to meet him here," Runyan said. "Something about the questions Sarah had given them."

"I asked about classified intelligence contracts that might be involved in the Palisar scandal," Sarah said from behind them. "They wanted the questions in writing. But I don't know why they called a summit meeting like this. I just took shots in the dark."

"I guess your aim was better than you thought," said Jones.

Sullivan drove past one nondescript building after another along a loop road before coming to the visitors' lot in front of the intelligence agency's squat, seven-story headquarters. After they signed in at the reception desk in the vast, marble-lined lobby, a somber-suited security officer took them in a key-operated elevator to the seventh-floor office of C.I.A. director Marvin Reynolds.

A short, bespectacled, nervous man, Reynolds was waiting when the elevator opened into his anteroom. With him was his boss, Phillip Vance, the director of national intelligence, who had come from downtown. He was tall and patrician-looking, with a neatly trimmed mustache and an assured manner.

"Phil." Runyan greeted Vance heartily, shaking his hand. "It's been a while since I've seen you in a suit."

"They play tennis every week at St. Alban's," Jones whispered to Sarah, who wondered how that would affect the meeting.

Reynolds led the group into his office and over to a conference table in front of a window that ran the length of the room. The view outside was filled with leafless trees on a dreary winter morning.

"Are we agreed?" Vance asked. "This meeting is off the record?"

"Yes," Sullivan responded, while Runyan settled casually into his chair.

"We are not able to answer any of your reporter's questions because they allude to highly classified operational information," Reynolds said, after getting a nod from Vance.

"Then why are we here?" Sullivan asked.

"We want to be sure you understand that any discussion by your reporter or her sources about any connection between the Palisar contracting and bribery investigations and any intelligence activities or funding could compromise ongoing operations, endanger lives, and violate espionage laws," Reynolds said purposefully, glancing down at a piece of paper on the table in front of him.

That sounded even more serious than Sarah had imagined.

"Hold on," Runyan interrupted. "Wouldn't it be the C.I.A. that was breaking the law if it or any of its contractors were involved in fraud or bribing members of Congress?"

"This agency has no responsibility for the activities of assets operating outside its control," responded Reynolds, who looked anxiously to his boss.

"Lou," said Vance, "your reporter has no

evidence of involvement of any intelligence agency in that sort of thing. And I'm sure you don't want her to run the risk of a subpoena or jail."

Sarah felt like a child who had become the subject of conversation at dinner, listening as the grown-ups talked about her in the third person.

"Look, we're not alone," Ron Jones broke in. "As you know, Justice and Congress have active investigations going."

"We have every reason to believe they will honor our requests not to get into matters of national security," Vance said.

Sarah noted that Vance had just confirmed what Chris Collins had told her a few nights earlier.

"It would help us," Mary Sullivan said, "if we could understand where our reporting might expose legitimate covert operations, which we do not want to do."

"The only way you can avoid that is to stop inquiring into any aspect of this affair that touches on the intelligence community," Vance answered.

"Come on, Phil," said Runyan. "If you don't help us, we'll have no choice but to make decisions on our own."

"Well, we'll just have to see about that, Lou." Vance rose from his chair, ending the meeting. "Thank you all for coming."

"What happened in there?" Sarah asked after they were all back inside Mary Sullivan's car.

"We called each other's bluff," Runyan said. "They warned us to back off. We refused. Now they'll be watching what we do. And we'll be waiting for what they try next."

"Where does that leave me?" Sarah asked him anxiously.

"Staying on their ass," he said, turning around in his seat. "That meeting got my juices flowing."

So much for tennis at St. Alban's.

As they drove back into the city, Sarah thought about Chris Collins, with whom she had now spent two nights, one at his town house and another at her hotel. In the company of her editors, she felt more than a little guilty about it. But she knew she would have to see him again.

Back in the newsroom after lunch, with time to spare before an appointment at the White House, Sarah checked her voice mail.

"This is Kit Morgan. I was expecting to hear from you by now," said the voice on one of the messages. "You said we'd get together. Give me a call."

Sarah dialed what appeared to be a local cell-phone number. She was ready to find out more about the woman Marge Lawson had described as a "ghost."

"Well, it's about time," Kathleen Morgan declared in the effusive way Sarah still remembered from the Democratic convention in Chicago. "Can I buy you dinner? I assume even busy journalists eat now and then. Would tonight be too soon?"

"Actually, I'll have to buy you dinner. Newspaper rules," Sarah said. "And tonight would be fine."

"Can the newspaper afford the Prime Rib? I've got a table there."

The Prime Rib, in the midst of the lobbyists' offices on K Street, was one of Washington's inner-sanctum restaurants. Regulars were treated like royalty. Interlopers were politely tolerated. *I've got a table there* sounded like royalty.

"I can be there at eight," Sarah said.

Soon afterward, she went to the White House to talk to Elizabeth Tawney.

"Thanks for seeing me," Sarah began. "We're off the record."

The two women were sitting in antique chairs in the chief of staff's corner office on the first floor of the West Wing. It was nearing dusk, and the clouds had lifted just enough outside for the sinking sun to tint the room with an eerie, yellowish glow.

"Your visit to Langley must have been inconclusive," Tawney said. "The D.N.I. has already asked the president to talk to your editors."

"Actually, that's not what this is about." Sarah was surprised, perhaps naïvely, that the White House was aware of the meeting at the C.I.A. "It's about the president's past."

Tawney looked puzzled.

"Remember Catherine Nichols?" Sarah asked. "The woman who blew the whistle on Michael Cameron?"

"I remember what she did," said Tawney. "But I'd forgotten her name."

"She called me recently, and I flew out to meet her in Los Angeles. She told me Susan Cameron knew all along about Michael's women, including her. She said that Susan — she kept using the president's first name — had tolerated it at first because she didn't want to risk their political future. But as Susan gained self-confidence in Washington, according to Nichols, she resented it more.

"So she confronted Nichols, who was an executive in Michael's venture-capital firm. They wound up trading information. Susan told Nichols about all the other women, which devastated her. Nichols told Susan about Michael's stock manipulation, which could have gotten both of them into serious legal trouble. So they decided to expose him and save themselves. They even scripted Nichols's television interview and Susan's public reaction to it."

"I don't believe this," said Tawney.

"I'm afraid Catherine Nichols is believable. The details check out. She told me she was pleased at first when Susan became successful in politics on her own. And Nichols did well herself as an investment adviser."

"So what changed?"

"When Susan became president, Nichols figured she had a friend in the White House. Although they hadn't been in touch for years, Nichols had contributed to Susan's campaigns. She wanted to visit the president here, maybe sleep in the Lincoln Bedroom. She tried calling and writing, but all she got back were form letters. She became frustrated and angry. Then she saw my stories about the contracting scandal."

Tawney leaned forward in her chair.

"So where are you now?" she asked.

"Nichols is still deciding whether she wants to go on the record," Sarah said. "She's worried about enduring the notoriety all over again."

"And your editors?"

"While we're waiting on Nichols, they want me to get the president's side of it."

"I'll have to discuss it with her," Tawney said. "I'll get back to you."

"Miss Morgan is expecting you," the maître d' at the Prime Rib told Sarah after she had identified herself. "Let me take you to her table."

"What a dress!" Kathleen Morgan exclaimed as Sarah settled herself into a high-backed leather wing chair across from her at a table for four, with two place settings, in the middle of the gold-trimmed, black-paneled dining room. "Red looks good on you. Even better than that black number in Chicago."

Sarah, surprised that Morgan remembered what she had worn so long ago, was no longer dependent on that black sheath dress. She had taken the time to buy some new clothes, including this one, a dark red dress with long sleeves and a high neck that was vaguely Asian in style and clung to her body. She had changed after work to blend in at the Prime Rib. And she had called Chris Collins to meet her afterward.

"The martinis and the prime rib, that's why we're here," Morgan said. She had nearly finished the martini in front of her. Just as in Chicago, Morgan was provocatively turned out in a low-cut dress — white this time — that exposed an extraordinary expanse of her freckled bosom. Instead of the silver cross, she wore pearls.

"You can get one of those fruit-flavored 'tinis if you want," said Morgan. "And they'll give us ladies' portions of the beef."

"I'll have what you have," Sarah said, eager to get down to business. "I know it was a long time ago. But you said in Chicago that you'd tell me back here what you do."

"Good memory. I work with government contractors, mostly defense and intel types, helping them make connections." Morgan took the last sip of her drink. "Considering what you've been writing lately, I thought that might interest you."

Judging by Morgan's presence at the A-list convention fund-raiser and her apparent status at the Prime Rib, Sarah guessed that she probably had money and influence. But her manner and dress, in addition to her absence from most of Marge Lawson's usually reliable databases, made Morgan a tantalizing mystery.

"What do you think would interest me?" Sarah asked her.

"I've got a Brit friend, a client of sorts,

who has competed against Palisar companies for Pentagon contracts," Morgan said. "He knows a lot about how they work."

"They've taken contracts away from him?"

"No, no, my dear, he's not a sore loser. He's had some very big contracts in Iraq. Tens of millions of dollars, everything from security to civil administration."

"Intelligence work, too?"

Morgan smiled indulgently.

"Intelligence gathering and analysis are integral to the security work."

"Does that include covert operations?"

"That's kind of a naïve question, isn't it?" The smile disappeared and Morgan's voice hardened a bit. "Obviously, anyone engaged in them can't talk about it."

Sarah was at a disadvantage. She usually knew enough to put people she was interviewing on the defensive, not the other way around.

"I guess I'm kind of confused, Miss Morgan."

"Call me Kit." She was smiling again. "Everybody does."

"Why did you want to talk to me tonight?"

"I really want you to talk to my British friend. I think he can help you."

"Who is he?"

"Jack Lassiter. Former S.A.S. — that's the

Brits' special forces. His company is called Saxon. You can look it up. Headquarters in London. Small government-relations office here. Jack gets to Washington himself every now and then."

Morgan cut off a small bite of her prime rib.

"He stays with me," she added, looking up meaningfully at Sarah.

Just then, the maître d' came into view over Morgan's shoulder. He was accompanied by a trim-looking man in a double-breasted indigo blazer, white-collared blue-and-white-striped shirt, and what looked like an English school or club tie. Sarah knew immediately that it had to be Lassiter. Morgan had set this up.

"I'm Jack," he said to Sarah. He leaned over to give Morgan a kiss on the cheek and sat down in a chair between the two women. "Please don't get up."

"I guess I don't have to introduce myself," Sarah said, a trace of irritation in her voice.

"Kit has told me about you," Lassiter said, "and I'm familiar with your journalism. But she didn't tell me how beautiful you are. I apologize for surprising you like this. It's a habit one forms in my line of work. Given what you've been writing about, it's not beyond the realm of possibility that you're the subject of surveillance."

As he spoke, Sarah noticed Morgan watching Lassiter with pride, if not adoration. With his Jermyn Street clothes, perfect teeth, and expensively styled dark hair, Lassiter looked every inch a very successful English businessman. Only the lines etched into his deeply tanned face betrayed any sign of age.

"Surveillance?" Sarah asked.

"They could be intercepting your mobile calls or monitoring your e-mail traffic with spyware," Lassiter said, lowering his voice. "I wanted to make certain no one knew in advance that I'd be talking to you."

"Why do you want to talk to me?"

"You want to know about the covert operations that are off-limits to your government's contracting investigations," he told her. "And I can tell you a bit about them."

"This is just for your guidance, Sarah," Morgan interjected. "You can't use anything Jack tells you unless you obtain it from other sources. You know, just like Deep Throat."

"Kit keeps me in line when I'm in the States," Lassiter said to Sarah. "You folks in the news media work differently here. There are ways to keep the press at bay at home."

"No First Amendment," Morgan added.

"So what can you tell me, Mr. Lassiter?"

Sarah asked.

"Jack, please," he said with a smile. "Your government is using some of those contractors to do what it is no longer able or allowed to do itself. Tracking down bad people. Getting them to talk. Eliminating them in some cases."

"Eliminating them?" Sarah hadn't expected this. "You mean like death squads?"

"Don't be so dramatic, dear," Morgan told her.

"Your military's counterterrorism task forces, run by something called the Joint Special Operations Command, already had the authority to eliminate terrorists and insurgents in Iraq and other places," Lassiter explained matter-of-factly. "And they used it, sometimes like a blank check. During the last American administration, the message from Washington was that anything goes.

"But, as you know, the war in Iraq became too unpopular. Congress switched parties. Interrogation rules were changed. Your military and intelligence agencies worried about recriminations. The brass knew it had already dodged a bullet with Abu Ghraib. The enhanced interrogation techniques used there came from the Joint Special Operations Command."

"You mean torture?" Sarah asked, knowing the answer.

"We avoid pejorative terms," Morgan interjected again.

"The point is," Lassiter continued, "they started farming out some of the dirty work to private contractors. Carter Phillips, who had been in special ops himself, created a network of companies to do the work and made sure they got the contracts."

"But Justice and Congress are staying away from that," Sarah said.

"Your government has understandable reasons for keeping a lid on those covert ops," Lassiter said. "Exposure would shut them down. And heads would roll."

"So why are you telling me this?"

"As I'm sure you'll discover, I'm no choirboy. But I've learned to take my contractual responsibilities very seriously. I work for more than one government, and mine has stricter rules than yours. So I'd obviously benefit from a more level playing field."

"Can you give me names of contractors?" Sarah asked.

"Linking specific contractors' names to specific covert operations could be illegal for someone in Jack's position — or mine," Morgan told her.

Or mine? Sarah still wondered what Morgan really did.

"Go back through everything Palisar owns," Lassiter told Sarah.

"Can I get back to you and confirm what I find?"

"You can contact me," Morgan answered for him.

"It's been my great pleasure to meet you, Sarah," Lassiter said. "But I don't want to overstay my welcome. If you don't mind, I'll say good night."

"I hope that helped," Morgan said to Sarah after he left.

44

Sarah had said good-bye to Chris Collins shortly before six in the morning. She had then set the alarm in her hotel room for eight because she was anxious to ask Marge Lawson what she could find out about Jack Lassiter.

"He's kind of an aging swashbuckler," Lawson told Sarah later in the newsroom after doing some research. "At least, that's the image Lassiter's created for himself. All you have to do is Google him. He's gotten a lot of ink in the British press over the years."

"What for?" asked Sarah.

"In his S.A.S. days, he was in a group of commandos who stormed an embassy in London that had been taken over by terrorists," Lawson said. "They killed all the bad guys without harming any of the hostages. When he got out of the military, he started his first company with some S.A.S. buddies."

"What did they do?"

"They called it security contracting. But it seemed more like mercenary stuff, mostly in Africa. Lassiter himself just managed to escape from Uganda after being involved in some kind of coup attempt."

"When did he start Saxon?"

"During the first Persian Gulf War. That's when he started getting contracts from the British and American governments," Lawson said. "By 2003, Saxon had become one of the companies with big jobs in Iraq. It did security for V.I.P.s, other contractors, supply convoys, and government compounds, including the Green Zone."

"Anything else?"

"Just some more derring-do. Lassiter went along on a joint American and Iraqi military operation that rescued several kidnapped Saxon employees who had been held in a house just outside Baghdad. Even though the kidnappers were gone by the time they stormed the building, Lassiter was lionized in the London tabloids. They called him Commando Jack."

"So Saxon's a serious competitor to Smith and Hawley?"

"Oh, yes. They've fought over contracts in Iraq. At one point, Smith and Hawley accused Saxon of shooting indiscriminately at Iraqi civilians. And Saxon complained that Smith and Hawley was getting preferential treatment in contract bidding."

"Which we now know may have been true," Sarah said. "I can understand why Lassiter would want to give me more dirt about his rival."

Pat Scully messaged Sarah later that day.

"what happened at agency"

"How do you know about that?"

"sources"

Sarah didn't know what to think about Scully anymore — or what to tell him.

"They want me to stop asking questions about intelligence contracts, but they wouldn't say why."

"what else"

"Why are you asking me? What do you know?"

"did you talk to brit"

Sarah guessed he meant Jack Lassiter.

513

Then she remembered what Lassiter had said about someone monitoring her e-mail traffic. Is that why Scully was being so cryptic?

"You know about that, too?"

"was he helpful"

Sarah decided she should be careful, too.

"He gave me the general picture, but no names."

"maybe later"

Was Scully somehow orchestrating all this?

"What are you up to, Pat?"

"still can't say . . . but I'm looking out for you"

"What does that mean?"

"be careful with congressman"

"What???"

"monocle"

That infuriated Sarah. How could Scully know?

"Aren't you his friend?"

"just be careful"

Sarah had no idea why Scully was warning her about Chris Collins. But she was beginning to worry about it. And she was beginning to worry about not telling her editors about Collins.

"Why am I only finding out about this now?" Susan Cameron asked angrily of Sam

Stetson.

The atmosphere in the Oval Office was tense. The president was seated behind her desk. Elizabeth Tawney, Stetson, and Philip Vance were all on their feet, facing her. Outside the windows behind Susan, the afternoon had grown dark and snowflakes were starting to fall.

"It's one of our most highly classified programs, Madam President," Stetson said. "I was informed about it when I was in the Senate. But I couldn't discuss it with anyone, not even you. I had assumed you would be told in your intelligence briefings when you moved into this office."

He looked over at Vance, who shifted his weight uncomfortably, but said nothing.

"Well, Phil?" Susan was visibly unhappy that she had to ask.

"I'm afraid it's a 'need to know' classification, Madam President, and you hadn't asked before now."

"How could I when I didn't know what to ask?" Susan shouted. She was ready to explode. "You've briefed me yourself every day since I became president."

"I see the problem," Vance responded coolly.

He had managed a multitude of intelligence activities during his career, which included two tours as ambassador to countries where he oversaw major covert operations to combat insurgencies against the host governments. He practically ran those countries at times, so he was certain he knew more than this inexperienced president about how to handle situations like this one.

"As I'm sure you know," he said, "the terrorist threat is probably greater now than ever before."

"I don't need a lecture, Phil. Get to the point."

"Yes, ma'am. When the C.I.A.'s interrogation centers overseas were shut down and the interrogation rules for the military and intelligence community were tightened, it was decided to contract out some of the detentions and interrogations of certain suspected terrorists."

"Counterterrorism was outsourced?"

"In a manner of speaking. It was decided that certain legal restrictions on government employees would not necessarily apply to private contractors."

Susan couldn't believe what she was hearing.

"Are you telling me," she asked, "that the United States government has outsourced torture?"

"We don't do torture," Vance answered quickly. "But we have been able to return to more robust methods of interrogation. That has enabled us to disrupt terrorist networks and prevent planned attacks. It is one of our most effective counterterrorism tools."

"Madam President," Stetson said in his formal way, "I suggested bringing Director Vance in today after he summoned journalists from the *Washington Capital* to Langley to discourage reporting that might lead them to these operations. He wants you to talk to them, too."

"I warned them of the serious consequences they could face," Vance said. "Without providing any information, I told them they were asking about highly classified activities. Any disclosure could irreparably damage national security."

"What were they asking about?" the president asked.

"Their reporter Sarah Page wanted to know about some of the contractors involved in these operations."

"Why?"

"Well," Vance said, shifting his weight again, "some of them may have been caught up in the contract-bribery affair."

Susan stared at him for a few moments.

"So these secret operations involve corruption," she asked Vance, "as well as questionable methods of interrogation, by contractors acting in the name of the United States government?"

"You see the problem."

"If I may, Madam President," Stetson broke in. "As I understand it, the Justice Department and Congress have agreed to limit their investigations to avoid revelation of these classified operations."

"Sam." Tawney spoke up. "Do you believe it's really possible, under these circumstances, to keep them secret?"

"I think so."

"And should we?"

"With your permission, Madam President," Stetson said to Susan, "I suggest that I find out more about this and report back to you before any decisions are made."

"I have no objection to that," Vance interjected officiously. "But, if I may, whatever questions you may have about methods being used or complications caused by the behavior of some contractors, it is vitally important to national security to keep this completely classified."

"I hear what you're saying, Director Vance," Susan said, no longer addressing him by his first name. "But I need to be a hell of a lot better informed about what I've inherited here. I like the vice president's idea. I expect you and your people to cooperate fully. And I mean fully."

"Of course, Madam President," Vance said.

"Sam," she asked, "is forty-eight hours too soon? I'm going to have to deal with the contracting investigation in the State of the Union."

"You'll have it before then," Stetson said.

"Thank you, Madam President," Tawney said.

"Do I still have a job?" Vance whispered to Stetson just outside the Oval Office.

"We'll see," the vice president said.

45

Sarah and Chris Collins had planned a romantic dinner at the historic 1789 Restaurant in Georgetown, where he had reserved a table near the fireplace in its antiques-filled main dining room. It was Friday night, and his housemate wouldn't be back from a weekend trip to his district until Monday.

Looking as youthful as ever, Collins conformed to the 1789's dress code with a dark blazer over a white button-down shirt. Sarah had selected from her new winter wardrobe a red, high-necked sweater and tight black velour pants.

They hadn't been together for several nights, and she could feel the electricity between them. But she had questions for Collins. And a confession to make. Nervous about how he would react to it, she waited until they had taken a few sips of Beaujolais and ordered rack of lamb, the house specialty.

"I've been talking to members of your investigative subcommittee staff, Chris," she said. "You'll be glad to know they're quite loyal to you."

"What?" He looked even more surprised and disturbed than she had expected.

"But I found a few who've been helping me," Sarah said, forging ahead. Her heart was racing. "I know Phil Vance talked to you this week, right after my editors and I met with him at Langley. And Elizabeth Tawney called you this morning about something urgent. Was it about the questions I've been asking about covert operations?"

"This week? This morning?" Collins kept his voice down, but his face had tightened. "You mean, while we've been, you know, intimate, you've been spying on me with my staff?"

"Chris, we've only been 'intimate,' to use

520

your word, for a week or so. I've been talking to your staff ever since you introduced me to them on the Hill. I got all their phone numbers. And I persuaded a few of them that they could help me without compromising your investigation. That's the way I work."

"So you've been playing me?"

"Chris, if you're talking about our personal relationship, the answer is no. I've kept that completely separate. If you're talking about our professional relationship, you called me first. Remember? We were helping each other."

"What else do you know?"

Whatever their relationship, Sarah had to be careful about how much she told him.

"Just what I've been able to piece together from various other sources. I know some of the contractors involved in covert operations started out supplying the C.I.A. with planes and crews for renditions of terrorist suspects captured abroad to friendly countries for questioning. Carter Phillips bought those companies and started some others specializing in that kind of work. It was easier to provide cover for each one of a bunch of small companies than for one big one. They eventually got much more deeply involved in terrorist hunting. And they've been doing it in ways that seem to have everyone scared."

"I'm not scared," Collins said. "I'm trying to be responsible, whether or not I'm comfortable with everything that's been going on."

Their food arrived, but neither of them made a move to eat it.

"So you *are* uncomfortable," Sarah said. "That fits the man I've been getting to know."

That seemed to relax him. They began to eat.

"Look, Sarah, here's what I can say. Vance told me he warned you and your editors to stay away from the covert ops. Tawney called to make sure we're staying away from them in our investigation."

They had had this conversation before, but Sarah wanted to try one more time.

"Are the covert operations illegal, Chris?"

"I'm not going to talk about it."

"But shouldn't that be weighed against claims of national security?"

"Speaking hypothetically," Collins said, waiting for Sarah to nod her understanding, "our government may have to use methods to fight terrorism that could be illegal, even repugnant. It might be the only way we can protect the American people."

"But shouldn't the American people decide whether they want to be protected that way? Like the C.I.A.'s secret prisons and the N.S.A.'s unauthorized interception of phone calls."

"Good examples," Collins said. "They raised legitimate questions about legality and values. And they were both modified after being exposed by the news media. But those stories led to real losses in our counterterrorism capabilities and relationships. And our failure to keep those secrets made it more difficult to convince potential allies to trust and work with us."

Impressed by his conviction, Sarah couldn't help asking, "Did you do intelligence work in the military?"

"As I think I told you," Collins said, "I was in a civic reconstruction unit, helping the Iraqis set up local government structures and rebuild."

Logical cover for an intelligence officer, Sarah thought. Was that why Pat Scully had been warning her about Collins?

"What about Pat Scully?" she asked.

"What do you mean?"

"How much are you in touch with him?"

The question clearly hit a nerve.

"What's bothering you, Sarah?"

"He already knows about us, Chris. He

mentioned the night at the Monocle in a message to me. He seems to know what I do and where I go."

"I don't know what that's about," Collins said. "And I don't like it."

After pausing, he added, "I can tell you what I do know about Pat, way off the record, okay?"

"Okay."

"He's C.I.A.," Collins said so softly that only she could hear. "But you can't repeat that to a soul. It's illegal to out a covert operative."

"I know. I remember the Plame case."

"Pat's been fighting Carter Phillips for years," Collins said. "When he found out that Phillips was dirty, he tried to stop the agency from doing business with him. But nobody would listen. So Pat set out to expose Palisar's corruption himself, working undercover on the Hill. He came to me, and I helped set him up."

"That's not exactly what the two of you told me."

"Operational secrecy," Collins said, smiling.

Sarah wasn't amused. Neither he nor Scully had been truthful with her.

"Why did he come to you?"

"My military background and committee

assignment. He took a chance."

"Because you were in military intelligence?"

"I just told you . . ."

"I know, Chris." Sarah laughed. She was certain now. "I just couldn't resist."

"As we did tell you, we kept running into brick walls on the Hill. Palisar was better connected than we realized. And ruthless. Some of Pat's sources told him about surveillance and threats. And he figured out he was being watched himself. So Pat disappeared. When you found him, he realized you could help us. And I agreed."

"So the two of you ran me like some kind of asset?"

It was Sarah's turn to feel manipulated.

"We didn't have much choice, given what we were up against," Collins said. "And you did your own reporting, way beyond where we pointed you. What I regret," he added, reaching for her hand, "was putting you at risk. I thought they'd leave a reporter alone, just as they've done with me."

"Where's Pat now? I can only contact him on the Internet."

"I really don't know," Collins said. "I just hear from him now and then. I'm not even sure he's in this country."

Sarah didn't respond. She was trying to

get everything clear in her mind.

"I guess we've had our first fight," said Collins. "Why don't we skip dessert and make up at my house."

Their conversation had raised new questions for Sarah about both Collins and Scully and her relationship with each of them. But she felt that she and Collins were on the same side somehow. She knew she was on dangerous ground, but her desire to be with him was too strong.

"Makeup sex?" She put her hand into his. "I've seen that *Seinfeld* episode a million times."

It was nearly noon on Saturday when Sarah awoke to the sounds and smells of cooking in Collins's kitchen. She put on a sports bra and running shorts, which she had brought in an overnight bag, and went into the kitchen.

"Eggs Benedict, complete with homemade hollandaise," announced Collins, who was wearing a long white terry-cloth robe bearing the insignia of the Ritz Hotel in Paris. "By the way, ace reporter, I bought this robe myself, although the government paid for the junket."

"The congressman's a chef." Sarah nuzzled the back of his neck as he took

English muffins out of the toaster. "Why didn't you stay with me in bed?"

"We've got all weekend."

"Not exactly. I've got a story to write."

"Something I said last night?" Collins asked.

"Was everything you said off the record?"

Collins carefully placed the poached eggs over slices of Canadian bacon on the muffins before turning to face Sarah.

"Seriously. I expect everything in our personal conversations to be off the record."

"Relax, Congressman. I'm using other sources for a story about how you and Justice are restricting your investigations."

Collins, who didn't seem bothered by that, carried their plates to the little kitchen table. "You were just testing me at dinner?"

"I wanted to get a better sense of you," Sarah said as they sat down. "As Pat Scully once said to me, things are not always what they seem to be."

46

"I'm sorry you had to come here on such a cold morning," Susan told her visitors as they filed into the Oval Office. She sat in one of the armchairs flanking the fireplace and motioned Lou Runyan toward its companion. Sarah sat with Mary Sullivan and Ron Jones on one of two cream-colored couches that faced each other between the fireplace and the president's desk. Opposite them were Elizabeth Tawney and Alison Winters.

"I know it's your job to decide what to publish in your newspaper, Lou," the president began. "I don't believe in trying to censor the press. And I admire what you've been doing, Ms. Page," she said, turning toward Sarah. "You're performing a real public service. I've been shocked by much of what you've written."

Alison reminded everyone that the president was off the record.

"You can report that I will talk about the defense-contracting scandal in the State of the Union," said Susan. "I'll announce that I'm creating an independent commission to assess the damage and recommend reforms. Alison can provide details later."

"That's on background," Tawney interjected. "Attribution to administration sources."

"Now, Lou," Susan said, "we understand that Ms. Page is writing a story speculating that contractors for the intelligence community are involved in the scandal. Nothing like that has come up in the investigations being conducted by the Justice Department and Congress."

Sarah thought, Didn't the president know?

"That's only because they've agreed to a request from your administration to stay away from contractors engaged in covert operations," she told the president.

"As I said, it isn't part of their investigations," Susan restated with a thin smile. "If any of those contractors *were* involved in covert operations, revealing it could almost certainly endanger lives and national security. I'm confident the commission I'm appointing can curb any abuses without running those risks."

The president was obviously trying to make a trade. The newspaper gets a scoop on news in the State of the Union address and, in return, it heeds her warning about Sarah's story.

"We understand your concerns, Madam President," Mary Sullivan said carefully. "We will keep them in mind. But we cannot make any commitments about what we will or will not publish."

"I appreciate that," Susan responded.

Remembering the tough talk at the meeting at C.I.A. headquarters, Sarah was surprised that the president did not press harder.

"Why isn't Phil Vance here this morning?" Runyan asked.

"We'll have an announcement soon about the leadership of the intelligence agencies," Tawney told him.

"Phil's out?" asked Runyan.

Sarah thought he seemed less than awed by the opportunity to sit next to the president in the Oval Office.

"Lou, you could say that personnel changes are under consideration by the White House," Susan told him. "I need my own team."

"Reynolds, too?"

"As I said, it's time that I had my own team."

"The president has decided to put in place people who will have her full confidence," said Tawney.

"Is that off the record?" asked Ron Jones.

"I believe the president intended for it to be on deep background," Tawney said, as Susan nodded her approval. "For attribution, without quotation, to sources familiar with the president's thinking."

"Let me see if I understand what's going on," Runyan said, turning to fully face the president. "You inherited some rogue covert ops run by crooked contractors. And you want to try to shut them down without the voters finding out about them."

Sarah thought of herself as an aggressive interviewer, but she couldn't imagine asking the president that kind of question.

Susan broke an awkward silence by laughing out loud.

"Lou, that's what I've liked about you ever since I first came to Washington," she said, reaching over to pat his arm. "No bullshit."

"So what's the story?"

"I really can't go further, at least for now. But you'll see that it's not about politics. Way off the record, we've got a problem I have to fix without jeopardizing national security. That's not rhetoric. Sam Stetson is running it for me. The commission I'm creating will report to him. Give us some time, Lou, and please be careful what you publish."

Sarah was impressed. Her editors and the president had just played the game at a very high level. Without explicitly making a deal, they had agreed on the rough outlines of the story Sarah would write. She had gotten more information than she had expected, while the president had sent several subtle messages. She had blamed inherited officials and policies for any wrongdoing. She had promised to clean it all up. And she had urged the newspaper not to reveal the private contractors' covert operations, without acknowledging their existence.

"Thank you again for coming," Susan said, extending her hand to Runyan.

"Thank you, Madam President."

As everyone stood up, Alison, who had not said a word during the meeting, took Sarah aside.

"Can I chat with you in my office for a minute?"

After telling her editors she would rejoin them in the newsroom, Sarah followed Alison down the hall to the press secretary's office.

"Governor Tawney told me about your conversation," Alison said, shutting her door. "And she discussed it with the president. As you heard in the Oval Office, the president has a lot on her plate right now. So what we're asking, what the president is asking, in confidence, is that you wait until after the State of the Union to discuss this with her."

"An interview with the president?"

"Yes. But only if the woman in Los Angeles is on the record."

"I'll have to talk to my editors," Sarah said.

When she returned to the newsroom, she did exactly that.

"She offered me an interview after the

State of the Union, but only if Nichols goes on the record," Sarah told Ron Jones, who had also brought Mark and Mary Sullivan into his office.

"Have you tried Michael Cameron?" Jones asked.

"Of course," Sarah said. "But he's traveling all the time."

"That man lives on his cell phone," Mark said. "He's ducking you."

"We're just going to have to wait," Sullivan said, "until Nichols makes up her mind."

Late that night, a sleepless Susan Cameron called Michael in California from her bedroom in the White House.

"Why are you doing this?" he asked. "We convinced Catherine to back off."

"Thanks. I really appreciate it. But it's much more than that."

"So how can I help?"

"That's why I called this time. I'm grateful for everything you've done for me, Michael. But I need to be completely on my own now."

"Understood. I knew this time would come. Stay in touch when you can. I'll be watching."

"Good night, Michael."

"Good night, Madam President."

Hours later, Sarah was awakened just before dawn by the first few bars of the *William Tell* Overture. It took her a moment to realize it was not coming from the clock radio. And it was not the ring tone of her own cell phone, even though the sound was coming from her purse, which was on the floor next to the bed in her hotel room. Finally, she remembered that Pat Scully had given her another cell phone more than a year earlier. She was amazed that it still worked.

"You may want to turn on cable," Scully began, without a greeting or an apology for calling so early. "CNN, Fox, it doesn't matter. They've all got it."

Sarah immediately recognized his voice from their one conversation in Union Station after Seth Moore's funeral. She was certain now that he was not the 4 a.m. caller.

"What's going on?" she asked as she fumbled for the television remote in the folds of her bedcovers.

"Carter Phillips. He's dead. Plane crash in Uzbekistan."

"What plane?" Sarah had succeeded in turning on the TV and was trying to punch the right number into the remote. "Where again?"

"Some small jet he must have swiped from one of Palisar's companies. The pilot hasn't been identified. They said it crashed well short of the runway while trying to land somewhere in Uzbekistan."

Sarah had the news on now.

"Why Uzbekistan?" she asked.

"Smith and Hawley and some of its subs did business there in the early fighting in Afghanistan and Iraq. It was supposed to be an ally. Phillips might also have had Uzbek connections from his Special Forces days. It was a logical place for him to hide."

"So it's an accident?"

"Too convenient. Phillips knew too much," Scully said. "The plane could have been knocked down by our covert guys or theirs. Or it could have been sabotaged."

"What are you suggesting?"

"Nothing I or anybody else is likely to prove. But, without Phillips, all those investigations will only go so far, especially since they've already been restricted. I saw your story on the Web about the president firing Vance and Reynolds. Now they'll be lawyered-up private citizens and unlikely to tell anybody anything for a long time, if ever."

"What about the president's commission?"

"Damage control. She appoints its members, so don't expect anybody who might rock the boat."

Sarah sat up in bed and turned on a light.

"What are you doing, Pat? Why are you using this phone now after only messaging me ever since we first talked? And why didn't you tell me you were a spook?"

"Too many questions, but I guess that's your job," Scully said, without a hint of surprise in his voice. "Did Chris tell you about me?"

"Some of it."

"Well, this isn't a good time to tell you more. And, remember, I said to be careful with him."

47

Members began gathering early in the House chamber on the last Tuesday in January to stake out the best seats along the center aisle for the State of the Union address. Reporters and photographers crowded Statuary Hall, through which everyone approached the chamber under the glare of television lights that brightly illuminated the statues of historic figures encircling the hall. Congressional staffers pressed against rope lines to take pictures with cameras and cell phones.

At the White House, Susan stepped into a presidential limousine on the South Drive for the motorcade ride along Pennsylvania Avenue to Capitol Hill. During the short journey, she took out her copy of the speech she was going to give and added a few words to a handwritten page she had inserted at the end.

"Are you sure you don't want that in the teleprompter?" asked Elizabeth Tawney, who was riding with her.

"Yes," said Susan, ending the discussion.

When the motorcade reached the Capitol, Susan was ushered into the ceremonial office of the Speaker of the House to await her entrance. At about the same time, members of the Senate began the traditional walk from their side of the Capitol. After entering the House chamber, they shook hands and chatted with the House members as they moved down the center aisle to their seats near the front.

The balcony filled with ambassadors and other dignitaries. In what had been designated the First Lady's Box in previous administrations, the White House had placed Susan's parents, her friend Amanda

Peterson, the mayor of Washington, several veterans of fighting in Iraq and Afghanistan, and three elderly women, recipients of Medicare and Social Security. In a tradition dating back to President Reagan, some of them would be singled out by Susan during her speech.

Shortly after 9 p.m., an assistant to the House sergeant at arms appeared at the back of the chamber and announced, one by one, the entrances of the senior members of the diplomatic corps, uniformed members of the Joint Chiefs, robed justices of the Supreme Court, and members of the president's Cabinet.

After they had made their way down to seats in the front row, everyone remained standing. The door from Statuary Hall opened again, and the sergeant at arms himself took a few steps into the chamber.

"Madam Speaker," he bellowed, "the president of the United States."

Wearing her favorite dark blue suit, Susan Cameron walked in confidently as members surged toward the center aisle to shake her hand. A long, loud ovation continued as she stepped onto the podium, turned, and reached up to hand ceremonial copies of her speech — without the page she had written by hand — to the vice president and

Speaker of the House on their perch behind her.

"Members of Congress," intoned the Speaker, banging her gavel as she recited the traditional introduction. "I have the high privilege and distinct honor of presenting to you the president of the United States."

This touched off more deafening applause until Susan raised her hands to quiet the chamber.

"Speaker Ames, Vice President Stetson, members of Congress, members of the Supreme Court and the diplomatic corps, distinguished guests, and fellow citizens," she began, looking at the transparent teleprompter screens in front of her. "Last year, our nation lost a beloved, distinguished leader who had devoted his life to the service of his country. This annual gathering of both houses of Congress, of Democrats and Republicans, of representatives from all three branches of government and our armed services, is a fitting occasion on which once again to honor the memory of the late president Monroe Capehart.

"Tonight, we dedicate ourselves anew to his values of bipartisanship and public service," Susan continued. "I agree with our predecessor from the other party, who said on this occasion a few years ago, 'To confront the great issues before us, we must act in a spirit of goodwill and respect for one another.'

"Because of what we have done together so far," she declared, "the state of our Union is strong. And we can and will make it still stronger."

Everyone stood and applauded.

"There is much to do," Susan said. "We must make certain the brave men and women of our armed forces have what they need to fight for our security overseas. We must strengthen homeland security to protect Americans from terrorist threats and natural disasters. We must build personal security for all Americans by confronting the crises in American health care and in our Medicare, Medicaid, and Social Security programs. We must protect our environment before the very survival of our species is threatened by pollution, depleted natural resources, and global warming."

Each declaration drew another standing ovation.

"As I stand before you, I recognize my unusual position as an unelected president. Therefore, I am departing from tradition tonight to lay out a plan of action, not just for this coming year, as is customary, but for all three of the years remaining in my term. I ask the American people to listen closely to what I say and to give me a mandate in this November's congressional elections to fully carry out these plans."

After nearly an hour of detailing her plans, Susan turned to the defense-contracting scandal.

"To make progress for the American people," she said, "we must get serious about corruption in Washington — corruption that has stained the White House and the halls of Congress. I will ensure that everyone in the executive branch cooperates fully with all investigations of the defense-contracting and bribery scandal. And I will create an independent, bipartisan commission to assess the damage that has been done and recommend remedial action.

"I call on members of Congress in both parties to work with me to enact real reforms to prevent repetition of this kind of corruption in the future. Changes must be made in how business is done in our capital. The cycle of wrongdoing in Washington must be broken."

Remembering that they were being watched on television, the members of Congress applauded politely.

Then Susan reached down to the lectern and picked up the page of her speech she had written by hand. A rustle of surprise rippled through her audience as she began to read it.

"I believe the plans I have presented tonight to the Congress and the American people are so important for the future of this great nation that I do not want them to become hostage to my own political future," she said. "I do not want to be tempted by personal political ambition to change course. Therefore, I am announcing tonight that I will not be a candidate for election as president in my own right."

Susan paused to let her audience grasp what she had said. Murmurs of shock rolled through the chamber.

"I will serve only the three years remaining in the term begun by President Capehart."

She paused again as the commotion in the chamber grew louder. Behind her, Sam Stetson allowed himself a slight, knowing smile. Susan raised her hands for quiet.

"I will make mine a different kind of presidency," she said. "A presidency without personal or partisan ambition. I will serve only the American people."

She looked up to find her place on the teleprompter.

"We Americans are optimistic about the

future. We believe in our way of life. We believe we can prevail over the enemies of democracy. We believe we can solve the problems facing us at home. We believe this is possible with leaders who are open, honest, and determined. I ask you to help me be that kind of leader. I ask you to work with me for the greater good of all Americans. Let us make this a new beginning.

"Thank you. God bless you. And may God bless America."

48

By the time Susan could be seen leaving the House chamber on C-SPAN, the *Washington Capital* newsroom had gone into overdrive. Mark Daniels wrote version after version of his State of the Union story for the Web site and the next morning's newspaper. Sarah recapped the corruption investigations and the president's comments on them in her speech. Other political reporters hurriedly produced sidebar stories and analyses.

After the last deadline for the printed paper passed, shortly before 2 a.m., and the bedlam in the newsroom had subsided, Sarah and Mark took stock with Ron Jones in his office.

"Why did she do it?" Sarah asked. "Was it Catherine Nichols? The contracting scandal?"

"You mean you don't believe what she said?" Mark responded sarcastically. "About not wanting 'to become hostage to my own political future'? That's a new one."

"What do you think, Sarah?" Jones asked.

Despite Mark's cynicism, Sarah was impressed with the president's words. But she was still skeptical about her motives.

"Nichols could go on the record at any time," she said. "And exposure of the illegal covert ops could make the corruption scandal much worse."

When Mark and Ron Jones left for home, Sarah went back to her desk to call Chris Collins.

"Did I wake you?" she asked him.

"I just got home from the Hill. We couldn't stop talking about it."

"What do people think?"

"It beats the hell out of everybody. She took us all by surprise."

"But you know the scandal could still get worse."

"Not on the phone," Collins said. "What are you doing now?"

"Going to get some sleep. We just finished here."

"I'd better do the same. Talk to you tomorrow."

The brief conversation left Sarah with an unsettled feeling she didn't understand.

Before she could leave her desk, the phone rang. It was Joni Parker.

"I knew you'd still be there, girl," she said. "Good story, right?"

"I'm wiped out. Where are you?"

"Police headquarters. Something's going down. I've never seen so many cops here. Langford came in after midnight, which means it's gotta be something big. And there are Fubbies all over the place."

"What?"

"F.B.I., including the agent in charge of the Washington field office."

"The task force?"

"That's my guess."

"Should I come?"

"Oh, no, darlin'," Joni told Sarah. "That would get me into big trouble and probably get us both thrown out. Langford promised me a heads-up, but not for hours."

"Call me on my cell."

Only a few late-shift editors were still in the newsroom when Sarah finally left. Bundled up against the cold, she had just stepped out onto the deserted street when she heard the sound of the *William Tell*

Overture again in her purse.

"Don't go to the hotel!" Pat Scully sounded agitated.

"How do you know I'm not already there? It's after two."

"Just don't go to your hotel. Stay in the newsroom for now."

"Why?"

"It's too dangerous."

Sarah stopped walking and looked around. She was still within sight of the security guard sitting at the desk inside the entrance to the newspaper building. A car passed in the street. But no one else was nearby. She thought about what Joni Parker had told her.

"What's going on?" she asked Scully.

"I'll tell you more soon. Please trust me."

Sarah didn't have much choice.

"Should I call the police?"

"I'm taking care of that."

Scully hung up before she could ask what he meant.

Sarah thought of calling her parents, but they'd probably be too alarmed to be of much help.

Just then a taxi turned the corner and started down the street toward her.

"You work late at the newspaper?" the taxi

driver asked Sarah as she got into the back-seat.

"Yeah. We had a big story tonight." She put the phone Scully had called on back into her purse and took out her own.

"I'll tell you where I'm going in a minute," Sarah said, dialing Chris Collins's number.

The driver was a middle-aged man with a mustache and a Middle Eastern accent. "I've got all night," he said.

"Chris, can I meet you at your place?" she asked. "It's kind of an emergency."

"Sure," he said. "My housemate's asleep upstairs."

Sarah gave his address to the driver.

49

It had happened again and again over the years, but it still irritated Ron Jones's wife to be disturbed early in the morning by a call for her husband. She shook him awake and handed him the phone.

"Ron Jones?"

"Yeah," he answered groggily. "Who's this?"

"Sorry to disturb you. It's Chris Collins. We've met a few times."

"Of course, Congressman," Jones said, his eyes still closed. "What can I do for you?"

"Congressman?" his wife said with disgust. "At this hour?"

"This is a little awkward, Mr. Jones, but I'm worried about one of your reporters, Sarah Page."

Jones propped his head up on one arm and forced open his eyes.

"What about Sarah?"

"Like I said, this is a little awkward, but she called a few hours ago to say she was coming over to my place. And she never got here."

Jones reached over to turn on a lamp, then started to get out of bed.

"Congressman," he said in his deepest intimidating voice, "why would my reporter be going to your house in the early hours of the morning?"

"It probably would have been better for Sarah to tell you herself," Collins said. "But we've been seeing each other for a few weeks."

"What the hell?" Jones roared.

His reaction sent his wife downstairs to the kitchen to make some coffee. Jones went to the closet and tried pulling on a pair of trousers with his free hand.

"Not even a few weeks, really . . . and she's been scrupulous not to mix business with . . . you know."

"I sure as hell don't want to know," Jones shouted into the phone. "But I do want to know where Sarah is. When did she call you?"

"Sometime after two. I'd gotten home an hour earlier from the House after the excitement of the State of the Union."

"I'm really not interested in your political life right now, Congressman. Where was she calling from?"

"She may have been getting into a taxi."

"Probably near the newspaper," Jones said. "I had left her there not too long before then. Why didn't she go to her hotel?"

"I don't know," Collins said. "When we talked earlier on the phone, after she finished work, she said she was going there. But then she called again to ask if she could come over. She said it was 'kind of an emergency.'"

"Congressman," Jones said in the tone he used to give orders to his reporters in a crisis. "I'm going to call the police. And I want you to stay in your house, by your phone, to answer their questions. Give me your address and phone numbers."

"Madam President, I came to offer my resignation." Alison Winters was standing with Elizabeth Tawney in front of Susan's desk in the Oval Office. "When you leave me in the dark about something as important as your announcement last night, I have to conclude that you no longer trust me. And when I can't explain why you did it, I lose credibility with the press."

The first light of the icy winter morning was breaking through the darkness outside the windows behind Susan. Her daily staff briefings were minutes away.

"I'm sorry, Alison," she said. "I do trust you. But I didn't want anybody to know before I told the American people. What I said in my speech is the only public explanation I can offer."

"It's not about Catherine Nichols," Tawney told Alison. "The president can deal with that if she has to, and everyone would understand. It would play much better than standing by the man who had wronged her."

"It has mostly to do with the defense-contracting scandal," Susan said. "What the vice president has told me is much worse than I had thought. And it poses an even greater threat to national security. I need the freedom from political considerations to do whatever is necessary to protect the country, even if it means risking accusations of a cover-up."

"I'm sure the American people would

understand that, too," Alison heard herself saying, without really knowing what she was talking about. There was nothing like working directly for the president of the United States to engender intense personal loyalty. "I guess you can't tell me anything more."

"I'm afraid I can't," Susan said. "But I hope you will stay on. You do your job well. And I need all the help I can get with our domestic policy initiatives. I meant what I said about that in my speech. We can still accomplish a great deal."

Alison was confused. Was she now part of some kind of conspiracy of silence about a national scandal, whether or not she stayed in her job?

"May I get back to you, Madam President?" she asked.

"That's fine. This is difficult for all of us."

Sarah rolled over, noticed the time on the clock radio, and panicked. It was after eight o'clock, and she was still in bed in the guest room of Kit Morgan's high-rise apartment in Arlington. Had Joni tried to contact her? Should she call the newsroom? She needed to find her purse and her cell phone.

She found a robe laid out at the foot of the bed and put it on. She pulled back the drapes, revealing a spectacular view of

Washington across the Potomac River. The monuments and the Capitol dome gleamed in the late-January sunshine.

"Good morning, Sarah. I thought I'd let you sleep a bit."

Sarah turned and saw Morgan standing in the doorway.

"I took the liberty of turning off your cell phone and hanging up your sweater and pants last night," Morgan said. "I apologize again for kidnapping you. You fell dead asleep as soon as you got here."

"When I couldn't figure out where we were going, the driver told me that you had sent him," Sarah said. "Who was he, anyway?"

"An old friend from Langley. Driving a cab is his favorite cover. He even learned the Knowledge, the almost impossible street-location exam for taxi drivers in London. He passes himself off everywhere as a Lebanese immigrant, even though he's a Jew from Queens. Served in the Israeli Army and trained with the Mossad before joining the agency."

"How did he know I'd be outside the newspaper building?"

"The special cell phone from Pat Scully that you kept in your purse," Morgan said. "It has an almost immortal battery and a sophisticated GPS chip. The best we have. Pat could follow your every move on a computer. Unfortunately, we think other people did, too."

"What other people?"

"The people who want to protect the contractors and their covert ops. Some of us in the intelligence community want to close them down because of all the corruption."

" 'Us'?"

"Sorry. I used to work for the agency. That's how I know Pat. Like I told you, I'm more entrepreneurial now."

"I'm trying to remember. Did Pat call you last night, too?"

"He said he was going to alert you. But I didn't think we should take any chances, so I sent for you myself."

"Why? What's going on?" Sarah asked anxiously. "I'd better get dressed and go to the newsroom."

"I think you still have some time," Morgan said in a way that made Sarah think she knew the answers to her questions. "Breakfast should be ready now."

When they walked into the kitchen, where Morgan's housekeeper was making breakfast, Sarah was surprised to see a man sitting at the table. He had graying hair, was clean-shaven, and wore a businesslike suit. Pulling the robe tightly around her, Sarah stopped. She recognized Pat Scully. Then she saw her open purse on the table next to him.

"Sorry, agency property. It's time to take it back," he said, holding up the cell phone he had given her. "I left yours in your purse."

"Why did you do that?" Sarah asked, as she and Morgan sat down. "Why did you track me?"

"To keep you out of harm's way," Scully said. "But it didn't work out so well. I wasn't always watching when you were in danger. And others could track you, too. Like that guy who made the early morning phone calls to you. When Chris told me about that, I found the guy and told him to stop."

"Who was he?"

"Military intel. One of the people who thought it was a good idea to privatize counterterrorism so contractors could do things we can't. They also thought it was okay to go into business with someone like Carter Phillips. They even thought it was okay to spread money around to make sure his companies got the contracts."

"This is all way off the record," Morgan

interrupted, in the same way she had laid down the rules with Jack Lassiter. "We just want to help you understand what's going on."

Sarah looked up at the housekeeper, who had started serving them scrambled eggs and English muffins. "She's okay," Morgan said.

"We're all spies here — except for you, of course," Scully joked, eliciting a stern look from Morgan.

"Off the record?" Morgan persisted.

"Yes," Sarah said. She knew she couldn't write about any of this anyway without confirmation from other sources and, most likely, negotiations between her editors and administration officials about national-security issues. "So, who are you, really, Pat?"

"He's high-ranking in the Clandestine Service," Morgan answered for him. "It's illegal to reveal that."

"I know," Sarah said.

"I went undercover on the Hill to fight Carter Phillips," Scully said. "Chris knew because he was in military intelligence in the Army. He's still in the reserves."

Sarah thought about how she still didn't really know much more about Chris Collins than about Pat Scully.

"Why did you tell me to be careful with him?"

"I eventually discovered he was on the other side of the argument. I don't mean he was compromised or anything. He just believed this was the only way we could fight the terrorists effectively, almost without rules. I believe in rules, and I didn't trust private contractors, especially Carter Phillips. He and I had become mortal enemies, even though I never met the man."

"You never saw him?"

"I didn't say that," Scully told Sarah with a slight smile. "We have our ways of *seeing* people, but I never met Phillips, you know, face-to-face, introducing ourselves to each other."

Sarah looked at Morgan, who clearly knew everything he was talking about. Like Scully, she was part of a Washington that remained a mystery to Sarah.

"After I left town, I found out that Chris had put me on his staff to monitor what I was doing," Pat said. "He lied to me about being blocked by more powerful members of Congress when I wanted him to hold hearings."

"Lied?"

This was hard for Sarah to hear, and her face showed it.

"Oh, don't worry about that," Morgan told her. "Lying is normal, even honorable, for people like us."

"He was the same with you, in a way," Scully said to Sarah. "He made sure his subcommittee investigated what you were writing about, so he could control it.

"And, I apologize for saying this" — Scully paused for a second — "so he could monitor you, just as he did with me."

"Spy versus spy versus spy," Morgan said, smiling.

But Sarah wasn't amused. She felt horribly violated. And foolish. She desperately hoped Scully hadn't told Morgan or anyone else that he knew she had slept with Collins.

"How many of you were opposed to contracting out counterterrorism covert operations to private companies?" she asked, changing the subject.

"Most of the people in the agency who knew about it, except for some cowboys in the Clandestine Service," Scully said. "It was pushed by the intel people at the Pentagon. And the D.N.I. okayed it."

"Phil Vance?"

"The one and only," Scully said. "Reynolds didn't like it, but he was overruled."

"Then why were they both fired?"

"They fell on their swords. But I don't

know how the White House is going to explain why they were fired without revealing what was going on. If the president's commission ever issues a report, it should make interesting reading."

"That's enough for this morning," Morgan said. "Sarah's going to have a lot of work to do again today."

"You haven't told me what was going on last night," Sarah said. "Why did you bring me here?"

"Some law-enforcement activity that I can't talk about yet. It'll be revealed later today," Scully told her. "One of the people who I believe was taken into custody had been making inquiries about you at the hotel."

"Anyone connected to what happened to me and my housemate? And Seth Moore? And Andy Foster and Derek Stevens?"

"Carter Phillips's palace guard was responsible for killing Seth and going after you," said Scully. "Most of them were arrested after he blew town. This is bigger than that."

"What about Foster and Stevens?"

"They're actually fine."

Sarah's face contorted in shock.

"I'm sorry," Scully said. "I wanted to tell you, but I couldn't compromise their safety.

Andy disappeared on purpose, just like I had, when he realized Phillips's people were closing in on him in Mexico. He didn't even tell his family until he could get them out."

Tears welled in Sarah's eyes.

"To where?"

"California. They've got new identities."

"The witness-protection program?"

"Something like that," Scully said. "Stevens just moved far away with his family after selling Falcon Services to Smith and Hawley. He had gotten some threats."

"Because he talked to me?"

"Most likely."

"That's a lot for me to digest," Sarah said. She hadn't touched her food. "I'd better get ready for work."

In the cab on the way to the paper, Sarah realized she hadn't yet turned her cell phone back on. When she did, she found messages from Joni Parker, Ron Jones, and Chris Collins asking her to call back immediately.

She tried Joni first.

"Ron Jones is looking for you. And he doesn't sound happy. He's been in the office since dawn trying to find you. Where are you, anyway?"

"I'll tell you later. What's going on where you are?"

"A bunch of arrests in the contracting scandal," Joni said. "I'm trying to get some of it from Langford before the big press conference at noon."

"I'll get to the newsroom as quickly as I can," Sarah said.

"You'd better call your boss first."

She did.

"Where the hell have you been?" Jones barked into the phone.

"At a friend's apartment in Arlington." Sarah didn't know how better to characterize Kathleen Morgan. "I didn't know you were looking for me."

"Arlington, not Capitol Hill? Which guy were you with there?"

That stung Sarah. Jones had never talked to her like that before.

"No guy. A woman friend. I crashed there for the night. Why did you say Capitol Hill? Why were you looking for me?"

"Congressman Collins woke me up at home to say you were missing. I had the police break into your hotel room."

"Oh, shit."

Sarah couldn't imagine anything worse. How could she have forgotten to call Collins back when she arrived at Morgan's apartment to tell him she had gone somewhere else? Did the whole city know about them now? She had to concentrate to hear what Jones was telling her.

"I want you in my office right now," he said. "You have a lot of explaining to do."

50

"I felt like a fool," Ron Jones said to Sarah as she walked into his office. "I called the cops. They went to your hotel. And just when they're about to start a citywide search some guy from the C.I.A. calls Charlie Langford to tell him he knows you're safe. By that time, I was already here."

"I'm really sorry, Ron. I'm not sure I was thinking clearly last night." Sarah paused. "And I'm really sorry about Chris Collins. It didn't last long. And I know now I made a big mistake."

"I'm not ready to talk about that yet," he said gruffly. "Shut the door and sit down."

Fearing this could be even worse than she had imagined, Sarah meekly did what she was told. Jones got up from behind his desk and took the chair nearest to the couch where she was sitting.

"Langford called me back again while you were on your way here," he said, as though she had never mentioned Chris Collins. "He said your friends from Langley did the right thing by taking you in. When the police got to your hotel room, they discovered that somebody else had already been there and gone through everything. Langford figured they were looking for notes or a laptop. I told him you hadn't taken anything like that with you when you moved into the hotel. He said he doesn't know who it was — or whether they were after you, too."

Sarah slumped limply on Jones's couch. Fear — then relief — took over. This was serious. Had Scully and Morgan saved her from real harm?

"Sarah," Jones said more gently than she had ever heard him. "I'm really glad you're safe."

"Thanks, Ron."

They sat silently for a few moments. Sarah calmed down. As though someone had flipped a switch, she returned to the story.

"Did Langford tell you what else the police were doing?"

"Arresting people who were named in indictments being unsealed today," he said. "The six members of Congress. Some administration officials. And executives of Smith and Hawley. They're putting on a show at the Justice Department."

"Then I'd better get to work."

"Sorry," Jones told her. "Not today."

"But I'll be all right. Working on the story will keep me from thinking about what happened at the hotel."

Jones shook his head. "We have plenty of people on the story. You and I," he said, "will now talk about Congressman Collins. You have to tell me everything this time. And I mean everything. Your job is on the line."

Later, alone at her desk, Sarah watched the press conference on her computer. It was the first time she had gotten a look at Lois Engle, her source on the Justice task force, who was telling reporters about the indictment and the arrests. While Engle talked, Sarah read the text of the indictment on the Web. There were no surprises among the members of Congress and senior government officials who were charged with bribery, conspiracy, and other crimes.

Elliott Bancroft, who was named as a conspirator in the indictment, had agreed to plead guilty to one count of bribery, which meant he was cooperating with prosecutors. Two unidentified employees of Smith and Hawley, whom Sarah guessed to be Cathy Adams and Monica Saunders, the accounting supervisor, were listed as unindicted coconspirators, as was an employee of Malin Associates, most likely Lucilla Brown. They had to be cooperating, too.

But Robert Malin apparently wasn't — at least not yet. He was indicted on multiple counts of bribery, fraud, money laundering, and income-tax invasion. With both Tucker and Phillips dead, Sarah figured the buck stopped with him.

And there were a few names she didn't recognize: Pentagon people charged with conspiracy. Was one of them the man who had asked about her at the hotel?

Sarah's phone rang.

"I'm watching the press conference on television," Chris Collins told her. "I want to congratulate you — and apologize."

"Apologize for what?"

She wanted to hear him say it.

"For telling your boss about us before you did."

"Well, there's no us anymore," Sarah said firmly. "So forget your apology."

"But he didn't sound so angry when he called back to tell me you were okay."

"He's still angry as hell with me. But that's not the point. I never should have gotten involved with you in the first place."

"Can we get together to talk about this?" he asked almost plaintively.

"No, Congressman."

Sarah was upset about him and herself, too. Why did romantic entanglements keep jeopardizing her work? Why did she keep ignoring the risks?

"I don't trust you," she said.

"Because I called your boss when I was worried that something had happened to you?"

"Was that really the reason? Or did you tell him about us to get me off the story? Was I getting too close to those covert operations for your liking?"

"Wait a minute," Collins said, with what Sarah heard as a hint of panic in his voice. "I don't like discussing this on the phone, but I've got to know what you're talking about."

"Pat told me you strung both of us along."

"Scully? When did you talk to him?"

"This morning, at the apartment where I spent the night. A woman named Morgan."

"Kit Morgan, for Chrissakes?"

"You know her, too?"

"Everybody does. She works for the agency. She's never registered as a lobbyist or a foreign agent while making a bundle lobbying here for foreign defense contractors."

"Is Saxon one of those contractors?"

"Kit's very tight with a Brit named Lassiter, who owns it. Wait a minute. Listen to this, Sarah."

"Yes?"

"What if Pat's a friend of Morgan, too, and they both have juice in the agency? Pat's been gunning for Carter Phillips for years, and for good reason. Now the covert-ops contracts may be taken away from the companies Phillips owned. Morgan could put Saxon in position to take them over. And she and Lassiter would be in fat city."

If he was trying to confuse Sarah, he was succeeding. She realized Scully and Morgan could have diverted her during the night so someone could search her hotel room. But why would they do that? And why would Scully then call Charlie Langford?

Sarah tried to stay on track.

"You misled Pat about why he couldn't get an investigation of Palisar off the ground when he was on the Hill."

"He said that?" Collins was silent for a moment. "I wanted to go after Carter Phillips just as much as he did, but I couldn't jeopardize classified operations. It's what I've been doing with my subcommittee staff, too."

"And what you did with me."

"Yes, I guess so, Sarah," he agreed in an irritated tone. "And you were working my staff without telling me. But I tried to keep our personal relationship separate."

Neither of us did, really, Sarah thought. We were just using each other.

"Well, that won't be a problem anymore," she said to Collins — and herself. "Let's just keep it professional. Are you going to fold your investigation now that Justice has gotten indictments without touching the covert operations?"

"We've been cooperating with Justice all along. I still want to hold oversight hearings on how to prevent this kind of corruption in the future. But that's off the record for now."

"Don't worry. I'm not on the story. Ron Jones put me on ice."

51

"Sarah," Pat Scully said as she approached a corner table in a busy Starbucks in Bethesda, "you remember Marvin Reynolds, don't you?"

Actually, she barely recognized the former C.I.A. director, whom she had met only that one time at Langley. He looked smaller than she remembered in loose gray sweat clothes and a wool knit Redskins cap. And he wasn't wearing glasses. Scully looked different, too, in a black running suit and an Orioles baseball hat pulled down on his head.

Scully had called Sarah the day before to arrange an early morning meeting for her with "a good source." Ron Jones agreed to it, even though he and Sarah hadn't yet talked to Lou Runyan about her future at the newspaper.

"Why are we here?" she asked briskly, still on her guard with Scully.

"I wanted to talk to you," Reynolds said. "On background."

"A former senior intelligence-community official with knowledge of certain covert activities," Scully said.

"So you want to be a confidential source, Mr. Reynolds?"

Sarah wanted to be precise about the ground rules.

"Yes," he said. "But you can tell your editors, if a court ever orders you to reveal your source, I'll release you from our confidentiality agreement and face the consequences. I want this out."

Sarah didn't know whether he was going to spin a cover-up story or become a whistle-blower. But, as Jones had said when she didn't know whom she'd be meeting, there was only one way to find out. She took out a small digital recorder and placed it on the table where her purse hid it from the view of everyone else in the coffee shop.

"Where do you want to begin?"

"There's a civil war going on in the intelligence community," Reynolds said. "I know that sounds melodramatic. But it's a fact. Pat has been on the front lines."

Scully's expression showed that he took that as praise.

"When I was recruited from Rand and appointed C.I.A. director by President Capehart, I inherited a dispirited agency," Reynolds continued. "Of course, it had had some successes, like helping overthrow the Taliban government in Afghanistan. But it also had monumental failures — not foreseeing an attack like 9/11 and not making clear, before the Iraq war, that there was no credible evidence Saddam had weapons of mass destruction or ties to Al-Qaeda.

"But the worst thing was that the last administration saw the agency as its enemy and relied on the military to hunt down and kill suspected terrorists. When restrictions were later placed on both the agency and the military, they hired private contractors to do what we couldn't."

"And they ran wild," Scully said with evident emotion. "Before, you had to go through the chain of command to take someone out, sometimes right up to the president. These guys acted on their own, like it was the Wild West. Indiscriminate killings. Bodies left in the streets alongside victims of the bad guys. They became government-authorized death squads."

Reynolds gave him an understanding but reproving look.

"Please keep Pat's intemperate language off the record," he said to Sarah.

"Sorry," Scully said. "Carter Phillips got the contracts for this dirty work by bribing and bullying whomever he had to — in Congress and the administration. Just as he had done with other Pentagon contracts."

"The D.N.I., too?" Sarah asked Reynolds.

"I don't think Phil Vance knew about the corruption," Reynolds said. "But he did approve contracting out covert counter-terrorism operations. And he knew what those companies were doing in the field, over my repeated objections after I found out about it."

"Is that why he was fired?"

"President Cameron dismissed him for not telling her what was going on after she took over from Capehart."

"Capehart knew?"

"Yes," Reynolds said. "While he was still in the Senate, he would have been one of the few people in Congress to be briefed about it, along with Sam Stetson."

"But isn't the vice president handling this for Cameron?" Sarah asked.

"Precisely. You can draw your own conclusions," Scully broke in again. "Remember, Elliott Bancroft recommended Stetson to be vice president, which meant that Trent Tucker and Carter Phillips were probably behind it."

"Pat has a conspiratorial mind," Reynolds said to Sarah, smiling briefly for the first time.

"Just because I see conspiracies everywhere doesn't mean they don't exist," Scully said. "It's like that kid in the movie who saw dead people."

"Why were you fired?" Sarah asked Reynolds.

"Vance told the president he wouldn't go quietly unless she got rid of me, too. He thought I sabotaged him. But he did it to himself by bringing you and your editors out to Langley and then asking the White House to lean on you. It got their attention. And Stetson told the president she had to do something."

"Nobody at the Pentagon was fired," Scully added. "They just shuffled some generals around, like they always do when somebody screws up."

"Until then, Pat and I were going along with protecting the covert ops from exposure, while we tried to close them down," Reynolds said. "Now that I'm out of the agency, I want to do what is in the best interest of the country, rather than the administration."

"Not that I doubt your word, Mr. Reynolds," Sarah said, "but can you give me anything to back up what you've said?"

"Documents?" he said, smiling again. "You reporters love secret documents, don't you? Let's go outside."

They put on their coats and walked a few blocks to a public parking garage and up two ramps to a weathered, dark green Subaru Outback. With no one else in sight, Reynolds unlocked the car, took a fat sealed envelope from the backseat, and handed it to Sarah.

"This should keep you busy," he said to her. "It forms a pattern showing what's been going on. By the way, the Justice task force has all this and more. That should make it more difficult to trace the source."

"I thought the task force was staying away from covert operations," Sarah said.

"That's the story for public consumption, but they're not fools," Reynolds said. "They can't be part of a cover-up. The White House knows that. Check it out. I need to go now. My phone numbers are in there, along with my lawyer's name and number."

Reynolds got into the Outback and drove away.

Scully asked Sarah to walk with him to the Metro station.

"Why is Reynolds doing this?" she asked him.

"Just what he said. He thinks he's acting in the best interest of the country. He was a military officer himself, and he hated it when he discovered what they were doing."

"You made sure he found out when he became director, didn't you?"

Scully smiled.

"You don't just see conspiracies," Sarah said. "You start them. You, me, Reynolds. Chris Collins, as far as he would go. Andy Foster, Derek Stevens, and who knows who else. All of us against Carter Phillips and the forces of evil."

"Sounds like a movie, but unfortunately it's real life. And it hasn't been much fun."

Sarah held the bulky envelope close while they walked. This was the nearest she was likely to get to knowing the real Pat Scully, she thought, and she wanted to tie up some loose ends.

"What did you do after you left Washington?" she asked. "And when did you come back?"

"I lay low in California until I was sure I could trust Reynolds. Then I went back to my day job, which I really can't discuss. Let's just say I traveled a bit, and I got back here some time ago."

"Without telling me."

"Or Chris, for different reasons. What I do is secret. I was unusually visible on the Hill for a while, but I was actually undercover there, if that doesn't confuse you."

"Not anymore. How did you stop that guy from calling me?"

"I said I'd tell you who he was, so you could write about it. And I told him you recorded the calls."

"So was he the one asking about me at the hotel? And who searched my room?"

"Definitely the former, which concerned me because I shouldn't have said you recorded him. So I warned you not to go back to the hotel until he was picked up."

"Which one was he?"

"Can't tell you. He wasn't in the indictment. The F.B.I. did me a favor. But you don't have to worry about him or anyone else anymore. In fact, you could move back home."

"I couldn't possibly go back *there*," Sarah said. "I'm staying in another hotel while I look for an apartment downtown."

She didn't tell him that it all depended on what happened to her at the newspaper.

They had reached the entrance to the Bethesda Metro station. Sarah was taking the subway, too, but she guessed Scully wouldn't want her to follow him inside. He said good-bye, turned and started down the escalator. It would be the last time Sarah saw him.

52

"So, Sarah," Lou Runyan said, leaning over his desk, "Ron's ready to fire you. And you go out and get the biggest story yet."

"I didn't say —" Jones began.

"I know, I know." Runyan cut him off. "You thought *I* was going to fire her. And maybe you, too. Tell me about the story first," Runyan said to Sarah. "Are the documents authentic?"

"Yes," she said, worrying about what Runyan would do. "I checked them last night with a source high up in the Justice task force. They've got them, too."

"The president told us the task force wasn't going there," said Mary Sullivan.

"Either she lied or someone misled her." Sarah was gaining confidence as they focused on the story. "The task force seems to be going all the way. My source didn't seem bothered that we might do a story about this. They may want to send some kind of message."

"So," said Runyan in his blunt way, "you have two high-level sources and supporting documents showing that the Justice task force is investigating corruption, torture, and murder by private contractors working for the U.S. government in Iraq and Afghanistan, among other places."

"Sounds like a pretty good lead to me," Sullivan said. "Sarah's got a little more reporting and a lot of writing to do. And we need to deal with the White House and show the story to our lawyers."

Turning to Jones, she asked, "Ron, do you think it could be ready some time tomorrow for the Web and the next day's paper?"

"Looks doable to me," he told her.

They have confidence in the story, Sarah thought, which gave her the courage to ask Runyan, "What's happening to me?"

"I really like you, Sarah," he said. "You're one hell of a reporter. And you're dedicated to your work. Maybe too dedicated. You don't seem to have a life outside this newsroom. So it's not surprising that you keep winding up romantically involved with colleagues or sources. I wish you could find someone who has nothing to do with your work and settle down with him."

"Colleagues are okay, Lou," Sullivan said. "It's just complicated if they're already married to someone else or one is reporting to the other. But, Sarah," she went on, "people you're reporting on are different."

"I know that," Sarah said. She made it seem as though she finally did.

"But you can't make any more mistakes like that one," Runyan warned, sounding very serious. "We have to put a lot of trust in a reporter who does what you do. The credibility of this newspaper and, frankly, the jobs of your editors depend on that trust. I know you're still young. But you're doing grown-up work. It can affect people's lives and even the future of the country."

"I understand everything you said," Sarah replied. "I want to do this kind of work. Nothing is more important to me."

"Then pay attention to what Ron and Mary tell you." Runyan had obviously made up his mind. Sarah had survived. "I don't want to have this conversation with you ever again."

53

Wearing White House press and visitor badges, Mark and Sarah followed Alison Winters to Elizabeth Tawney's corner office in the West Wing. Because they had been summoned to a meeting with the chief of staff before the noon press briefing, they feared that Tawney would warn them not to publish Sarah's story, about which she had notified Alison, for national-security reasons.

"Sarah," Tawney said after they had all sat down, "I thought you deserved a heads-up that the president will take the podium for the briefing today. The president will announce actions she's taking in response to an interim report from the Stetson commission on the defense-contracting scandal, following the indictments unsealed earlier this week."

Sarah didn't understand what that meant, but Mark did. And he was angry.

"You're preempting Sarah's story," he said to Tawney. "Is that what she deserves for being responsible enough to give you a summary of her reporting and time to prepare a response?"

"I'm sorry." Tawney was still talking directly to Sarah. "But this is a matter of grave concern to the president. She believes she must act immediately to shut down these covert operations before any more damage is done."

"That can be on the record after the briefing," Alison said.

"Thanks for nothing," Mark said as Sarah sat in silence. "You're trying to limit the political damage to the president by getting out in front of the story."

"This is not about politics, Mark," Tawney said.

"It's all about politics. The president's trying to inoculate herself against future political damage from the scandal by taking the heat now."

"You're mixing your metaphors," Tawney said. "Look. Let me talk to you on deep background. No quotes. No senior White House officials. Only for your thinking, if you wish."

Mark nodded.

"I think this means that she's finally decided to fully take the reins of the presidency, even though she wasn't elected to the office. She's making a very hard decision here. She's leveling with the American people. It's fully consistent with what she said in the State of the Union. What's different is that I'm not sure she really understood then what it meant to be president in a situation like this, even though that was only a week ago. She was almost thinking out loud in that speech."

"Including when she said she wouldn't stand for election?" Mark asked.

"Maybe. But this has nothing to do with that. This is about taking bold action in a crisis."

Sarah knew now that the president of the United States was taking away her story by making it her own, and there was nothing she could do about it.

"We've saved a seat for you next to Mark at the briefing," Alison told Sarah.

"I need to make a phone call first."

She wanted to tell Ron Jones what was going on.

"Sorry," Alison told her. "Not until after the briefing. What we've said in this room is embargoed."

Sarah smiled nervously.

"Even in jail," she said, "I'd get one phone call."

All of the forty-nine journalists' seats were filled in the press-briefing room, and photographers buzzed around behind them as Susan walked in. In the midst of the con-tracting scandal, with more members of

Congress and administration officials under indictment than at any time in the country's history, a feverish anticipation of big news permeated the crowded room.

"Good afternoon, ladies and gentlemen," Susan began. "Following the unsealing of indictments in the defense-contracting investigation, I have received from Vice President Stetson an interim report from the commission I appointed to advise me on this matter. Its conclusions are disturbing. Its recommendations require immediate action, which I will announce today. Summaries of the interim report and the steps I'm taking will be available afterward."

"Which means everyone will have the same story you were working on," Mark whispered to Sarah, "except the president will be the lead."

"The commission has found that among the companies being investigated for corruption are a number with contracts from the Department of Defense to carry out covert counterterrorism operations," Susan continued as the journalists stirred. "Some of these companies have used unauthorized methods to apprehend, detain, and interrogate terrorist suspects, which in some cases resulted in unexplained injuries and deaths."

"That's about as abstract and bureaucratic as you can make torture and murder," Mark said to Sarah amid a din of clicking camera shutters and muffled conversations.

"Today," Susan declared, her amplified voice rising, "I am removing all secrecy classifications from these contracts and activities. I am ordering the Departments of Justice and Defense to investigate fully what these companies have done and whether they or their employees have violated any laws or international agreements. I am also ordering that the investigations extend to government officials who granted and oversaw these contracts. I expect everyone who has committed illegal acts to be prosecuted to the fullest extent of the law."

"Saint Susan to the rescue," Mark said to Sarah.

"Although I inherited these covert operations when I became president, and knew nothing about them until recently, I accept full responsibility for closing them down. And I apologize now to the American people for whatever damage has been done to our nation's good name and the struggle against terrorism."

"Good politics. Whatever is revealed after this will not be blamed on her," Sarah told Mark before he could say it to her.

"We cannot fight terrorism effectively if people acting in our name behave no differently than the terrorists," the president said. "The protection of freedom and human rights is just as important in this fight as the most sophisticated armaments."

When the briefing ended, the president left the room and everyone stood up. Just then Sarah saw Catherine Nichols standing in the back, a White House visitor's pass dangling from her neck. Sarah tried to push through the crowd to reach her. Before she could make much progress, she found Alison Winters at her side.

"Hold up a minute," she said to Sarah. "We promised her privacy."

"What's she doing here?"

"Completely off the record," Alison said. "You can't tell Mark or your gossip columnist or anyone else until I figure out how to deal with this."

"What's she doing here?"

"Like any good friend of the president," Alison told Sarah, "she's spending a couple of nights in the Lincoln Bedroom."

ACKNOWLEDGMENTS

This book would not have been possible without the steady encouragement and guidance of Amanda Urban at I.C.M. and the patient tutelage and remarkable editing of Jonathan Segal at Knopf. I admire and greatly benefit from their professionalism. Kate Norris copyedited the manuscript with great care and sensitivity. *Washington Post* colleagues Phil Bennett, Bob Kaiser, and Steve Coll helped considerably with their comments on early drafts, as did friends Ann Ryan, Susan and Jim Holt, and Marsha Muawwad, and my son, Joshua, and daughter, Sarah. My wonderful wife, Janice, has been my indispensable partner in this adventure, as in all things, as reader and editor.

A NOTE ABOUT THE AUTHOR

Leonard Downie, Jr., has worked since 1964 at *The Washington Post,* where he has been a prizewinning investigative reporter, a principal editor of the paper's Watergate coverage, a foreign correspondent, managing editor, and, for seventeen years, executive editor, succeeding Ben Bradlee. He is now a vice president of The Washington Post Co. and an author and lecturer. This is his fifth book and first novel. He lives with his wife, Janice, in Washington, D.C.

The employees of Thorndike Press hope you have enjoyed this Large Print book. All our Thorndike, Wheeler, and Kennebec Large Print titles are designed for easy reading, and all our books are made to last. Other Thorndike Press Large Print books are available at your library, through selected bookstores, or directly from us.

For information about titles, please call:
    (800) 223-1244

or visit our Web site at:
    http://gale.cengage.com/thorndike

To share your comments, please write:
    Publisher
    Thorndike Press
    295 Kennedy Memorial Drive
    Waterville, ME 04901